Tales of Two Sisters

A Novel

By D. M. Dubay

Obenhoff Press

Tales of Two Sisters
A Novel
By D. M. Dubay

Cover and author's photographs by René Dubay

ISBN: 0692252630
ISBN: 9780692252635
Library of Congress Control Number: 2014913015
Obenhoff Press
13740 36th Avenue NE
Seattle, WA 98125

To all my sisters

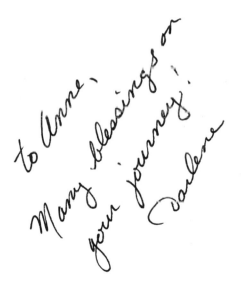

to Anne~
Many blessings on
your journey.
Darlene

Acknowledgments

As I attempt to express my gratitude, many adages and truisms come to mind, but they are flat and lifeless on a printed page. As President John F Kennedy said, "As we express our gratitude, we must never forget that the highest appreciation is not to utter words, but to live by them." I am trying, by completing this project, to live up to that high ideal.

We are meant to share our gifts, and to all the people who have so generously shared their gifts of encouragement, expertise and love with me, I am deeply grateful. "At times our own light goes out and is rekindled by a spark from another person. Each of us has cause to think with deep gratitude of those who have lighted the flame within us. – Albert Schweitzer.

So for the rekindling…

Thank you, Bud for believing in me.

To my first writers' support group in Anchorage, Barbara Husereau and Patsy Romack, I owe a debt of gratitude for getting me started on the right track.

Thank you, Sno-Island Writer's Group—Melba Burke, Morna Frazier, Bruce Lawson, BJ McCall, Judy Price and Mary Ann Schradi—for your encouraging words, editing skills and kind and gentle critiques. I couldn't and wouldn't have done it without you.

Thank you also to the Hard-Nosed Zealots Writing and Critique Group—Mary Ann Hayes, Gloria MacKay, Erika

Madden, Margo Peterson, Lani Schonberg, Val Schroeder, Mary Trimble and Peggy Wendel. Your professionalism inspired me to try harder and to believe in my own voice.

For Joan Landis who eagerly read every word I sent, a big thank you.

I am grateful to Paul Johnson for his careful reading of a manuscript way out of his comfort zone of sports and numbers.

Meister Eckhart said, "If the only prayer you said was thank you, that would be enough." I say that prayer often, humbly, with the knowledge and understanding that only by grace, and the love of others, can I be and do my best. So, thank you. Thank you all.

"Hope is the thing with feathers
That perches in the soul
And sings the tune without words
And never stops at all"
Emily Dickinson

Chapter One

Meet Nikki

"That's it, Gerik!" Elsa yells in the direction of the family room as she enters the house. "I've had it!" Gerik sits there, watching television. Elsa slams her keys down rattling the ceramic dish. "That was the finishing touch: the last straw, the coup de grace."

Gerik's eyes are glued to the screen. "What now?"

Elsa enters the room and stands between Gerik and the television. "I'm changing my name, so don't even try to talk me out of it."

"What on earth has gotten into you? Change your name? That's stupid! Nobody in our family does that. And what's wrong with Elsa?" He cranes his neck, trying to look around her to watch the last inning of the ball game.

"Well, nothing until I married you."

"What do you mean by that?" He wrinkles his brow—looks her straight in the eye.

"Your last name Selzer—do I have to spell it out for you?"

"What's wrong with Selzer?"

"Come on, Gerik, get a clue."

Elsa remembers her embarrassment at the latest cutting, mean remarks about her name. She can still hear the woman she met at the quilting club earlier today saying,

1

"Did you say Alka Seltzer?" Leila overheard the woman's whispered remark, "At least it's not Rolaids or Maalox, but if it were me, I'd dump that name." Remembering this still makes Elsa blush with fury.

Her face red, Elsa continues, "Every time I introduce myself the comment is, 'Did you say Alka Seltzer?' and I have to explain, No, it's Elsa—E L S A—Selzer. If I hear that stupid remark one more time, I'll throw up. I'm so tired of people making jokes about my name."

Gerik grumbles, "Now that you've interrupted the last inning of the game, at least tell me what you plan on changing it to."

"I've been thinking Nicole would be nice. You could call me Nikki; doesn't that have a nice ring? Nikki Selzer of N S Designs. I like it."

"But, nobody in your family is called Nicole. How did you come up with that?"

"Well, I..."

"And, what in the hell is N S Designs?"

"It's my new..."

"Besides, you were named after your grandmother. Don't you think she would feel bad if you changed it?"

"She's not even alive, and she wasn't saddled with the name of an antacid. Her last name was Pedersen. And you forget—my grandfather's name was Nicolas. So, I would still be keeping it in the family."

"Whatever!" And with a shrug, he picks up a financial magazine from his lap. As the television blares with post-game commentaries in the background, the air-conditioner hums a continuous monotonous tune. Outside, the afternoon sun is white hot in the front yard, while in the back the slightest hint of the evening shade creeps around the edges of the grass.

Danny bounds into the kitchen, grabs a peach out of the designer glass bowl on the granite counter. With his mouth full he yells, "Hey, Ma, where'd you put my baseball cap?"

From behind the magazine Gerik's voice interrupts. "What ever happened to, Hi, Mom, how are you?" He slams the magazine down to glare at his son. "Show your Mother some respect."

"Oh, he didn't mean anything by that, Gerik. Did you honey?" Elsa turns towards Danny with a smile. *He is getting to be so handsome. He looks just like Gerik did when he was in high school. I hate to think of sending him go off to college this fall.*

"Okay, okay!" He looks toward his mother. "Hi, Mom, how're ya doin'?" He grabs his cap from the back of a chair where it is hanging and rushes out of the room before waiting for an answer. "Gotta go. I'm late for practice."

"Be sure you come straight home afterwards, we're having your cousins over for dinner. It should be cool enough to eat on the deck," she says to his disappearing back.

Elsa spots a brilliant red cardinal at the birdbath as she looks through the French doors of the dining room. She's glimpsed the large male several times in the past weeks, but today he splashes and hops around, looking like he owns the place and has no intention of leaving.

"Ah, this lighting is perfect," she whispers.

She forgets all about the tension in the house and her embarrassment about her name. She grabs her Canon Rebel XT and silently slips out onto the deck. The cardinal is still splashing. She aims the camera and gets several close-ups of him before he flies off, clean and refreshed. As she walks back inside, she looks at the pictures in the viewer.

"Yes!" she whispers. "These are exactly the colors I want for my next design. The way the deep red and shades of green accent the whites and greys of the birdbath! Wow! That's stunning."

She stops in the kitchen to put some potatoes on to boil for a potato salad. As she passes the foyer on the way to her office, she looks up at the king size quilt recently hung there. She stands with pride as she remembers how thrilled she was when it won best of show in a Chicago area contest. The local paper declared it a *Masterpiece*. And although she had been offered $5,000 for it, she could not part with her favorite creation.

Elsa continues up the stairs to her office, dinner forgotten. She downloads the pictures and opens the design program to manipulate the images, playing with different combinations of repeats and washes.

Forty-five minutes are gone before she hears, "Elsa, where are you? Something's burning."

Elsa takes a deep breath. Her shoulders sag. *Why is he so helpless? Can't he help around here at all?*

She saves her work and rushes into the kitchen to see the pot of potatoes billowing smoke. The water has all evaporated and the stench is sickening.

Seeing the mess on the stove and Gerik sitting nearby oblivious to all but his precious financial magazine makes something snap within her. "Why in the hell can't you ever do anything around the house? Can't you even watch things for a few minutes? You sit there on your ass when you get home from work like a king on his throne, while I wait on you and do all the menial chores around here. Don't you think I work too? Maybe you should hire a maid."

Everything piles up on her: Gerik's malaise and lack of interest grate on her nerves. That old, dark, energy-sapping heaviness makes the colors of the day go dull. The hopelessness of their relationship hits her full-force. *How did we get here? Why can't we talk anymore? And why is it that he is always so mad at Danny?*

"I don't know how much longer I can take it. We live in the same house, but that's about all we share. Can't you see that I need help to get this dinner ready?"

"Come on, Elsa, I'm not the one who invited all the relatives over for dinner on a week night." He lifts the magazine and buries his head in it until Elsa grabs it from his hands and stands square-shouldered before him. Her eyes are narrowed and her eyebrows are raised in *that* look—the look she knows he dreads.

"Oh, oh! What now? What are you so touchy about?" He pauses, "Okay. Okay. I'll help. What do you want me to do?"

"You can start by peeling some potatoes—about fifteen—and putting them on to boil. Then you can make sure that the grill has enough gas to cook the steaks and corn. You can check the beer cooler in the garage and. . . ."

"One thing at a time. Who do you think I am, Superman?"

"Gerik, please...let's not get into it again. Your sister Jill and Mike and the kids will be here in an hour. I don't have time to argue." *Or the energy.*

On the verge of tears, Elsa scrubs the blackened pot, slams it down and gives up as she leaves it to soak. She grabs the vacuum to do some last minute cleaning.

By the time the guests are expected to arrive, the sun is low in the sky and the temperature is down to eighty degrees, but the humidity makes it feel hot and sticky—a typical Midwest summer evening. Sweat is running down Elsa's back as she rushes outside to put the dishes on the picnic table in the corner of the deck. The shade of the house has cooled the back yard a little. Cumulus build-ups can be seen in the distance with a far-off rumbling from time to time. *I hope it doesn't rain.*

Elsa lights the grill. For a moment she stands still, admiring the back yard. All the recent rain has made the grass thick. A few of the delphiniums are still in bloom. She muses *I love their dark purple and lavender spikes. They look so regal.* The white chrysanthemum border contrasts with the deep green of the Arborvitae behind. The hedge between their yard and the neighbor's is now tall enough to give them privacy. The door slams as the guests arrive and wakes her out of her reverie. She goes into the house to greet her in-laws.

As they finish dinner, Gerik looks around the table and smirks. "Hey, did you hear what Elsa is going to do?" His voice is edged with sarcasm. "She's going to change her name to Nellie or Nasturtium or something like that. Maybe we could call her *Nasty.*" He laughs. "Have you ever heard anything so ridiculous?"

Heads all turn; questioning eyes stare at Elsa.

Elsa, with a dramatic sigh, raises her eyes to the ceiling. "It's Nicole. I think it's a beautiful name and it's certainly better than Elsa Selzer! Jill, you know how my business is taking off. I already have invitations to speak at seven quilting workshops and seminars in the next nine months. I want to be taken seriously and I can't have people laughing at my name. Image is very important. I want a modern sounding, catchy name, but one that says stability."

"But why change your name? That's pretty drastic." Jill looks at Elsa, incredulous.

"It's not like I just thought of it. I have actually been thinking of it for a long time. It's just that now with my new business getting started it seems like a good time to make a change. So, once it's official you can call me Nikki, or Nicole. I won't respond to Elsa. In fact, tomorrow I'm going down to the courthouse to fill out the paperwork. It's quite simple."

"But what about all of your correspondence? Have you thought about all of the things that will need to be changed?" Jill asks.

"There's a checklist for all of that. The court paperwork explains everything."

The discussion goes on throughout dessert, until Danny jumps up and says, "Hey, Jason, Mick, Andrea, how about throwing the disc for a while? There's still enough light. Em should be home in a few minutes, too."

"How about an 'excuse me,' please?" Gerik says as Danny and his cousins leave the table in a rush. They ignore his comment.

"Those kids! They show no respect. When I was that age, I trembled in my shoes to think of what my father would have done if I left the table without asking to be excused or thanking my mother for a wonderful dinner."

"Oh, Gerik," Elsa looks at him. "They're just young and energetic. Let them have some fun." *Why is he so hard on those kids? You'd think he was never a kid himself.*

She gets up from the table, grabbing a few dishes to take into the kitchen. "Come on, Jill; let's get started on the dishes. I want to show you some of the designs I've been working on."

Gerik and Mike sit in silence while Elsa and Jill make several trips to the kitchen.

"Where's Emma tonight?" Jill asks as they finish clearing the table.

"She works at Right Way Camp six days a week now." She was only part time 'til she learned the ropes, but she's picked it up quickly for someone so young...they say her age is an asset for working with teenage drug users."

"Really? Well I hope my kids never have to go there. I don't know how she can stand to work with those hoodlums."

7

"She's good at what she does."

In the kitchen, away from their husbands' ears, Jill asks, "Come on, Elsa, really, why do you want to change your name?"

"Remember. After tomorrow it's Nikki."

"Okay. I'll try to remember." Jill smiles, then turns serious. "I know my brother can be a jerk a times, but really, he does have a point."

"Well, it's partly about the business image thing, but I've always hated the name, Elsa. It sounds so old fashioned. It's not me. I remember when Leila and I were kids. She always lorded it over me and teased me to the point of tears about everything. But what I hated most was when I tried to get back at her, I would say, something like *you better stop, or...*and she would say *or what? Or else, Elsa?* Then she'd call me Else. I can still hear her saying *Else, Else, or Else!* with that sneering tone of hers. I hate it."

"Speaking of Leila, how is she doing since her husband— what was his name—was killed in the airplane accident?"

"Pete, uh...Peter. I guess she's doing okay. I don't really talk to her very often. We don't have much in common, other than being sisters."

Jill shakes her head. "I can't imagine not talking to my sisters. They're my lifelines."

"Well, it's her fault. Since she decided to make her home in Alaska, she hasn't been back to visit for more than a couple of days at a time. She's always in a rush to get back to Alaska. You'd think she would at least have come to help when Mom was so sick. But, no, she's always too busy with their stupid charter business. You'd think after Peter died she would have given up on anything having to do with airplanes."

"What about life insurance?"

"How would I know?"

"Well, even if he left her with anything," Jill continues, "she still has to work to support those three small kids. And it is something she knows. It only makes sense for her to stay and run it. From what I hear, it is quite a successful business."

"The kids are not so small any more. In fact, Rudy is about to start his third year of college. Danny idolizes him. You should hear him talk about their adventures when he gets back from his annual visit to Alaska."

"How about her other children?"

"Leila's second child, Ana, is working as a cook on the North Slope in one of the oil camps."

"She is?"

"Yeah, I hear she's a great cook." Elsa stands with her hands on her hips, looking around the kitchen for any dirty dishes."

"Was she the one who went to culinary school?"

"She did. She used to call me all the time asking about which school would be the best. She settled on the program at the University of Alaska in Anchorage because it was close to home and inexpensive. But she could have gone anywhere."

"Yeah. But it probably doesn't matter if you have talent."

"Well, good credentials never hurt."

"How about Leila's youngest?"

"That's Natalia—she's still at home. Emma used to spend summers with her in Alaska. They were best friends until a couple years ago."

"I suppose that's when Emma started working at the camp, huh?" Jill asks.

"Yes. But I still don't see why Leila can't come and visit. She doesn't need to be at that stupid office all the time. Rudy pretty much runs the business now. He flies non stop all summer when they're busiest."

"Well, someone has to take care of the office, I'm sure. What about all the scheduling and maintenance, keeping the books straight and all that stuff?"

"I suppose you're right, but I still don't see why she can't come home once in a while." Elsa refuses to let it go.

Changing the subject, Jill says, "Hey, I just joined the Downtown Athletic Club."

Elsa puts soap in the dishwasher. She turns it on, looks at Jill with eyes wide, "You what?"

"I joined the Athletic Club. They're having a summer special to get people in. No initiation fee, and the monthly rate is reduced if you pay by the year. You can't beat that. A couple people from the office joined and I thought, *what the heck?*"

"What kind of stuff do they have?"

"They have all the regular equipment for weights, lots of aerobic machines and all kinds of classes. I'm planning on water aerobics and I might even try yoga. I do need to lose a few pounds."

Elsa looks at their reflections in the window and then sneaks a sideways glance at her sister-in-law, thinking, *she must weigh almost 200 pounds. It makes me feel positively thin.* "Oh, Jill, you look great," she lies. "You shouldn't over do it, though. You've never exercised before in you life, so be careful. Besides, when are you going to find the time?"

"I haven't told you, but, I've been walking at the mall three mornings a week with a couple of friends. So, I'm just going to substitute water aerobics for walking. They say three times a week is all you need to improve your fitness."

Elsa has always been slightly overweight. In high school she put on a few pounds and when she went away to college, added a few more. Then, after Danny was born, she never quite took off all the weight she gained. When she got pregnant with Emma, her weight ballooned. Now, every once in a while, she tries the latest fad diet, but can't stick with it and always gains a few more pounds after she falls off the wagon. *But it doesn't matter. In fact, I'm the slimmest one in the entire quilting club.*

She and Gerik enjoy eating out. She tries to analyze the recipes and duplicate them at home. Gerik's praises of her culinary expertise are the only positive comments she receives from him nowadays.

She always does most of the cooking and baking for family gatherings and special occasions. Other than quilting, it is how Elsa expresses her creativity. Everyone raves about the table she sets and she secretly craves this admiration even more than she craves the food. Her mother put her in charge of the kitchen when she was twelve years old when Leila proved to be inept at anything having to do with food. The attention she got buried her feelings of inferiority. *I have a special gift. So what if I'm a little overweight? I'll lose weight someday. There's plenty of time to change.*

That night after everyone leaves, Gerik watches the news in his office. Elsa slips out of her sleeveless dress and heads for the shower. She catches sight of herself in the full-length mirror in the dim light of the bedroom and stops to take a good look. "You don't look too bad for forty-two," she says to her reflection. Turning sideways she sucks in her stomach and throws her shoulders back. "Breasts are a little saggy, but the butt...Oh, who am I trying to kid?" she whispers. "I'm fat and old looking. Maybe Jill is right. Maybe I should start exercising."

In the bright light of the bathroom she examines her face and hair in the mirror. She sees her mother's double chin starting to show and the laugh lines around her eyes and mouth are deeper than she had realized. Her dishwater blond hair has streaks of white. *Just from the sun,* she rationalizes. *But when do I ever spend any time in the sun? I'm an indoor person. I even avoid walking from the car to the grocery store as much as I can. I always sit under a protective awning at Danny's baseball games because my skin burns so easily.* "I am going to dye my hair and get a new style—tomorrow," she says aloud. "I'll have a new name and a new image."

As she falls asleep she resolves to stick with her plan in spite of what anyone might say. In her dreams that night she is on stage under hot lights, prancing to seductive music in a skimpy costume. Gerik is in the audience laughing so hard that tears are running down his cheeks and he falls into the aisle, holding his side. She wakes up grabbing at the sheets trying to cover her rolls of belly fat in spite of the sweat drenching her.

Elsa gets out of bed not daring to look at her image in the mirror. *I'm fat. I'm dumpy. No wonder Gerik...* she shakes her head. *No, I'm not going to go there.*

Well, at least I am creative, Elsa muses. *Everyone raves about my quilts. I remember the first quilt I made when I was pregnant. That kit I found was pretty babyish, so I improvised with colors and textures to make the simple design look more interesting. What I made had depth and character. I remember throwing out the fabrics from the kit and adding colorful material left over from my own clothing projects. When I used it to wrap Danny during those cold winter months, everyone asked me where I got it. Before long, I had been talked into making quilts for all my nieces and nephews. But I always loved the feel of the fabric slipping through my fingers. I still do. I love it when people "ooh" and "aah" over the beauty and craftsmanship of my quilts. I feel so sorry for women who are inept and have no domestic talents.*

The next morning, Elsa remembers her plan to get a new hairstyle and decides to try the new salon in town. She heard it was expensive, but wants the latest style. She feels like doing something daring, reckless.

At breakfast, Gerik starts again, "Why on earth do you insist on doing something so ridiculous? Changing your name is pretty drastic, you know. You could just use your middle name. But, it's obvious you'll do what you want, anyway. I can't figure out what has gotten into you."

Elsa listens in silence until he jumps up from the table and rushes out the door. "I don't care what you think," she says to his retreating back, "I'm doing it." She adds, "Don't you ever think of anything but work and those precious stocks that you follow like a religion?"

As soon as she hears him back the car out of the garage, she picks up the phone and calls Salon Bleu. *I've got to do this before I chicken out.* "I need an appointment for this morning for a haircut and color," she says into the phone. "No, it doesn't matter what time and with whom. I just have to be done before three p.m. Well, I guess one o'clock is fine. You say he is your color expert? Great! My name?" She decides to practice her new name. "It's Nikki, Nikki Selzer. That's N I K K I."

Nikki spots the exact hair cut she wants in one of the hairstyle magazines as she waits for her stylist. She has always worn it shoulder length with a part down the middle and the ends curled loosely. Sometimes she pulls it back into a loose chignon at the nape of her neck. She is startled when a thin young man calls her name and escorts her to his station. He is wearing tight black jeans and a lavender shirt, open at the neck. His hair—black with red streaks—stands straight out from his head. She thinks, *Whoa, that's pretty avant-garde,* as she appraises his hair and attire. *I wonder where he's from. I don't know if I'm ready to go that far, but…here goes.*

"I'm Jonathon, the stylist. You must be Nikki. Please have a seat Ma'am."

He runs his fingers through her hair. "You have really good hair, but the ends are frayed and something shorter would be much healthier for it. Oh, yes," he exclaims as she shows him the picture. "This will be perfect for your hair type and the shape of your face. The bangs must be short, though, ending just above your eyebrows. Got to accentuate them. I've never seen such perfect eyebrows."

Two hours later Nikki stands up feeling pampered as she never has been pampered in her entire life. As she turns and sees her image in the mirror, she gasps.

Jonathon looks worried. "Don't you like it?"

"Like it? No, I love it."

"I must say, I love the transformation in you. You ought to be on a magazine cover."

"Oh, Jonathon, you're just saying that, but—thank you. You are a genius."

Nikki glows as she remembers Jonathon's running conversation about her good qualities, her skin, and the ease of working with her hair. She thinks, *he makes me feel special, unique—beautiful.*

Nikki surprises even herself when she gives him an enormous tip.

"Oh, please, come back, Nikki. I love working with you."

"I will, I definitely will." Her smile is so big she can hardly talk. Nikki knew it would be expensive, but when the cashier hands her the bill, she looks it over with a fine-toothed comb to be sure she is seeing it correctly.

The cashier smiles and asks Nikki to turn around. Nikki obliges.

"Isn't he great! The color, the shape the texture—everything is perfect. You look stunning!"

Nikki pays the bill with a smile and walks out of the shop floating on air. As she walks back to her car she catches her reflection in a store window and doesn't recognize herself. Her hair—dark red, chin length, shiny—accentuates her green eyes and ivory complexion; the bangs hang straight across to fall just above her perfect eyebrows. Her hair swings as she turns her head and she feels absolutely coquettish. She wishes she had worn something a little more attractive. Her lavender slacks with the elastic waistband and the long, matching Henley shirt with raglan sleeves make her body look like an Easter egg. The shape does nothing to complement her new hairstyle.

I'll deal with that later, she thinks as she gets into her car for the short drive downtown. Once parked at the courthouse, Nikki sits in her car for a few minutes. Taking a deep breath and feeling very self-conscious, she braces herself for imagined stares and then bounds out of the car with a pretended confidence in her step. She strides into the courthouse to fill out the paperwork for her name change. She feels like everyone is looking at her, but standing in line at the window, she notices all of them are wrapped up in their own affairs. The clerk behind the counter has a look of distain and barely looks at the people he is serving. When Nikki's turn comes, he has his head down, involved with paperwork, and says in a tone that connotes total boredom, "Next."

Nikki steps up to the window with trepidation but as the clerk looks up, she notices his raised eyebrows, wide, admiring eyes and slight smile as he meets her gaze. His face lights up in genuine admiration. "Well, now," he says. "Can I help you?" sounding like he really means it.

With a coy smile and one shoulder raised she says, "I think you already have."

Chapter Two

Leila Lives in the Past

It is late afternoon in August when Rudy rushes into the office of their air taxi business on Lake Hood, adjacent to Anchorage International Airport.

"Mom, get your sleeping bag. We're going out to Alexander Lake. I have an overnight charter with the Beaver and there are only two fishermen—the others canceled at the last minute. They don't mind if you come along for the ride. And since they want to return first thing in the morning, I thought that we may as well stay overnight too. That will save us flying out and back twice. What do you think?"

Leila gasps. "I need time to think about it, Rudy. You can't just spring it on me like that."

Her heart is beating fast and she can't get a deep breath. The room closes in on her. "I can't just leave the office." She reasons. "What about all the customers who depend on us being here?"

Leila has not been in a plane since Peter died two and a half years ago. She didn't plan to avoid flying. It just happened. After the funeral she had all the work around the charter office to do. The responsibilities at home piled up, too, and she didn't have time for flying. By the time a spare minute presented itself, the horrible details of Peter's crash built up so much in her mind, she could not bear the thought of ever getting into a plane again. She always had the perfect excuse for Rudy whenever he brought it up.

Today, though, Rudy is persistent. "But, all of the charters are out for the day. We have no planes left on the ground. We have the answering service to handle new orders. It's perfect, Mom. You haven't been camping all summer and this will be like a free trip. The customers are paying all the expenses. I won't take no for an answer."

Rudy grabs the camping gear, along with Leila's sleeping bag, from the storeroom and loads it into the plane. He comes back in to get some freeze-dried meals and butter from the refrigerator for the fish he hopes to catch for dinner. Stopping at Leila's desk, he grabs her by the elbow.

"Wait, let me close all these files and, hey, what about emergencies or accidents?"

"The Rescue Coordination Center or the FAA will get ahold of us. Anyway, there's nothing we could do until morning, anyway."

"Well, let me at least get my jacket."

"Okay, but I have everything else. Let's go."

Rudy ushers her out to the plane at the dock and puts his hands on her back as he shoves her in. The fishermen are eager to get their lines in the water at Alexander Creek and don't even notice the struggle going on between Rudy and Leila.

Leila gives up the front seat of the Beaver to the larger of the two men. She and the other fisherman sit on the bench seat behind the pilot. Her usual friendliness has given way to monosyllabic answers to their questions. As Rudy taxis out into the water lane and waits for clearance to takeoff, Leila clenches and unclenches her hands. The tension around her eyes and the tightness in her throat and chest make her feel as though she will burst out crying if anybody says a word to her. The fisherman sitting next to her is looking out the window taking in all of the exciting scenes before him and doesn't seem to notice Leila at all.

Traffic on Lake Hood at six p.m. on a summer evening is heavy and Rudy looks around, watching one plane after another apply power for takeoff. Leila notices the wake behind each plane get smaller and neater as it accelerates on the step and lifts off. When it is their turn, Rudy lines up for takeoff. He pushes the throttle forward as he lifts the water rudders in a smartly choreographed move. As the powerful radial engine of the DeHaviland Beaver lifts them into the air, Leila feels a passing thrill as the plane breaks free of the water and surges forward. She smiles in spite of her anxiety. *Yes, I understand why they love it so much.*

The momentary thrill of takeoff disappears as the dread of flying returns. Leila looks around instinctively, almost frantically, for other airplanes. She does not notice the spectacular scenery surrounding them as they climb. The corridor in which they fly beneath the Elmendorf Air Force Base approach course is busy with floatplanes leaving and approaching Lake Hood for landing. Fighter jets speed overhead across their flight path and giant cargo aircraft leaving Anchorage International Airport rumble alongside of them. The mixture of different types of aircraft requires a special Federal Aviation Regulation to enhance safety in the airspace surrounding Anchorage. A unique combination of air traffic—general aviation planes from Lake Hood and Merrill Field, commercial cargo and passenger jets from the domestic airport and military aircraft all follow specific flight paths and altitudes to assure separation.

When her fellow passenger nudges her arm and points, Leila at last looks to the north to see Denali shimmering in the afternoon sun a hundred miles to the north. The look of awe on his face reminds her of the feeling she had when she and Peter stood on its summit—breathless a world of white stretching out below them and off in the distance, green slopes fading off into the haze. Her entire attention is riveted on the mountain. She can see the Kahiltna Glacier where they were dropped off for the start of their climb, but their path to the summit is in the shadow.

The sound of the big radial engine and the chatter on the intercom between Rudy and the passengers fades into the background as something about the quality of the light takes her back to that day they left Talkeetna in the Cessna one eighty five. She once again feels the thrill of landing with a ski plane at 14,000 feet on a glacier. The difficulty of climbing recedes into the background and only the final ascent remains fresh in her mind. Her memory is so vivid, it seems as though it happened only yesterday. The scene plays in her mind...

"I can't do it, Pete. Just let me rest here. You go on to the top. You're not suffering from altitude sickness like I am. My headache is just too much. I don't want to spoil your chance to summit."

"No, I'm not going without you. We trained for this together and you're coming with me even if I have to carry you."

Pete picked up her pack and pulled her to her feet. "But, Pete, I don't think…"

"Nonsense! I saw you jogging up to the top of Flattop with your heavy pack. Don't even think we went through all that preparation for you to stop three thousand feet short of the summit. Come on."

⟜⟶

Leila remembers when she first met Pete and smiles as the image of him dressed in a light tan hiking shirt and black fleece comes into focus.

⟜⟶

At a gathering of the Chugach Mountaineering Club Leila noticed a member she had not seen before. *I wonder who that hunk of a guy is. He seems so shy.* She asked her friend, Leisl, "Can you introduce me to that black haired guy over there? I hope he's going on the hike to O'Malley Peak."

"Of course he's going. Isn't that what this meeting is all about? Come on, I'll introduce you."

Pete formally shook Leila's hand when they were introduced. "Pleased to meet you."

To Leila his touch was electric and she did not let go of his hand right away. She looked up into his dark brown eyes. "Have you hiked up O'Malley Peak before?"

"Many times."

Still holding his hand, Leila asked, "How about if we stay together on the hike? I'm a little apprehensive about the rocky area near the top. I could use a strong arm to lean on."

Pete didn't seem to notice that she was still holding his hand. "Sure."

At a small deli on the Seward Highway after the hike, Leila dragged information out of Pete. She didn't mind his brief, sometimes one-word, answers to her questions. She didn't notice the music playing in the background until Pete said, "Is that the Gloria from Mozart's Requiem?"

Leila listened for a few moments, and then nodded. "You're amazing. I didn't even notice there was music playing."

"I guess I'm tuned in to Mozart right now. We have a concert coming up in October—mostly Mozart."

"What instrument do you play?"

"The oboe."

"I'm impressed."

Pete shrugged his shoulders.

"How could we have so much in common? You grew up in Alaska and I in the Midwest. We both love hiking and classical music."

"Yeah."

"How did you get interested in classical music?"

"My grandmother forced us."

"But playing the oboe, that's a bit unusual."

"I like challenges."

"Well, the hike today didn't seem to be much of a challenge to you."

"Nah."

The silences in their conversation felt comfortable. Leila enjoyed just looking at Pete. She noticed his thoughtful expression. He looked as though he just solved a complex philosophical question and was excited about its implications.

Holding his sandwich with both hands, he looks at Leila. "How about hiking the Resurrection Trail next weekend—just the two of us?"

Leila's heart leapt at the suggestion. "I'd love to."

As they finished their sandwiches, they planned all the details of the upcoming hike. They took their time. The lights dimmed in the deli and soon Leila noticed the manager hovering near their table, trying to get their attention.

"I hate to interrupt you two lovebirds, but we closed a half hour ago."

Leila looked at her watch. "Oh, my gosh, where did the time go? I've got to get back to the apartment and do some studying."

Pete took Leila's elbow, helped her to her feet and walked her to the door. Leila noticed her legs were a bit stiff after the steep descent from O'Malley Peak.

That summer, every chance they got, they rushed down the Seward Highway to one of the trailheads and spent entire days discovering new things in nature and about each other. One cloudy, windy day they huddled together on the leeward side of a ridge gathering warmth from each other's body before continuing to the top. On a sunny day on Bird Ridge, they lay in a high alpine field of fireweed, forget-me-nots and lupine to gaze at the clouds speeding by above, the sun warming their tired bodies. The appearance of a golden eagle rounding the hillside delighted them. He soared in the updraft along the mountainside coming so close they saw his shiny amber eyes looking directly at them.

During their first winter together, they hiked or skied every chance they got. On one winter hike, they surprised a flock of nearly invisible ptarmigan that took off with a flurry so unexpected they both shrieked from the shock of the sudden noise and movement. They fell down, laughing, in each other's arms in the deep snow. He taught her about the medicinal plants his grandmother collected and dried to ward off a variety of ailments from menstrual cramps to fever. Leila was amazed at the things he knew and took for granted.

Still lost in thought, Leila reminisces about a special hike—one that changed the course of her life. She romanticizes the scene. From the perspective of time, everything takes on a warm, idealistic glow.

Leila suspected something unusual as they hiked along the Crescent Lake trail that day. "How come you wouldn't let me carry any of the food today?"

"This is an experiment. Just want to see if I could do a gourmet overnight hike."

They found a perfect spot to pitch the tent. Leila wandered off to collect wildflowers. She picked some greens to add to the salad while Pete prepared their dinner.

As she approached the campsite, Pete scurried around. Two low camp chairs with backs sat side by side next to a white tablecloth set with small china plates and crystal wine glasses. Pete was opening a bottle of wine and as he spotted her, he poured a generous amount into each glass. He set the bottle down and embraced her. He picked up the glasses and handed her one.

"Here's to us."

Leila's eyebrows lifted in a question. Looking at the dinner spread out on the cloth before them, she gasped.

"Sushi! How did you know I love hamachi?"

"I pay attention to important details."

"And what is *that?*" Leila pointed.

"Escargot. I thought for sure you'd know what it is."

"I've never..."

"You're going to love it."

Leila lifted the bowl to her nose. She closed her eyes and inhaled deeply, getting a strong whiff of garlic. "I do love garlic, so it can't be all bad in spite of how it looks."

"Trust me."

"But what's the special occasion, Pete? You've never packed this kind of stuff before. Your pack must have weighed a ton. I don't know how you got all the stuff in it."

"It wasn't too bad, besides, I just wanted to see if it could be done."

Leila sipped the wine, savoring its rich flavor. "Don't tell me this is that special Pinot Noir you were saving."

"It is."

"What's going on?"

Leila knew Pete was up to something, but the wine began to relax her and she sank gratefully into the camp chair. "This is so beautiful." Tears sprang to her eyes. "It's paradise. How blessed we are to have it all to ourselves."

Long shadows made the dwarf trees seem enormous. The breeze blowing a strand of black hair across Pete's forehead felt warm. A loon called in the distance, sounding eerie, lonely.

Pete scooted his chair closer to Leila to put his arm around her shoulder. "That's the sound of my heart calling to yours, Leila."

"I don't know what I did to deserve this—or why you've been so secretive. If I didn't know you better I would say you are showing off. What do you have up your sleeve?"

Pete smiled. "That reminds me. I've got to get the dessert. But first, a little more wine?"

Leila nodded and held out her glass. "You're too good to me."

After pouring the wine, he added some wood to the campfire, and then walked towards the tent where his backpack was stored under the rain fly. Leila watched, trying to guess what other surprises he had in store for her, but Pete positioned himself with his back to her as he rummaged in his pack.

He returned carrying a box wrapped with a huge red bow in one hand and in the other, a brocade, beaded pouch. He held out the box. Leila took it in both hands.

"Sweets for my..."

"No. Don't finish. It would be too corny."

She untied the red bow and lifted the lid. "Peter, how did you know? I love these Godiva truffles. Don't tell me. Let me guess. I bet they're..."

"Of course. They're mocha and hazelnut. Dark chocolate of course. Rich and intense like you."

She offered him the box, letting him make the first choice. The sun was about to disappear behind the mountain and the air grew noticeably cooler. Leila huddled nearer to the warmth of the fire, loosening her boots, allowing her tired feet to breathe. Pete handed the box back to Leila. She chose a truffle, sniffed it and took a tiny bite. "Wonderful! The only thing that would improve this would be a sip of wine—oh, yes, I have some here. You think of everything." She reached for her glass and took a sip. She closed her eyes, as she usually did to savor the combination of tastes. "Heavenly!"

She opened her eyes to see Pete kneeling in front of her holding out the beautiful brocade pouch.

He whispered, "Leila, I love you so much, will you always be with me? Will you be my lover forever? Will you be my wife?"

Leila opened the pouch to see the golden ring with a precious stone glittering in the firelight. The light was fading, but she noticed the intricate carvings on the band of intertwined figures of bears, fish and ravens.

She opened her mouth to answer, but no sound came out. "Oh, I," Leila sputtered as she lifted the ring from the pouch. "It's…" She held it between her forefinger and thumb closer to the firelight. Then it slipped from her hand down into the sandy beach.

"Don't move!" Pete tried to follow its path in the dimming light, but Leila jumped up, stamping her feet, scattering sand.

"Oh, no. I've lost it."

"Stand still, will you. Damn! I'll never be able to find it if you keep jumping around!"

Shocked at the harshness of his voice, Leila stumbled away towards the tent with one hand covering her mouth to stifle the cries welling up in her throat. Her other hand clutched her side to squelch the sudden cramps in her lower abdomen.

I've ruined everything. How could he be so angry sounding when he just told me that he loved me? I didn't know that he could sound so mean. Maybe he's right. Maybe I am a klutz.

She found a log to sit on and dug the heels of her boots into the soft sand. She picked up a stick and started mindlessly drawing figures in the sand. The magic was gone. Numb and cold, she shivered involuntarily and when she looked down, she saw that she had drawn a heart shaped figure in the sand with a jagged line dividing it in two from top to bottom. *Why am I so stupid? How come I ruin everything?* Leila gave in to her sobs, which became louder and louder. She looked up to see Pete walking toward her. His arms were hanging down at his sides; his shoulders were slumped.

"Did you find it?"

"No, but it doesn't matter. What matters is how much I love you. It was just a symbol. The real love is in here." He tapped his chest with his fingers. "Please forgive me for being so harsh. You surprised me. If I promise to never again talk to you that way again, will you say yes? I need you to make me complete. You haven't answered me, Leila. Have I spoiled everything?"

It was more than he had spoken at one time since Leila met him. His nearly incoherent rambling touched something in Leila. She looked at his earnest face, his eyebrows knit into single brow, his eyes wide and dark, their brown looking almost black in the dim light, a strand of black hair falling across his forehead. Her heart melted and she smiled at him, closing her eyes as she leaned into him for a soft, almost sisterly kiss on his lips.

"No, I mean, yes. Yes, I do forgive you. Yes, I do want to marry you. I love you and need you, too."

Pete impulsively lifted Leila into his arms and staggered on the uneven ground the short distance to the tent. Before the door he fell to his knees with Leila still wrapped in his arms and unzipped the door.

"I want to carry you over the threshold," he breathed as Leila tried to struggle away.

A part of her thought, *this is not right*. But as she looked into Pete's eyes everything *was* right.

She heard the wind rustling the dry leaves in the trees and an owl's cry as they lay together. In their nearness, Leila could not tell where she began and Pete ended. His skin next to hers was hot and smooth. Their passion spent, Pete gently stroked Leila's back and shoulders. They talked quietly of the future and the children they would have: of their many dreams.

When Pete disengaged from Leila and got up to leave the warmth of the tent, Leila cried, "Oh, please, don't go now. Stay and hold me."

He kissed her gently on the lips. "I only need to make sure the fire is out. I'll be right back. Keep the sleeping bag warm for me."

He grabbed the flashlight and crawled towards the door, pushing aside their clothing and lifting Leila's boots to the side so he didn't have to crawl over them.

A sudden gasp from him frightened Leila. "What is it, Pete, a bear?"

"No," he laughed, it's only a ring."

"What are you talking about?"

"A ring," he said, "as in engagement ring. It must have fallen into your boot and came out when you took them off. Now we really are betrothed. The symbol and the reality are one."

<hr />

Leila wakes from her reverie when she hears the power decrease and feels a sudden deceleration as the flaps go down.

Where have I been? She wonders, returning to the present. She is surprised to realize that her fear of flying has all but disappeared. She can see the buildings of Alexander Lake Lodge as Rudy makes his final approach to the lake. His touchdown on the glassy water is so smooth, she doesn't realize that they are on the water until she feels the plane fall off the step and settle into the water for the short drift to the shore. With his door already open, Rudy pulls the mixture control full aft and the huge radial engine winds down. The propeller stops as the floats nudge the dock and Rudy jumps out to grab the bow rope to fasten it to a cleat. The fishermen are eager to get out and after a short flurry of activity unloading their gear and some shouted instructions about when and where to pick them up in the morning, Rudy and Leila get back into the plane to taxi to the other side of the lake. A small stream runs in to the lake from the west. The silver salmon spawn in its upper reaches, but it is too small for boats to navigate so it gets very few fishermen because of the great abundance of fish elsewhere. Rudy shuts down the engine and they drift to shore where he leaps out into the water—already attired in chest waders—to pull the aircraft to shore.

After securing the aircraft and getting the camping and fishing gear out, Leila and Rudy head up the trail along the creek. They make their way carefully amidst the ruts, stepping over exposed roots. Rudy carries the heaviest pack while Leila carries only her sleeping pad and bag. Memories again assault Leila as she remembers her first time along this trail with Pete.

⟅⟆

Six months pregnant, awkward and heavy, Leila trudged through the rain on a narrow path through the woods.

29

Branches slapped her face. Her pants, wet from the tall grass near the shore, clung to her legs.

"I can't believe that anything could be worth this much trouble. I can hardly stay upright with all this mud."

"Just wait. It's not much farther. It's worth it. I promise."

"If I didn't love you so much, I would turn around and sleep in the plane. At least give me a hint as to what is so special about this place. And how are we ever going to set up our tent with everything so wet."

"You'll love it. Have I ever let you down before?"

"No, but..."

"Just wait. It's only a couple more minutes."

"We've already been hiking at least an hour."

"No, Leila. It's been ten minutes and..."

Leila gasped at the sight before her. A rock formation the size of a small house rose up out of the woods; at its base on one side there was a bend in the stream that formed a small pool about fifteen feet across. With a sly grin, Pete took her hand and led her to the west side of the stone formation. Eons of flowing water eroded the lower portions of the rock, leaving an overhanging ledge, resulting in a small, dry room, open on two sides. Obviously others had used it as a shelter and a soft layer of dry mosses and grass lined the part closest to the wall. At the rear it was only high enough for a person to sit upright, but it was dry and cozy. They left the backpacks under a tarp and crawled in to listen to the rain splashing into the water. "I love you so much, Leila. I just had to have you share this with me."

"I have to admit, I was doubting you there for a while. But this is awesome. I feel like the whole world belongs to us."

"It does."

They lay down on the moss and Pete protectively rubbed Leila's protruding belly. "I can hardly wait for the baby to be here. But I don't want to share you with anyone, Leila. Promise me that you'll always have time for just me."

"Oh, Pete. How could anyone—especially a child—ever come between us? I'm sure you'll love the baby as much as you love me."

"It will change things, though."

"Yeah, but it will only be better."

His gentleness warmed Leila's heart. He didn't force himself or ask her for anything beyond what her condition allowed. Their lovemaking was delicate but passionate. Afterwards they lay in each other's arms stroking each other's body and humming softly.

Pete kissed Leila's ear and she recognized a theme from a Rachmaninoff Concerto.

"That's Rachmaninoff, isn't it?"

"Yup."

"Tell me about your audition, Pete. You've been pretty quiet about it. Did you get the part?"

"Well, I was going to surprise you, but since you asked... yeah, I got the solo oboe part for the fall concert. Some of the symphony board members wanted to hire a pro from New York, but I guess I wowed them with my expertise."

"I wish I could say you are too humble, but..."

"Come on, give me a break. You know how hard I worked to master that piece."

"You sure did. But that's how you do everything."

"Well..."

After dinner, Leila looked out to see blue sky through the trees. Pete disappeared while Leila cleaned up the campsite. She heard the most beautiful melodic sound coming from above. "Pete, where are you?" No answer. *Where is he?* She walked a short distance from the shelter of the rock, looking, but saw no sign of him. Then she spotted the burgundy colored low-bush cranberries practically turning the floor of the forest red.

Wow, I've got to get some of these. She turned back towards the rock formation to get something in which to pick the berries. None of the cooking pots had covers, but she found a plastic bag. *This ought to work well enough.* She looked up towards the top of the rock to see Pete, sitting at the very edge, wrapped up in his playing.

Leila screamed. "Be careful, Pete. You're right at the edge. Come on down. It makes my stomach queasy to see you up there."

"But you should see the view of the Sleeping Lady from up here. None of the trees are in the way and the color is spectacular. It's inspiring," he accentuated his words with a series of improvised scales and practice intervals. To Leila he sounded like the most beautiful bird in the world.

"I hope our children inherit your musical talent. That is the most beautiful sound I have ever heard."

"Well, you're not so bad yourself. It's a shame, though, that you never put your music education to work teaching others. But I'm glad for all the accounting classes you took, otherwise you wouldn't be able to help in our business."

"Yeah, well, as much as I disliked accounting, I am glad to be working next to you all day. We make a good team."

"Your advisor was very wise, but not necessarily for the right reasons."

Leila laughed. "Who would have thought that accounting would make love grow?"

Leila hears someone stomping through the woods towards the shelter and wakes with a start. It's Rudy. She realizes this was all a memory. *But it seemed so real.* Sadness hits her with such force that she can barely push herself away from the tree she is leaning against.

"Hey, Mom...MOM. HELLO!" Rudy's voice gets louder as he approaches. "Where do you want your sleeping bag?"

Leila shakes her head. "I'll take care of it, Rudy." She busies herself with her sleeping bag and pad.

Trying to cover up her inattention, she says, "You know the first time I was here with your Dad was only a few months before you were born. He made me trudge through the woods from where we parked the plane. I was as big as a house. Of course he wouldn't tell me anything about it until I saw it for myself. I could have killed him when he forced me to traipse through that dense, wet underbrush. But when I saw this spectacular monolith, I knew that it would become our special place. The summer after you were born, we took you here on your first camping trip. It was raining again and the sound of the rain on the water put you right to sleep. After that, we came here every chance we got. It *was* our own special place. I know other people used it, but we never had to share it with anyone. This spot was your introduction to camping and you have loved it ever since."

"I knew that, Mom. Dad told me how much this place meant to you. He told me all about that first trip. That's the main reason I conspired to get you here today. I had it all planned out, but I had to pretend that it was a last minute thing so you wouldn't have time to think."

"I sure didn't."

"It was the only way to get you in a plane again. This is the first time since the accident, and it's been over two years. But aren't you glad you came?"

"I am, Rudy. I really am."

"You have to get your life back, Mom. You can't just mope around the office all the time. I miss Dad so badly; it feels like my right arm has been cut off. But we're still living. It hurts me just as much to see you wandering off in a daze all the time. Sometimes I have to say your name three or four times before you come back to the present and reality."

"I'm sorry, Rudy, but I miss your dad terribly. We did everything together. He was my life. I never had time to prepare." Leila swallows, smiling through her tears. "But you know, you are so much like him. You remind me of him every day. When you were born only a couple months after that trip, I knew from day one that you were your father's son. When you were a baby, you cried for him, rather than me, to hold you."

"I don't remember hearing that before."

"It's true. You know, he was the first one to make you laugh out loud. Only he could comfort you when you suffered from colic. I was beginning to get jealous and felt guilty about being a bad mother, but when I saw how you adored him and that special bond you had with him. . . . ." Leila wipes her nose and continues, "Ana and Nat always clung to me, but you..."

Rudy reaches out to put his hand on Leila's shoulder.

"As soon as you could toddle around, you followed him around the office when he wasn't flying and hung on his pant leg. Do you remember that wooden airplane tricycle he made for you when you were three years old?"

Rudy smiles. "Uh-huh."

"You always insisted on bringing it everywhere you went. You threw tantrums if we couldn't fit it in the car right next to you."

"I do remember. Whatever happened to it?"

"I think it's somewhere in the crawlspace. I was so glad when you finally outgrew it."

"We'll have to dig it out one of these days."

"Yeah, one of these days. But remember how he took you everywhere with him?"

Rudy nods.

"He even made you a booster seat for the Super Cub so you could see out the window when he took you flying."

Rudy clears his throat and roughly brushes his sleeve across his eyes to hide his tears. "I'd better get a line in the water if we are going to have dinner." He grabs his fishing gear. "Just relax, Mom, I'll be right back."

Walking quickly towards a small clearing upstream from their camp, Rudy reminisces about flying and fishing with his dad. He laughs to himself as he remembers his first solo flight.

"I'm lucky Dad didn't ground me for good after that misadventure."

Chapter Three

Nikki and Daphne

Home at last from the courthouse, Nikki rushes to her room to look for some suitable clothes. With almost all of her clothes out of the closet—either tried on or tossed aside as being too old fashioned, she gives up on the short shorts and has slipped on a pair of black capris that visually slim down her wide hips. In the back of the closet she notices, next to Gerik's shirts, a sexy top she bought last winter during their vacation in Hawaii. Never having the nerve to wear it, she still didn't have the heart to give it away. Nikki struggles into it and appraises her image in the mirror. The top is a soft mint green with a subtle, barely visible, flowery pattern in aqua and teal. Beneath the bust, sheer organza fabric drapes in a flounce that hides her stomach and calls attention to her cleavage. The narrow shoulder straps accentuate the pale skin of her shoulders.

Wow, would I ever dare wear this is public?

Thrilled about the look of her hair, she visualizes herself thirty pounds thinner, thinking about all of the new fashions she will be able to wear. The doorbell rings and she hears the front door opening.

Who in the hell? She rushes to the foyer. Her best friend, Daphne, has let herself in and is heading for the kitchen with an armful of sunflowers, dahlias and snapdragons, baby's breath and daisies.

"Oh, I'm sorry." Daphne frowns. "I didn't mean to barge in, but I didn't think anyone was home yet. I didn't see any cars in the driveway and Elsa told me she was going to the courthouse this afternoon. Is she at home?"

"Daphne, it's me! Didn't you recognize me? It's me—Elsa AKA Nikki—the new me."

She turns around in a pirouette. Her hair swings back and forth.

"Ta daaa. What do you think?"

"Oh, El, I mean, Nikki, you're beautiful. I love it." She rushes over to embrace her, flowers and all.

Daphne looks towards the kitchen. "Has Gerik seen it yet? What does he think?"

"Oh, he's not home yet. He's hardly ever home this early."

"Yeah, I should have known."

Daphne has been Nikki's best friend for a long time, although they have seen some rocky times. Nikki remembers meeting her in the eighth grade when Daphne's family moved to Caraville from Chicago. They sat next to each other in their homeroom because their last names, Pedersen and Penndel, are next to each other alphabetically. She remembers the home economics class she and Daphne took when they were sophomores. The class was a snap for Elsa. She did most of the cooking at home. Nikki can still see the approving look on the teacher's face when her soufflé turned out like a dream.

⌒

"Elsa, that's impressive. Have you done this before?"

"Not really, Mrs. Erickson. I just know how to follow recipes, I guess."

"It's more than that. You have real talent for someone so young."

"Thank you."

Mrs. Erickson took her aside one day when the rest of the students were struggling to follow a recipe and making massive messes in the kitchen. "Elsa, would you please help that group over there while I try to get these three straightened out?"

"Sure."

"It's so nice to have someone to rely on in this class. It seems all the other students have two left hands."

The others in the class resented her "brown-nosing." They avoided her, making suggestive gestures behind her back. Daphne—the most popular girl in the sophomore class—usually snubbed Elsa. She apparently didn't want to be seen talking to a plain, frumpy goody-goody. But one day after class, Daphne begged, "Elsa, can you please help me with this pattern? It makes absolutely no sense to me."

Daphne sounded desperate. Her obvious interests were boys and art, not home ec. She confided in Elsa that her goal was to date every boy on the football team. "I love that attention. It makes me feel smart—like you."

⟨ ⟩

Snapping back to the present, Nikki takes the flowers from Daphne to the kitchen to arrange them, smiling at Daphne's ineptitude. "I don't understand how an artist like you still can't arrange flowers in a vase. I guess if it was a canvas, you would have no trouble."

Daphne laughs. "Yeah, well, I guess we all have different talents. Remember how you helped me with all the projects in home ec? I'm glad the teacher never found out I didn't actually do any of them. You were a lifesaver. I'm sure the old bat would have made me take the class again if she knew."

Nikki nods, but still has bittersweet feelings about their friendship, remembering how she helped Daphne with all her projects—even doing some of them entirely alone. By the end of the semester they were best friends, talking on the phone for hours. One conversation stands out in Nikki's memory.

Sitting on the steps with the phone cord stretched around the corner so her family—especially Leila—would not hear, Elsa and Daphne talked until Elsa's father finally said, "That's enough. Someone else might want to use the phone."

"Okay, Dad."

Before hanging up Daphne said, "Hey, how about if we do a double date this weekend? Joe Cummings asked me out to the dance on Friday night. You and that gorgeous guy of yours would make it a lot more fun. Gerik's laughter and voice are so sexy. You lucky dog!"

"I'm so glad to have him as my steady. He really is a hunk."

"He sure is, too bad you found him first."

"Well, we've known each other all our lives."

"Wish I had met him earlier."

"I couldn't avoid it since our mothers were best friends. I used to think he was my brother."

"Aren't you glad he's not?"

"Yeah. I remember crying for days when he started kindergarten and I couldn't go with him. I thought he didn't like me anymore."

"He sure does now, though. You are so lucky."

"I guess we were childhood sweethearts. At least that's what everybody said."

"Didn't he ever go through that ugly, girl-hating stage?"

"No, we've always been close."

Elsa's father appeared around the corner with his hands on his hips. He looked like he would grab the phone from Elsa's hands. "Come on, that's enough for tonight. Don't you have homework to do?"

"Okay, Dad. I'm off. Bye, Daph."

"Don't forget about Friday night."

As Nikki remembers bits and pieces of her conversations with Daphne from high school, she kicks herself for not recognizing the signs of things to come sooner. A whiff of anger meets her nostrils. She conceals the sudden rage arising within by stuffing the last snapdragons into the vase. She steps back to admire her artistry. She sticks her chin out. *I'm glad that's all in the past. But how could I have been so stupid to think we were engaged when I left for college. He hadn't even given me a ring. I should have known they would see each other with Daphne being so near in Chicago. Best friends forever—ha! I should have guessed at what she meant when she said she would take care of Gerik for me.*

Daphne admires the flower arrangement, too. "I don't know how you do it, Elsa. You make everything look so easy."

"Not everything."

"But you're so competent. I don't think you ever fail at anything you try."

"My sister never thought so. She always had to ridicule me—no matter what I did."

"Well, she's an idiot. Gerik says she still treats you like a child. The other day, when we..." Daphne stops abruptly.

"When what?"

"Never mind." Daphne looks away. Her neck reddens. "Hey, may if I use your computer for a few minutes? I need to print something and my printer stopped talking to my computer."

"Sure, go ahead. You know where it is."

Daphne rushes out of the kitchen towards Elsa's office.

Elsa's mind starts wandering as she prepares dinner. Conversations from the past play back in her mind as though she is watching a movie.

⟜⟶

"Don't worry about Gerik, Elsa. I'll take good care of him for you. You know I'll be close by in Chicago. I'll get back to Caraville all the time. How could I miss out on partying with the old crowd?"

"But, I'll be way off in Michigan. I'll only get home on the longer breaks. And now Gerik says he's taking a year off from his studies at Loyola because his dad is so sick. He says he has to help his mom take him to chemotherapy."

"Like I said, I'll keep him company."

⟜⟶

Nikki washes the vegetables without thinking, her mind a million miles away. When she hears footsteps behind her, she startles and drops an overripe tomato. It splatters, leaving tomato juice, seeds and pulp all over the floor and cabinets.

41

"I didn't mean to surprise you," Daphne apologizes.

"No, no. That's okay. My hands were just slippery. You didn't really surprise me."

No, Daphne. Nothing you do will ever surprise me again.

Chapter Four

Rudy's First Solo

R udy walks down the path a little way remembering how his dad had shown him how to fish for Dolly Varden trout.

A typical four-year-old boy, Rudy loved running through the woods, chasing squirrels and jumping over roots and stumps. Rambunctious and overly active—even for a four year old— Rudy wanted to please his dad, Pete, but his attention wandered to other, more exciting things. He tried many times to get the tiny lure to the spot his dad had pointed out, but some of his casts didn't even make it to the water. Finally he got the lure to settle into the smooth water just under the trees across the stream. As he pulled it back toward shore, he felt a tug on the fishing line. A fish jumped out of the water, flashing its silvery belly. Rudy dropped the fishing rod, but his dad's hands were right there to catch it.

"Put your hands back on the pole, Rudy. Start winding. Steady, now. Keep winding. He's a big one. Looks like a granddaddy, all right."

They worked the fish together, bringing it closer and closer. By the time they got the fish to shore, Rudy was hooked on fishing. From that day on, they spent many happy hours fishing together.

Remembering that day, Rudy prepares his fishing rod and finds a comfortable place to sit.

"This could be the very spot," he thinks. "It looks familiar."

Rudy also remembers fishing for king salmon on the Kenai River when they lived in Kasilof. His mind wanders to the old Piper PA-12 tied down in the backyard of their house on the bluff north of Kenai. His dad said he would of restore it to flying condition one day, but he never found the time. The dull white fabric—ripped and in need of paint—flapped in the breeze in many places. Rudy doesn't remember if it had a propeller or whether or not it even had an engine. He does remember how beautiful it looked to him.

Rudy spent countless hours sitting in the plane, pretending he was flying. On windy days the plane almost seemed like it wanted to fly. Rudy rushed out to the plane whenever he heard the southwesterly winds pick up. He learned that if he lengthened the tie-down ropes a little, the plane would actually lift off the ground momentarily in a gust. He moved the controls forward and aft, left and right. The plane would lift a little and he would bank it to the right or left and the gear would touch down with a thud. Again and again he tried to make it smooth and hoped for a steady wind so he could keep the plane airborne for more than a few seconds. By the time he was eleven years old, he had more time in that cockpit than many pilots have in a lifetime of flying. Sometimes his friend Jimmy sat in the front seat and Rudy would pretend to give him instruction. They took turns handling the controls.

When the boys turned twelve, their dads tried to turn their attention from flying to the more practical pursuit of trapping.

"There's plenty of time to fly, Rudy," his dad, Pete, said. "Now, you need to learn how to make a living. I'll show you and Jimmy how to set the traps and check them. Next winter you should be ready to run a trap line by yourself and you can use the snow machine each weekend to check it. Any money you make above expenses, you can save for flying lessons. By the time you are fifteen, you should have enough for a private pilot certificate. Does that sound fair?"

"Sure, Dad," Rudy said. "Me and Jimmy can check it right after school on Wednesdays, too."

"Jimmy and I," Pete said, smiling.

"Right, Dad, Jimmy and I," Rudy laughed.

Pete's family had run trap lines as long as he could remember. When the price of beaver pelts dropped, he gave up trapping as a way to make a living, but continued to set traps for wolverines so he could provide furs for his grandmother's crafts. Her beautifully handcrafted fur parkas, beaded slippers, hats and mittens graced the stores in popular tourist stores in downtown Anchorage and commanded top dollar.

The excitement and responsibility kept Rudy on task that winter and the next. He handled the trapped animals—mostly lynx, beaver and muskrats—with trepidation at first. Checking the trap line only on Saturdays generally assured the animals would be frozen and easy to release from the traps. The first wolverine he encountered, though, was still struggling in the trap. One of its front legs was caught in the spring trap. Rudy and Jimmy kept their distance. Its beady black eyes, snarling teeth and long claws looked like they could rip through thick leather.

"I wouldn't want him to get a hold of me, Jimmy. I think he'd rip me apart as mad as he is."

"They are pretty mean, all right. My dad says wolverines are ten times stronger than an animal twice its size."

"Why are they so mean?" Rudy asked.

"I don't know, but they sure have beautiful fur." Jimmy replied.

"Yeah, my grandma always makes the ruffs of her parkas out of wolverine fur. She says it's the best for warmth because it doesn't frost up like other furs."

Jimmy hopped on the idling snow machine to head to the next set of traps. "Well, I'm not going to try and touch him today. Maybe my dad or yours will help us next time we come out." He said as they zoomed down the trail. "Sure, but I think we can handle it on our own. I wouldn't want anyone thinking we were sissies." Rudy bragged— his courage boosted by the increasing distance from the angry animal. "How hard could it be to bag a forty pound animal?"

As they sped away from the angry wolverine, Rudy remembered the twenty-two rifle on the sled. He tapped Jimmy on the shoulder and said, "We've got to go back, Jimmy. We can't leave that animal suffering like that—even if he is mean. I'll use the twenty-two to finish him off."

Jimmy slowed down, saying, "You couldn't possibly hit him without damaging his pelt. He was thrashing around something fierce."

"Don't worry. I've been practicing. I think I can do it. At least I have to try."

They turned around and drew near to the trap with the wolverine. Rudy noticed the animal lying there very still. The snow around the trap was tracked and scratched; looking like the wolverine had tried to escape.

"I think he's dead, Jimmy." Just then the animal moved and sprung towards the boys—snarling. Both Rudy and Jimmy jumped back, almost falling off the snow machine.

Rudy got the twenty-two rifle out of the sled, checking to make sure it was loaded. He switched the safety off and braced himself against the machine to look steadily through the sights. His heart was pounding. The vibration of the running engine made it difficult to hold the gun still.

"Shut down the engine, Jimmy," Rudy ordered.

"But my Dad said never to shut down this far from home."

"You're right. We'd hate to be stuck here all night with this wounded animal nearby. Look, there's a stump over there I can use."

Rudy started towards the stump and sank thigh deep in the snow. "Looks like I need to get the snowshoes on. Boy, this is taking longer than I thought. I hope we make it home before dark."

By the time he got the snowshoes on and braced against the stump for his shot, his confidence had returned. He waited until he could get a clean shot and then fired two quick shots into the wolverine's head, one of them hitting him right in the eye. It dropped and lay very still. The boys waited for at least five minutes watching the animal closely to be sure it didn't move. They approached it cautiously with Rudy holding the gun ready to fire if it moved at all. It didn't. They released the wolverine from the trap, loaded it onto the sled, reset the trap and hurried away. Rudy knew he had done the right thing.

He and Jimmy trapped and sold enough pelts to more than cover their meager expenses and saved most of what they earned. Rudy was getting close to having enough for flying lessons and he would be fifteen in a few months.

One February day while passing a private airstrip on the way back from checking their traps on the snow machine, Rudy noticed a ski plane tied down that hadn't been there before. They swung over to look at it, driving the down the center of the snow-covered airstrip.

Jimmy leaned to one side to get a better look. "Wow, cool! Maybe we can get in it and check it out."

"We'd better not, Jimmy, this is private property, remember. We probably shouldn't even be here. But it is really cool."

As they admired the plane a grey bearded man dressed in heavy duck Carharts and Sorrel boots silently walked up behind them and growled, "She's a beauty, isn't she?" Rudy and Jimmy jumped as they turned around to face him. "How would you boys like to fly her?"

Both Rudy and Jimmy were too stunned to speak. They had expected to be in trouble and instead were being offered the chance of a lifetime.

"That would be great," they both said at once.

Sitting in the left seat, the old man—Gustaf—let Rudy take the controls for a few minutes and was impressed with Rudy's ability to fly.

"Where did a young whippersnapper like you ever learn to fly?"

"Oh, I've been flying for a long time," Rudy fibbed. "My dad runs a flying service."

After landing and tying down the plane, Rudy asked if they could come back sometime and maybe exchange some work for time in the airplane. He was ready to do anything to get his hands on the controls of an airplane again.

"Oh, I don't really own the plane," Gustaf said. "I am just watching it for a guy in Anchorage who is looking to sell it. He likes me to run the engine every once in a while to keep it lubricated and I figure I may as well fly it since the engine is running. No point in wasting perfectly good fuel. Besides, it gives me a way to check my trap line from the air. You'd be amazed how much ground you can cover in a plane in a very short time. But, maybe in a week or two, you can stop by again. If it is still here we can take her for a ride."

"Wow that would be great." Rudy smiled. "Thanks a bunch."

Rudy thought of nothing but flying for the next two weeks. He remembered how the airplane felt when he moved the controls. He wanted nothing more than to go back and fly the old T-Craft. He dreamed about owning it. Even running the snow machine across the frozen lakes at full throttle didn't hold the thrill for him that flying did. He imagined soaring over the mountains and seeing the wilderness from a different perspective. While it was true that he had been flying for a long time, it was with his father at the controls. Now he wanted to be in charge.

The next week no planes were on the airstrip as Rudy and Jimmy went by on their way to check the trap line. The money Rudy had secretly withdrawn from his savings was burning a hole in his pocket. Then two weeks later, there she was. It looked like Gustaf was about ready to get in the plane and take off. Rudy raced the snow machine over to the airstrip, kicking up snow as they swung alongside the taxiing plane. Jimmy hung on to Rudy with one arm, waving frantically with the other to get the old man's attention. About ready to give up and turn away, he noticed the plane slowing down and coming to a stop in the middle of the airstrip.

A complete stranger jumped out as the propeller was winding down. He was shaking his fist and yelling, "What in the hell are you doing? Do you want to get us both killed? Hasn't anyone ever explained to you the dangers of being in the vicinity of an airplane with its engine running? I've got a mind to haul you both in to town and report you to the sheriff for trespassing. Now get your butts off this strip before I throw you off!"

Rudy squared his shoulders and took a deep breath. "Now, sir, I just wanted to make sure that nobody was stealing my plane. It looked like you were about to take off with her."

"Your plane? Hah! This is *my* old beat..., aah—beauty, kid. And, what in the hell, you couldn't own a plane anyway, you're just a kid."

"Well, I told Gustaf that I wanted to buy it. In fact, I brought along $2,500 today to sew up the deal." Rudy hoped he would have an opportunity to make an offer on the plane. He had no idea what a plane like that would be worth, but he had overheard his father talking about an old T-craft that he had picked up for parts for $1,500. He thought maybe $2,500 for an operational plane might be about right. With false bravado he reached into his back pocket and pulled out twenty-five carefully folded one hundred dollar bills.

"Are you the owner, sir? If so, we can settle this right here." Jimmy made choking sounds beside him and Rudy elbowed him in the ribs as he said to the man, "Just sign over the title to me and it's a done deal."

On seeing the cash, the man's demeanor changed. "Sure, kid, why don't we just head inside and talk it over." They walked to the small shed alongside the strip. "I've got to get back to Anchorage pretty quick, though. Look, I've got the title right here in my pocket. We can take care of the details if you would give me a ride to Anchorage after we sign the deal." He grinned like a fox discovering a hole in the wall of the chicken coop.

The papers properly signed and money exchanged, the guy said, "Okay, let's get a move on. It'll be getting dark in a few hours. Time's a wasting."

Rudy's heart was pounding, but there was no way he could back down now and admit that he didn't know how to fly an airplane. His mind raced. *How am I going to get the plane back here? What will I tell my dad? What about the trap line? I don't even know if the plane has a radio.*

On the outside, he was all calm and collected. "Now, Jimmy, you finish running the line and then go to my house and tell my dad I'll be home in a little while. Then come back here and pick me up around seven o'clock. I should be back by then."

Pulling him aside so the guy wouldn't hear, Rudy whispered to Jimmy, "Now, don't tell anyone anything until we have a chance to get our stories straight. We'll figure something out."

Jimmy looked like he would cry and Rudy shoved him in the chest, "Come on, Jimbo, we're in this together. Think of all the fun we'll have with the airplane. Don't spoil it now. Just think of the places we can explore!"

With that he turned towards the plane and hopped in the right seat. Relieved to see the previous owner planned to fly it to Anchorage, Rudy relaxed a bit. That would give him time to figure things out. He watched carefully as they took off from the small airstrip. He concentrated so hard on trying to remember everything the pilot was doing, he hardy heard his animated conversation.

The pilot shouted above the noise of the engine, "Yeah, she's a good old bird, just needs a little TLC. I was going to fly her back to Anchorage today—since Gustaf never sold her—and put her on the sale lot at Lake Hood, but lucky for you, you got her first. The buddy who dropped me off will be flabbergasted when I return with the money I owe him. Times are tough since the price of oil dropped and my job up on the Slope was cut. I just don't have the money anymore to support an airplane along with my other habits, Ha-ha. Yeah, we had a lot of fun with this bird. I'm going to miss her."

Some thing in the guy's voice and nervous manner made Rudy uncomfortable, but the thought that he now owned the airplane overshadowed any uneasiness he might have felt. At least the guy could fly an airplane all right. He seemed a little rougher than Rudy's dad, but safe enough. The man talked on about trips he had taken all over the state with the plane. He described some narrow escapes and encounters with bad weather, laughing them off as though that was a normal part of flying in Alaska.

When they crossed Turnagain Arm, the little plane descended towards an airstrip on the south edge of Anchorage.

"We'll land at O'Malley strip," the guy said. "That's where I left my car."

Again Rudy appreciated the fact they didn't have to land at an airport where there would be a lot of traffic and air traffic controllers to deal with. He was accustomed to small bush strips from all the flying he'd done with his dad. He knew O'Malley strip was a small airport with no control tower and only a few private airplanes.

The guy flew over the airstrip to check the windsock. A fresh layer of snow made it difficult to recognize the edges of strip, but the airplanes parked along one side outlined one edge.

"Not much of a wind, kid. You can just take off to the north after I turn her around. If you don't mind, we can just leave the engine running and I'll jump out, that way you can take right off again and get back to Kenai before dark," the guy said, sounding eager to get away.

"Yeah, that sounds great," Rudy said, thinking of what a stroke of luck it was that the guy had his own worries and didn't notice his nervousness. The man landed the plane with a thud causing Rudy to bite his tongue. He taxied to a wide spot at the end of the strip where a red Corvette was parked. Unbuckling his seat belt as he turned the airplane around to face back down the runway, the guy turned to Rudy.

"Been a real pleasure dealing with you, kid. If you ever want me to show you some action around town, give me a call. I know some hot chicks who can show you a good time, if you know what I mean." Roughly shaking Rudy's hand, he winked and jumped out of the plane. "Next time!" he said, bounding away from the plane.

Rudy wanted to get away as soon as he could. He slid over to the left seat and buckled his seatbelt before pushing the throttle forward. The skis stuck to the snow-covered runway and Rudy had to push the throttle all the way forward before the skis broke free and the plane moved forward. He realized he was now committed to continuing the take off. Looking down the runway, Rudy noticed the plane veering to the left. Instinctively, with all his might, he turned the control yoke to the right. Nothing happened. Then he remembered his dad saying something about steering the plane with the rudders, and just as the plane was about to go off the left side of the runway, he stomped on the right rudder. The plane yawed suddenly to the right and then left again as Rudy reversed controls. His left hand tightened on the yoke and he pulled back as the plane neared the left side of the runway for the second time. Suddenly he was airborne.

"Yahoo, I'm flying!"

The trees surrounding the runway brushed by as Rudy pulled the yoke harder and harder. Something didn't feel right. The plane wasn't climbing like it should. A horn was blaring in Rudy's ear. *Oh, man. I can't do anything right. What's happening? I don't want to wreck my airplane.*

Rudy's hand relaxed a little on the yoke, and the airplane began to climb away from the trees. *Okay, that's better. Now, let's get her turned around. Let's see, if I keep the mountains on my left, after I cross the inlet I can follow the shoreline. That should take me back to the airstrip where we took off. I think I'll be able to recognize Johnson's Road from the air and the strip is right at the end of the road.* Rudy relaxed a little and looked around. He noticed for the first time, the large jets approaching Anchorage International Airport. *I'd better stay low and out of their way.*

The inlet looked much wider than it had on the trip north. Rudy forgot to look at his watch when he took off, but he looked at it now. *Man, it's already five-thirty. I didn't think it was so late. I can't remember exactly when it gets dark now, but I'm sure I have plenty of time. It can't take much more than an hour to get back to Kenai.*

When he came to the shore of the inlet, he turned the plane to the west and flew right over the shoreline. A westerly wind picked up and it seemed that he was barely moving forward. He felt like he was suspended in midair. After what seemed to be an eternity, he reached Point Possession and turned south towards Kenai. *Now I'm home free. I should be there in no time.* But the wind was now a quartering head wind and his ground speed was only a little better than it had been when he was heading west. He looked at his watch again. *Six fifteen! How did that take me so long? I wonder how much gas is in this thing.* Beginning to look around inside the plane for the first time since he took off he couldn't find any gas gauges. *Well, there must be enough.*

The sun settled towards the horizon and nothing looked familiar to Rudy. Flying at less than five hundred feet above the snow-covered terrain, he could not tell frozen lakes from swampy areas. They all looked the same.

What have I gotten into? Well, I'll just have to keep the shore on my right and keep going. I will certainly know when I cross the Kenai River. If that happens, I'll know that I went too far and turn around. This thought comforted him for a while. Although, when he glanced at his watch again, it was six forty-five. The deepening twilight lengthened the shadows and things again looked different.

"At least it's a clear day. Thank goodness for small favors." Just then, the engine made a sputtering sound and Rudy grabbed the yoke more tightly.

Sweat ran down his face in spite of the cold air blowing through the cracks around the edges of the windows. He looked down towards the throttle and noticed another knob that was labeled "heat." He pulled that out hoping to get some air circulating in the cockpit. The engine noise got worse and he was tempted to reverse what he had done. *No, I'll leave it on. I need heat. I don't want to be cold if I crash.*

He still tried finding something familiar. In his fear, he had climbed a little higher and with a wider perspective he could identify some buildings.

"Oh, there's the Radcliff's fishing cabin. Yeah, all right! There's the wrecked boat on the beach. I know where I am. Yahoo!" The engine noise smoothed out and Rudy breathed a sigh of relief.

He turned the airplane around—circling higher and higher—looking for Johnson's road and the airstrip. He still could not identify the strip. His eyes were straining to see something—anything. His throat was dry and his head hurt from trying to concentrate.

"I don't know what to do, Dad," he said aloud. Tears welled up in his eyes. For the first time since taking off, he thought about how mad his dad would be. Fear of punishment added to his anguish.

But, Daddy is always fair. He always helps me out of scrapes.

He imagined his dad giving him advice now like he always did. He could almost hear his soothing voice.

Stay calm, Rudy. Think. What are the positives in this situation?

These words always helped him to deal with situations ranging from a thorny algebra word problems, to dealing with his sisters, to diagnosing engine problems on his snow machine. Maybe they could help him now. He took a deep breath and focused.

What are the positives? Well, for one thing I'm still airborne. I sort of know where I am. The engine is still running. The weather is good. The wind has calmed down. With each positive statement his thinking cleared. His confidence returned.

What else did his dad always say? Rudy imagined his dad sitting next to him.

How can you best handle the challenges? Use your head. Don't rely on feelings or be discouraged by momentary frustration.

Okay, now. The challenge is finding the airstrip. He scratched his chin. *How can I solve this problem?*

It occurred to him that flying a pattern or grid from a known point could narrow his search area. He flew back to the beach and located the wrecked boat on the shore. *I know the airstrip is about two miles east of the shoreline and I figure it's a little south of the wreck. I'll fly east for a couple minutes, then turn right and fly west to the shore and then repeat until I see Johnson's Road.*

On making his first turn back to the west he noticed lights of a moving vehicle on the ground. They appeared to go straight for a while then circle around a few times then straight in the opposite direction. He flew closer to the moving light and could see that it was a snow machine racing along a wide expense of white.

It must be Jimmy. Bless his soul! He's showing me the strip.

Rudy wagged the wings of the plane and turned around to get lined up with the airstrip, trying to remember exactly what his dad did when approaching to land. He remembered him bringing the throttle to idle and using the trim wheel.

Now where is the trim wheel in this thing?" I guess I don't have time to look right now.

It was getting more difficult to keep the airplane in a level flight attitude. Rudy pulled harder and harder on the yoke as the plane lost altitude and settled towards the ground. Before he realized it, he was over the airstrip still moving—too fast—over the ground. He gritted his teeth and braced for the impact. About half way down the strip the plane settled down on to the snow. At first Rudy did not realize he had landed. Although the snow covered runway slowed him a little, he was still moving quite fast. The skis slid easily on the slippery snow. Out of the corner of his eye, he saw a snow machine with its lights on. He went by it. The snow berm at the end of the strip was getting closer. Rudy reached down and pulled the mixture control aft. He had seen his dad do that in the floatplane when approaching the shoreline. The engine quit abruptly. The propeller stopped turning. All he could do now was hang on and wait for the momentum of the airplane to slow. He knew a ski plane would have no brakes.

In what seemed to be slow motion, he hit the berm and the airplane began to tip up on to its nose. He thought for a moment that it might flip over completely on its back, but he was powerless to do anything about it. He was just along for the ride. The plane gradually came to a stop in an almost vertical position with the propeller and spinner wedged in the snow bank. It was very quiet then and Rudy could hear his heart pounding in his ears. Suspended from his seat belt, he carefully reached to open the door and grabbed the door-frame. Releasing his seat belt and bracing his feet against the instrument panel, he jumped down to the ground.

Jimmy stood there, wide-eyed. "Gee whiz!" He said. "I thought you were going to kill yourself."

Rudy laughed almost hysterically. The relief of surviving his first solo flight and the sight of the airplane with its nose stuck in the snow struck him as very funny.

"What a trip! Next time, it's me and you, Jimmy. What a blast!"

"We better get this thing out of the snow bank before anyone sees it. I'll get a rope around the tail and we can pull it down with the snow machine." Jimmy dug a rope out of the sled. He lassoed the horizontal stabilizer and hooked the other end to his snow machine.

Rudy by now had calmed down and cautioned Jimmy, "Be careful. Go slow. Wait! Maybe we can just pull it down ourselves. We don't want to damage the tail."

They both grabbed the rope and pulled with all their might. The airplane did not budge. Then Rudy thought maybe they could dig out around the prop and nose of the plane. They ran to the front of the plane and started digging snow with their bare hands.

Jimmy stopped digging. "Hang on; I have a shovel in the sled." The work went much faster with the shovel. Before long the snow was cleared from around the nose of the plane. As they walked towards the back of the plane, tired from their efforts, they heard a creaking noise. The plane teetered and slowly began to settle down. It picked up momentum and the tail wheel slammed down onto the snow, barely missing the snow machine.

"I guess we should have moved the snow machine out of the way," Rudy cringed. "But since we have the rope tied on, let's tow it over to the parking spot and tie it down. We have to get home before my mom and dad get suspicious."

"No worries," said Jimmy. "I told him that we were going to study together at my house until at least eight o'clock and that you would have dinner at our house. Then I told my parents that I was going to study at your house. We should be okay as long as they don't talk to each other."

"Good thinking, Jimmy. Just wait 'til I tell you about my trip. Maybe we can find some excuse to come out here tomorrow and take her for a ride."

The next day after school Rudy told his mom he and Jimmy needed to go back along their trap line to pick up some supplies they had left.

"We had to leave some stuff cuz we had so many pelts. It was at the end of the line, too, so it might be a couple hours."

Leila nodded, barely pausing from her dinner preparations. Rudy raced to Jimmy's house with the snow machine and together they headed out to the airstrip. On the way they planned their flight and laughed with excitement.

"When we get there, Jimmy, see if you can round up Gustaf and ask if he has any fuel to spare. We can pay him back with our trapping money. I'll untie the plane and look her over to make sure that we didn't bend the tail feathers or anything last night. It was so dark by the time we got her out of the snow bank; I couldn't tell if anything was bent. Then we'll just take her for a short ride and I'll see if I can get the landing a little better."

As they approached the airstrip, their conversation grew more animated with Rudy shouting over his shoulder so Jimmy could hear. Rudy did not notice his dad's blue pickup truck parked next to the shed. They slid to a stop with a spray of snow just as their fathers stepped out of the cabin with Gustaf.

"Uh, Oh," Rudy looked back at Jimmy, his shoulders hunched as though to deflect a blow. "We've been had!"

Rudy had been fishing absentmindedly as he relived his first solo flight and now looks down to see four beautiful trout in his creel. He doesn't even remember catching them. *Talk about Mom being lost in thought! I guess I could compete for top prize in that department as well.* He laughs as he anticipates sharing this memory with Leila.

Approaching their campsite, Rudy whistles "The Gypsy Rover" intentionally off key. It was a game he and his sisters played on Leila whenever they were learning a new song. They would see if they could sing it very slightly off key, pretending not to notice the difference. Leila always corrected them. *That last note was just a little under pitch, Rudy.* Then one day she overheard the three of them singing in perfect harmony and knew they had been pulling her leg. But she was a good sport about it. Since Pete's accident, Rudy tried to get Leila to laugh at his off key singing, but she never even noticed. Today, however, as soon as she hears him, she laughs. "That last note was a little flat, Rudy."

He hurries over to her and gives her a big hug. "That's more like it, Mom. I knew this camping trip would be good for you." He hesitates. "You know, I was just thinking about the time I bought that old T-Craft. Remember?"

Leila nods with a smile.

"I don't know if Dad ever told you the whole story about my recklessness—he probably didn't want to scare you—but he dragged every detail out of me when he found Jimmy and me at the airstrip that day."

"Your Dad and I shared everything. Of course I knew the whole story."

Rudy grimaces. "I thought he was going to tan my hide for sure. But the way he handled it made me respect him and his judgment more than anything. I'm sure that sleazy character who sold me the plane was just hoping to unload an out-of-annual old junker. He must have needed money desperately, too, to sell it so cheaply."

"I bet he was."

"So, when Dad told me all about the investigating he had done that day to make sure everything was legal and discovering what an incredibly good deal I had made, I was relieved and ready to face my punishment.

You know, he could have grounded me for good, or scared me speechless, or tried to turn me away from flying forever. But I think he recognized in me that same love of flying that he had. He knew that I would fly with or without his blessing."

"Yes."

"So, first, he made sure I fully understood the seriousness of what I had done. He told me how much you both loved me and how much it would hurt if anything had happened to me on that flight—which it so easily could have. I was shaking in my boots by the time he finished with me."

"He always tried to teach you to be responsible."

"I know. And, as I look back, his punishment was certainly fair enough, but at the time I thought my life had ended. I couldn't imagine how I would live without using the snow machine for a whole month."

"It was even harder for him to ground you like that."

"I can see that now. You know, something he said then has stayed with me all these years. I don't think I fully understood its meaning, though, until after he died. He said—and I don't remember the exact words—but it was something like, 'Live each day fully, Rudy, but always consider how your actions will affect others. Whether you fly, or build houses, or become an accountant, do it to the best of your ability, always with others in mind; because it is in our relationships with others that love blossoms and grows and our lives become full and rich.'"

Rudy clears his throat and unashamedly wipes tears from his cheeks with the back of his hand. Leila reaches over to put a hand on his arm holding the creel.

"He really lived that way, didn't he, Mom? "

She nods silently and smiles.

"Well, I'm doing my best to honor his memory by doing the same...Hey, how about getting these fish on the grill? I'm starving."

Chapter Five

Nikki's Past Revisited

Until recently, Nikki rarely gave a thought to her history with Daphne. Now, with Gerik's attitude grating on her nerves and Daphne seeming to pull away from her, she can't help but wonder. Her mind wanders back to those difficult years and she creates scenarios that make her blood boil. She shakes them off and returns to the present. How much of it is true? What is simply jealousy or insecurity? She doesn't know. She does know that when she went away to college in Michigan, Daphne and Gerik gravitated towards each other. She remembers a mutual friend asking her if she and Gerik had broken up.

"Hey, what's between you and Gerik? Have you broken up?"

"No, why do you ask?" Elsa was curious.

Well, I wasn't going to say anything, but he and Daphne seem pretty close these days."

"Sounds like she just wants to keep him from getting lonesome."

"But, you should have seen the low-cut blouse she had on the other day at a party. Her boobs were practically in his face. You know how persuasive she can be. It looks to me like she is after him—seriously."

Elsa chose not to believe any of the reports and buried herself in her studies. She cherished each conversation with Gerik and never brought up anything about Daphne, but a hint of suspicion surfaced. She suspected that Daphne had a secret crush on Gerik and imagined her pursuing him.

One evening when Elsa called to talk to Gerik, his mother said that he was out for the night. "You should have seen him; all dressed up like a Tomcat strutting around. He told me he was going out with the guys and wouldn't be home tonight. Said he was spending the night at Bill's house, right near his job so he could just go straight to work in the morning."

"I guess Bill does live close to Evanston."

"He just seems to be doing a lot of partying these days. But at least he's always here to help me with his dad. He's faithful about getting him to chemotherapy every week."

"Yes, he is a hard worker, isn't he?" Elsa believed in him.

During the summers, when Elsa was at home, Gerik spent most of his time with her. Daphne was not in the picture, or so Elsa thought.

Gerik praised Elsa, making her feel as though she was the only woman in the world. "I love how you believe in me, Elsa. I feel like I can accomplish anything with you behind me."

"You can! And I love how you're so good to your parents, Gerik. You're so smart. I know when you go back to school in the fall, you'll do great. I don't know how I got so lucky to have you notice me."

"Well it's not like we just met, is it? You've always been a part of my life."

"I just hate it, though, that you have to work such long hours. But I guess the money is good with all that overtime you're getting. You are lucky to have an uncle in the construction business."

With Gerik lavishing attention on her, Elsa had no clue about what he did on nights he claimed to be working late and couldn't make it back to Caraville. Only later did she understand that Daphne's presence in her Chicago apartment must have drawn him like a magnet. Only later did she imagine Gerik rushing to meet Daphne and making love to her, oblivious to anything else.

After that fateful day Elsa tortured herself with imagined conversations... *Oh, Daphne...* Elsa heard his deep voice in her imagination: *My love. Your naked body thrills me to no end. I just can't get enough of you. You're so free and uninhibited. Your laughter during sex drives me wild. Oh, oh ooooh, man, Daphne, my love. Oh, yes. YES.*

But that was only after she discovered the truth about their affair. Summers in Caraville were busy with Elsa holding down two part time jobs. Gerik spent most of his free time with Elsa. They talked about the future and Gerik confided in her that he had doubts about his career choice. "I don't know how I can finish with a double major. It's not like either on of them is a snap."

"But, Gerik, think of what a great job you'll have with both an engineering degree and an MBA. I just know you'll be CEO of a big company someday."

"That's only because you're behind me one hundred percent."

Elsa never suspected that after dropping her off at home, Gerik would be heading to Chicago and Daphne, losing himself in the passion of their affair. If an impartial observer could see the entire picture they would note Gerik's selfishness and immaturity. But Elsa saw only his devotion to her and his parents and Gerik obviously never thought rationally enough to consider how it looked to anyone else, or the consequences.

On Christmas break during her senior year at Wayne State, Elsa surprised Daphne by dropping in on her at her apartment in Chicago. When she rang the bell and Gerik answered the door, he gasped, "Elsa!" He was dressed in Daphne's burgundy terrycloth robe—a gift from Elsa.

She was livid. "What are you doing here? You, you—fraud!" She caught sight of Daphne in bra and panties trying to sneak out of the living room.

"And you! I can't believe it! So this is how you sneak around behind my back while I'm working my butt off to graduate. Best friend? Is that what you call this? You are both the lowest of the low. If I never see you again in this lifetime, that will be too soon. Working long hours, huh? I can imagine the type of work you do around here. You're despicable!"

Gerik stood there, mouth open, unable to speak.

Elsa left without waiting for an explanation. She broke off all contact with both Gerik and Daphne. Their betrayal was inexcusable. In her last semester of college, she did not speak to either of them and frantically struggled to finish her degree but with an overriding sense of futility. Her graduation present from her parents was a month's vacation in Italy. She and Gerik often discussed how he would join her in Florence, but after that fateful afternoon, that idea made her stomach roll. She went alone instead. For a while, she was able to forget about his betrayal. She loved the chaotic energy and the abundance of art in Rome and Florence. Everywhere she looked, great sculptures and paintings spoke to her innate sense of style and design. It was a time of soul searching and she found that maybe she could survive alone. But she returned to Caraville out of malaise. She didn't have enough energy to investigate other options. A teaching job at a junior high school was open, and she fell into it without even considering anything else.

Elsa had been back in Caraville for a month before she ran into Gerik. She spotted him one day while waiting in line at the bank. She was in a hurry and ran inside thinking it would be quicker because of the long line at the drive-through window. Inside the cool lobby, there were only two people in line in front of her and she noticed Gerik instantly. He was first in line. Her heart raced and she felt flushed.

Please, let him just leave without seeing me, she silently prayed. As he finished his transaction and started to turn around, she meant to turn away so he would not notice her, but could not tear her eyes away from him. His look of surprise unsettled her as she tried to look casual and smile. Conflict overtook her emotions. On one hand, she wanted to slap his face and humiliate him in public for the hurt he caused her; on the other she wanted to rush to him and hold him close.

Just as he approached her in greeting, the teller said loudly, "Next in line, please," and Elsa turned to take care of the deposit she had come to make.

She calmed herself a little by the time she walked out of the bank, breathing almost normally. Still annoyed with herself for letting him affect her so, she fought to control her thoughts. *How can I live in the same town with him, if every time I see him I almost have a heart attack? I've got to get over this.*

The words of her sister Leila echoed in her mind. *There are other men around. He's not the only pebble on the beach. Get a life.*

As Elsa left the bank Gerik approached her from where he was waiting in the shade. He held both hands out and grabbed hers before she could resist. He looked into her eyes, his own eyes shining with the start of tears.

"Elsa, how *are* you? How was your trip to Italy? Where have you been hiding?"

A long moment passed while Elsa's mind raced with thoughts of what she wanted to say, but none of them would come out. Those hazel eyes compelled her to return their gaze.

"I am so sorry," Gerik finally whispered. "I have been kicking myself over and over for letting you slip away. I know it is entirely my fault and I just want to say that I never meant to hurt you."

"What a bunch of crap!"

"I don't blame you for doubting me. I am stupid. I've been immature, thinking only of my own desires and immediate gratification and if I ever have a chance again I will be a better person. I can't explain how and why I have been such an ass."

"You can say that again."

"Elsa!"

"Well, it's true."

"You know, these past few months while I watched my father slip away and observed the love and patience my mother showed through all the difficult times, I have thought again and again of what we had together. You helped me to see my own strengths. You always believed in me even when I did not believe in myself. It was that kind of love that helped my mom and dad through his final ordeal."

"We can't talk about this here," Elsa interrupted. "I have a million things to finish before my first day tomorrow. I'm... What's this about your father?"

"He passed away yesterday," Gerik said. "I thought you knew."

"Oh, Gerik, I am so sorry. I hadn't heard. How is your mother doing?"

"She's doing as well as can be expected. Actually in a way it is a relief. He suffered so much in the last two months. And I'm handling it okay, it's just that when I think of his final moments, I can't...I just can't..." and he looked down, swallowing hard.

"Oh, Gerik," Elsa hugged him in a long embrace, patting his back as she felt his silent sobs.

When Elsa got home, she told Leila—who was visiting from her home in Alaska—about meeting Gerik. She told Leila that she planned to meet him for dinner on the weekend.

Leila frowned. "Oh, don't be so stupid. He's the kind of guy that would chase any skirt that comes along. Let him go. And I don't think too much of your *best friend* either for going behind your back like that. Don't do it, Else. He is bad news."

"I don't know why I bother telling you anything," Elsa said. "You are about as sympathetic as a door knob. Since you've moved to Alaska, you're more out of touch than ever. "

"Well, it's the truth. You've got to learn to handle the truth and get on with your life. You are wasting yourself here in Caraville."

"Me, wasting myself?"

"Yeah. With your creativity you could make a name for yourself, or at least have an adventure. Of course, I guess you were always Mama's girl and can't leave her apron strings. At least I am going to see the world and experience things before I get too old to appreciate them. I can't wait to get back to Kenai and our new business. When Pete, Rudy and I take off for Alaska in our new Piper Cherokee, I won't look back. In fact, I can hardly wait to leave this stick-in-the-mud place. I'm glad I decided to go to UAA instead of a dull Midwest college."

"I still don't know why you decided to marry that primitive backwoods guy before even graduating from college. If you want to see the world, you could have at least waited to have a family."

"Rudy is the joy of our lives. Besides, Pete and I are having adventures together with him."

Elsa turned and left the room without answering and was more than ever resolved to make up with Gerik.

Why should I listen to her? She never did understand me. And look at her marrying that low-life with no future and no culture. Talk about a stick-in-the-mud! At least Gerik has a great job with Ellis Manufacturing.

She went directly to the phone and called Gerik's house to offer sympathy to his mother. She wanted to finalize plans for Saturday.

Their getting back together was rocky, but Elsa was determined to make a go of it and Gerik certainly seemed contrite, so they wasted little time in reestablishing their connection. Elsa became pregnant before they even had a chance to talk about getting married. She couldn't get enough of him. He vowed that he's always loved her. All of her frustrations of college and their separation disappeared when they were together and Elsa wanted nothing more than to make a comfortable home with Gerik. She dreamed of a beautiful place on the lake and Gerik coming home to her for scrumptious meals waiting on the table, wine poured, spending luxurious evenings in each other's arms. She would listen sympathetically to his problems of the day. They would spend weekends searching for the perfect furnishing for their home. Later on, she will watch the kids running through the grass, and they will come in to a meticulous house with beautiful hand-made tapestries, homemade decorations everywhere, and 'home-maker of the year' meals and activities. Everything will be perfect. Their home will be always neat—never any crying or messy scenes.

Elsa's reconciliation with Daphne took a lot longer. But in a small town like Caraville, it was impossible to go anywhere without running into her, or someone who knew her. At first, when the three of them were in the same room, the awkwardness was palpable. Elsa tensed up and clung to Gerik as though her life depended on it. She invited Daphne to their wedding, but did not include her in the wedding party.

Elsa was relieved when Daphne moved to Chicago and wished she would move even further away.

One evening after Elsa had put both Danny and Emma to bed, Daphne called. " Elsa, I'm getting married next month. Will you be my Matron of Honor?"

She planned to marry a fellow artist, Dennis.

"Why me?"

"Elsa, please. I don't know anybody else who can do it and our friendship goes back so far."

"I can't, Daphne. It would be a charade. I don't think you love him anyway."

Gerik stepped in. "Come on, Elsa. Get over it. Daphne needs you now."

"How would you know anything about that?"

"Well, at least she's willing to let bygones be bygones."

"Meaning...?"

Gerik walked away, shaking his head.

Elsa suspected the marriage was one of convenience and was doomed from the start. Daphne's pregnancy was evident as she walked down the aisle. Elsa barely talked to her during the wedding reception—even though they were seated next to each other. When Gerik asked Daphne to dance, Elsa couldn't watch and had to leave the room. She came back too soon—they were still on the dance floor in an ardent embrace, Gerik's right hand caressing Daphne's derriere, his lips nuzzling her ear and neck.

Elsa demanded they leave the reception immediately after that dance. "Let's go, Gerik, I've got a terrible headache. We have to get home to check up on Danny and Emma."

"They'll be okay, Elsa; your mother is the best baby sitter in the world. Come on, let's party a little longer."

"If you're not leaving, I'll go home without you." She grabbed her purse and left.

Elsa went home and cried herself to sleep. She awakened when Gerik stumbled into their bedroom three hours later, but pretended to be asleep. He snuggled next to her, running his hand along her thigh, then along the inside of her legs. He breathed heavily and nibbled on her ear, licking it noisily. Elsa began to feel aroused, but held herself stiffly— every muscle tensed as though ready to spring.

"Come on, this is a wedding night. Let's have a little fun." Gerik slurred his words together.

"It sounds like you already have had your fun tonight," Elsa hissed. She pulled the blankets more tightly around her. After a while Gerik gave up, rolled over and fell asleep.

She was cool towards him for the next few days, but they eventually made up. They never discussed what happened at Daphne's wedding, but the memory of Gerik and Daphne pressed against each other in a slow dance still made her so jealous, she couldn't focus.

When Daphne called her a month later, Elsa was shocked to hear her voice. Daphne was crying. It to her several minutes before she was able to blurt out the problem.

"I've had a miscarriage, Elsa. I just had to tell someone who cares. How am I going to go on living? I see you with your adorable kids and I want that so much for myself. Now it's not going to happen."

Elsa's heart went out to her. "Oh, Daphne! I am so sorry to hear that. I know how much you wanted this baby."

Elsa offered to meet her for lunch and shopping and listened sympathetically to Daphne's expression of desolation. She tried to distract her from the loss by asking her advice about several of her quilting projects. Elsa's artistry is with fabrics and textures but Daphne's sense of perspective and color is impressive. She offered advice and affirmed Elsa's creativity and genius. Once they exhausted the subject of art projects, however, their conversation became awkward again.

With time, Elsa managed to put any thoughts of Gerik and Daphne out of her mind. She was busy with two toddlers and spent her spare time designing and making quilts to sell. Daphne was rarely in Caraville and the few times Elsa did see her around town, she was able to talk to her with civility.

Nine months after that miscarriage, Daphne called Elsa again, "Oh, Elsa, what am I going to do? I've lost my baby! Again!"

"I didn't even know you were pregnant, Daph."

"I didn't want to tell anyone until I was at least twelve weeks along. I didn't want to jinx anything. Now it's happened again. There must be something wrong with me. Dennis says if only I would take better care of myself..." Her voice trailed off into a whisper. "I'll never be a mother."

"It's not your fault, Daphne. Don't give up." It took Elsa longer that time to help Daphne out of her depression.

Daphne moved back to Caraville the following year and opened a small studio on Main Street. She gave art lessons to a limited number of promising students. Her original paintings were in demand. Their prices kept climbing. Dennis stayed in Chicago, and although he and Daphne made a show of being the loving couple, Elsa knew there were problems.

One night Elsa sat down at her desk with a glass of wine to work on a quilt design. The kids were both tucked into bed. The doorbell rang. "Would you get that, Gerik? It must be one of the neighbor kids soliciting donations for something."

She continued working on the design but stopped when she heard a woman's voice—almost hysterical—crying, and Gerik saying, "Just shush, baby. We—you'll be okay."

"What is it, Gerik?" Elsa asked as she walked towards the front door. Rounding the corner, she saw Gerik and Daphne in a close embrace. Daphne's hair was disheveled. Her face was flushed and her eyelids puffy and red. Elsa's first reaction was one of jealousy.

"I thought it was over between you two. Now you have the nerve to cling on to each other in my own house! Get your hands off my husband, Daphne."

"No, Elsa, it's not like that. Gerik has been a real friend to me in the last few months. But I don't know if anyone can help me now. I've had another miscarriage and Dennis says he's had enough of my drama and has filed for divorce. He didn't even bother to come to Caraville to tell me. He just left a message on my phone. He says he doubts this last pregnancy was his doing. We haven't been really getting along for quite a while. He's accusing me of infidelity. How could he? I can't handle any more of this. I just don't want to go on."

Daphne walked into the living room and collapsed into an overstuffed chair. She looked small and helpless. Elsa's heart went out to her. She felt a twinge of guilt for accusing Daphne and Gerik. She felt guilty for her good fortune in marriage and for having two healthy children. She sat on the arm of the chair next to Daphne. Gerik stood by awkwardly, looking embarrassed by the whole situation.

"Let me talk to her privately, Gerik. Please, get us both a glass of wine."

He looked relieved to be excused from the room and rushed out to the kitchen for the wine. After serving it to both of them, he excused himself and left the room.

Elsa and Daphne talked until midnight. Elsa's sympathetic and nurturing side took over. Her overriding emotion was one of pity for Daphne's condition. By the time Daphne left that night, they had agreed to work as partners in their artistic pursuits. Daphne needed someone to believe in her and push her through dark times when she totally lost her inspiration. She minimized her gift as an artist even though her talent was well known. She garnered thousands of dollars for her original paintings. Elsa, on the other hand, knew her quilt designs were original and inspired but thought they had little value to anyone else. Daphne respected Elsa's creativity with fabrics.

In the fifteen intervening years Daphne has supported and encouraged Elsa's attempts at marketing her designs, urging her to advertise her genius at quilting conventions all over the country.

One evening over a glass of wine, Elsa muses about the good times she and Daphne have shared.

"You know, Daph, I really owe you for getting me that ad in the Midwest Artists magazine. I was just thinking about our collaboration over the past fifteen years. I don't think my business would have ever gotten off the ground if you hadn't helped me."

"It's great to see you getting the recognition you deserve. And I'm thrilled that you're in such demand as a speaker and can travel all over the country."

"Yeah. In fact, I have a convention next month in Chicago. Maybe we can meet the day after to go shopping."

"Sounds good to me."

Later that summer, Nikki is confident as she presents her talk at the largest Midwest quilting and craft convention in Chicago. Her new hairstyle and her new name engender self-assurance. Her quilt designs are in great demand and she realizes for the first time that she has attained a great deal of fame, at least in quilting circles. She schedules an extra day in Chicago to shop for some new clothes with Daphne, but when Daphne calls her hotel in the morning to cancel their day together, she shops alone on Michigan Avenue. Her frustration builds as she tries unsuccessfully to fit into the latest styles. Then, giving up without one purchase, she drives away from the city in the light traffic before noon, vowing to lose twenty pounds by the end of the year. Daphne's car is in the driveway as she pulls in and Nikki briefly wonders what she is doing here at this time of day, especially when she couldn't meet her in Chicago. As Nikki opens the door from the garage leading into the house, Daphne is rushing down the stairs from her office, arms full of file folders and swatches of fabric. Her face is flushed and her one-piece sundress looks like it is on backwards, but with Daphne's slender body, it is hard to tell for sure.

"I had to get these for a client I have to see this afternoon," she says hurriedly, "And since you weren't home, Gerik was good enough to come and show me where you keep them. Gotta run. Give me a call later."

Gerik, coming down the stairs from their bedroom with bare feet, dressed in shorts and an old Loyola t-shirt only partially tucked in, looks like he's ready for yard work.

Elsa looks at him with astonishment. "What are you doing at home at this hour? Aren't you working today?"

"You heard her. I had to come home and show her where you hide things. And since I am home, I decided to take care of some of the weekend chores. It's not like anybody else around here will do them. They are too damn busy with sports." Gerik mutters angrily as he marches out the back door.

Nikki shrugs and makes a face at his retreating back. She has not forgotten about her promise to lose twenty pounds and as soon as Gerik is out of hearing distance, she calls Jill to find out about joining the Athletic club.

"Great," Jill says. "They're still offering the summer special and a new water aerobics class is starting on Monday. Why don't you join me? It's early, though. It starts at six thirty a.m."

"I'm gonna do it, Jill. I'm ready for a change. See you Monday."

Chapter Six

Leila Meets Dom

During February in Anchorage, daylight hours increase by at least thirty-five minutes a week. Even when temperatures dip below zero, the sun gives an illusion of warmth. Leila gazes out at the sun shining on the frosted trees visualizing the time she and Pete snow-shoed to Swan Lake on the Resurrection Pass Trail. They spent the night in a Forest Service cabin.

Leila remembers the scene as vividly as a movie playing on the wall. Breathless from climbing in bone-chilling fog, they break out into the sunshine. The hoarfrost-covered trees and shrubs in the foreground sparkle like diamond-studded bottlebrushes. Rugged peaks with snow cornices materialize out of the mist. It looks like she could just reach out and touch them. The sun turns the grey cliffs a brilliant bronze. The deep blue of the sky almost hurts the eyes with its intensity. Leila gasps with delight. "Wow! Look at that."

Leila can almost smell the hot chocolate as she remembers pausing to drink from the thermos and to snack on trail mix. Standing in silence, taking in the scene, labored breathing punctuates the stillness.

The ringing phone interrupts the movie playing in her mind. It is Rudy calling from the university, apparently on a break between classes. He is breathless as though he has been running. With excitement in his voice he asks Leila, "Hey, Mom, how would you like to go camping near Port Alsworth this weekend?"

"I can't, Rudy."

"At least listen to the plan before you answer."

"Okay."

"Celeste and I are going to try out the ice boat. The other day Lake Clark looked really clear when I flew over it, miles and miles of clear ice. So I landed near the west side to check it out. It hasn't been this smooth in years. We're just going to spend one night out."

"I don't know, Rudy. The symphony is on Saturday night and, besides, I really haven't been winter camping for years. Where on earth is all my gear stored? How could I get it together before then?"

"But we'll be staying in Tallman's cabin, so you won't need much. And, hey, don't you remember the great time we had last summer camping at Alexander Lake? It'll do you good to get out."

"Well...maybe."

"Good. Celeste's uncle from Chicago is visiting. She'd like to give him a memorable Alaskan experience. You could keep him company and show him how a real outdoorswoman does it."

Leila feels a spark of excitement about camping again. "If we leave Sunday morning, I guess I could go, as long as we get back before noon on Monday."

"All right, Mom, it's a deal. Celeste has to be at work by eleven and I have a class at two o'clock. So we should get back to Anchorage before ten. We'll leave at the crack of dawn on Sunday."

Rudy, Celeste, her uncle Dominic and Leila agree to have dinner together at a seafood restaurant overlooking Cook Inlet that Friday. When they meet in the lobby, Celeste hugs Leila and says with excitement, "Leila, this is my Uncle Dominic Perfetti. He's been eager to meet you since I told him about our camping adventure and your expertise."

"Call me Dom," he says as he, too, embraces Leila.

Leila, not accustomed to such an overt show of affection, stiffens and pulls way. "Pleased to meet you."

Dom is as wiry and energetic as Celeste. The family resemblance is striking: The same dark eyes, the same auburn hair, and the same quick smile. Dom, a non-stop talker, starts right up. "Did I hear that you grew up in Caraville? You know I spent a lot of time there myself after graduating from college. My uncle had a pizza place there that I managed for a summer back in the eighties. Did you know a guy named Jesse Miller?" Leila shakes her head. "How about Frankie Sturgelewski? We called him Ski. Man could he dance. We'd go out after the pizza joint closed and hit all the bars. We had a great time. There were a bunch of us who hung around together. How about Harry Bourgeois? Adam Cicely? Jason Whitcomb? Benjamin Hanson?"

Leila shakes her head after each name.

"Hey, how did these youngsters here meet?" He grabs Celeste and pulls her to his side, while looking at Rudy. "Don't they look good together? I didn't think my favorite niece would ever find her match."

"They met at the university when they were both taking a ground school class. I think it was for the commercial written, wasn't it?" Leila looks from Celeste to Rudy.

"Yeah, I wowed her with my knowledge of the regs."

Celeste punches Rudy in the arm. "It was more about his bravado than anything else."

Rudy and Celeste have been dating for a couple of years. She admitted to Leila that she is not as enthusiastic about hiking and camping as Rudy, but goes along to be near him. But it was their common interest in flying that cemented their relationship. At a ground school class for commercial pilots, Celeste—according to Rudy—looked baffled by the problem scenarios of the Federal Aviation Regulations.

"What on earth are they talking about? Rudy, could you explain this question to me?" Celeste asked him one day after class.

"That's simple," he said. "How about if we go over to the cafeteria and I'll show you how to interpret the regulations and put 'em in plain language. These regs were written by lawyers. They must think we're all fresh out of law school and can make sense of them as they're written. Nobody can. But my dad always explained them to me from a practical viewpoint."

That was the start of an on again, off again relationship. Celeste complained about Rudy's single-minded devotion to flying, but Rudy egged her on by showing off his expertise, knowing that she loved challenges. She did, and flying provided her with unlimited challenges. There was always something more to learn.

Celeste turns back to her uncle. "When I saw Rudy in that class, I wanted to meet him and had to act like I needed his help. He fell for it."

"Oh, yeah, Missy." Rudy pronounces the last word with emphasis.

"Don't start that with me." Celeste gives Rudy a stern look, and then grins at him.

Rudy smiles back and gives her a kiss on her forehead.

"Anyway, Dom, you know how I hated it here when my parents dragged me away from La Jolla."

"Yeah, your mom was wringing her hands with your whining and complaining. She said all you talked about was boys and clothes. It was your dad who thought maybe flying would be a good diversion for you. And wasn't it your brother who dared you to take your first lesson?"

"It was, but when I found out how much fun it was, I was hooked. I love challenges. Maybe that's why I love this guy so much. It's a real challenge to keep him from pulling stupid pranks."

"Me? Stupid pranks? I'm just trying to liven up a boring, think everything through before acting, character flaw. I've never known such a perfectionist."

"Now, kids. Let's get back to important matters—like how glad I am to finally meet you, Rudy and you, Leila. I couldn't be more thrilled. I never imagined meeting such an enchanting woman in the frozen north." Dom moves towards her with outstretched arms, looking like he might hug her again.

Leila blushes and excuses herself to visit the restroom. When she returns Celeste is saying, "Our table is ready, come on Uncle Dom, give someone else a chance to break in."

"What do you mean? I've let you guys talk my ear off." He turns to Leila, "They were just telling me about that fishing trip you took out of Whittier last summer. Celeste says she was the only one to get a halibut that day and it was a monster, besides."

"It was."

"I don't believe it. How could this skinny young thing land a monster halibut? Look at those scrawny arms."

"Don't let her looks fool you, Dom. She's pretty tough. She actually landed that 140 pound halibut without any help. I could hardly bear to watch. It was quite a fight." Leila looks at Celeste. "Those skinny arms are all muscle."

Dom continues his talk when they are seated, breaking only long enough to order.

"Now, back to Caraville. Leila, don't you miss it?"

"No, I can't say that I do."

"But the lakes and water skiing and summer evenings, man, I remember water skiing on Meyers Lake. One day we nearly ran over some old fart in a rowboat. When I went to apologize after he rowed to shore, I met his daughter, a knockout gorgeous blond named Daphne. We dated for a while, but she had bigger fish to catch."

"I do know a Daphne." Leila manages to say.

Dom starts talking again. "Well, I'll tell you..."

"Please, Uncle Dom."

Dinner arrives and Rudy dives into his prime rib with gusto. Dom looks at the halibut cheeks on his plate. "This fish must have had an enormous face to have such big cheeks. You're not pulling my leg, are you? These can't really be cheeks of a fish."

"Well, they are. At least that's what the menu said."

Dom takes a small bite and rolls his eyes. With his mouth still full he mumbles, "Wow, delicious!"

"Uncle Dom, remember your manners."

After swallowing the first bite, he spears another piece and chews it with obvious pleasure. "That, my dear niece, is the finest seafood I have ever eaten. I'm glad you recommended it. The texture and flavor are out of this world. Is everything in Alaska so magnificent, including the beautiful women?"

Leila looks away from Dom's insistent gaze. She pretends to be studying the wine list. "What was that wine you ordered? It's very good."

"It's the Domaine Drouhin Pinot Noir from Oregon. I thought it would go well with whatever we ordered."

"Good choice."

"I thought you'd like it. But really, Leila, isn't there anything you miss about the Midwest?"

"I do sort of miss the huge thunderstorms. Watching them approach from the protection of our huge porch swing thrilled me. Alaska just doesn't have that brilliant lightening and pounding thunder. Oh, we do get some mini-storms, but after one clap of thunder and a spattering of rain, they're done."

Dom leans closer to Leila. "I love them, too. You should come back sometime in the summer to see one."

Leila leans away from him. "But I hate to leave Alaska in the summer. The long days, the pleasant temperatures and the fresh, dry air are pretty hard to beat. I don't think I could take the humidity in the Midwest anymore."

"I know what you mean. The humidity can be pretty oppressive." Dom moves closer to Leila again. "Summers here must be awesome with the long days. I've never been here in the summer. In fact, this is my first trip to Alaska."

"Celeste tells me that you are taking a tour to Seward on Saturday. Well, you're in for a treat. You will see some of the most spectacular scenery in the world."

Dom and Leila find so much to talk about that when dinner is over, Rudy and Celeste quietly excuse themselves to find their own way home. They leave Leila and Dom to catch up on their memories of the Midwest.

Dom insists on attending the symphony on Saturday evening, giving up a chance for a sightseeing trip to Seward. "I would get back too late for the concert if I went," he persists when Leila tries to talk him into going on the tour.

"But the scenery is so spectacular on the drive down. Seward is such a quaint town. And you would miss the Sea Life Center."

"Oh, I'll be back to see it some other time. Besides, our camping trip on Sunday will more than make up for any scenery that I would miss. And it's not every day that I get a chance to hear a world class cellist," Dom grins.

Leila, responding with an exaggerated show of tolerance, says, "The soloist is a violinist, not cellist."

"I meant you," he says, "I want to hear you play."

Sunday morning, the sun is bright. Leila hums phrases from the symphony she played last night; but as she descends to sea level, Leila's shoulders slump and the music stops when she notices the fog rolling in off the inlet. Her lightness turns to melancholy and she realizes that she was actually looking forward to this trip.

Rudy, Celeste and Dom are already in the hangar preparing the DeHaviland Beaver for the flight. "Have you looked outside?" Leila asks when they seem totally unconcerned about the weather.

"What are you talking about? It's a beautiful day for flying," Dom says as he heads towards Leila, arms outstretched. Leila manages to sidestep his intended embrace by picking up her sleeping bag and slamming it into the baggage compartment of the plane.

"Rudy, did you check the forecast? Didn't they say anything about fog?"

Rudy looks down at his feet and mumbles, "I meant to, Mom. I was going to do it after I checked over the plane. Besides, it looked so nice when I got up, I wanted to just rush right over and get going."

"Well, it doesn't look like we will be going anywhere anytime soon. Look outside," Leila barks.

They all rush to the hangar door and look out to see the visibility reduced to hundreds of feet as though they are in the middle of a huge bowl of milk. The ice crystals hit Rudy's face as he looks up to see if he can determine how thick the fog is.

Rudy sounds embarrassed. "Okay, I'll give Flight Service a call and see how long this is expected to last."

"We could go over to that café you talked about with the killer cinnamon rolls. Don't they make a mean cup of espresso? Maybe by the time we have a meal to hold us over, the fog will be gone," Dom says.

"What do you know about Alaska weather?" Leila snaps.

Celeste steps in tactfully. "That's a wonderful idea Uncle Dom. Rudy was in such a rush this morning that we didn't take time for breakfast. I think things will work out better this way. I am sure when we finish eating, the fog will lift and then we will be able to take off with full bellies. We won't have to cook as soon as we get to Lake Clark. We can start right out with the iceboat. Just wait until you see what a thrill it is!"

They walk to Dom's rental car after securing the hangar door, Rudy and Celeste holding hands with Leila lagging behind. At an old-time Alaskan restaurant on Spenard Road they eat massive, gut splitting breakfasts: hotcakes overflowing the edges of a twelve inch plate, reindeer sausage, eggs and toast spread with sticky lingonberry jam. They order two cinnamon rolls and share one between the four of them at the restaurant, taking the other along with them in a doggie bag.

Dom turns out to be right. The sun is shining on beautifully frosted trees when they leave the restaurant. The startling white light and brilliant blue sky causes them all to grab for their sunglasses. The coffee in the restaurant was not quite what they expected, so they stop at an espresso stand on the way back to the airport for lattes to go. They pour them into a heated thermos bottle so they can drink them when they get to Lake Clark.

Arriving at Lake Hood, it takes only a few minutes to get the Beaver out of the hangar and prepare for takeoff. Rudy and Celeste are in the front seats, sharing the flying duties and Leila sits next to Dom in the back. She is still not comfortable in the air, but will not admit her fear to anyone. Leila realizes that she is holding her breath as they taxi out to the airstrip and exhales as Celeste applies power for takeoff. As they climb out, a small jolt from wake turbulence shakes the plane and Leila instinctively reaches for something to hold on to. She hangs on for dear life and finally, when they are safely across the inlet and the air is smooth and calm, she realizes sheepishly that it is Dom's hand that she is holding.

"I was wondering when you would notice," Dom grins. "I kind of liked it myself." Then, more seriously, "Are you okay, Leila, I mean, really okay? I don't understand how someone from a family so involved in aviation can be nervous about flying."

Leila wants to say, "It's none of your business, you insensitive jerk!" Her face contorts when the memories of Pete's crash push into her consciousness. She bites her lower lip and finally turns to see the look of concern on Dom's face. As she sees him trying to keep the smile on his face—but failing—she says quietly, "I'm all right. Really. I'll tell you all about it some day."

She tries unsuccessfully to put some of the overwhelming memories of Pete's crash out of her mind. She doesn't want to talk about it at all and especially to a pushy, loud, shallow jokester like Dom. He is the exact opposite of Pete in so many ways that she regrets having agreed to this trip at all.

Well, it's only overnight, and then I won't have to deal with him again, although, I do hate to think of hurting Celeste's feelings by snubbing her uncle. She's almost like a daughter to me.

Chapter Seven

Nikki Takes up Exercise

Nikki joins the Downtown Athletic Club and the following week meets Jill at the six-thirty a.m. water aerobics class. As she puts on her new swimming suit, she is embarrassed at how she looks and enters the pool deck wrapped in a towel. She glances at the other women in the class. *Looks like I don't need to hide my few extra pounds. These other women make me look thin.*

Someone yells towards her as she feels the water with her big toe. "Welcome to the class. You're going to love it."

One woman shouts towards Nikki over the music, "You don't look like you need exercise. Look at how thin you are!"

The instructor bounces with enthusiasm. Lively music blares and reverberates off the concrete walls. Class time passes quickly. It is much more difficult than it looks, and after three weeks Nikki begins to feel some results of the exercise. But then the music starts to grate on her nerves. The repetitive movements and inane jokes of the instructor set her teeth on edge. One day as she gets out of the pool she tells Jill she is not coming back.

Jill frowns. "Oh, don't give up so easily. You'll learn to love it."

"No, it's not that I'm giving up, Jill. I just need to find something else. Maybe I could start walking. Do you still walk in the mornings?"

"Well, I'm only walking one day a week since I do the water aerobics three mornings. But you are welcome to join us. The weather's been nice so we meet at the track over at Curtiss Jr. High. We walk for an hour, starting at seven on Saturday mornings."

"That's a bit early, but maybe I'll give it a try."

That Saturday, Nikki is at the track before anyone else arrives. She walks around the track once and loves the rhythm of it. Although only 5'2", her legs are proportionately long and her stride is smooth and easy.

"Wow, you look like a natural," the young woman in running shorts says as Nikki comes around the final corner.

"What's that?" Nikki asks as she prepares to go around again.

The woman falls in beside her. "I said your stride is real natural. Where did you learn speed walking?"

"This is just my normal walk. I'm trying to get some exercise and lose weight."

"You should join our speed walking group. Most of us meet on Saturday mornings and we also have a track workout on Tuesday nights. We have a great mixed group and a very encouraging coach."

"I don't know. I'm new at exercise."

"You would fit right in. Oh, excuse me. I didn't introduce myself. My name is Nancy. Nancy Brace." She reaches out her hand to shake Nikki's.

"I'm El-Nikki Selzer. Nice to meet you."

"What was that again?"

"Nikki." She was about to explain her name change but let it drop.

90

"Yeah, well, in any case, we meet here every Tuesday for intervals and then several of us meet at various places during the week to walk together. We even have a website you can check to see where people are meeting each week. It's called Walker's Walkers."

"How did you come up with that name?"

"Our coach's name is Mike Walker, so we call our group Walker's Walkers."

"Cool."

"In fact, this morning I am heading out to Myers Lake with Kim and Joellen to walk on some of the hills around the lake. I think some others from the group will be there. Would you like to join us?"

"My sister-in-law will be here in a few minutes. Can you wait until she arrives so I can tell her where I am going?" Nikki stalls, not sure she wants to join a group of speed walkers.

"Sure, I got here early anyway. We will just walk to the start from here; it's only a half-mile. We'll meet the rest of the gang and we'll be out about an hour and a half to two hours."

What will Gerik think when I'm gone that long? Oh, to hell with him! She looks at Nancy. "That will be quite a test for me. I am not used to walking more than a few yards at a time. My daughter Emma keeps bugging me to get more exercise, but... I guess I'm game, as long as I don't slow you down."

When Jill arrives, Nikki asks her if she wants to join the speed walking group on the hills, but Jill says she has to be home in an hour, so she'll stay at the track. Nikki heads to the lake with Nancy. Four others show up at the lake and Nikki struggles to keep up with them, especially when they add several bursts of speed going up the hills. The group members vary in ability and Nikki finds a partner to stay with her when the rest of them complete an extra loop. She manages to walk continuously for almost an hour and a half but she is panting and breathless at the end. Her feet hurt. Back at the parking lot, she feels as though she won't be able to make it the last few yards to where her car is parked. Sweat pours down her face and her legs feel like she can hardly lift them to slide into the car seat. A feeling of exhilaration passes through her as she realizes for the first time in her life, she has accomplished a physical feat she thought far beyond her capability.

"I think I overdid it for the first time out," she laughs. "But, hey, I want to do it again."

"Great." Nancy smiles.

"I'll join you Tuesday night. What time did you say it was?"

"We meet here at six p.m."

"See you then."

Nikki quickly grasps the technique of speed walking. As Nancy had said, she was a natural. The group turns out to be a very competitive group and several members participate in races all over the country. Nikki has to work hard to keep up with them, but within a couple of months, her natural talent enables her to walk right along with the leaders. She can walk a mile in just over nine minutes. The coach encourages her to enter some races.

"The record holder in your age group walks under an eight minute mile," he says. "Her time for a 5K is only twenty-three minutes."

"Oh, I'm not ready for racing. I'm nowhere near that fast," she says.

"Yes you are, Nikki. I bet you could beat anyone around here. I bet you could finish a 5K in less than twenty-eight minutes."

By the end of August, she decides to give racing a try. She loves it. On the finishing stretch of her first 5K race, she pushes past at least twenty other racers and crosses the finish line exhausted, but exuberant.

"I did it!" she says, hugging the woman next to her in the finishing chute. When her name is announced at the awards ceremony as the first place finisher in her age group, she doesn't know what to do.

Nancy nudges her, saying, "Get up there for your prize."

Nikki stumbles up to the podium to polite applause. *If only Gerik could see me now.*

When she gets home and tells Emma about the race, Emma hugs her. "I'm so proud of you, Mom. First place! Wow!"

"It was only first in my age group, not overall."

"But that's a really competitive age group. All the best speed walkers are in their forties. I'm going to come and watch your next race for sure."

The other benefits of speed walking begin to show. Without even dieting, the pounds start to fall away and her clothes feel looser.

Just wait, next time I go to Chicago, I'm going to buy a whole new wardrobe.

As the weather turns cooler, Nikki enjoys the exercise even more. The cool, fresh air and fall colors are inspiring. She had heard of a *runner's high* and for the first time experiences it on returning from a lengthy training walk. She bounces into the house feeling like all is well with the world. Her outlook is optimistic. She loves everybody. All is beautiful. Even Gerik's gloomy frown and negative jibes don't affect her.

Winter training is a different story. The Tuesday night interval workouts end on October 31st and the group disperses. Many of them still meet on Saturday mornings regardless of weather. The pace is a little slower in the winter due to slippery surfaces and the pervasive wind. Nikki tries it several times, but gives up after nearly suffering frostbite one morning. Her light jacket and skimpy gloves were not adequate for fifteen degrees with a twenty-knot north wind. She was shivering uncontrollably by the time she got back to her car and had trouble getting the key out of her pocket.

"This is definitely not fun," she says to Nancy on the drive home.

"Well, we could walk at the McGinn Arena. They have a walking track around the indoor ice rinks; it's almost a quarter mile around."

"Maybe," Nikki hesitates.

"If you buy a pass, it's only twenty dollars a month and you can walk any time between five a.m. and ten p.m. How about joining me there on Tuesday about six?"

"I guess I can try it. Although it sounds kind of boring just going around in circles."

"It is, sort of, but we can make a game of it and do some intervals. I walked there a lot last winter and you'd be surprised at how fast the time goes with a partner."

"I'll try it," Nikki stalls, "but I'm not making any promises."

"Great!"

By the end of February, Nikki is eager to walk outdoors. On nice days she meets the Saturday group. They are all eager to begin the track workouts again. Nikki feels as though she is one up on them because she has been doing intervals with Nancy at the indoor track.

One Tuesday as she is warming up before the workout, she falls in with a couple of women who are talking about the rock climbing gym in town.

"Yeah, I went to their introductory class. Wow! What a blast! I loved the rappelling. My hands were sweaty and my legs were shaking after climbing that first wall, but the exhilaration was addictive. I signed up for a six-week class starting next week. It includes all of the classes at the gym, plus two free solo sessions a week and an outing at some rock faces along the Mississippi after the end of the class with two instructors."

Nikki interrupts. "That sounds pretty cool. Do you need any experience to take a class, or do they take beginners? Since my sister climbs mountains, I've thought about rock climbing, but I'm afraid of heights."

"Oh, no." says the first walker—Val. "You don't need any experience at all. It's for beginners and to tell you the truth, I am afraid of heights myself. I wanted to overcome that fear and that's why I'm taking the class. Why don't you join me? I think there's still room in the class."

"I'll have to give it some thought. "My husband likes me to be home in the evenings and we usually have dinner together. But since our son, Danny, went away to college, meal times are a little more irregular and casual. Our daughter Emma is a senior and has a part time job, so she is hardly ever home. Maybe my husband wouldn't mind spending some evenings alone."

"Gerik," Nikki says as soon as she enters the house after the track workout, "What do you think about me taking a rock climbing class?"

"What next? I suppose you'll take up sky diving pretty soon. What has gotten into you? You're not the same person anymore. Your hair and your clothes are different. I never know what to expect. But you'll do as you please, anyway, so why ask me?" He pauses. "Actually, it will be nice to have some peace and quiet around here. Go ahead. In fact, I'll probably spend a couple evenings at the office while you're at class to catch up on work."

After her conversation with Gerik, Nikki is more determined than ever to take the rock climbing class. *I don't know why he loves that office so much. He is hardly ever at home anymore anyway and I have to have something to do with my time. Emma is always busy with sports and school and work. Danny is off at college. I just drift aimlessly around the house with nothing to do, nobody to cook for. Why not have some fun?*

She talks Daphne into taking the class with her, telling her that she will pick her up for the first class.

They walk in together—late as Daphne usually is—to hear the instructor saying, "Okay, everyone, pick two partners about your size. I've shown you how to fasten the harnesses and tie the knots. Now I want you each to watch the others put them on again and I will come around and check. Let's get started."

Nikki looks around the gym. The fake rock structure overshadows everything else in the room. The ceiling is barely visible and the huge windows overlooking the river give one the impression of being outdoors. The floor beneath the climbing wall looks like it is covered with small black stones, but as Nikki steps onto them they feel soft and squishy. They smell like ground up rubber tires. Cabinets along the wall hold shoes and climbing harnesses. They had walked through an area that had climbing gear for sale but Nikki did not pay much attention. She is fascinated by the rock wall and notices little else.

The instructor turns to Nikki and Daphne. He grabs them around the shoulders and ushers them to the supply cabinet.

"You must be my last two students. Let's get you some shoes first. What size do you wear? There. Try those on. Next, the harness. This looks like it should fit you. Slip those on while I check their knots. I'll be right back." He goes off to help the other students.

Daphne in her black, lycra knee length pants and fitted V-neck knit cotton shirt is dressed appropriately for climbing. Nikki, however, is wearing tan cotton slacks and a sleeveless cotton blouse that does not give or stretch. Luckily, they are both loose enough so they will not restrict her movements.

"What a hunk!" Daphne says as he walks away. "Look at those bulging arm muscles and that tight ass."

"Shhh." Nikki says, "He'll hear you."

"Oh, all men want to be admired," Daphne grins. "Why do you think he wears such skin tight pants? I wonder how old he is. Maybe he's not too young for me. He looks about thirty-five or so. I wonder what he is doing after the class. Maybe he would like some company."

"Is that all you ever think of, Daph?" Nikki says with exasperation. "Let's get this stuff on before he comes back."

Nikki struggles to get her legs into the right straps of the harness and has everything twisted around so as she tries to stand up, the tangles cause her to lose her balance. She stumbles towards the shoe rack. Suddenly she feels strong arms around her from behind, helping her to her feet.

"Oh, I'm sorry I'm such a klutz," Nikki says to the instructor as she turns in his arms to face him. "This is not going very well."

Daphne in the meantime has gotten her shoes and harness on and is gazing admiringly at him. She steps towards him and places a hand on his forearm.

"You'll have to excuse my friend," she says, "She's a bit nervous about taking this class." He pulls his arm back, ignoring her advance.

Turning back to Nikki he says, "I'm sorry, I didn't introduce myself. I'm Grant Tobin, but my friends all call me Granite.

And you must be Nikki Selzer. You missed some of the important instructions at the beginning, so let's go over it now."

He turns to Daphne and says, "It looks like you already know some of the basics. Why don't you join Mary and Hannah over there," pointing as he says, "Hannah is the one with the bright blue shirt. She'll fill you in."

Granite helps Nikki through the first class and encourages her to keep trying when she panics on the wall and can't find a hand or foothold. The first time she makes it to the top of the beginner wall and rings the bell at the top he yells, "All right, I knew you could do it. Great job! Now push off and I'll support you as you rappel down."

Nikki's heart is pounding as she clings to the wall, afraid to look down. Her throat constricts. She can't even get a word out to say that she can't do it. Her fingertips are tingling and her legs are starting to shake. It seems as though an eternity goes by before the sound of Granite's voice penetrates her consciousness. It is a soothing voice: deep and even—confident—sure—believable.

"Come on, Nikki, I won't let you fall. I'm holding you all the way. Just take a little step. Relax into the harness. There. That's it. Come on. Let yourself fly a little. Feel the thrill of the descent. That's it. That's it! Great! You look like a pro!"

Tears are streaming down her face as she reaches the floor. She stumbles and Granite catches her.

"I'll never get it," she cries.

"But you did it, didn't you?"

"Yes, I did. And I have to admit, that last part *was* fun, once I let go."

Granite is all business. "Your reactions are completely normal. It's good to have a healthy respect and even a healthy fear of the unknown. I wouldn't want anyone on a rock face who did not admit to the danger. It's the overconfident and cocky students who worry me. You will do just fine. I'm looking forward to your outdoor climb at the end of this class."

Nikki looks at the floor, embarrassed. "Thank you for having confidence in me. I've never done much physical exercise before this. In fact, I just recently have gotten into speed walking, so it's nice to know that there's hope for me." Nikki blabbers nervously. "My husband thinks I'm uncoordinated and won't even let me play golf with him. Our son, on the other hand, can do any physical activity he sets his mind to and excel at it. He's on a baseball scholarship at the University of Illinois in Urbana. He must get the coordination from his father."

"Don't sell yourself short. You've got strong legs and good balance. If you spent a little time at the gym lifting weights, your arms would be as strong as your legs." Granite pinches her biceps. "Yes, you've got the makings of a great rock climber." The rest of the evening flies by and Nikki is beaming as they leave the rock climbing gym.

In the car on the way home, Daphne complains about the instructor spending the entire class with Nikki.

"Well, I needed help. I didn't have much confidence starting out and I needed extra attention. But wasn't it fun? I saw you laughing over there with your two partners. You looked like you were really getting into it. I think you're just jealous that Granite spent that time with me and not you. I saw how you were physically attracted to him."

"He is a hunk, isn't he?"

"Yeah, but you're not used to having any man ignore you. They all love you, Daphne. When they don't fall for you it's notable. So, get used to it and, welcome to the real world." Nikki pauses, glances at Daphne and says, "How do you think I feel when we're together and men we meet act as though I am invisible?"

Daphne, sounding repentant and remorseful, says, "Nikki, I'm so sorry. I didn't know that was happening. Maybe I have been a little self-centered and thoughtless."

Nikki takes Granite's advice and starts lifting weights at the Athletic Club. Staff members at the gym familiarize her with the machines that provide a full body workout. She eagerly goes to the next climbing class—alone. Daphne says she has an evening meeting she can't get out of. Nikki gets there early so she can buy shoes and a harness. She admits that she is hooked on the idea of rock climbing and decides that she will continue even if Daphne drops out.

Granite smiles broadly when he sees her. "I was wondering if I would ever see you again," he says. "You seemed terrified at the first class, but I'm glad you came back. You showed real promise. And I'm glad you wore a little more appropriate clothing. I meant to mention that before you left last time. It looked like your clothes were hindering your moves."

Nikki answers with a laugh. "Yes, I certainly was terrified. I had totally the wrong clothes, but I think I am addicted to adrenaline. The more I thought about it, the more I liked the idea of rappelling. You're a good teacher, Granite. Can you help me pick out some shoes?"

"Hang on just a sec," he says. "Let me finish with this customer and then I'll be right with you."

"Yes, I'm good at hanging on," Nikki says. "Remember last week?" Granite walks back to the checkout counter, laughing.

By the time class time rolls around, Nikki has her shoes and harness and other supplies that Granite recommended. She has made a couple of climbs up the beginner wall with him belaying and she rappels down with confidence. Tonight she will progress to an intermediate wall. She finds that the walls are graded according to difficulty, pitch and number of handholds. This gym uses a grading system based on the Yosemite Decimal System of difficulty with certain modifications. The routes range from a simple positive slope with plenty of artificial handholds and footholds evenly spaced, graded as a 5.0, to a negative pitch with only natural notches and crevices to grasp which are difficult to find. These are graded as a 5.11. Outdoors there is no limit to the difficulty of climbing, but in the gym under controlled conditions, a 5.11 is as difficult as they get. On her second attempt at the wall graded as a 5.4, she makes it to the top. Half way up she learned first hand what Granite meant by "sewing machine" leg. Her leg shook with the strain of supporting all her weight on a precarious perch. Before it gave out entirely, she managed to find a good handhold and gave her fatigued leg muscles a rest before continuing to the top.

Nikki thinks about little else during the six weeks of the rock climbing class. She even goes several extra times to the gym for her solo climbs and is disappointed the one time that Granite is not there to belay her. Daphne continues with the class, but has missed at least half of them. She always has an excuse. She does meet Nikki at the gym once or twice to belay, after being signed off to climb without an instructor.

Granite's encouragement and smooth sounding voice pop into Nikki's mind and she finds herself daydreaming of mountain climbing scenes with fresh air blowing through her hair and reaching the apex of a tough wall with Granite waiting for her at the top.

At home, everything—even the granite counters in the kitchen—reminds her of Granite. She smiles to herself and her heart beats a little faster to think of his words of praise for her. She imagines romantic scenes in mountain meadows: birds singing, flowers blooming, Granite gazing proudly at her, saying, "*Yes, Nikki, I knew you could do it. I knew that you would love it as much as I do.*"

Aroused at the thought of his nearness, her face reddens as she stands at the counter slicing onions. She doesn't hear Emma enter the house.

Emma walks into the kitchen looking for a snack. She gives her mom a hug. "Hey, it's not that hot in here, Mom. How come you're beet-red?"

Chapter Eight

Ice Boating at Lake Clark

As they gain altitude and turn west, the air becomes smoother. Leila relaxes, getting a book out of her bag so as to avoid talking to Dom. Entering Lake Clark Pass, they see the blue ice of the glaciers peaking through here and there, but it is mostly covered by brilliant white snow.

Dom's head turns from side to side. He leans forward to shout, "Be careful, Celeste, don't get too close to those hills. Isn't this amazing! Wow! I must have died and gone to heaven. Watch out, Rudy. Don't let it get away from you. Where's my camera?"

He turns to Leila. "I can't believe I left it in the baggage compartment. Why didn't you warn me? Oh, my God! This is better than any roller coaster ride I've ever had. Amazing! Wow! Look at that glacier over there." He points, knocking the book out of Leila's hand to her lap. She picks it up.

"Whoa! It looks like we're going to run into that hill. Are you sure you've been this way before? You seem to be lost. Was that a moose down there? Leila, look at that. Look. Look!"

Dom grabs Leila's arm. "How can you just sit there reading? This has got to be some of the most spectacular scenery in the world. You act as though you see it every day. Well, I guess of course, you do. But, wow, open your eyes and look. We could practically reach out and touch that mountain. Not too close, Celeste! Are there other planes in here? How would there be room for us to pass?"

Celeste sighs with exasperation. "Uncle Dom, please. I know you're excited, but you are distracting me. This corner can be turbulent and I want to make sure everything is under control. I need to make a position report to Kenai radio over a Remote Communications Outlet, an RCO. Can you speak a little more quietly?"

On hearing that, Dom continues his monologue but whispers it into Leila's ear. Leila grits her teeth and smiles tolerantly over his enthusiasm. She remembers her first trip through this pass with Pete at the controls of their J-3 Cub. She was in the front seat and was terrified that he could not see where they were going. The pass appeared to be too narrow for them to navigate through, but as her time in the air increased, she learned that appearances could be deceiving. Dom continues to describe every new scene and Leila finally begins to see it through his eyes.

It is beautiful. We are so blessed to see these great wonders of God's creation. Maybe I have taken it for granted.

They land on the windblown ice near a cabin on the west shore of Lake Clark. The ice is smooth and thick and the plane slides to a stop noisily, its skis clattering on the ice. It takes Rudy and Celeste little time to get the iceboat out of the plane and set it up. Then, before Leila realizes, they have jumped into the iceboat and are speeding across the lake, leaving her and Dom to take care of the plane and haul the supplies up to the borrowed cabin. Leila gets the covers from the baggage compartment and asks Dom to help her fasten the engine cover over the plane. As they struggle with the wing covers, Dom asks, "Is this really necessary? I don't see any clouds or snowflakes."

Leila responds impatiently, "We are staying here overnight and there might be an accumulation of frost. It's just a sensible precaution. If there is frost, these will save us a lot of time in the morning when we get ready to take off."

"Oh, yeah. Good idea."

"Would you get that catalytic heater out of the plane and start it up, please? I'll slip it in under the cover so the engine will stay toasty warm."

Holding the heater, Dom looks puzzled. "How do I do that? I've never seen one of these contraptions before."

"Never mind. I'll do it. Just fasten the rest of these wing covers."

When they have completed all the necessary chores and have made a small fire in the cabin, Leila pauses to take a deep breath. She feels good after the flurry of activity and is energized by the bright sunshine and the coziness of the cabin. She smiles at Dom. "Time for coffee, Pete." Realizing her mistake as she sees Dom's confusion, she continues, "I'm so sorry. I forgot for a moment where I was." Sadness hits her like a great weight. She smiles, but her eyes are pinched, her forehead, furrowed.

Dom walks over to her holding two mugs. "I knew you would need this after that work party. Here," he says, holding one mug out to her. He bends over and kisses her on the forehead. "Don't worry your pretty little head over it. I do that all the time." He keeps up a running chatter, telling stories about his trips to Northern Wisconsin in the wintertime.

Leila, again lost in thought, barely hears most of it. After he is quiet for several minutes, he finally chokes out the words, "I know how it is to lose somebody. I'm with you, Leila."

She breaks free from her reverie and looks at him, seeing him—really—for the first time. She sees his thin face with the laugh lines around his eyes and the almost permanent smile etched into his wrinkles. The empathy on his face softens her heart a little. She manages to get out of her own suffering to consider that he, too, might have some pain in his life.

"Thank you, Dom," she says slowly just as the door bursts open and Rudy and Celeste tumble in.

"You've got to try it! What a blast! I think we got up to seventy miles an hour once. The ice is absolutely perfect. Only a few open holes to watch out for. What do you say, Mom? Do you and Dom want to try it?"

"I think I'd better go with someone experienced," Leila says. "It's been years since I've handled the boat. Why don't I go out with Celeste while you and Dom get the cabin ready for the night? Are we all going to sleep in here, or are you going to set up the tent?"

Rudy glances over at Celeste and says, "We'll discuss that while you're gone. Maybe we can all fit in here, but nobody would have any privacy."

"Well, whatever you decide...Let's go, Celeste, before I lose my nerve. Just give me a minute or two to get my warm clothes on." They rush out the door as Rudy and Dom busy themselves with the supplies.

When Leila and Celeste return to the cabin they see a small tent set up about eighty yards down the shore. Spruce trees and willow bushes surround it, making it look like the small opening was made expressly for a tent that size. Rudy has carefully brushed the snow from around the bottom edges of the tent making a small mound all the way around. A well-packed path near the opening makes it look welcoming and neat. He certainly has his father's sense of respect for the wilderness.

"Celeste and I will sleep in the tent, Mom." Rudy says quickly. Leila frowns at him. Even though she knows that they live together, they have had many discussions about the sanctity of marriage and he knows she does not approve of the arrangement.

He has argued in the past "We're engaged, Mom, we just have to wait for the right time to get married. I can't support someone until I finish my degree. And how can I ask her to support me through graduate school?"

Leila grudgingly acquiesces and notices that her sleeping bag is already spread out on the bunk closest to the stove. "Looks like I was kept out of the loop again," she says.

Rudy and Dom rush off to get in a quick ride before dark. By the time they return, the sky to the southwest is a deep red with gold layers fading into a soft peach color, becoming grey, then purplish blue and finally a deep blue-black with the first stars appearing in the eastern sky. The temperature has dropped to near zero.

Dom is shivering with the cold—and excitement. His cheeks are red and tears are streaming from his eyes. "You know, I always watched people ice-boat on Green Bay, but never could afford to do it. Why have I waited all my life to have such an experience? That was more of a thrill than my first—oh, sorry, there are ladies present." He elbows Leila in the ribs and gives out a hearty laugh.

Leila shakes her head in mock disgust. "Men!"

Leila has a pot of soup simmering on the stove and the smell permeates the cabin, giving it a homey glow. As she rummages through their supplies and the shelves to find enough bowls and spoons, Rudy digs a bottle of brandy out of his pack. He pours a small amount into four canning jars, which will serve as glasses and hands them around. "Here, Mom, Dom, here's to another first." They raise their glasses, smiling. The warm amber liquid warms Leila as it goes down. She dishes out the soup and as they eat noisily in the dim light from the kerosene lamp, that is the only sound in the small cabin. They rip pieces of crusty bread from the loaf to sop up the last of the soup from their bowls. Finally, they slow down.

Dom says, "Man, I didn't realize that I was so hungry. That cold, fresh air sure works up one's appetite. What a day! This will certainly go down as one of the best days of my life." Everyone nods in agreement, not wanting to spoil the mood with extraneous conversation.

"More brandy, anyone?" Rudy asks as he pours himself a second glass.

"Sure, why not?" Leila says as she leans back, totally relaxed and satisfied for the first time since... An intense sorrow presses against her consciousness. *Oh let it go. Just let me be in this moment. It IS good here, now.* She hears Pete's voice in her head, *just do it. Let yourself be lost in the moment. Go with what feels good to you.*

He had actually said something like that talking to Leila about her cello playing, encouraging her to let herself be lost in the music and to let her feelings show through. It had been a breakthrough for her at the time. Even though she was a perfectionist and technically, the best cellist in the orchestra, she seldom let the music pull at her emotions to allow them to be expressed. Once she let go, everyone noticed the change. At home, in her practice, she often was lost for hours in the joy of playing. Once she mastered the technical aspects of a piece, her interpretation was so gripping that anyone listening had chills running through his body. She smiles. *Yes, this is good.*

Leila closes her eyes in the silence. "Rudy, remember how we always sang songs around the campfire? The girls and you harmonized so well. I loved hearing you sing your three-part harmony. Wouldn't it be great if you had your guitar and..."

"Mom, where have you been?" Rudy interrupts. "We were just talking about singing and I regretted that I didn't throw my guitar in the plane. But Dom here has a harmonica. Let's listen to him play a few tunes."

"Oh, I'm not really a musician," Dom shrugs. "After hearing you play last night with the symphony, I'd be embarrassed to play anything. I can't even read music. I just play by ear and only know a few songs."

Celeste begs him, "That's not true. Please, Uncle Dom. I know you're really good. I've heard you play at family reunions. We used to sing and dance for hours to your music. Please. Pretty please. Play that one about the mountain man. I'll sing."

"Let me get it warmed up first. Here's one everyone might know." Dom pulls the harmonica from his pocket and warms it in his hands before putting it to his mouth. The crackling of the fire in the barrel stove provides a subtle percussive accompaniment to the sweet chords of "Georgia." Leila had never thought much of harmonica music before. She barely tolerated anything but classical music. But as she listens to its full sound in the small cabin, she appreciates the unique artistry of a harmonica for the first time. Dom is certainly a master. He sounds like a whole orchestra. He closes his eyes and, sitting upright on the edge of his chair, sways with the music. The builds and crescendos, the dramatic pauses, the pleading quality in the sound say more than any vocalist could ever say—including Ray Charles himself.

"Wow!" Leila says as he finishes. "That was beautiful. I have never heard a harmonica played like that. Of course, I can't say that I've ever actually listened to harmonica music before. But I didn't know what I was missing."

"Okay, now the mountain man song," Celeste says. Her clear soprano voice soars above the quiet chords in a song that Leila had never heard before. Leila didn't know that Celeste could sing.

Chapter Nine

Nikki's First Outdoor Climb

Nikki finishes the six rock climbing sessions at the gym and eagerly awaits the outdoor climb scheduled for next weekend. Only three others in the class elect to do the outdoor climb. They have the option of driving to the site on Saturday morning or on Friday afternoon. It is a three-hour drive, so Nikki and Michael opt to leave Friday afternoon with Granite and stay overnight in a motel near the site.

Nikki has to be back in Caraville on Saturday evening for a mandatory dinner party Gerik's staff is throwing for their retiring boss. Gerik has been promised the position and really must attend. Nikki says she will be back in plenty of time. She's arranged to ride home with Val after the climbing expedition.

Gerik grumbles as Nikki prepares to leave. "I can't imagine why you're going off on a wild goose chase on one of the most important days of my career. Don't you realize that a stable marriage is one of the reasons I got the promotion? The other contenders are all wrapped up in ugly divorces and can't give 100% at work. I need you to be by my side and show your support."

"It always has to be about you, doesn't it? Well, screw your fancy career and appearances. I need to do this to prove something to myself. This day is about me, too."

Gerik takes a step toward Nikki and fingers the jade sculpture on the counter. He glares at her.

Nikki backs away from him and continues. "A wife is more than a cook and homemaker and doormat, someone to clean up messes while you do the important work. We're partners, Gerik. It's time you respected my contributions to this relationship. They are more than the menial chores I do to make this place a home. And, besides, you didn't hear, I said I'd be back in time for your stupid party. When people see my new dress, and new figure, I'm sure they'll *oohh* and *aahh* and turn green with envy. I'll be the hit of the party and not jeopardize your career." She turns towards the door. *You jerk.*

In his van during the drive up to Central Wisconsin, Nikki glances across the front seat at Granite's profile, admiring his posture. Seated behind the wheel, he has the look of a bodybuilder. His brush cut hair seems incongruous with his sleeveless t-shirt and jeans and the rock music blaring from the speakers. He taps the steering wheel as he dances in his seat to the music. Nikki loves admiring his strong arms and shoulders as the muscles ripple with his dance. As Granite turns and catches her watching him, he smiles with that broad toothy smile she has come to love. Nikki forgets all about her argument with Gerik. She is caught up in Granite's enthusiasm. His love of climbing exudes from his person like a strong fragrance. This is his element. Rock climbing is his passion. It feels good to be with someone who is passionate about something so exciting.

They have dinner together at a small town diner. Michael, who had eaten his huge lunch during the drive, says that he needs a good night's sleep and declines the dinner invitation. Val and Jeff will drive up in the morning. Nikki orders *the best red wine you have,* and laughs as the screw-top mini-bottle of sweet wine arrives at the table.

"Here's to a great climb," she toasts to Granite's mug of draft beer. "I wish I had ordered the beer."

Granite takes a big swallow and breathes a satisfied sounding, "Ahhhhh. That's good. Here, have some of mine, I'll share."

"Oh, you just want to get me drunk and take advantage of me." Nikki jokes. She leans towards him, but stops her hand from reaching out to stroke his leg.

"Oh, no, don't worry about that tonight. You'll need to get plenty of rest. Tomorrow will be a challenging day and you'll need all your strength and balance. No extra-curricular activities tonight. I'll make sure that you're all tucked into bed by nine."

Nikki imagines him smoothing a satin sheet over her body. *I wish you would.*

The next morning Nikki wakes before five a.m. Her mind spins with worries about the climb. She has never actually seen a rock wall that one would climb outdoors. If she has, she did not recognize that it could be climbed. She imagines sheer cliffs with drop-offs into churning waters or boulder fields below that would break a leg or even the neck of someone weak or clumsy enough to miss a hold and fall. Before long, she has herself convinced that this is much too dangerous and decides to tell Granite she just cannot do it. She dresses for the climb, however, and packs the essentials—the climbing shoes and harness—and attaches the drying bag to her belt loop.

In the coffee shop, Nikki wrinkles her nose at the luke-warm, weak coffee she is served as she studies the menu and wonders what might be appropriate for a last meal. She spots Granite through the restaurant window walking towards her. Her heart does a little flip as he opens the door, looks her way smiling, and gives her a wink.

"Good morning, Gorgeous. I'll bet you're ready for the thrill of your lifetime."

"Well, actually, I've decided not to do it. I can't..."

"No, no, no. I don't want to hear any excuses. I've been around the block a few times, and—just so you know—I've heard them all before." Granite shakes his head. "Have you decided what to have for your last meal?"

Nikki laughs, "How did you know what I was thinking?" She spots Michael approaching their table. "Come and join us, Michael. Granite is giving his pep talk."

"Sure. I guess I'd like company for my last meal."

"You guys!" Granite explains patiently, "Look, everyone is nervous about their first outdoor climb. Remember what I said after that first class? It is good to have a healthy respect for the wall and admit to a little fear of the danger. If you were overconfident, I would be worried. You're both going to do just fine."

He reaches across the table and squeezes Nikki's hand. "These fingers will serve you well today. Trust me."

Nikki decides on the French toast and a large glass of orange juice. The toast is surprisingly good and she eats every bit of it. Both Michael and Granite order four-egg omelets with all the trimmings and wolf them down.

The group gathers in the lobby at eight o'clock. Jeff and Val drove together from Caraville. Nikki guesses by their nervous laughter and inane chatter they feel as she does. Val is pacing back and forth. Michael keeps clenching and unclenching his hands into fists.

Granite takes a deep breath and begins, "Hey, relax everyone. This is going to be a piece of cake after the tough wall at the gym. Come on, pile into the van. I'll brief you during the drive. Gus from the gym is going to meet us there and he will help with belaying. Every person will have someone they trust on the ropes."

"How will we know where to go?" Michael asks.

"Okay, first things first, let's just take it one step at a time. We'll do some bouldering when we get there to limber up. There's nothing comparable at the gym, but it's fun and easy. You will feel like little kids."

"What on earth is bouldering?" Val asks.

"It is basically scrambling to the top of a rock pile on all fours. There's no real technique, but agility and flexibility help. The boulders in this area are an ideal size and the rock piles are stable. So the greatest danger is going too fast and twisting an ankle."

Nikki grimaces. "So what then? I'm still concerned about the wall."

"The route we will climb first has been climbed a million times. It is challenging, I won't kid you there, but there are pitons in place and I will go up first and place the rope at the top. Thank goodness it's nice and dry today. The morning sun has warmed the rock and dried up any dew from the night."

Granite turns and looks Nikki in the eye. "Then one at a time you will attach the rope to your harness, Gus will belay so when you get to the top you can rappel down. You are going to be hooked, I tell you, just to feel the wind on your face and the solid rock beneath your fingers and feet.

"I can't wait," Jeff says. "Can I go first?"

115

As they drive up and park, the wall seems much less intimidating than what Nikki had envisioned. But still, the thought of climbing it makes her knees a little shaky. She follows Granite's advice, though, and takes one thing at a time. Once there, they pile out of the van and at the sight of the sofa size boulders, begin scrambling to the top. They are all laughing with excitement.

Upon reaching a high point, Nikki stands—legs outspread, arms lifted to the sky. "I'm an amaaa-zing woman!"

Everyone laughs. Granite turns to look. "Okay, Wonder Woman, let's get started."

They scramble down like little kids and gasp as they look up and see that Granite has already begun to climb the eighty foot cliff and he pauses to smile down at them. "See, it's easy." Gus is holding one end of the rope and Granite has a carabiner, which he clips on to each piton as he passes it. When he reaches the top, he loops the rope through the top piton and throws the loose end down.

Jeff grabs it and fastens it to his harness. "I'm ready." He scales the lower half of the wall, looking like he is simply walking up a set of stairs.

"Piece of cake," he says. But from there the pitch steepens and handholds are scarcer. He reaches a little too far to his right; his foot slips and he loses his balance. He slips from the rock face and falls about five feet before the slack in the rope catches and holds him in place. Nikki can't see his face, but as he hangs there immobile, she thinks she hears him crying. Granite is coaxing him from the top.

"Come on. Reach your left foot up about ten or twelve inches and scoot it over. There, do you feel that ledge? Okay. Get your right hand on the wall. Feel for that crevice. There. You're back on. Now take it easy and be sure you have a definite hold before you let go of the last one."

Jeff's cockiness is gone and he meekly follows Granite's advice. Inch by inch, foot by foot, he gains altitude as the others watch from below. Nikki realizes that she is holding her breath and when he reaches the top and slaps Granite's palm in a *High Five,* she exhales through pursed lips. As Jeff rappels down with ease she thinks, *I should go next before I lose my nerve.* But Val is already saying, "My turn. My turn."

Val is cautious, but confidently competent. She looks like a nimble monkey as she reaches for handhold and foothold, one after another, pausing for only brief moments to evaluate her route. She arrives at the top almost as quickly as Granite had.

She yells "Wahoo!" As she rappels down she sings, "What a day this has been, what a sight I have seen, why it's almost like…"

"Being in love," Nikki finishes. She flushes with embarrassment, but no one notices her gazing at Granite. She is not ready to climb yet and is glad when Granite says, "Okay, Michael, you're next." Nikki hardly notices him climb. Her arousal and conflicting emotions demand all of her attention. *How can I do this?*

Her desire not only to climb the wall, but to get to the top—and Granite—drive her to fasten the rope to the harness as quickly as she can when Michael reaches the bottom. She is aware only of the heat from the rock face and from her body as she climbs mechanically, carefully. Her focus is on Granite and she hears his voice, coaxing her, urging her on.

Oh, God! I'm really doing this. I'm alive! Wow! I don't remember ever feeling like this before. This is great!

She is so near the top she can see Granite's blue eyes and smell his peppermint breath when her right foot slips. She screams, "Granite, help!" She begins to panic.

"Left hand," he yells.

Her focus narrows and she feels a solid hold with her left hand. Her right hand is on a crevice only large enough for two fingers. She hangs on until the muscles in her left forearm are screaming for relief. The lactic acid burns as she tries to think what to do next.

"You know what to do." Nikki is not sure whether Granite actually said the words, or if she imagined them. She takes a deep breath and looks around. There are plenty of good choices of which way to go. The adrenaline rush has her muscles pumped up and strong. Her mind is clear. She climbs with a determined set of her chin and a confidence in her ability that she never before realized she had. Then she is at the top and sees Granite's hand raised to give her a 'high five'. She gives one last push from the ledge with her right leg and instead of a high five slap, she grabs for Granite's hand. He is surprised by her maneuver and almost loses his balance before thrusting his weight backwards and pulling her up over the top with him. He falls backwards with Nikki landing on top of him. In her excitement, Nikki grabs his neck, pulls his face to hers and kisses him with abandon. Coming up for breath, she says, "Oh Granite, I did it. I love...this!" And she kisses him again.

"I knew you would," he whispers. Then, as though realizing the awkwardness of their position, says, "Whoa, Nellie. We've got plenty more walls to climb today. We can't keep the others waiting. Let's continue this some other time."

Nikki jumps up and motions to Gus over the wall. "I'm ready to come down." She feels as though she is flying as she rappels down.

The rest of the day passes too quickly for Nikki. She dreads the drive back to Caraville and the mandatory party at the Country Club. She wants to stay here and not ever have to think about her troubles with Gerik again. She climbs to the top of the rock face several times gaining confidence with each ascent. Then, after lunch, they move to a different part of the wall and try a couple of more difficult routes. She can hardly believe the thrill she feels in looking down from the top and having no fear. The freedom is exhilarating.

There are no more opportunities that day for Nikki and Granite to be alone together, but Nikki is convinced that Granite is gazing at her with the same desire and excitement she feels. She climbs with a buoyancy and lightness that surprises her.

Nikki glances at her watch after a challenging climb and says, "Val, we've got to go! It's almost three o'clock. If I'm not home and ready to go by six-thirty, Gerik will kill me."

They rush to Val's car, waving good-bye.

Nikki is wrapped in her thoughts during the drive. Several times Val tries to start a conversation and talk about the day, but Nikki barely hears her. Instead, she relives that first ascent and the delight of reaching the top and embracing Granite. On reaching home, she briefly thanks Val and says "See you at the gym next week." Then as she slips her hand into her pocket to get the house key, she looks at her fingers reaching for the lock. She remembers grabbing Granite's neck and pulling his face to hers. *Yes, these fingers served me very well today. I can't wait to give them another chance.* She floats through the front door, smiling. As she walks by the kitchen, she notices Gerik standing at the bar, a half-filled glass raised to his lips. He sets it down with a clunk and glares at her. She feels as though a lead blanket is thrown on her. Her shoulders sag and the smile fades into a blank expression.

"Well, it's about time, Adventure Girl. What took you so long? It's time to go."

Chapter Ten

Sharing Stories

After singing every song they can think of, it gets very quiet in the cabin. They all sit staring into empty brandy glasses; Dom, for once, is silent. Rudy stands and says, "It's too quiet in here. Sounds like everyone is tuckered out from all the fresh air. I'm going to bed." Arm in arm he and Celeste leave the warmth of the cabin for their tent.

Leila busies herself with clearing the table and putting a kettle of water on the stove to heat for washing dishes. She avoids looking at Dom and can think of nothing to say to him. *It's a relief to have a break from his non-stop talking.*

She walks self-consciously to the window to look out. As her eyes adjust to the dim light from the half moon she notices a movement along the shore. *What is that?*

She whispers, "Dom, come here, quick!" and motions for him to join her.

"What?" His voice rattles the windows.

"Shhh, you'll scare him. Just come and look."

Joining her at the small window, he puts his arm around her—his face next to hers as they peer out into the darkness. "What do you see?"

"He's gone behind a drift, but we should see him come out soon. I am pretty sure it's a lynx."

His voice unaccustomed to being quiet is a low and rumbling, hoarse whisper. "Wow! A wild lynx? I didn't realize there were lynxes in Alaska. I've never seen one before. How big are they? What would he be doing out there in the cold? Are the kids okay in the tent? Should we warn them? Do you think I could get a picture if I stepped outside? Just wait until I tell Maria, she's not going to..." Leila hears his sudden intake of breath and sudden silence. She feels his large hand grip her shoulder. She doesn't want to say anything or even look at him right now. She senses a deep pain in him that he does not want to show. She can feel his shoulders heaving and she involuntarily tenses her entire body.

He's such an extrovert, I'm sure he would say something if he wanted me to know what's going on. She stands without moving and continues to squint out the small window with Dom's ragged breathing in her ear. She doesn't realize she is holding her breath until Dom whispers, "I see him. Look over by the plane."

Leila breathes out silently. The lynx circles the plane and then returns to its hunting along the shore. He crouches down, waiting, patient, almost invisible in the deep snow, then without warning leaps up and pounces on his prey.

Leila keeps her eyes on the lynx. "Looks like he was successful. Isn't he magnificent? He's curious, too. Must have smelled something in the plane."

After the lynx disappears, Leila turns to Dom. His eyes are shining. Leila smiles. "Wasn't that a treat? Lynxes are such solitary creatures."

"Sort of like me, huh?" He turns back to look out the window. After a long and uncomfortable silence, Dom begins to talk in a soft voice. Leila has to strain to hear him.

"I always wanted to marry her."

Leila wants to ask, who. But she says nothing as Dom continues.

"But in spite of her compassion and generosity, she could be very rigid. I never could figure it out. I got used to not bringing it up, but I couldn't help myself sometimes. I know that she loved me, that wasn't it. Our match was made in heaven. I know there were never two people who were more compatible. We were together for eighteen years. When she died it was like my heart was cut out. I felt like an empty shell walking around—when I could finally walk. At first all I could do was lay on my back, eyes open, looking—without seeing—at the ceiling. It still makes no sense. How could the God she loved so much do something so cruel? I asked over and over, *what kind of a God are you to let one of your best creations suffer?* I shook my fist and ranted and raved and even swore to get even, but you know, I never stopped believing in God's ultimate love. Crazy, huh?"

Leila looks at Dom. They are still standing at the window but he looks like he is gazing at a distant scene.

"No, not so crazy. I've done my own share of complaining to God. Suffering never makes any sense."

"No it doesn't. But, you know, even after three years, I still can't believe she's gone. It took at least a year and a half before I stopped seeing her everywhere. I still see her sometimes, at the oddest times, and my heart stops. I'll say, *Oh, Maria!* And most of the time just that phrase is enough to bring me back to reality."

"I do that too. I thought at first I was hallucinating."

"I know what you mean. But in a way it is comforting."

"Yeah. But, hey, speaking of comfort, why don't we sit down? My back is getting sore from hunching over this window."

"Sure."

They move to sit opposite each other on benches on either side of the table.

Dom continues. "She was Catholic, you know. One of the most generous and caring persons you would ever meet. And devout! I don't think she ever missed daily mass. She just couldn't bring herself to get married outside of the church's blessings and since I had been married before, she couldn't marry me in the church without me having my marriage annulled. I don't even know what that means. I don't know why she didn't insist on it."

"That is strange."

"Anyway, I made some stupid mistakes when I was in college and got married on a whim. The young fool left me after a few months to marry her high school sweetheart. She never intended to stay with me. She just wanted a name for her baby. In any case, that short relationship caused me years of grief and agony. I begged Maria to marry me. *It doesn't look right for us to live together,* I would say. *I'll study your religion and give it a chance, even though my mother is dead set against it. Our kids can be raised in the Catholic faith. Please Maria.* But my begging did no good.

"How sad!"

Dom is quiet for a long time. He shakes his head and wrinkles his brow. He swallows, closing his eyes, and takes a deep breath. "My mother, God rest her soul, was devout in her own way, even though it was a bit on the fanatical side. Growing up in a southern Indiana Pentecostal family, she used to call on God for every little thing. She quoted scripture at me from the time I was a toddler. Every situation had some scripture or verse applied to it. My dad used to leave home for days at a time to get away from all the preaching. He always came back, though. They would kiss and make up and he would ask her to forgive him. She always did. They loved each other, I am sure, but it was a rocky relationship—full of passion. I covered my ears to the yelling, often running to my room to put a pillow over my head."

"Oh, my!"

"She forced him to abandon his Catholic faith and he went along with it, because he loved her. There were some things so deeply ingrained, though, that occasionally he would slip up and murmur a particularly onerous—to my mother—Catholic prayer. Something like, *Holy Mary, Mother of God, pray for us*. And she would yell, *Mary is not God that we should pray to her*."

"So many people misunderstand a Catholic's relationship to Mary."

"I guess. In any case Mother never really accepted Maria. When Maria was diagnosed with a brain tumor, Mother said, *I knew all that praying to false Gods would come to no good. She is reaping the fruits of her stubbornness.*"

"How awful!" Leila reaches across the table to pat Dom's arm.

"Yeah. Mother was as rigid in her lack of compassion as Maria was in holding on to her faith. Isn't that strange: that two women could be so obviously and externally devout with blind spots wider than a mile. My heart just aches to think that they never really *knew* each other. They never saw each other's beauty. Maria was by far the more tolerant of the two, but Mother would not allow her to get close enough to see her goodness."

"My family never really warmed to Pete, either—especially my sister. She said some hurtful things about him. I have a hard time letting that go. But at least they were civil. It helped, I think, that we lived in Alaska. I never had to deal with conflict on a regular basis."

"That's one good thing about being separated by a great distance."

"I guess, although Pete always tried to get me to make peace with my sister. He was such a tolerant, forgiving person. I could never explain to him what drove us apart. We're just so different..." Leila's voice fades away.

Dom looks uncomfortable. Glancing toward the window, he clears his throat and begins, "I'm sorry. Here I've been rambling on and on. I haven't let you get a word in edgewise. I'll shut up now. I know I could talk for hours, but I'm sure you don't want to hear any more of my sob story; although it does feel good to get it out in the open."

"But I do. When you talk I can identify with your pain and your depth of feeling is very moving. It helps me to realize what I have been missing since Peter died."

Leila shifts her position to rest her elbows on the table. Dom leans over the table and grasps one of Leila's hands between his own and she puts her other hand on top of his.

Leila stares at their intertwined hands. "I have been living wrapped up in a cocoon. I have not allowed anything to touch me. I have stifled every honest emotion and blocked myself from even thinking—period. I don't know what I have been living on, but hearing you talk just now awakened something within me. I am not a very expressive person—never have been. I have always wanted to be in control of everything. When I couldn't control my emotions, I buried them. Please, go on, I want to hear about your life. It sounds much more real than mine has been."

"No, I've said enough. I want to hear your story, that is, if you are ready to share it. I know it took me at least two years before I could even talk about Maria's death. I sobbed and sobbed on the first telling. The sad thing, though, is that I could never talk about it with my family. But, please, if you can, tell me your story."

"I don't know, Dom. The pain is still so fresh. Pete and I had such a good marriage. I am sure it was like you and Maria. Ours was a match made in heaven. He was a very quiet and private person. I guess we matched in that way. We hardly ever had any arguments. Somehow, we just agreed on all the important things."

"Yeah, I know what you mean."

"Although when Natalia—our youngest—started to use drugs, we sometimes would yell at each other in frustration; we were so afraid for her. We had no control over the situation. I hate it. It's idiotic. How can she be so controlled by drugs? Rudy and Ana have always been so focused and responsible. We didn't know how to deal with Nat. I still don't."

"I haven't met Natalia or Ana yet. I want to hear more about them, but I must say Rudy has made a big impression on me. I can see why Celeste loves him. Her mom—my sister—worships him. I never knew her to get excited about any of Celeste's boyfriends before. But Rudy's a special guy."

"He is... He's so like his dad in many ways...yeah, he's special. Pete and I did argue a little about his education. He was always asking Pete's advice about staying in the flying business and Pete never discouraged him from considering it."

"Well, I'm glad he stuck with it long enough to meet my niece."

"Yeah, me too. The flying community in Alaska is pretty small, though, and they were bound to meet sooner or later. But, you know Rudy is a gifted naturalist and really should continue to work on his master's degree."

"Nothing wrong with a little education."

"Pete always said he should be able to make his own choice. In fact, we were arguing about just that the day Pete died—one of our rare arguments. We parted with bad feelings between us. It was something we had never done before. The guilt I feel... If only I had gone with him. I didn't tell him often enough how much I loved and needed him."

Leila pulls her hands away from Dom's hold and massages her forehead with them both.

"I'm sure he knew it, Leila."

"I didn't realize how much he needed me, too. If I had not been so stubborn and had gone with him that day, he might still be here. That's the hardest part, Dom, the guilt. Sometimes I feel like it will bury me."

Leila stands and begins pacing to the door and back. She stops suddenly, looks at Dom sitting by the table and with a shaky voice, she begins to tell Dom about the day Pete died.

Dom follows her movements with his eyes, a helpless expression on his face. As Leila returns to sit across from his again, he reaches out to touch her arm, but she moves to avoid contact.

"It was a beautiful spring day. April twenty fifth. It had been an unusually warm and early spring. The ice went out of Lake Hood much earlier than usual that year and Pete had just put floats on the Cessna one-eighty-five."

"Floats?"

"Yeah, you know, like for landing on water."

"Oh, I thought they were called pontoons."

Leila smiles and then continues. "Pete liked to do maintenance test flights himself after annual inspections, before releasing planes to the line. He asked me to go with him, but, like I said, we were arguing. I said I was too busy to go."

"What did you say?"

"I don't remember exactly, but Pete's last words to me were, 'okay, suit yourself. I'm just going over to Twin Island Lake for a few landings. I want to give the engine a good workout. Maybe next time you won't be too busy to come with me.' I didn't even answer him." Leila walks to the window and looks out into the darkness.

"I never said good bye." She closes her eyes to quell the start of tears springing up. "I heard him taxi away from our FBO and I continued working on the books, almost relieved to have him out of the way." Leila blinks several times and bites her cheek.

Dom, taking advantage of the pause, asks, "What in the heck is a beo?"

"A what?"

"You said f-beo. I was wondering what a beo is and why you would say it was an f- beo, that's all."

"Oh, Dom. I don't know why I find you so amusing. What I said was *F B O*, as in Fixed Base Operation. That's what they call a small flying service like we have."

"Oh, sorry. I won't interrupt again."

"That's all right. I needed a breather. Anyway, I was thinking, I don't know why he has to be so stubborn. He never listens to my side of the story. You know how you get irrational when your feelings are hurt. Pete was a good listener but I was just so angry."

"I've been there."

"I was absorbed in filling out some tedious payroll reports when I hear the front door open. I am not sure how much time had gone by, but it seemed only minutes. I thought... he's back rather quickly. I wonder if something went wrong. I went back to my work, trying to decide whether or not I was still angry with him. I heard the buzzer on the counter out front ring three times—one short and two long. It had been our special code to each other. You know, to let me know it was Pete—and vice-versa—not a customer. I smiled to myself, pretending to be absorbed in my work, just waiting for him to come and give me a bear hug, lifting me off my chair, and telling me how sorry he was."

Dom looks as though he can't wait for her to continue.

"The door to the back office opened tentatively, then a voice I didn't recognize began, 'Mrs. Pletnikof.' I heard him clear his throat, and say again, 'Are you Mrs. Pletnikof?'"

Chapter Eleven

Nikki's Night Out in Chicago

After the outdoor climb, Nikki thinks of nothing but Granite and climbing. Even her quilting designs fail to keep her interest for long. As she enters the climbing gym one day, she notices a flyer advertising a climbing excursion.

A trip to Bend, Oregon! Great! I've got to go. That's where all those great granite walls are. People go there from all over the world.

Nikki climbs the most difficult wall that morning imagining another outdoor adventure with Granite. She rereads the notice before leaving the gym and sees in the small print at the bottom that only people who have completed a level five advanced class, or have a minimum of five years of experience, can sign up for it. She turns around, looking for Granite to talk to him about a class and the trip. He is busy with another client so Nikki signs up for the first available class without consulting him or giving any thought as to what Gerik might think. The class requires a partner and Nikki knows she will be able to talk Daphne into it, even though Daphne is not too keen on climbing.

Later that day she begs Daphne, "Come on, Daph, I need the moral support. You don't have to do the trip to Oregon, just go through the classes with me. It helps when you have a partner you trust."

Daphne wrinkles her nose. "Okay, okay, I'll do it, but just for you. But you know that I am really busy at the gallery right now. I have a big show coming up and I am working a lot of nights to get ready, so, I might be a little late for the first class. You can fill me in on everything when I get there."

"All right, but honestly, Daph, I don't know how you do it. Your schedule makes me tired just thinking of it. You must have fifty things going on at once. But, I'll fill you in, as long as you promise to stick with it."

The following week—the first night of the class—Nikki walks into the gym a little early, dressed for climbing. She sees Granite and his buddy, Dave, near the counter, going over some paperwork. Granite has his back to the door.

Nikki is about to say hello when she overhears one of the men saying, "Is that klutzy old broad with the red hair gonna be in the class? I thought I recognized her name on the class list. What is it, Nellie? No, Nikki. Man, I don't know... she might be dangerous on a tough wall. She doesn't have enough experience."

Nikki's face falls and her energy falls with it. Her ears are burning and she can feel her cheeks getting red. Old feelings of incompetence pile up on her. Not waiting to hear a response, she turns and hurries out to her car. She bursts into tears as she opens the car door. *How could Granite say such a thing? I thought he found me attractive.*

Convinced of Granite's callousness, she can't think straight. She feels as though a cold, hard stone has settled in the pit of her stomach. Her thoughts are all in a jumble and in a daze she pulls out of the parking lot not noticing that Daphne is pulling in as she leaves. Distraught, Nikki drives without any awareness of where she is going. *I thought he liked me.*

She grows angrier and angrier as she drives. Somehow she ends up on the expressway headed for Chicago. The trees alongside the road blur as Nikki grips the steering wheel, her foot heavy on the accelerator.

"I'll show him! Klutz, am I? He can take his climbing and shove it." She is passing cars right and left and suddenly finds herself behind a slow car in the right lane. As she slams on the brakes to avoid hitting it, she hears a siren and sees flashing lights of a Highway Patrol car behind her. Glancing down at the speedometer she notices that even after slowing down, she is going eighty-five miles per hour. She clenches her teeth and prepares to face the cop for the ticket she is sure she will get. Then the police car goes by her, picking up speed as it does.

Whew, that was a close call. I'd better slow down.

She continues to drive at a more conservative speed and as she passes the next exit, she sees the flashing lights of several police cars, a fire truck and an ambulance.

"Oh, my God! That looks really bad. Better slow down a little more."

But, soon the merry-go-round of thoughts in her head returns. She speeds up automatically, unaware of her surroundings. She is driving as though she is on autopilot. Near the city she gets off the expressway heading for Chicago's city center.

Nikki notices a familiar landmark. *Oh, there's that bar I stopped in when I found out about Gerik cheating on me—with Daphne, of all people. I think I need a drink.* She pulls into a parking place right outside of the bar on Hubbard Street.

It is still early evening, so the bar is almost deserted. She takes a seat at the bar and orders a martini, extra dry. It goes down so smoothly she orders another. As the alcohol begins to relax her, her anger flares again and as soon as the second drink arrives, she gulps it down without tasting it.

"I'll have another," she says to the bartender.

A few people have been trickling in and the bartender's attention has been directed elsewhere.

When he finally places the drink in front of Nikki, she mumbles, "It certainly takes a long time to get served around here."

A man sitting next to her at the bar overhears her mumbling. He puts a hand on hers to get her attention. "Well, let me order you another right now so you don't run dry. We wouldn't want you to get thirsty, would we?"

Nikki turns towards him, trying to focus, but having a hard time, and nods, "Good idea," she slurs.

When her fourth drink arrives, Nikki says to the guy who bought it, "Thanks. I needed that."

Then she turns her back to him to quietly sip the martini in solitude. When she has finished it she looks up towards the mirror behind the bottles lined up on the shelf. *Whoa, who is that gorgeous redhead with that hunk of a guy leaning over her shoulder? I didn't notice her when I came in.*

She squints in order to focus better, closing one eye. The rest of the room is out of focus and the football game on the television is blaring, making the music in the background barely discernible.

"Hey." Nikki turns and bumps into the guy on her left, "Who…..? Oh, excuse me, I'm sorry. You're the guy, but, oh, no, it's me, I had forgotten that I dyed my hair."

"That's okay, Honey, you've got beautiful hair." He runs his fingers through it, slipping his hand around to cradle the back of her head as she allows her head to rest on his hand.

"That feels good. I didn't realize I was so tired. Just let me rest here a minute. Maybe I should get something to eat. I never drink on an empty stomach. Oh, too late for that I guess," Nikki giggles.

Her tongue feels like a thick wad of cotton in her mouth. She has to speak slowly in an attempt to enunciate every word. "I'm Nikki, by the way. I'm sorry; I didn't get your name."

"Mitch," he says. "Nikki, that's a beautiful name. It suits you perfectly. Do you live around here? I don't think I've ever seen you in here before and I certainly would have noticed."

"Oh, no I'm from out of town. Here on a convention. It's been a rough day. I had to get away from it all."

"Well, I was supposed to meet a few friends here to go dancing at the new place up on Rush Street, but they're an hour late. I guess they stood me up. Why don't you come along with me? You seem like the dancing type. Everyone says it's the hottest new place in Chicago." Mitch leans close to her so he can hear her response over the background noise.

"I'm not much of a dancer. But, hey, why not? I like to watch. Maybe you could teach me a few steps. How far is it from here? Can we walk? I don't know if I should drive just now."

Nikki slides down from the bar stool, trying out her balance and weaves back and forth.

Hanging on to her elbow, Mitch says, "It's about eight blocks, I guess we could walk. It would do us good. But we need to get there before ten o'clock; otherwise, you can't get in the door. On second thought, let me drive. We'll get there quicker. We can always come back later and get your car."

"Why don't we just take mine? It's right outside the door."
Nikki is eager to get moving. She hands Mitch the keys. He
opens the door for her and helps her into the passenger
seat. Her shoulders slump down and her head falls against
the back of the seat. She closes her eyes as Mitch pulls out
into traffic in her new black Jetta. Her body feels warm and
relaxed. The motion of the car makes her head spin. She
feels like she is floating.

"Thanks for driving, Granite, I mean, Mitch. This is
soooo relaxing. Oh, are we already here? That was quick,"
Nikki says as she feels the car come to a stop.

Mitch is handing the keys to the valet as Nikki opens her
eyes, and before she can move, he is opening her door and
helping her out of the car.

"Come on; let's get a table before they're all gone," Mitch
holds her elbow and ushers her into the bar.

The beat of the music is overpowering as they walk to
their booth close to the back. From there they don't have
a direct view of the band, but the sound is good, bouncing
from the hardwood floor and concrete walls. A tenor sax
begins a solo and Nikki closes her eyes letting the pure feeling of the sound carry her.

"Let's dance," she says, "Who needs to eat when you
can feed on music like that?" So before even sitting down,
they head out to the dance floor, swaying to the rhythm as
they go. On the dance floor, Mitch grabs Nikki and pulls
her close. Her mind is riding on the repetitive waves of
the sound. She allows her body to be led to the pulsing
beat.

"You're absolutely right. This band is world class. It is so
danceable. It just carries you along with it. And I don't even
know how to dance."

Her mouth is only an inch from Mitch's ear. As Mitch responds to her comment, she can feel his breath tickling her neck. Their bodies are moving together and suddenly, she can feel his arousal and pushes against him, laughing as she does.

"Does that feel good?"

He groans and says, "How about if we go somewhere a little quieter?"

"No, no. I want to dance," Nikki says looking up at him and then attempting to give him a little kiss on the cheek, hits his mouth instead and the kiss takes all of her attention away from her dancing. They stand together, feet locked in place, swaying back and forth, pressing into each other, not even noticing when the music stops. Another couple bumps into them as they are exiting the floor. Nikki look around and realizes where she is. She grabs Mitch's hand and leads him back to their booth, saying, "I've got to get something to eat, or I'll pass out."

Nikki plops down onto the bench seat of the booth and leans over to a reclining position. It is a great effort for her to pull herself up to a sitting position. She leans her elbows on the table and cradles her forehead in her hands.

"Are you all right?" Mitch whispers into her ear.

He has slid in next to her and has his left arm around her shoulder. His right hand rests on her thigh. His fingers inch up.

"Yeah, I'm fine. I'll be just great when I get something to eat."

"You're already great," Mitch says as he strokes her leg.

The waiter yells above the music, "Anything to drink?"

"Yes, two double martinis," Mitch says.

The waiter turns, saying "Right on."

"Wait, wait," Nikki yells. "I need a hamburger, too. I don't think he heard me. Would you run after him, please?"

Mitch rushes off after the waiter and disappears around the corner. When he doesn't return immediately, Nikki scans the area near their table and notices the restroom sign to her left. "I've gotta go," she says aloud. She staggers up from the table and weaves her way to the restroom. The brightly lit room is spacious and decorated with a sofa and several overstuffed chairs. Nikki sits for a moment on the sofa and leans her head back. Then remembering why she came in, rushes to the toilet stall.

"What a relief! Whoa, am I drunk, or what?" As she washes her hands she notices her reflection in the mirror. "You are a doll, Elsa, I mean Nikki."

Then turning around, she notices a telephone on the table next to the sofa. She sits again and says, "I have got to call Daph. She would love this band." Her fingers automatically dial the familiar number and as she hears Daphne's voice she yells, "Daphne, you have got to hear this band. You love jazz and this is absolutely the best. Come down here immediately. I met this hunk of a guy and..."

"Where are you, Nikki? It sounds like a bar. Are you drunk?"

"I'm in Chicago, some jazz club on Rush Street. I think it's Rush and, oh I don't remember the cross street, but Daphne, I tell you, it's the greatest. And I don't give a damn about Granite. He can take his rock climbing and shove it."

"What's that about Granite? He was wondering where you were tonight."

"He can take his carabiner and...Nikki begins to laugh, near hysteria. When she pauses for breath, she hears

Daphne's voice so quiet now that she has to press the phone against her ear to hear what she is saying.

"Don't go anywhere, Nikki. Stay right where you are. I am going to call my brother to come and get you. He lives downtown about a mile from where you are and you need help getting home. I don't know what has gotten into you. Did you hear me Nikki? Give me a call when you get to his house."

But Nikki had let the phone slip to her lap. The door to the bathroom opens and a young woman in a classic little black dress comes in. Nikki hears the band, back from their break. She places the receiver back in the cradle and rushes out the door.

"Where have you been?" Mitch asks when she gets back to the table.

"Oh, you know, little girl's stuff."

The martinis and two oversized hamburgers sit on the table in front of her.

As she eats her hamburger, Mitch watches her with a smile. "You must be famished."

Nikki begins to feel as though Mitch is a long lost friend. She feels like she could tell him anything and he would understand. The incident with Granite pops into her mind again and she starts to cry.

Mitch slides a little closer to her and puts his arm around her, patting her shoulder like a brother. "What is it?"

"Oh, Mitch, you have been a life-saver." Nikki leans her head on his shoulder. "You know, I am really tired all of a sudden. Would you mind if I just took a little nap? I've got to tell you what happened, but right now I am just too tired."

She is leaning into him and can smell a faint, arousing scent of a men's cologne mixed with the pungent body odor emanating from his damp clothes.

"What is that scent? I love it. It really turns me on," Nikki whispers as she inhales noisily at his neck.

"Oh, just something I picked up at Niemen Marcus. Glad you like it."

The band, back from their short break, is louder than before. Mitch has to shout with his mouth close to Nikki's ear.

"How about if we go up to my condo? It's only a couple of blocks from here. It is much quieter and you can tell me your story over a glass of port and some cheesecake I just happen to have. How about it?"

"That would be great, Mitch." They make their way to the door through the crowded dance floor and the noise. Nikki is leaning on Mitch to keep her balance.

Mitch calls the valet to bring Nikki's car out and as they wait, he turns Nikki and they press together in a passionate embrace. When they part to take a breath, Nikki notices a tall, blond-haired guy stepping out of a double-parked car. He looks somewhat familiar. He rushes up and grabs both of Nikki's hands.

"Elsa, how are you? I was hoping that I would find you here. But I almost didn't recognize you with that red hair. It's fabulous on you. I'm glad Daphne told me about your new look. She called and..."

"Hey, buddy, watch who you're grabbing. You must have the wrong lady. Her name's Nikki. So get lost, unless you want me to call the cops."

Nikki looks from the blond to Mitch and back again. Her confusion intensifies as they argue, Mitch referring to her as Nikki and the blond referring to her as Elsa. The valet opens the door of her car stopped in front of the bar and signals to Mitch. Nikki feels as though she is being pulled apart. She struggles to stay upright as Mitch puts his arm around her shoulder. She feels someone tugging at her but is too drunk to offer any resistance. She closes her eyes and falls into the front seat of a waiting car. She dimly feels the thrill of the car accelerating with tires squealing.

Chapter Twelve

Leila Continues
Her Story

Leila speaks softly and slowly, pausing for long periods to gather her thoughts. She can still hear the man's voice as he burst into the office, disturbing her reverie. The shock of his news still hits her full force. It seems as though that terrible day happened yesterday. But she cannot grasp the feelings she had *before* that day. She can only see, hear and feel the pain of the memory playing over and over in her mind. She sits down next to Dom.

"I was so irritated that it was not Pete, I snapped at the guy who was sticking his head through the open door, 'Yes, what do you want?' I had been looking forward to our reconciliation and now a stupid customer was interrupting my daydreams. I couldn't be civil. It's amazing what details I remember about that day. Some things are burned into my memory and others are gone forever. I remember wondering how on earth this jerk knew our special buzzer code. Stupid, huh?" Leila bends over and rests her elbows on her knees. She holds her head in her hands and takes several deep breaths. She closes her eyes and relives that terrible afternoon.

Dom puts a hand on Leila's shoulder. "You don't have to go on if it's too hard. We can just sit here quietly and enjoy the fire."

"No, no. I need to get it out. But it's hard."

Leila tries to continue but the memory is playing in her head. Dom waits, saying nothing. Leila sees the scene as though she is watching a movie in which she has a role to play.

⟨⟶

"I am Richard O'Hara from the NTSB. Do you own a Cessna one-eighty five, tail number November 4532 Papa?"

"Yes, what's the problem?"

"I'm afraid it has been involved in a collision. Do you know who was at the controls?" O'Hara asks.

The earth drops out from under her feet and the air in the room is suddenly thin. Leila gasps and gulps to get enough of it. "My husband was flying it on a maintenance flight. What happened?"

"We are not sure of all the details yet, but the one-eighty-five sank before anyone could get to it." he says, matter-of-factly. "The tower controller said the plane belonged to Pete's Flying Service."

Leila then notices Father Ignaty standing, with a look of compassion, behind the guy from the NTSB. "Father, what's happening? Tell me. Nothing happened to Pete, did it? It can't be. Pete is the best pilot in the world. Please, God, no."

She tries to stand as Father Ignaty walks around the desk and he catches her in his arms as her knees buckle. "No, no, NO. It can't be." Father Ignaty holds her, patting her back.

⸻

A strong arm is encircling her back. Leila blinks, stifles her sobs and sees Dom looking at her. For a moment she doesn't know who he is. She must have been lost in her thoughts, not speaking, but staring—sightless—at the dark window. They sit there for several minutes until Leila calms down enough to talk again. "I'm sorry Dom. I didn't mean to break down. I've never talked to anyone about that day. Not even Rudy. I screamed and yelled at first, but by the time I told the kids, I had everything under control. People were amazed at how well I functioned. I handled all the funeral details, made all the business decisions, talked to insurance agents…Oh, God, how could I have been so cold?"

Dom interrupts, "Don't beat yourself up. Your reactions were perfectly normal. Grief has many stages and some people take a longer time with one phase or another."

"I know all that, in my head at least."

"Then you know living in the past is one way of remaining in the stage of denial. But it sounds like you're ready to move on. Having been through it myself, I know how long the grieving can go on. I'll be glad to help however I can. You don't need to tell it all at once. I'll be here to listen whenever you are ready." Dom continues to sit close to Leila with his left arm around her shoulder.

"Somehow I feel relieved just to hear that, Dom." Leila begins again to relive that terrible day in her mind when she snaps out of it and realizes that she must speak it out loud. She knows it will be a part of her healing process. She starts talking without raising her head, without making eye contact with Dom. "When the NTSB guy barged in, I intuitively knew something was wrong. He had the air of officialdom about him. By snapping at him, I think I was trying to protect myself from the inevitable truth. I knew it was something serious. You know how you get those gut feelings, like sometimes when the phone rings you just know it's bad news before you even pick it up? We had been through that often enough with Natalia. It was like that—but worse."

Dom rubs her shoulder.

"When he asked me who was at the controls of the plane—our one-eighty-five—I knew it was bad. He rattled off the details so coldly and calmly; he might have been talking about the price of milk in the store."

"I don't know why all those government inspectors seem to lack compassion."

"Me neither, but he *was* pretty cold. He told me about a Beaver breaking free of its tie downs while a mechanic was running it up for a maintenance test. None of it was making any sense to me. When I noticed our priest there, something snapped. I remember screaming and screaming, then trying to run out to where it had happened. Father Ignaty held me and talked soothingly. I have no idea what he said. It could have been in Russian for all I know."

"I bet his presence there was both distressing and comforting."

"It was. I remember the NTSB guy continuing on and on. I wanted to shut him up, but his monotonous voice droned

145

on. I can still hear his voice. 'Eyewitnesses say the one-eighty-five had just come out of the channel hydroplaning at high speed on the step. Once airborne, just above the water, it was hit by the errant Beaver on the left side, just aft of the wing. Apparently your plane tumbled and plunged nose first into the water.' I wanted to scream."

"How could he say something like that so casually?"

"I don't know. It was like a nightmare. But he wasn't done yet. It seemed like he took delight in telling me all the grisly details. He said, 'there may have been survivors of the collision, but by the time the rescue crews could get to it, it was submerged in twenty feet of water. Rescue divers found the wreckage so tangled they could not enter it and had to wait for equipment to pull it out of the water. We'll need someone to identify...'"

"Oh, my God." Dom squeezes Leila's shoulder.

"I remember yelling—finally, *Can you shut him up. I can't take any more. Get him out of here.* Then miraculously, the official was gone and Father Ignaty—what a saint—sat with me while I ranted. My throat hurt and my eyes were almost swollen shut by the time I finished. Looking back, it seems that as suddenly as I broke down and lost control, I regained it. When I heard Father say, 'Do you want me to notify the kids?' Composure and certainty came over me like another presence. I was performing almost robotically. I said, NO, I have to do it myself."

"I had the exact same reaction when Maria died. I watched her take her last breath and couldn't believe she was gone. I raged at the nurses to do something. I was about to lose it, but a presence took over and I was able to tell her parents gently—compassionately—even though her mother hated me."

"That must have been hard. I, at least had Father Ignaty. He was kind enough to pick up Nat at school and notified Rudy who was in a class at the University to tell him to come home. Ana was already there. He didn't give them any details, but they knew before they got there.... Oh, this is the hardest part. When I saw the look on Rudy's face a red-hot spear went right through me. It felt like someone was strangling me. Pressure behind my eyes was excruciating. Fortunately, Ana was on her week off from her North Slope job. I don't know what I would have done if I had had to tell her over the phone.

Somehow I managed to get the words out and told them how much I loved them. But even then—maybe especially then—the words sounded unreal. It was as though I was talking about someone else. I remember telling them how we would have to stick together to make it through this. And they *are* my whole life now. I have never really had a close female friend or confidante; Pete was that for me. He was everything. Why did God have to take him? Nothing makes sense." She stops talking.

After a long pause, Dom says, "I am amazed at how similar we are, Leila. At least deep down where it matters. At first, after Maria died, I could not imagine why or how I could go on living. There just seemed to be no purpose to it. I've moved on, though. I had to. I'm still alive. The pain is still there, but I can function and love life even in the middle of the pain. Like today! What a gift that was to me! I have not felt so alive in years. Seeing this magnificent country, feeling the thrill of speed in the iceboat with Rudy, being next to you, singing with my favorite niece... How could I ask for more? And now with my arm around an incredibly sexy woman in a cozy cabin—alone..." Dom winks at Leila and smiles.

"How do you do it?" she says laughing through her tears. "You manage to be irreverent and caring at the same time, and make it seem okay. But honestly, I don't think I have laughed since Pete died. It *does* lighten the load on my shoulders."

"I guess that's why I'm here: to lighten your load. And I must say it has been a pleasure. But remind me never to go backpacking with you. I would end up carrying everything."

"You are an insensitive jerk! And what makes you think I would ever want to go backpacking in the wilderness with you, anyway?"

Dom looks penitent. "I'm sorry, Leila. You see that's my problem. I never know when to stop. I always go too far. I tried to make you laugh, and succeeded. But I couldn't leave well enough alone, could I? I am so sorry. I of all people should know that it takes time. This healing process happens in small bits. Can we go back to a few minutes ago, please? Try to forget about what an oaf I am and continue with your story. I want to hear as much as you are willing to tell. My heart hurts for your pain. I understand. I know that sounds trite, but it's true."

Leila is silent for a few minutes gathering her thoughts. It doesn't seem that there is any appropriate place to start. *Where have I been for almost three years since Pete died? The seasons have gone by without my even noticing the changes. I've been in denial: numb. But now I feel like a chick ready to break out of her shell. Maybe life does have color after all.*

"What is *that?*" Dom asks looking towards the window. "I thought I saw something flash."

Leila walks over to the window and peers outside. The Northern Lights are huge curtains of light sweeping across the sky. Leila had seen the Aurora countless times, but tonight they seemed brighter and closer than ever before. With no ambient lighting for hundreds of miles, the darkness accentuates the brilliance of their pale green, white and yellow, and occasional starbursts of red.

"Get your coat on, Dom. This is going to be a great show."

They rush outside and stand, transfixed by the wonder of the mysterious light. Dom is silent. Just as the show appears to be over, another burst of light appears and Leila points. "Wow!" they exclaim simultaneously.

"This is incredible. Should we wake the kids up?"

"No, Rudy has seen this many, many times. I want to share this with you." Her hands are freezing and she notices for the first time that she has forgotten her mittens. "I'm going to have to go in, though, Dom. My hands are freezing."

"No, no, can't we stay out a little longer? Here, put your hands inside my coat. I'll open the zipper so you can put them under my armpits."

"But then you'll freeze. It must be twenty-five below."

"Not if you're standing in my arms. We can look over each other's shoulders and keep turning around so neither of us misses a thing."

"Okay," she says as she slips her arms under his coat. Standing wrapped in each other's arms, they turn in circles in a slow dance, looking up in awe.

"What are the kids going to think?"

"You just said you weren't going to wake them up. And who else is out here to see or even care about us keeping each other warm, except for one solitary lynx. Besides, I've never danced under the Northern Lights before. Another first!"

"You are absolutely incorrigible."

"But you love it, don't you?"

Leila and Dom finally come back in to the cabin, stomping their feet. Their cheeks are red and eyes watering. "Boy, I think I froze my nose. Does it look frostbitten?"

Dom is keyed up and paces around the cabin, bumping into things. "Wow! That was some display! I had no idea that the Aurora was so bright and moved so fast. Do you see it all the time? When I saw it in Wisconsin it was just a band of light close to the horizon in the north, looking kind of like the glow of a distant city. This was, Wow! I can't believe it. This day will certainly go down as one of the best in my life, at least the most memorable. Leila, you are so lucky to live in Alaska. It's so big. It's so spectacular. It's so…"

"Dom, please. I need to settle down and get some sleep. It's almost one o'clock. Rudy and Celeste will be up by six to get the plane ready. You know Celeste has to be back in Anchorage before ten to go to work. We'll only have time for coffee and oatmeal before we take off."

"Forgive me, Leila, please. I'm sorry to go on and on, but this is so exciting. I don't think I'll be able to sleep at all."

"Good! Then you can keep the fire going." Leila steps behind the curtain and slips into her fleece pajamas. Her toes are still numb from the cold so she changes into dry woolen socks, also. She gets into her down sleeping bag and curls up with her back to the fire. "Yes it was a good day, Dom. I had fun." As the warmth of the cabin overcomes her, she begins to drift off to sleep. "Sorry, Dom, I just can't keep my eyes open another second. I'm exhausted. Good night and God bless you." Her familiar good night greeting to Pete slipped out without her even being aware of what she said.

When Dom says, "Good night, Leila, and God bless you, too" she realizes what she had said, but fatigue prevents her from caring. She drifts off to sleep trying to identify the feelings overwhelming her. It has been so long since she felt the spark of joy; she no longer can identify it. A peaceful drowsiness envelops her and without turning over once, she falls asleep.

Chapter Thirteen

Nikki's Morning After

Nikki opens her eyes to bright sunlight streaming in through the small opening in the heavy drapes. Putting her hand over her eyes to quell the pounding in her head and to stop the room from spinning, she looks around. She does not recognize her surroundings and does not remember how she got there. *What have I done?* She remembers bits and pieces of the previous night: groping and grabbing, feeling aroused. Embarrassment makes her clench her teeth. *What was his name and where did I meet him? Was it a dream? Is this his condo?* Nikki is full of questions, but more pressing is her need to get to the bathroom, quickly. She sees bathroom fixtures through an open door and stumbles out of bed to make it there before heaving her stomach's contents into the toilet. The taste in her mouth is disgusting and she feels like vomiting again as she swallows. She searches for a glass to rinse her mouth. She scrubs her hands and rinses them with cold water, splashing some on her face, running wet fingers through her hair. The sparkling white bathroom light hurts her eyes and she squints, letting in enough light to see her features in the mirror. "You look like hell, Elsa," she says. After cleaning up as best she can, she makes her way back to the bed. She is wearing only a man's large white t-shirt.

The room is still spinning as she lies back on the bed. The blankets are rumpled, making the bed look like a bunch of children were having a pillow fight. She smoothes the blankets and pulls them over her head.

"Are you awake in there?" a voice outside the door whispers.

Not wanting to acknowledge her behavior to anyone yet, Nikki does not answer. She can't face whoever it is outside the door. If it's the guy she met in the bar, she never wants to see him again. And who else would it be? She wracks her brain to try to remember what happened after she went to the jazz club. She remembers laughing and dancing with abandon. She remembers feeling beautiful and attractive. She remembers the thrill of arousal and desire.

She pulls the pillow over her head thinking, *I've got to sort this out before I face anyone. Hell, I don't even know what my name is anymore. Elsa? Nikki?*

Her emotions are as jumbled as the blankets on the bed and the spinning of her head and the queasiness of her stomach do not encourage any deep thought. Surviving the next hour is foremost in her mind.

Nikki holds her breath when she hears a voice from the other side of the closed door. "I have to go to work. There is some breakfast on the table and coffee ready to be made in the coffee maker. I'll check in on you later and leave a note. Stay as long as you like and maybe I'll see you tonight."

Nikki strains to hear what he is saying. She continues to hold her breath as she hears him walk away and quietly close a door. She remains motionless for a long time. Finally, she throws back the covers and grabs the bathrobe from the bedpost. She slips it on, making her way to the bedroom door. Noticing a clock on the bed stand, she sees that it is eleven-o-five. *I am so ashamed. Have I regressed to one-night-stands? What will Gerik think?* Then a sudden dawn of realization...*Gerik! He didn't even know that I was going anywhere except to a climbing class. What will I tell him?*

Her memory of the climbing class and how she ended up in Chicago is even more upsetting to her. Granite's put down still makes her cheeks burn. She thought he had felt the same about her as she did about him. Wasn't he always encouraging her to take more classes and join in on the outings? What about her first outdoor climb along the Mississippi River? Her emotions are jangled. She goes from feeling like telling him where to shove it one moment and the next wanting to look into his pale blue eyes and smile. Even in her anger and hung-over state, she finds herself excited to think about him. She remembers the sound of his voice and the way it makes her feel she can do anything.

Nikki walks to the bedroom door and opens it a crack, not sure if anyone is still in the condo. She peeks out and does not see anyone. The kitchen is as immaculate as the bathroom. Modern and stark, it suggests an artist had a hand is designing it. One solitary painting hangs on the rich maroon wall opposite the sink. The modern lines remind Nikki of Georgia O'Keeffe's style. A colossal flower adorns the unframed work of art, which covers almost the entire wall. A lush, tan oriental rug with an intricate design of purple, maroon, red, black and an occasional glimmer of a shimmery gold lies in the center of the room. Two chairs with clean lines sit next to the small table on which a placemat matching the rug sits. It is elegantly set with a place setting for her breakfast. A single red rose is in a crystal bud vase in the center of the table.

Nikki finds the coffee pot ready to go and turns it on. She wanders back to the bathroom to see if she can find any pain relievers in the medicine cabinet. The sudden jangling of a phone makes her head start to pound again. *Should I answer it? No, it's probably that stupid guy from the bar and I don't want to talk to him ever again. What was his name? What did I find attractive about him? How much did I have to drink? I have never felt this bad from a hangover before. I've got to get out of here before he comes back. I wonder what I did with my car.* She hears a man's voice on the answering machine telling the caller to leave a message. *Oh, no! It must be that guy's place.*

Then from the other room she hears a familiar voice, "Are you there, Nikki? Did Eric find you all right? I have been so worried. Call me as soon as you get up. Don't worry about Gerik. I told him that you had an important meeting and you didn't have time to get in touch with him. I reached him at the office last night before he had a chance to worry about where you were. We had dinner together. What do you want me to tell him about when you will be home? Anyway, call as soon as you can. I'm at the studio."

"Oh, my God, it's Daphne." Nikki rushes to the phone. She catches it just as Daphne is finishing her message and says, "Daphne, thank God it's you. How did you know where I am?"

"Boy, you must have been a lot drunker that I thought. What has gotten into you? I have never known you to have more than a glass or two of wine. What on earth have you done? I asked Eric to call me when he got you safely to his place, but I must not have been home when and if he tried to call me last night."

"So, what are you telling me? That I am at your brother's condo? I should have guessed." Something snaps inside Nikki and the anger she has been suppressing for so long rises to the surface. "You always have to interfere with any fun I might want to have. Why did you have to get your brother involved in this? I'm an adult and have the right to

155

enjoy some fun, too. It's not like you are any stranger to a little fling now and then. I'm sure that's why your husband couldn't take it any more." Nikki's head throbs and bile rises in her throat. All of the hurtful things that Daphne did to her pile up. She can't let go of the thought of Daphne and Gerik together in Daphne's Chicago apartment. She wants to hurt her back. "I'm surprised that you can even keep your hands off my husband, if, in fact you are. I wouldn't put it past you to be sneaking behind my back. You even want to grab Granite's attention away from me."

"Granite was asking about you last night. He wondered where his favorite student was."

"I'm sure, after he got done laughing about my klutziness. The stupid remarks he makes behind my..."

"No, he was really concerned...Elsa, I mean, Nikki, what is going on? What remarks are you talking about? Why are you acting like this?"

"Don't *Elsa* me. Just leave me alone, would you? I don't want to face this right now. You can tell Gerik that I'll be home when I am damn good and ready...maybe tomorrow or even the next day. What does he care anyway? And what do you care?" Nikki hears the beginning of Daphne's stammering rebuttal as she slams the phone down to cut out her voice.

Nikki stomps to the bedroom, dresses in her climbing clothes, leaves a note that says only *THANK YOU* in large letters and rushes out of Eric's condo. The coffee and breakfast are left untouched on the table. After closing the door behind her, Nikki realizes that the bathroom was left with the mess she made. *Oh, well,* she rationalizes as guilt gnaws at her, *they have no right to interfere in my life.* Arms pumping, she walks to the lakeshore and heads north into a stiff breeze. Waves of nausea sweep over Nikki as she walks. She is breathing heavily and her pounding head leaves little room for any reflective thought. She meets joggers, bikers and people on roller blades. They are all smiling and looking as though they are enjoying the sunshine. Nikki's thoughts are an angry jumble. *What are they smiling about? Don't they see how stupid this life is? How could Granite lead me on like that? I always knew that I was just a klutz. I suppose Daphne came on to him during the class last night in my absence. I hate her and her man-grabbing ways. Why did I never see this before?*

A man on roller blades brushes past her and she gets a whiff of his cologne. It reminds her of the bar scene from the night before.

I hope I didn't do anything embarrassing last night. But wasn't that guy a hunk? I wish I had gone home with him. Why did Daphne and her stupid brother have to interfere? How can Gerik be so insensitive? He never listens to me. What ever happened to the great sex we used to have? I remember when we were first married, the weekends spent in bed, only getting out long enough to answer the door for the pizza delivery. All he thinks about now is work. You'd think I was his mother, the way he treats me! But maybe he is getting it elsewhere.

Nikki is huffing and puffing. Sweat is rolling down her face and back. A thought hits her like a blow to the stomach. She stops in mid-stride and looks around. A young couple standing near a water fountain, locked in each other's arms is oblivious to the commotion around them. A blond, pre-school boy is running back and forth carrying handfuls of water to splash on his little sister, who is screaming, "Mama, Mama!" A line has formed behind the couple waiting for a turn at the fountain. The concession stand nearby is mobbed with people. Tinny, carnival style music is blaring from an unseen speaker. To Nikki it sounds like the grating of someone's first attempt on a violin.

Nikki's breath is coming in short gasps—like she has just finished a five K race. She finds a bench and sits down, panting. *It must be true, but I can't believe it. How did I not see it coming? Of course, it makes sense.*

Nikki remembers Gerik's affair during her college years. *If she's leading him on again, I'll kill her. But a leopard doesn't change its spots.* Nikki imagines the worst and the same feelings she had as a college student come back to overwhelm her. She feels like a fool. *I thought I was over all that. How could I be so stupid? I know I'm fat, short and ugly and never have been good at exciting Gerik or any man for that matter. I am no match for Daphne with her long sexy legs and those dark eyes and blond hair. Just her presence turns men on. I'm sure the only reason Granite even talks to me is to get near her.*

Nikki crumples against the back of the bench. Her shoulders sag, her mouth turns down and she closes her eyes. *What a loser I am! Even my worthless husband doesn't want me.*

"Well, well, well! This must be my lucky day." She hears a somewhat familiar voice very close to her, but she does not open her eyes. The darkness she thought she had overcome hits her anew. Her stomach rumbles and she presses her fist into her belly below her sternum to ease the pain. She breathes deeply through her nose and clenches her teeth.

Why don't these insensitive people just go away? She turns her head away from the voice and prepares to get up to continue walking. She doesn't know where she will go, but she needs time to think.

"It is Nikki, isn't it? I thought I would never see you again after your abrupt departure last night." Nikki turns and recognizes the man she met in the bar last night who is now very close to her. An involuntary gasp escapes her. *Wow, he's more of a hunk than I remember. He looks even better in the daylight.* She remembers his name as soon as she sees his face.

"Mitch!" She smiles, then remembering how bad she must look, frowns and looks away. "I must be a real mess."

"No. Oh, no, no! You are just as beautiful as you were last night. When that guy rushed off with you I almost called the cops, but the way he acted as though he knew you, I figured he was your husband or something and decided to back off." He pauses and then goes on. "He's not, is he?

"Not what?"

"Your husband. Please say he is not. I need to know you better. Last night you made me come alive like I have not been alive in years. Your laughter went right to my heart. There hasn't been much of that in my life lately." He smiles a sad smile. "I know I must sound like a flake, but honestly, I went into that bar last night wanting only to get drunk, stumble home and sleep in oblivion. That's what I do when the pain gets to me. But when I saw you there, looking so beautiful and lonely, *my* problems went right out the window."

Nikki looks at him skeptically and says, "If that isn't the corniest pick up line I've ever heard, I don't know what is."

The corners of his mouth turn down and Nikki tries to make up for her rudeness. She doesn't want to hurt him; she just wants him to go away. "But I did have fun last night. I never realized before that I could dance. Thank you for showing me that, at least. Now, if you will excuse me, I've got to be going."

"Please let me at least walk with you for a while. I have no more clients this afternoon and would love to spend it with you. I promise that I will not say anything or grab at you or interfere with you in any way. I'll be a perfect gentleman. I just want to be near you so I can think and clear my mind. Your presence seems to have that effect on me. But if you tell me to leave, I will. I will not force my presence on you ever again."

No wonder men are turned off by my behavior. I do everything I can to push them away. Why am I so insecure? What is wrong with me?

Her heart melts as she looks at Mitch and sees the earnestness on his face. He sounds sincere and he has kind eyes. Nikki forgets how unattractive she feels. She forgets her embarrassment. She puts aside her dark thoughts.

"Well, I guess it wouldn't do any harm for us to walk together. This is a public place, so I guess I'm safe. I need to do some thinking of my own. Just don't expect any stimulating conversation."

I'm doing it again. Why can't I say nice things? Why am I always so negative? At least he still wants to walk with me. Just keep your mouth shut, Nikki, and you'll be okay.

They walk along the lakeshore in silence. Nikki's mind is in turmoil and so many questions arise, she begins to lose track of where she is. *I've got to get a handle on this. My life is such a mess right now. I don't even know who I am or what I believe in. Maybe that's where I should start. I need to write some of this down.* Energized with a new resolve, unconsciously she picks up her pace.

"Hey, I didn't think this was going to be a race! Slow down, would you, or I'm going to be left in the dust."

Chapter Fourteen

Lake Clark to Anchorage

Leila wakes to the smell of coffee and the sound of a fire crackling in the stove. She hears Celeste humming quietly and dishes plunking onto the table. As she looks toward the small window, she can see a pink blush in the sky. It reminds her of Dom holding her under the Northern Lights. Not fully awake yet, she smiles, trying to separate her dream from the reality of last night.

In her dream just before waking, she was a Geisha traveling to Chena Hot Springs in an iceboat, pulled by three lynxes. Their fur rippled as they ran. Dom was next to her in the boat. *We're almost there. It's where we can consummate our marriage if only the Northern Lights come out again. We must have the Northern Lights.* Leila looked into his eyes and desire came over her in waves. *No, we don't need Northern Lights. We only need each other.* They floated on silently over the snow towards a castle made of ice but glowing with fiery warmth.

Wow, where did that come from? I'd better get up before I have any more silly dreams. She reaches one arm out of the sleeping bag to grab her pants and sweater.

"Hey, do I hear someone rustling in there? It's almost sunrise. We've gotta get a move on."

"I'll be dressed in a minute."

"Celeste has oatmeal ready to go, and coffee."

"I know. The smell woke me up."

"Rudy's already loaded the plane with his tent and sleeping bags and the boat. We have the wing covers off and..."

"Okay, okay. I'll be ready in a minute."

Leila pushes the curtain aside and steps into the main part of the cabin.

"Good morning, beautiful." Dom heads towards Leila, smiling.

Leila's first instinct is to back up, but remembering last night, she smiles back at him and accepts his embrace. Celeste raises her eyebrows and shrugs her shoulders. When Rudy walks in a moment later, she nods her head towards Leila and Dom who are whispering to each other. He shrugs his shoulders also.

After breakfast and a quick sweep of the cabin to make sure the fire is out and everything is put away, they all load into the plane. Celeste climbs into the left seat. Her handling of the plane is smooth and confidence exudes from her as she takes off and climbs towards Lake Clark Pass.

Dom looks from side to side taking in all the scenery again, but on this flight he is quiet and his gaze includes the inside of the plane as he looks at Leila from time to time with a smile.

They arrive in Anchorage before ten o'clock and park the plane in the hangar. Rudy rushes off to his class. Celeste is in a hurry to get to her job.

"Leila, could you entertain Dom today? His flight is at eight o'clock and I have to work until six. I hate to leave him stranded alone in my apartment all day."

Leila nods.

"He can just stay here and help you unload the plane so I can go straight to work. Then maybe you could show him around town a little before his flight. I'll meet you at my apartment after work. You know, he might like to see the aviation museum at Lake Hood."

Dom grins. "Are you kidding? I'd love to see it. I hear they have some famous photos of the early Alaskan bush pilots and displays of the planes they flew. It's like something out of the barnstorming days of the 1920s. Celeste has told me many times about all the women pioneers in Alaskan aviation. Maybe I'll get to read about some of them. Real gutsy women, she tells me, sort of like someone I met this weekend."

Leila begins to protest, but Celeste jumps in and says, "Just ignore him, Leila, he means well." She gives her uncle an affectionate hug. Turning to Leila, she embraces her, whispering, "Thank you so much, Leila. I know, he wears on me a little, too, but I love him. He has a good heart. And I love you, too. Thanks, again, see you tonight."

Leila hoped to have some time alone to reflect on Dom's story and consider how she felt about having shared such personal things with him. *Did I go too far? I've never shared the things I told him last night. I don't want to get into it again. But with his incessant talking, he's likely to blurt out some things I don't want to hear right now.*

Celeste turns back to Dom. "We'll have to talk about your trip this summer. You've gotta come, Uncle Dom. May and June are beautiful here. We'll show you some killer trout fishing streams. Look, I've gotta run. See you later today. Have fun. Love you." Celeste gives him no chance to respond before rushing to her car and speeding away.

"Well, she sure takes after my sister. She's one of the few in my family who doesn't even let me get a word in edgewise.

Did she ever tell you about her first flying lesson? That kid's got real balls, if you'll pardon the expression."

Leila rolls her eyes, "I did hear something about her putting some guy in his place, but, no, I never heard the whole story."

"If you'd like, I'll tell you over a cup of coffee. Do you have a favorite place?"

Leila, busy loading the camping supplies into her car, nods. "Yes, I do. There's a great little place on the Old Seward Highway. Get in. I'll drive."

Thinking that it would be best to have him talking about something other than Pete's death and reopening painful memories, Leila says, "I would like to hear about Celeste's first flight. I'm really fond of Celeste. Rudy is a lucky young man to have found her."

"They both are."

"I agree. She treats me so well, much better than my own daughter, Natalia, who is spaced out most of the time. But that's another story, which I really don't want to get into now. So, let's hear about Celeste's flying lesson."

As they get into the car to drive towards the Old Seward Highway, Dom begins. "Well, as she tells it, her parents almost forced her to take the lessons. She was moping around after moving here from Southern California. She hated Alaska. It was *so backward, so boring*—her words."

"You'd never know that now, the way she loves seeing it from the air and hiking with Rudy."

"I know, but my sister said Celeste talked on the phone constantly to her friends in La Jolla and was losing interest in school. Her mother—my sister, Rosa—had finally had enough and challenged her to find an extracurricular activity that might interest her. From what Rosa said, Celeste responded sarcastically with, 'Yeah, like, how about learning how to fly so I can get out of this stupid place.'

'You're on!' my sister said, and arranged for her to have her first lesson at a flying school on Merrill Field. Celeste said when she walked in, a bunch of guys were gathered around the coffee pot telling stories and bragging about their exploits."

Leila pulls out on to Minnesota Drive and speeds up.

"Hey, this isn't the Seward Highway. Where are you taking me?"

"This is a shortcut. Besides the expressway is quicker."

"All right. Anyway, Celeste said she felt awkward and out of place. The guys were talking in what seemed to be a foreign language. She didn't understand any of it. One of them finally noticed her and asked if she was there to apply for the scheduler position. She said she was too embarrassed to say anything."

"I can imagine her reaction to that. She must have been steaming."

"Yeah. Well, then the tall guy telling the story nodded in her direction and told her he would be right with her—as soon as he finished with his students. He continued his storytelling."

"What nerve! How could he ignore such a beautiful young woman?"

"He must have been a self centered jerk. Celeste tried to find something to read to occupy her time but everything seemed too complicated. Her frustration was mounting and she was on the verge of tears. Usually she can handle any social situation, but those guys were just plain rude. She said she could barely read through the tears welling up in her eyes."

A noisy diesel truck pulls alongside Leila and Dom. Leila cannot hear what Dom is saying. "I missed that last part, Dom. That dang truck is pretty loud."

Dom speaks a little louder. "Yeah, well, Celeste was out of her element and practically burst out crying, but since she had bet her brother that she could solo in less than a month, she wasn't about to leave. She said that one by one the students left until only the tall guy, a blond haired man, the secretary and she were in the office. Still, nobody paid attention to her. She was furious by the time the tall guy finally talked to her. She said he actually called her Missy."

"I did hear that part. Sometimes Rudy calls her Missy now to get a rise out of her. She takes it in good humor and calls him Neanderthal."

"That sounds like her all right. Anyway, apparently that's when she lost her cool. She told him where to go and asked to talk to the manager. The secretary stepped in and said that this jerk *was* the acting manager. So Celeste turned to walk out, but the blond, who was also an instructor, saved the day."

"I wonder if she would have gone back if she *had* walked out."

"I guess we'll never know, because the blond instructor calmed her down and took her up for her first lesson."

"They make quite a pair—she and Rudy. He, of course, has been flying forever, but his first solo scared me to death. It's a wonder he survived. Did you ever hear about it?"

"No. I don't think Celeste has either."

"I'll have Rudy tell you about it sometime, but I want to hear more about Celeste's first lesson."

"I really couldn't do it justice. Maybe Celeste can tell you later on our way to the airport."

Dom looks around to discover that Leila has parked the car in front of a small café. "Oh, my gosh! I didn't realize we were here already. Let's go in and get a bite to eat."

After ordering, Dom continues, "She was hooked, right from that first lesson. She laughs now about that male chauvinist who gave her such a hard time, but I think it still irks her a little. Thank goodness for that other instructor. He now works for Alaska Airlines, by the way."

The day, instead of dragging as Leila feared, passes quickly. Leila shows Dom around the Aviation Museum. The people working there all know Leila, and Dom notices how everyone treats her with deference.

"Do you know everybody?"

"Anchorage is still a small town and of course everyone in business here on Lake Hood knows everybody else. We all help each other out."

"That's so much better than a big city, and, wow! What an exciting place to live!"

"I guess I do sort of take it for granted. It's refreshing to see it through the eyes of an outsider."

"What do you mean *outsider?*"

"That's just what we call anybody who doesn't live in Alaska. They live *Outside* of Alaska, so they're outsiders."

"Strange. So, I suppose you also know all the stories of these old-timers."

"Not all, only the most colorful ones. This one, for example."

They are standing in front of a collection of old photographs. Leila points. "This one is Bob Reeve and here's Mudhole Smith. They both founded airlines and each had some unbelievable flying exploits back in the thirties and forties. You should read some of the books about Alaskan aviation in the early days. Those pilots sure knew how to handle adversity, and with such primitive equipment. They had to be pretty tough."

"It seems like you still have to be pretty tough to fly around this state. It's so big."

"But at least we have good navigation equipment and weather reporting and..."

"Well, it just seems so complicated to me, and dangerous."

Leila and Dom spend several hours at the museum. Dom asks questions of the mechanics doing restorative works on an old Stinson until Leila pulls him away. "Come on, Dom. Give these guys a chance to get some work done. They are volunteering their time, you know. We don't want them to waste it."

"I'm sorry, but this is so fascinating. I've never even seen a plane this old, much less expect that it could ever fly again."

One of the mechanics mentions, "You could come and give us a hand sometime. We always need gofers around here. You don't have to be a mechanic to volunteer."

"Hey, now there's a thought."

"But you don't even live here, Dom."

"You never know..."

Leaving the museum, Dom and Leila walk to her car without talking. As they get in Dom asks, "Where to now?"

"Are you up for more museums?"

"Nah. One museum a day is my limit."

"Are you hungry? Ana made some fabulous borscht I could warm up."

"Does that mean just you and me alone together at your house?" Dom grins, waggling his eyebrows like Groucho Marx.

"But, no, that sandwich is still sticking to my ribs. Besides, I really should stop at a gift shop to pick up something for my sister."

"I know some great shops downtown."

"That's what I need—my own personal shopper."

Leila continues. "No, on second thought, why don't we go to the Alaska Native Hospital."

"What? I'm not feeling sick or anything. Are you okay?"

Leila laughs. "What I meant was, we could go to the gift shop at the hospital. When people from the bush come in to the hospital, they bring Native arts and crafts to sell."

"Really? That's cool."

"It is, and the art is authentic. The prices are the best in town."

"Wow, who would have thunk…"

"Wait till you see it. You'll appreciate what I mean."

The quality of the art impresses Dom. After buying several baskets, a small ivory carving and an intricate baleen weaving, he joins Leila to look at the display near the lobby.

Leila grabs his sleeve. "Come on. Let me show you something."

They ride the elevator to the top floor and Dom gawks at the exhibit in the display case next to the elevator. Leila leads him down the stairway to the next floor, where another showcase captivates him. Each successive floor holds his interest. Dom is in no hurry as they admire the artistry of the exhibits.

Finally Leila says, "I thought you had had enough museums for one day and here we've spent an afternoon looking at Native art."

Dom looks at his watch. "Wow! Look at the time. I had no idea…"

"We better head over to Celeste's. She'll be home any minute, and you've got to get ready to go to the airport."

"If I must."

Leila and Dom rush across town to Celeste's apartment just in time to catch her pulling into her parking spot.

"Come on in, you guys. Are you hungry?"

They walk in to Celeste's tiny apartment. Leila notices Rudy's parka hanging on a clothes tree next to the door. She shakes her head.

Dom pats his stomach. "Now that I think of it, yeah, I'm starving. This woman kept me on the go all day." He elbows Leila in the ribs.

"I..."

Celeste, ignoring her uncle, interrupts, "I have some spaghetti sauce I can warm up. I'll throw some pasta on to cook and we should have a meal in a few minutes. You can pack, Dom, while I get it ready. Leila, would you set the table?"

Dom turns to leave the room. Leila asks, "Will Rudy be joining us?"

"No, he has a class at seven. He'll be home later."

"Oh." Leila is clearly uncomfortable about Celeste's choice of words. She sets the table with no further questions.

As they sit down to eat, Dom, oblivious to any tension in the room, asks his niece, "Hey, Celeste, why don't you tell Leila about your first flying lesson? I told her about that first instructor writing you off as someone applying for a secretarial job. So, how did you get hooked up with the other guy?"

"The first guy was a complete jerk. He was the most egotistical, self-centered, insensitive... I was really pissed. Mike, the other instructor, was totally different. He interrupted Big Shot and told him he would take me up for a lesson since his student had just cancelled. Mr. Big Shot gave me a look like I was a bug to be squashed under his foot. Then he just turned back to the schedule board and said, 'whatever.'"

"It's a wonder he had any students at all if he treats everybody like that!"

"It was only women he treated like that. He must have been really insecure. Anyway, Mike took me by the elbow and led me into one of the briefing rooms. He closed the door behind us so we could see, but not hear, what was going on in the office. He tried to apologize for the other instructor but I could tell he didn't think much of him. He said he was tired of making excuses for the guy's rudeness. He told me he'd be glad to have me for a student. He saw my teary eyes and tried to cheer me up. He said, 'you showed real balls standing up to him. His size alone can be intimidating.'

I was sniffling and trying to keep from crying. He told me I'd have to develop a thick skin because even in these modern times, men can feel threatened by a woman who can fly as well—or better—than they can."

"What is it with these guys?" Dom looks puzzled.

"Thank goodness everyone is not like him. Mike was so nice. By then I had gotten my confidence back and I really wanted to show that jerk I could fly. Just thinking of his macho attitude made me feel like spitting and kicking. So I agreed to go with Mike for my first lesson and am I ever glad I did. He had me handling the controls right from the start. My first takeoff in that little Cessna one-fifty felt like flying the space shuttle. I could tell I was going to love it."

Chapter Fifteen

On the Lakeshore

Nikki looks out at Lake Michigan sparkling in the sun and notices Mitch walking beside her. He is breathing heavily and sweat covers his face. "I'm sorry. I didn't mean to speed up so much. It's just when I start thinking, I forget where I am and I revert to my race walking pace."

Suddenly it occurs to her that Mitch is the exact person to whom she can tell her problems. She has always been good at thinking aloud. Things seem to come into perspective as she hears them spoken. At this point, Mitch is a complete stranger and she can choose to disappear from his life after a therapeutic release. It will be sort of like the confessional: dump your problems without giving any personal, identifying details and walk away absolved. She feels lighter already.

"Mitch," she says, "I apologize for how I've been acting. It's just that I have a lot of problems on my mind. I've really needed a listening ear to sort it all out, but I have had no one to turn to. How can I say this?"

Nikki walks on, sorting her thoughts, then blurts out, "I suspect my best friend is sleeping with my husband—just like she did almost twenty years ago, and who knows how much of the intervening time...I'm getting old and dumpy. My kids don't need me anymore. I don't even know what it means to love and care for someone. Everything seems like a farce. When I think of all those wasted years, I feel like throwing up." She rushes towards the bench beside the path and sits with her elbows on her knees, her head in her hands. A sob escapes her throat. "I don't know what to do or where to turn."

Mitch sits next to her and without saying a word, puts his arm around her shoulders. It is a long time before Nikki lifts her head and looks at Mitch, mortified at her boldness. Her eyes are red and puffy. Her nose is running. Mitch takes a handkerchief from his pocket and carefully wipes her eyes. He gently rubs the streaking mascara from her cheeks and allows her to blow her nose. "How about if we start at the beginning?" he says.

"I don't know why you would want to listen. I get sick thinking about it myself and wouldn't want to burden anyone else with such foolishness. And, why would you care, anyway? I'm just some bimbo you met in a bar and will never see again." She leans into his shoulder and starts to cry again.

"But I do want to hear it. Start from the beginning. I'm not much for giving advice, and I don't think that is what you need right now. You need to get this all out in the open and I'm here to listen. That is one talent I do have."

"Where to start...God...I don't even know that." Nikki whispers.

"How about if we start walking...slowly...and just let whatever comes to your mind come out. It doesn't have to be in any sort of order."

As they get up from the bench, Nikki is already talking. "I don't know why she always hated me. She was always the best at everything: cheerleading, school work, debate, sports. She didn't have to rub it in my face that I was fat and homely.

She didn't have to make fun of the things I liked to do. She always thumbed her nose at those beautiful desserts I made. 'Fattening,' she'd say. She hated the way I decorated our room. She even made fun of my name. That's why I changed it, you know. I couldn't bear the thought of her sneering about my name. I could hear her sarcastic voice every time I introduced myself to someone new. I hate her! She deserves the hard knocks that have come her way." That familiar feeling from childhood rushes upon her. She chokes back the rising bile as her acid stomach churns. Nikki suddenly feels as though she weighs five hundred pounds and can hardly lift her feet. She stops walking and stares out at the sailboats on the lake. They remind her of other painful memories.

"It's just like the time Dad bought us a catamaran for sailing around the small lake where we lived. Leila picked up sailing like she had been born on a boat. I, even after months of lessons, could never make it across the lake by myself. I always had to have someone help me. Mom made light of my failures and encouraged me in the talents I did have, but I always sensed disappointment from my dad. He and Leila were so close."

Nikki pauses for breath and starts again, "I don't know why I even thought of all that. I try not to think about my sister, and most of the time I can ignore that she is even alive. Since she lives so far away, our paths seldom cross. And, actually, I have many more pressing problems right now. Like, how can I face Gerik with my suspicion that he and my so-called *friend* are cheating on me? I don't know if it's true, but as I think about it, there have been warning signs. She's a smooth operator—bringing me flowers, hoping that I won't be there so they can have their little tryst. I am so dense. I've been wrapped up with my own stuff. Why did I ever believe him back then? Has it always been a lie?"

Nikki is suddenly very angry. She stops and grabs Mitch by the shoulders, forgetting herself. "How can they do this to me?" She notices Mitch smiling and the shock of it compels her to drop her hands. She is even angrier now and reaches up to slap his face. "I will not be laughed at! I thought you were a good listener, but now you are making fun of me. How could you?" Mitch catches her hand before it makes contact and begins to speak. But Nikki pulls her hand away and stomps off gaining speed with every step. Her thoughts are so muddled they make no sense at all. So she simply puts one foot in front of the other, pumping her arms and swinging her hips. She is gasping for air. The effort reminds her of her last speed-walking race where she was in third place with only a hundred yards to go. She sees a runner on the trail ahead and decides to make an effort to pass her, just like she did in that race. She is gaining ground on the jogger and begins to feel the thrill of winning when a large hand grabs the back of her shirt, making forward movement impossible. She turns around.

Mitch squints at her, saying, "What on earth got into you? What did I do wrong?"

Nikki struggles to free herself. "I'll scream," she says and opens her mouth to yell for help.

Mitch steps closer until his face is inches from hers, "Now, now, let's talk this through."

He leads her to a nearby bench. As she tries to swing her arms, he loses his balance and plunks down onto the bench with Nikki on top of him.

"You certainly are a wild tiger," he says. "I didn't know you had that much spunk. Now I want you to listen to me. First of all, I was not laughing at you. I was simply relieved that your problem was no different than my own. I have learned to deal with it and so will you. I smiled because I saw how much

175

I admired your spirit. I've never met anyone quite like you. You are so real and honest and..."

"And stupid for letting you sweet-talk me like this."

"Is that what this is? I thought I was doing the listening. I wasn't going to say a word until you had it all out. I do have to admit, though, that I sometimes have a hard time following your train of thought. But, what do you say? Can we continue? I want to know exactly where you are and how I can help. I really want to be your friend. I know it seems foolish, but I already know that you will be a very important person in my life."

"Let's not go there quite yet," Nikki says, still hoping just to dump her feelings and run. She doesn't share that thought with Mitch, however, and searches for the right words to begin again. Her anger is somewhat abated as she begins to realize she has choices. She moves away from him on the bench and sits with her arms crossed over her chest.

"I need to do some thinking about what my next steps should be. I'll tell you one thing: my business has become very successful and I could walk out on him and never need him for anything ever again. He certainly has not been an emotional support to me for years, anyway. And as for companionship, I may as well be married to a photograph. Sex, it's been non-existent for so long, I've almost forgotten what it's all about. So do I really even care if he is getting it on with Daphne? Ha! But I still have needs. Can't he see that? Does he think I am simply a domestic device that turns out meals and somehow gets the house cleaned and laundry done and the kids taken care of? What about my desires?"

She catches a glimpse of Mitch's raised eyebrows and says, "Now, don't think I'm talking about you—or us. If you want to be my friend, let's just keep it on a platonic level. That's how I got into trouble so many years ago with that jerk of a husband. Our son was born six months after the wedding. Then another one was on the way before long and there we were, stuck in a marriage that neither of us probably wanted. We never really thought it through. Although I suppose we were compatible enough at first. But we were so busy making a living and raising kids; we never gave a thought to what might have been. Now that our kids are leaving home, there is plenty of time to think, at least for me. But Gerik never has time for anything other than his investments, his job and now, of course, Daphne."

Nikki has finally run out of steam and sits staring up at the oak leaves moving in the wind. A sad smile plays across her face.

With a crooked index finger, Mitch strokes Nikki's jaw line from her ear towards her chin. "Such a beautiful, strong chin," he says.

"Please, Mitch. Don't do that. I couldn't handle you taking advantage of me. I don't want to be attracted to you. Can't we just leave it at this? I appreciate you listening to me and I already feel better. At least my mind isn't racing a mile a minute. And I can actually take a breath without it hurting. Silence is not at all characteristic of me, but can we just walk without talking? I want to be totally aware of my surroundings for once; to smell the fresh earthy smells and feel the wind on my face and hear waves crashing and the seagulls crying. I want to see the young men on their roller blades and the kids playing with reckless abandon. I want to experience the deep blue color of the sky and feel the goodness of my legs walking. Oh, I know I go on and on. Gerik always tells me to shut up already, so I will. But can we walk together just a little longer? You've been a life saver."

They walk in the direction of the Navy Pier. Nikki remembers why she ran off to the city and is about to share it with

Mitch, but then thinks better of it. She realizes she knows nothing about him and is now curious. She feels peaceful in his presence. She feels accepted and appreciated. She feels that she can be totally herself and he would understand. She begins to express these thoughts, but as she opens her mouth, says instead, "I really never even told you what precipitated my bar hopping in downtown Chicago last night. But now it seems so unimportant. What I want to know is why you were there. I haven't heard anything about you."

"It's a long story. If you let me treat you to an early dinner at McCormick's, I'll tell you all about it."

"We'll see. Let's just walk back to the city for now."

Chapter Sixteen

Dom's Summer Visit to Alaska

After Dom's February visit to Alaska, he calls Leila weekly. He always jokes with her and manages to get her out of her frequent gloomy moods.

Early in June, during one of their many conversations, Dom surprises Leila. "I'm going to be coming up to Alaska next week, Leila. I want to see the summer solstice and the midnight sun. Maybe I'll even see you while I'm there."

"You're in luck. Rudy has a charter to Barrow next week and you might be able to ride along. I'll check into it."

"Do you think you could go, too?"

"I'm pretty busy this time of year, but we'll see."

Leila still has trouble admitting to anyone that she is attracted to Dom, but secretly she hopes he will move to Anchorage so she can see more of him.

It will be a miracle if she can get away from the office next week when he visits, though. June is always busy at Pete's Flying Service. The three DeHaviland Beavers are booked every day. The Cessna 185s on floats are kept busy with fishing charters and the DeHaviland single-engine Otter is on the ground barely long enough for routine maintenance inspections. The temporary pilots fly only one type of plane.

The five, year-round pilots fly two types. Rudy flies all of the planes, but the Otter is his favorite.

On Wednesday Rudy plans to haul a load of time critical construction material to Fairbanks on his way to Deadhorse where he will pick up three marine biologists from Western Washington University.

Tuesday night, when Dom arrives from Chicago, Leila, Rudy and Celeste meet him at the airport. "Wow, what a welcoming committee! I was wondering if anyone would show up at this hour. It's almost midnight and I still need sunglasses. Cool!"

Celeste hugs her uncle. "Yeah, we love it, Uncle Dom. All this daylight gives us enough time to get things done in the summer. But you'll have to get used to getting a little less sleep."

Rudy gives Dom a quick hug, saying, "Hey, Dom, I just thought of this, but how would you like a ride up to the North Slope tomorrow morning? I have a charter to pick up some guys from Western Washington University with all of their equipment. It would be a great chance for you to see some more of Alaska. The Brooks Range is spectacular and the North Slope has a beauty all its own. The vastness is mind-boggling, hard to comprehend."

"Well, my mind is a little boggled right now just thinking about it in my exhausted state. I guess I'm game, but it sort of depends on whether or not my favorite cellist is going along."

"I don't know how I could, Rudy—Dom," Leila says, looking from one to the other, "and besides, there wouldn't be enough room for us both to return with you."

Rudy's eyebrows go up as he observes his mother gazing at Dom. "Hey, you could take advantage of our inter-line fares and get a ticket to ride back from Deadhorse on Alaska West Airways. They always have room on their flights midweek."

"I'll have to think about it."

"Let's talk about it over a glass of wine at the Homestead," Rudy takes Dom by the elbow and ushers him towards baggage claim.

After getting Dom's luggage, they crowd into Celeste's Subaru and head toward the popular watering hole at the east end of Lake Hood. On the Homestead's deck overlooking the landing lane they sample the salmon mousse and order two dozen Alaskan oysters on the half shell and a bottle of merlot. They pour four glasses and propose a toast to the midnight sun.

Leila is troubled by Dom's apparent lack of interest in her. He seems cold and indifferent to her overtures of friendship. He is quiet, very unlike him, and appears thoughtful, but then his chin drops to his chest and the sound of snoring comes from his side of the table. Rudy, Leila and Celeste simultaneously put their fingers to their lips but finally unable to control themselves—they laugh aloud.

Dom raises his head and blinks his eyes, looking around.

"Are you flaking out on us, Uncle Dom? You must be getting old and can't take the night life anymore."

Sheepishly, Dom wipes the saliva from the corner of his mouth. "I must have dozed off momentarily. And yes, of course, I am not used to staying up until," looking at his watch, "three a.m. You forget about the time change. My body is saying that it's been up for almost twenty hours."

"We better get you to bed, then. We'll talk in the morning. I don't leave for Fairbanks until noon tomorrow. But please come. I'll find some way to talk Mom into riding along."

The next morning Rudy walks in to the office with a sly, cat got the bird grin on his face. "It's done, Mom. I got you and Dom tickets on the flight back from Deadhorse tomorrow. It helps to have connections at Alaska West. Now you cannot possibly refuse."

"Rudy, you are impossible." Leila is unable to suppress her smile.

"I knew you would see the light, Leila." Dom walked in, hidden, behind Rudy when he presented the tickets to Leila. "Speaking of light, I was up at the crack of dawn. I got maybe three hours of sleep. How do any of you sleep with all of this infernal daylight?"

"It might help if you closed the darkening shades," Rudy says. "Celeste said you went straight to your room and just plopped on to the bed without even changing your clothes."

"Are there no family secrets held sacred anymore?" Dom chuckles. "I'll get back at that impudent young niece of mine for telling on me. But at least I did get a little sleep before the bright sun hit me in the face. I can see there are some advantages to all this daylight, but I must say, I prefer the long nights when I can snuggle up to someone inside a warm cabin." Dom walks around the desk to Leila, pulls her to her feet and gives her a long embrace. "We neglected to say a proper hello last night at the airport. It's good to see you, Leila."

Momentarily flustered, Leila doesn't know what to say. She looks Dom in the eyes and sees the sparkling of tears springing up. A barely discernible smile that would look like a smirk on anyone else makes Leila laugh and the awkwardness of the moment is erased in another, mutual tender embrace. They both hear the office door closing behind Rudy as he leaves them alone to catch up for lost time. Rudy is all business now as he readies the plane for the trip to the North Slope.

"I'll have to run home and get a few things for the trip, Dom. Could you just watch the office for a few minutes until

Ana gets here? She usually helps with scheduling and dispatching when she is not working on the slope."

"Sure. Is there anything I need to do?"

"You can just let the answering machine get the phone calls. And if anyone walks in, tell them that Ana will be here in a few minutes. I don't know what Rudy was thinking when he insisted I come along. Summers are so busy here; I barely have time to breathe. But I guess it will be nice to take a little break and have some fun. It's been years since I've been to the North Slope. I always love flying through Anaktuvuk Pass, or along the pipeline. The mountains around Galbraith are so beautiful. They remind me of the Canadian Rockies."

"It will all be a thrill to me. What I have seen of this state so far has been amazing. But, really, there are no words to describe it adequately. When I told my friends back in Chicago about the trip to Lake Clark, I could see their eyes glaze over when I tried to explain the color of the glaciers. Even my pictures look so flat and lifeless compared to seeing it real life, in all its Technicolor magnificence."

"You sound like a tourism ad," Leila laughs. "But I will admit, the beauty has never dulled for me. Well, maybe it did for a while after Pete died, but that was mostly because I refused to even look at it. Now you have made it come alive again. I love seeing it afresh through new eyes. Thank you for that, Dom."

"Don't mention it. I always love sharing how much I appreciate beautiful things—like you, Leila."

Rudy walks back into the office in time to hear the last comment. "Looks like you talked her into it, Dom. Well, Mom, you'd better hurry and get your bags packed. I want to leave in a couple hours, so we can drop off the stuff in Fairbanks and then spend some time camping along the Colville. I heard that a few peregrine falcons are nesting near the cliffs south of Nuiksit. It will be a rare chance to watch them hunting. You know, they are the world's fastest raptor, reaching dive speeds over 200 mph. Wouldn't that be a cool thing to see? We'll get to Deadhorse tomorrow morning and then you and Dom can take the evening flight back to Anchorage. That will give you time to see a few of the sights around Deadhorse."

Leila grabs her purse, heading for the door. "Okay, I'm outta here. I'll be back within an hour. Do you want me to pick up some lunch for the trip?"

"Why don't I do that after Ana gets here," Dom says. "I saw a great little deli along Minnesota Drive." Then, in an aside to Leila, "Maybe I'll get a little wine to go along with the lunch for you and me. No reason why we can't imbibe. We're not flying the plane."

"I shouldn't, but I guess a little would be all right."

Leila stops by the counter to double check the schedule. Just as she is about to walk out, she overhears the conversation between Rudy and Dom.

"So how is the master's program going for you, Rudy? Celeste says you are a natural naturalist. That is not actually what she said, but I thought it had a nice ring. Get it? Natural naturalist. Isn't that a simile? Or is it onomatopoeia? I always get those figures of speech mixed up."

Rudy rolls his eyes is mock disgust.

Dom continues, "Anyway, I know you will do great things for the world with your degree in Environmental Engineering."

"Well, Dom, I've decided not to go back to school in the fall. Flying is in my blood and I could never be happy at a desk job, even if it involved fieldwork from time to time. I've decided to stay at Pete's Flying Service and run the place. I've got some ideas on how we can expand our operation. I'd like to try them out. I don't know how Mom will take it, but I'm sure my dad would have approved. He himself could have been a professional musician, but gave it up to keep flying. Of course, he always enjoyed music, but it became his avocation rather than his vocation. And he was good, really good, at both flying and playing the oboe." Rudy looks out the window towards the lake, bites his lower lip and says, "I still can't believe he's gone." Then changing his tone, "I see the materials are here for loading. I'd better go and supervise. Weight and balance is crucial in that plane. You can come out and watch after Ana gets here."

Leila's response to Rudy's revelation leaves her breathless and shaky. The mention of Pete's death brought back all of the anguish of the past years. And now, to think that Rudy would expose himself to the same risks day after day is more than she can bear. She drives home in a state of lassitude, unaware of how she got there as she pulls into the driveway. She almost calls the office to tell Dom and Rudy that she has changed her mind and then remembers that they wouldn't even answer the phone. So she packs a few things and rushes back to Lake Hood.

Anxiety is written on her face in the furled brow and downward slant of the corners of her mouth as she returns to the office. Dom, who has driven up behind her, notices her slumped shoulders as she gets out of her car.

"Hey!" he says, observing the tension in her face. "What's going on? It looks like you've got the weight of the world on your shoulders. I thought you were eager to have a little escapade with me at the top of the world. What's happened?"

"How can he do this to me? I had hoped that he would have sense enough to get out of this business while he's young and has his whole life ahead of him. How would Celeste deal with it if he were ever in an accident—or worse? He is so ungrateful! He only thinks of himself and what he likes to do. Oh, Dom, please talk to him."

"Wait a minute. Let's back up a few steps. Who and what are you talking about? You left here an hour ago looking forward to our flight—and happy. What on earth happened?"

"It's Rudy. I heard him telling you that he's dropping out of school and will be flying full-time. He can't do this to me! He's going to end up dead and I'll be left alone again. I can't take it, Dom. I just cannot take it." Leila leans against Dom and lets him rub her neck and shoulders. The tightness in her chest is almost painful. Her throat is so constricted it is hard to breathe.

"Relax, Leila. Just take a deep breath and relax. You're as tight as a drum." Dom feels her shoulders relax. "There. That's a little better. I'll be here for you, Leila. Listen, I'll talk to him. I'll do whatever I can. Have a little faith why don't you?"

Chapter Seventeen

Getting to Know Each Other

Nikki walks in silence with Mitch at her side and tries to organize her thoughts. *First things first. I've got to start with where I am and work backwards. Okay, I'm upset because of Granite making fun of me behind my back. I thought he was attracted to me.* Her face reddens as she remembers that first outdoor climb. *But I am aroused just to think of him. His encouraging words have made me come alive. I have a new confidence in myself. He's shown me thrills I never before thought possible.*

With that thought her steps feel lighter—stronger. Suddenly a dark cloud descends on her. *But what about Gerik? How did we ever get to where we are now? Why does he seem to hate me so much? And how did I end up walking down the lakeshore with this hunk of a guy?* Nikki glances over at Mitch.

This is not like me at all. His presence, though, does have a calming effect on me. And I guess I never thought before about how I might have that effect on someone else. What harm would it do to get to know him a little better? But what would I tell Gerik? I still can't believe how drunk I was last night. I don't remember ever drinking that much before. What must he think of me?"

As though reading her mind, Mitch, walking silently beside her, says, "Nikki, I don't want to interrupt your thoughts, but I just have to say that I know your behavior last night is not the real you. I can tell by the speed you're walking that you really work at staying fit. I've been huffing and puffing to stay up with you, and I'm no slouch myself. Can you please slow down a little again?"

"Oh, sorry!" Nikki slows her pace and looks at Mitch. "What are you, anyway, a mind reader? I was just thinking how you must think I am a real lush the way I gulped down those martinis last night. Never before in my entire life have I had more than one martini in an evening. I don't like the taste of them, but they certainly went down easily last night." She blushes. "I hardly remember everything I said or did. How embarrassing! I hope I didn't do anything too stupid. I hate to even think about it." She glances away, afraid to meet his gaze.

"I'm afraid I wasn't a very good influence, either. I misjudged you. And I'm *so* sorry. You must have had a tremendous hangover. How about we start over and forget that last night ever happened? If you've decided to join me for dinner, you can tell me what you're really doing in Chicago—or whatever—and I can tell you why I was so determined to get drunk last night. At least consider it before you say no. Just think about it. Okay?" Mitch pleads.

"All right, I'll think about it, but give me a few more minutes to gather my thoughts. My mind is in such a jumble and the hangover is just now beginning to let go. Let's just walk without talking for a little bit yet. I'll slow down. I promise."

"Okay, I'll hang in there, and maybe if I'm around you long enough I'll get in better shape."

Nikki laughs, wrinkles her nose and sticks out her tongue at him.

Mitch shrinks back as though deflecting a blow and laughs. "Sorry, not another word out of me."

Confusion clouds Nikki's mind and Mitch's conversation adds to her anguish. Her heart leapt when he mentioned talking over dinner, yet she didn't want to appear too eager. She still is not sure that she should continue to get to know him better, but there is something about him that's so appealing.

What has come over me? I used to be such a homebody. I remember how Daphne would laugh at me and try to get me to loosen up a little.

At the thought of Daphne, Nikki's anger resurfaces. *That slut! Why can't she keep her hands off my husband? I should never have trusted her again. I wonder how long they have been sneaking around behind my back. I can just hear her sultry voice, faking innocence and concern, 'Oh, Elsa, I am so sorry. What can I ever do to make it up? You're my best friend in the whole world.'* Nikki grimaces. *It makes me sick.* She quickens her pace again. Swinging her arms, her legs blur with speed. Breathing heavily she mutters, "I'll find a way to get back at her, and him. They won't get away with it this time."

Mitch, jogging to keep up, says, "What was that? I couldn't hear you over my heavy breathing. Besides, you promised that you would slow down. It's hard jogging in this suit."

Nikki's chaotic emotions calm down as she focuses on Mitch's face. She watches him run his fingers through his sandy brown hair and wipe the sweat from his forehead. Sweat darkens his shirt. She feels the breeze cooling her. She notices the bright white sails of the small boats speeding by. The skyline of the city looks almost magical—like a fairy tale castle soaring into the brilliant blue afternoon sky. *That would make a striking quilt design.* She reaches for her camera only to realize that, of course, it is not with her. *Well, I'll just have to come back and get a picture of this some other time.*

Wanting more time to think things through, she decides to accept his dinner invitation. He is, after all, a good listener. "All right, Mitch. I'll have dinner with you. But first, can we stop at that health food store next to the Cheesecake Factory? I need some good old-fashioned hair-of-the-dog remedy. My stomach is still whirling around. "

"Sure, it's still early. I don't think they serve dinner before five anyway."

Soon they are near the Magnificent Mile. They turn from the lakeshore to enter the busyness of the city. Sirens scream, horns honk and pedestrians rush by, intent on making it across the intersection before the light changes. Nikki feels the calming presence of Mitch near her right elbow and allows herself be guided through the crowd.

The health food store has a juice bar and Mitch suggests having something after Nikki makes her purchase.

"Good idea," Nikki says. "Something with ginger sounds good."

They study the juice and tea menu for some time before the attendant interrupts with a suggestion. "Did I hear hangover? We have the perfect thing. How about an Elixir of St. Bernard?"

"What on earth is that?" Nikki asks.

"First you start with a few sips of orange juice with a dash of apple cider vinegar and soda bicarbonate. That's not very pleasant, but the St Bernard is delicious—no brandy in it, though—but lots of people without hangovers drink it."

"Give us two, then." Mitch orders.

They sit at a tall bistro table and when the waiter brings two small glasses and two steaming mugs, Nikki makes a face. "It smells awful."

"It's worth a try though. Let's see if we can at least take a few swallows, but first the juice." Mitch tastes the liquid in the tiny glass. "Not too bad."

"Here goes." Nikki raises her glass to her lips and takes a small sip. "Yuk, this is like medicine."

"It is."

Nikki finishes the juice in one large gulp and then picks up the tea. She takes a sip. "Oh, this is better than it smells. I taste some thyme in it and the ginger is mild. Yum."

Mitch agrees. "See. Medicine doesn't always have to be bad."

Feeling somewhat better as they leave the juice bar, Nikki strolls beside Mitch the few blocks to McCormick and Schmick's restaurant. The quiet of the restaurant sooths her as they enter. Dark paneling and crisp white tablecloths with booths tucked discretely into the corners express an understated elegance. The music is quiet with a definite, strong beat. It reminds her of dancing with Mitch last night. Her knees feel like they will buckle when a spark of desire flows through her as he touches her elbow to lead her to the booth on their right. *What is going on with me? I'm acting like a teenager.*

Outwardly composed, but shaking inside, she glances down towards her shoes. "Oh, Mitch, I just remembered how I must look in these grubby climbing clothes. This is not quite appropriate for such a nice place."

"You're fine," he says, "in fact you're more than fine. You're beautiful. You are the best dressed woman in this place."

Leaving them standing near their table facing each other, the host turns away to seat other customers.

"Oh, for crying out loud! Don't do that. Please! I don't need any false compliments. I want only honesty between us."

"I meant it, Nikki. Your inner beauty shines through and I'm sure even rags would look gorgeous on you. I have the feeling that you were sent to me last night to save me from myself. I want to know you better."

He pulls her close and kisses her on the forehead. Nikki is unsteady as they separate and leans against the table to calm her pounding heart.

The wine steward comes up behind her and clears his throat. "Would you two lovebirds like anything to drink before dinner?"

"I thought you'd never ask," Mitch says as he sits down, "How about the 1998 Mondavi Chardonnay, with your finest Crème de Cassis for an aperitif. We'll order our wine with the main course."

"Of course, Mr. Holden. Good choice." The sommelier turns away.

"Do you come in here a lot? He seemed to know you."

"My office is right around the corner and of course, I frequently entertain clients here. So, I guess they do know me. Can I recommend my favorite?"

"By all means," Nikki says. "I don't want to brag, but I am somewhat of a gourmet cook myself and I am always inter-ested in trying something new."

"They are famous for seafood here, but my favorite is the boeuf bourguignon. If you insist on having seafood, the cala-mari appetizer with an aioli sauce is the finest in Chicago."

"Now that you mention it, I am starving. I sort of skipped breakfast and haven't had anything to eat since that greasy hamburger last night. I should have had something with the ginger tea."

"I didn't think of it at the time, either."

Nikki studies the menu. "I think I'll have the boeuf bour-guignon. It's one of my specialties and it would be interesting to compare it to my own. There is nowhere in Caraville that even pretends to cook French cuisine."

"Aha, Caraville! I knew you had to be from around here. Your accent gave you away."

"Yes, I'll admit it. I live only an hour's drive from here and I really was not attending a convention in Chicago yesterday. But I haven't heard anything about you. Where are you from?"

"I've lived near Chicago all my life. My ex-wife talked me into buying a condo downtown. By the way, our divorce was finalized yesterday. I thought I wouldn't care, but it was like having my heart ripped out and stomped on, but more on that later. Anyway, I thought I'd hate living in the city, but I love it. It's the one thing we had in common. Every other part of our relationship was unbelievably messy."

He looks directly into Nikki's eyes as though trying to judge if she wants to hear more. She leans towards him, not taking her eyes from his, "You can tell me whatever you need to. I haven't always been a good listener, but I'm learning. I am finding that empathy comes more easily once you've suffered yourself."

"I knew you would understand, or at least try to; but let's not get maudlin; I want to hear about something you like to do. I want to know what makes you happy."

"Is that one question, or two?"

"Well, it was actually two, but since I like to eat, let's start with—what is the best meal you ever had?"

"That will take some doing to come up with only one. I've had so many. I love to cook *and* eat. I especially love to cook for other people and set a table that enhances the appreciation of the food. Presentation is very, very important to me. Atmosphere can make the simplest meal seem elegant. I used to play that trick on my kids all the time. We'd have a simple meal like chili con carne and I would serve it by candlelight in shallow bowls garnished with shredded cheese and daikon curlicues and a sprig of watercress. We'd have fresh green salad from the garden and of course, fresh, homemade bread. The Virgin Sangrias were the kid's favorite part of the meal."

"Umm, that sounds good. Chili is one of my favorites on a cold, windy day."

"But chili is not the best meal I ever had. I think, considering the whole meaning of sharing a meal, my favorite or best meal ever was the Seder dinner we had five years ago. I prepared the entire meal, from the gefilte fish to the lamb and charoset, desserts, appetizers, all the ceremonial foods, everything…including setting the table with all the special dishes."

"What do you mean, ceremonial foods?" Mitch is curious.

"I'll get to that. Anyway, our family usually shares in the preparation, but I wanted to do it all by myself that year. I had spent a week re-writing the entire ceremony to make it more relevant and I wanted it done exactly like I had planned."

"Wait, can I ask? What is a Seder dinner?"

Nikki takes a deep breath. "I get that question all the time. It's okay. Seder basically means order. It is a ritual meal with a definite order of prayers, blessings and foods. It is an ancient ritual celebrating the Passover of the angel of death and the release from slavery of the Jewish people."

"So you're Jewish, then?"

"Oh, no, no. I'm Catholic. But our roots, of course, are in Judaism. After all, Jesus grew up as a Jew."

"I never thought about that."

"Most Catholics celebrate something similar to the Seder on Holy Thursday…when Jesus celebrated the Last Supper. Some parishes even have a Seder meal for all parishioners."

"Well, I'm Catholic, too. But I've never heard about this Seder."

"I think you'd like it. During the course of the meal there are four blessing cups—that's four glasses of wine. It really is a celebration. But let me get back to why that particular meal was the most memorable of my life. Our immediate family—my two kids and husband—a cousin, his wife and three kids and two other couples were there. One couple—our next-door neighbors—had never been to a Seder before."

Mitch smiles. "That must have been quite an experience for them."

"Oh, yes, it was and they have celebrated it with us every year since then. For the rest of us it was a tradition we wouldn't want to miss. We'd done it together for years. That year, though, when the thirteen of us gathered at the table and we lit the ceremonial candles and said the traditional prayers, everyone was suddenly uncharacteristically quiet and reverent."

"Amazing."

"Maybe it was the rewritten ceremony, I don't know, but spontaneously, one by one, everyone around the table shared how grateful they were for the many blessing in their lives."

"Yeah, gratitude. Too many of us forget to show it." Mitch interjects.

"You're right. But that night the gratitude and unity at the table was palpable. It was as though we were united in the long history of all the people who had ever celebrated the Passover. The stories we read, the prayers, the remembrances, were all especially meaningful and the food, oh, my, it was perfect."

"I'm sure."

"Everyone raved about the lamb. The food seemed to flow onto the table without effort...usually I am all frazzled by the time a meal is over, but that evening, it just seemed to happen by itself. The ceremony had no awkward moments, no irrelevant episodes. We sang songs. We laughed. We were really blessed. We lingered over dessert. Even the teenagers stayed and joined in the conversation."

"That's a miracle in itself."

"It sure was. I felt so grateful for the whole thing: grateful for the tradition, the history and the inclusiveness. I felt grateful, too, for my cooking and entertaining abilities."

"Well, that's a gift more people should have."

"At the end when we raised our glasses and said, next year in Jerusalem, I cried tears of gratitude to realize that my talents *were* meaningful—that they could create a grace filled place. I hated for it to end. Other Seders have been good, yes, that's the word—good—but that one was special. I keep trying to recreate that feeling, but maybe I should just give thanks that it did happen once."

"Wow! That makes me want to celebrate a Seder. I've had some great meals, but the focus has always been on the food. Can I join you next year?"

"Let's not get ahead of ourselves…one step at a time. Now tell me about your favorite meal ever."

The waiter discretely places their aperitifs on the table and takes their dinner orders with a minimum of conversation.

"Before I go on, let's toast to our serendipitous meeting last night. I know it was not the romantic, charming type of encounter I would guess you prefer, but there was something compelling about it." Mitch raises his glass, "To more nights of dancing and fun."

"To more knowledge and self-awareness."

"Wow, that's heavy. Is that what you think last night was all about?"

"Well, it's just that without letting loose like I did last night, I might never have had an opportunity to look at my life and its problems in a new and different light. I think going a little wild and acting outside the box made me realize what's been happening."

"And what is that?" Mitch asks.

Nikki pauses to take a sip of the aperitif. She closes her eyes and breathes deeply. "Ah, that is *very* good!"

"You haven't answered my question."

Nikki's head is down, her eyes closed. Tears squeeze out of the corners of her eyes.

"Oh, Mitch, I am not ready to deal with this. I need thinking time *and* I need to confront some issues head on. I am not very good at confrontation. I'd usually rather just smile and say everything is wonderful and sweep things under the rug. I can see now that's how I've survived all these years."

"We all do that."

"But it's not a good way to live. It's as though I have been only partly alive."

"We don't need to go there—yet."

The waiter approaches the table with calamari for Nikki and a bowl of lobster bisque for Mitch and places the dishes on the table unobtrusively. He seems to know that Nikki and Mitch do not want to be interrupted. He disappears without a word. The mood shifts.

"Hey, why don't I tell you about my favorite meal?" Mitch digs into his soup with gusto.

"Okay, I'm all ears."

Chapter Eighteen

Trip to the North Slope

The loading and flight planning goes quickly and before Leila realizes it, they are piling into the Otter. Dom wants to sit up front so he can see the scenery, so she gets into a seat behind them.

As Rudy starts the engine, Dom keeps up a steady banter, asking questions about his every action. "I promise not to touch anything—even this fancy looking steering wheel in front of me."

"That's the yoke, Dom. It controls the elevators and the ailerons. Plus, it has buttons for radio transmissions." Rudy patiently explains every procedure, until finally, he says, "No more questions now. I've got to focus on taxiing and getting this plane in the air. We can talk once we get airborne and out of the Anchorage area. I'll show you how to work the intercom. But for now, why don't you put the headset on so you can hear the controllers?"

"Great." Dom turns around to talk to Leila. "Isn't this great! I've never been in an Otter before. This is quite a plane. See how Rudy operates it so smoothly. He looks like he was born at the controls of an airplane. You're lucky to have such a competent son. I'll bet you're proud of him."

Leila's face is tense. She has her arms crossed over her chest and frowns at Dom's nonstop conversation. "Let's be quiet now, Dom, so Rudy can hear the instructions from the air traffic controllers. He needs to focus on what he's doing. Just watch for a while." She is glad when Dom faces forward. She's not yet over her upset about Rudy's decision and wants to stew for a while. The noise as Rudy pushes the throttle forward for the takeoff makes further conversation impossible without an intercom, so Leila just looks out the window. She has a headset on, but has the volume turned down.

When they level off at 2500 feet, Rudy turns the intercom on. "Okay, we've just left the departure control frequency and will be flying VFR—that's under visual flight rules—so we can talk to each other over the intercom. The mikes are voice activated, so just talk into it. Don't press the button on the yoke, Dom. That's the transmit button and you don't want our conversation broadcast to the whole world."

"Okay. I think I can handle that."

"We'll be flying low today, through Windy Pass on the way to Fairbanks. It's a perfect day for flying...clear and calm."

"How far away is that big snow covered mountain?"

"That's Denali. It's over a hundred miles away. We'll get a close-up view of it when we pass Talkeetna."

As usual, there is a lot of air traffic as they climb out of Anchorage. Denali shines in the distance in the noonday sun. There is a cloud near the top of the mountain making it look like it has a hat. Dom is pointing and Leila sees his mouth moving, but since her headset volume is turned down she cannot hear what he is saying.

Rudy points to the cloud near the top of Denali. "That's a standing lenticular cloud, which means there is a lot of wind up there. We might get bounced around a bit when we get closer to Windy Pass, but I haven't heard any reports of significant turbulence. We'll just keep our seatbelts tight and wait and see. This plane is built like a tank and can handle anything."

Air turbulence does not bother Leila. She has experienced plenty of it in her years of flying, but Dom grips the armrest with white tipped fingers. "Is there any danger of a downdraft making us crash into the ground? Maybe we should go higher so we can't get slammed into a mountain."

"It would only be worse up higher, Dom. Don't worry. We'll turn around if it gets too bad, or if we hear anyone up ahead reporting severe turbulence. And like I said, this plane is well built and can withstand almost anything."

Dom is quiet for a while as he looks around taking pictures. Leila is reading the morning paper and is relaxed as the plane drones on and the light rocking motion almost puts her to sleep. Her reverie is interrupted when Dom suddenly shouts, "Wow! Look at that! It looks like we could reach out and touch that mountain. Is that Denali?"

"It sure is! We're not all that close, it is sort of an optical illusion and, actually, this is about as close as we get to it along our route today. Once we get into the pass, we won't be able to see it at all from our altitude. But you'll be impressed with the mountains through the pass."

"It will be hard to top the trip to Lake Clark. I thought that was the most beautiful place on Earth. So this ought to be good."

All is quiet again for a while, then just after passing Cantwell, the wind begins to increase and Rudy struggles to keep the wings of the Otter level. He flies from one side of the canyon to the other searching for smooth air. Dom looks around frantically, turning around in his seat to make eye contact with Leila. She smiles at him and turns the volume up on her headset. "Don't worry, Dom. This is nothing. I've been through a lot worse than this, and I'm still here to talk about it. Just relax."

"Look who's telling who to relax! Miss Tension herself. What if you had...oh my God!" Dom screams. As the plane banks suddenly to the left, he strains against his shoulder harness. Papers and charts float around in the cockpit. Leila casually reaches for the newspaper, which has fallen from her lap. Dom grabs the yoke as the bank approaches ninety degrees.

Rudy is trying to level the wings from the sudden upset and yells at Dom, "Get your hands off the yoke. What are you trying to do, kill us?"

Dom lets go of the yoke. He puts his hands under his thighs and sits on them so as not to grab the yoke again. He lowers his head to his chest and closes his eyes. He is mumbling into the intercom and Leila hears "full of grace the Lord is with thee... Pray for us sinners now and at the hour of our death. Hail Mary..."

Once the wings are straight and level, Rudy glances back at Leila with a quizzical look and shrugs his shoulders. The air is smoother now with only an occasional light bump. "It looks like we've gotten through the worst of it, Dom. I'm sorry I yelled at you, but you were working against me as I tried to level the wings. This plane, strong as it is, is very slow to respond to aileron input. I was trying to bring the left wing up with right aileron—by turning the yoke to the right—and you were trying to turn it to the left. You're pretty strong, you know." Rudy laughs.

Dom's expression is grim. He stammers, "No, don't apologize. I'm the one who is sorry. I was just so scared. I had to hang on to something. I didn't know what I was doing. I'm embarrassed. I must look like a real baby."

"You just don't know what to expect. That's normal. What you need to do is take flying lessons, so you will know what to do in unusual circumstances."

"I never thought of that before, but what a great idea." He turns around to smile at Leila. "Wouldn't Celeste be pleased? We would be a real flying family."

Now it is Leila's turn to be tense. The turbulence didn't bother her, but the idea of both Rudy and Dom flying fills her with dread. *I can't live with a constant fear of losing them.* Then, realizing what she has just thought, smiles. *I didn't realize how much Dom has come to mean to me.*

For the rest of the flight, Rudy and Dom chat on the intercom constantly, while Leila is lost in her thoughts. Her imagination devises scenarios involving Dom. When they arrive in Fairbanks she is surprised at how quickly the time passed.

Fairbanks is hot and sunny. The unloading of the construction materials is efficient. During the process, Dom follows Rudy around, asking questions and Rudy—businesslike now—responds tersely. But Dom is not deterred. He seems excited with the idea of learning how to fly. Leila is left to her own devices and wanders into the waiting area of the Fixed Base Operation where they have parked to unload.

"That Otter is a real beauty," one of the men in the office says. "Is it from the company in Anchorage that lost their director of operations a while back in some freak crash? I hear they have plans to expand their operation. Do you know anything about that? I hope they don't plan on competing with us. They're a real professional outfit from what I hear. Our business couldn't stand up to them if they moved into Fairbanks."

Leila feels as though she has been body slapped and the whiplash of conflicting emotions leaves her standing with her mouth open trying to catch her breath. The sudden reminder of Pete's death followed by the suggestion of a larger operation and then the indirect compliment about her flying business leaves her feeling as though she is caught in a whirlpool, out of control. She says nothing, but walks towards a seat near the window where she can watch the unloading of the Otter.

The man follows her to the window. "I'm sorry, ma'am. I didn't introduce myself. I'm John Nesgaard. I'm the chief pilot here. And you are?"

"I'm Leila Pletnikoff from Pete's Flying Service."

"Pleased to meet you." He stops abruptly and gasps. "Oh my, I *am* sorry. I didn't realize… me and my big mouth."

"That's okay, there is no way you could have known that it was my husband who died in that crash. I've had a long time to get used to it and we're doing well. Life goes on, you know."

"I should watch what I say though. The Alaskan flying community is pretty small and you know how rumors fly around—much faster than the planes we fly," John smiles, looking pleased with his analogy.

"That's true," Leila smiles back at him. Her emotions have calmed a little, but her heart is still beating fast and her breathing is shallow. She knows nothing about any plans to expand, but is not willing to share that knowledge with a competitor. Then she is surprised by the sudden taste of anger in her mouth. *That Rudy! I'll bet this has to do with his quitting school. Well, we'll see about that! I am going to have to talk some sense into him.*

The man changes the subject and allows the matter of expansion to drop so she does not have to evade any of his questions. As though he wants to cover up his faux pas, John offers Leila a cup of coffee, which she refuses. "Well, at least take some fresh fruit for your trip. There's a basket of apples there on the counter. You're welcome to take as many as you'd like."

"Thanks, I'll do that. Oh, it looks like they're done. We should be off. We've got a three hour trip ahead of us," Leila says, standing abruptly and rushing out the door. She strides across the ramp to the plane with determination.

John runs to catch her with a paper sack in his outstretched hand. "Here, you forgot these." He hands her a bag of apples. "It was a real pleasure to meet you, Leila." He puts an arm around her waist. "And again, I am so sorry. If there is anything I can do, just give me a call." His face is very close to Leila's. "Maybe next time you pass through Fairbanks, I can buy you lunch."

Dom jumps out of the plane in time to witness this exchange and places a protective arm around Leila's shoulders. "Rudy says it's time to go. Come on, we don't want to hold him up." Then, helping Leila into the plane, Dom mumbles possessively, "What was that all about? It looked like he was trying to put a move on you."

Leila pulls away and says, "And so what if he was?"

Dom is speechless. They both strap into their seats angrily. After completing his preflight inspection, Rudy hops into the pilot seat and begins his before-start checklist. Focusing on his duties, he does not notice the tension between his mother and Dom.

"This should be a real treat, Dom. The weather is just perfect for a flight through the Brooks Range. Luckily, we can fly VFR the whole way. And that's a good thing, too. The mechanics didn't have time to finish all the inspections to make the plane legal for instrument flight."

"That's good." Dom's response is brusque.

Rudy doesn't seem to notice. He puts his headset on after starting the engine and calls for a taxi clearance. The absence of conversation in the noisy cockpit speaks louder than the irritating chatter from the previous leg of their trip. But again, Rudy is intent on his flying duties and ignores the strained silence. He takes off towards the north on runway zero one and makes a slight turn to continue on course towards Anaktuvuk Pass. When he levels off at 3500 feet, he at last seems to notice the lack of questions from Dom.

"Hey, what's up? Are you tired of flying already?"

"No, just a little tired, I guess. I still haven't adjusted to the time change and remember, I didn't get much sleep last night."

"Well, if you're going to doze, you'd better do it now. Once we get into the mountains, you won't want to miss the scenery. Do you have your camera ready this time?"

"Oh, shoot. I put it back in my bag. Why did I do that? It's in the back seat." He turns around and asks Leila if she can get it for him.

She rummages in his backpack and hands it to him without a word.

Rudy notices the strain between them. "Whoa, what is going on between you? It looks like a lover's spat, or something. Did he insult you, Mom? Are you mad about sitting in the back?"

"Why don't you just fly, Rudy? That's all you ever want to do anyway." Leila refuses to let go of her anger and determines that she will put her foot down with Rudy as soon as they land and insist that he continue with his schooling. She will not let him devote his life to flying.

Rudy shrugs and turns around to engage Dom in conversation. Dom's answers are curt at first, but before long he and Rudy are talking and laughing non-stop. Dom apparently has forgotten his sleepiness.

Chapter Nineteen

Mitch Tells His Story

Mitch smiles, remembering. "Well, my favorite meal was on my twenty first birthday. I'll never forget it. Sadly, my family was never one to make a fuss about birthdays—or holidays for that matter. They were usually just another day, so I had not given much thought to it being my birthday."

"We're just the opposite. Holidays are pretty festive around our house." Nikki looks sympathetic.

"I guess it's all in what you get used to. Anyway, I had just graduated from Marquette University and we were spending a long weekend at my uncle's cabin on Sadie Lake."

"Cool."

Mitch continues, "Yeah. It was a perfect summer day. My fiancée was visiting for the weekend. I'm sure she was the one who put them up to it. They would have never thought of it on their own. My cousins, friends, fiancée and I had all bunked together in the dormitory style room—not much privacy for any hanky-panky. All of us guys were up at the crack of dawn to fish for rainbow trout and came back with enough for breakfast."

"That sure sounds like a wonderful meal: yum, fresh rainbow trout pan-fried in butter."

"But that wasn't it. The real surprise—and my favorite meal—came later. Let me finish."

"Okay."

"I'm probably romanticizing it, but that day was about as perfect as they come. Everybody pitched in and helped with the cooking and cleaning up. We ate, lounged, played tennis and baseball, swam, water-skied, drank a little beer..."

Nikki raises her eyebrows at the last remark.

"Okay, it was more than a little beer. But with all the activity, it wore off quickly. I didn't notice any strange happenings during the day—like anyone trying to keep a secret. But looking back, I do remember everyone doing their best to keep me away from the cabin and the beach to the south. There was always someone there to steer me to another activity."

"Sounds like they were pretty sneaky."

"They were. Then, towards dusk, Eddie, my cousin, said, 'Hey, let's take the boat to the marina store and get a little vino for a birthday toast. You want to ski there and back, Mitch?'

Always willing to get in a little more water skiing, I agreed. Nancy and I both skied on the way there. When we got to the store, Eddie went in while Nancy and I sat in the boat and made-out. She was pretty hot in her skimpy bikini. I didn't notice that Eddie was gone for an inordinately long time. That must have been part of the plot."

"Likely story."

"So when he came back with several bottles of wine and lots of snacks, it was a little too cool to water ski on the way back. But since Nancy was at my side, I didn't mind. It was good just to sit next to her and keep her warm. As we approached the cabin, no lights were visible except the marker light at the end of the dock. I told Eddie to be careful because it was so dark. I wondered where everyone went."

"Then, as we were about to dock, the lights went on. It looked like the Fourth of July. There were lanterns all over the place and I thought I even saw fireworks or sparklers. A crowd of at least a hundred people was jam-packed around the tables on the beach. Corn on the cob was roasting on a fire. I saw baked potatoes wrapped in foil and steaks sizzling on the grill. As Eddie cut the throttle on the motor, I heard what sounded like the Mormon Tabernacle Choir singing 'Happy Birthday.' I was glad that it was dark, because I was so choked up, I couldn't talk. Nancy hugged me and wished me a happy birthday and then, as I stepped on to the dock, people swarmed and hugged and congratulated me. And of course, with all that, it could have been dry bread or crackers and it would have been the best meal of my life."

"What a great story! And what a wonderful memory to have!" Nikki says.

"Yes, I am choosing from now on to remember only the good times. And as far as lessons learned from the bad times, those will become good memories, too."

"That sounds like a good bit of wisdom—hard to remember in the midst of life, but…Oh my gosh, Mitch, I forgot all about my car. What did I do with my car last night? How am I going to get home? As much as I hate to, I *have to* go home tonight. It's time to face the music—or lack thereof.

"You mean you honestly don't remember where you left your car?" Mitch asks as he finishes the last of his bisque.

"No, I only remember being at the bar with you and then some big argument out on the street about who I would ride home with. Then the next morning I woke up at Daphne's brother's condo. I wasn't sure where I was. Oh! I must have left it at the valet parking at that jazz club. But, no, it was out on the street. I do remember that because the parking attendant had brought it out and that's why I was so confused about where I was when I woke up. I didn't remember who I had ridden with." Nikki sounds more and more frustrated.

"Well, you needn't worry. I'm used to taking care of things like that."

Nikki wrings her hands looking down at her lap. Her frustration builds. "Oh, Mitch, I'm so ashamed. You must think I am a real fool." She adds, "You have to know that I am not like this. I have never before in my life drunk so much that I couldn't remember what I had done. I am a responsible mother and wife. I don't run around picking up men in bars. This is not me. You don't know who I really am. How could you want to spend more time with me?"

"Look, Nikki, I just know that you've been hurt and need a sympathetic ear. You've done nothing to be ashamed of. I'd like to say that I am a good judge of character. I usually am— except in the case of my ex-wife. But let's give this a chance. I feel a connection to you that I have never felt with anyone else. I think we were destined to meet."

"Maybe." Nikki sounds doubtful.

"No, really. Sure, I know that you are married and I will wait to see what happens with that; but can we just be friends?"

The waiter appears with Nikki's boeuf bourguignon. The aroma is rich and meaty and Nikki puts her nose close to the steaming bowl and inhales. "Wow! I hate to admit it, but already I know this is better than mine. The smell is so rich, so balanced—mmm. What did you order, Mitch?"

"I usually get the beef, but I just couldn't resist the fresh wild Alaska king salmon. We don't get it very often here in the Midwest and they always do an outstanding job with sea-food here."

"Well, let's dig in. We don't want our food to get cold. We'll discuss details later about how I am going to find my car."

"I told you not to worry, Nikki. I took care of it. When you rushed off with that other guy last night, I followed you in your car. The valet had given me the keys; I guess he thought it was mine. I followed you into the parking garage at the condo and left it there with the keys hidden under the mat by the driver's seat. I didn't know what else to do. I thought it would be safe there. Sure enough, I went by the garage at lunchtime before I took a walk along the lakeshore and it still looked okay. My condo is close, and I mostly walk everywhere anyway, so it was no problem to get home from the garage."

"You must be my guardian angel, Mitch. Thank you for looking out for me." Nikki takes another bite of her food and closes her eyes, savoring the flavor. "This is fabulous. I have never tasted anything as good."

"Oh, come on, I'll bet you put on some sumptuous meals yourself. I'd love to try some of your cooking. Nancy wasn't much of a cook. She mostly opened cans and ordered take-out food. Luckily, Chicago has great restaurants and we ate out quite a lot."

Nikki looks at him and notices the corners of his mouth turn down as he remembers his failed marriage.

"Are you ready to tell me your story, Mitch? I'm willing to listen to as much as you want to share."

Mitch is silent for a long time. His gaze is far off. Nikki notices his expression change from thoughtful, to angry, to pained. A questioning expression narrows his eyes. He bites his lip as he squints, trying to blink away tears. His fork is stopped half way to his mouth as though he has forgotten all about eating. Finally he takes a deep breath and begins.

"She left me for a woman, Nikki. How could I have been so blind? I thought we had a good sex life. At least she seemed to be happy enough with that part of our marriage. I thought it was normal for drive to cool somewhat, but she... Oh, I don't need to go into all the details, but, looking back, I think that our arguments, although they were never about sex, really originated with the disparity of our needs. My frustrations mounted over the years and I'm afraid that I wasn't the ideal husband either. We're both to blame. But I never cheated on her like she did on me. I was so stupid!"

"Don't blame yourself, Mitch. How could you ever have even suspected such a thing?"

"It's not like there weren't signs. I would often come back from a business trip and would find her and a girlfriend sleeping in our bed. I thought she just wanted company and wanted to feel safe. I get sick just thinking about it."

Oh, Mitch," Nikki reaches over to pat his hand, "I'm so sorry."

"When I finally began to suspect something was wrong, I still did not expect it to be another woman. Her partners were nice girls—co-workers from the hospital. They didn't look or act like I thought lesbians would act. In fact, it never even occurred to me. We often even had dinner together. But again, looking back, I recognize signs of physical attraction between Nancy and her partners, even in my presence. The way they would stroke each other's faces and embrace each other, kissing on the lips for what I thought was an inordinately long time; I should have recognized some of the signs." Mitch pauses again to take a bite of his cooling dinner.

Nikki waits for him to continue, sensing he has more to say.

"Eventually, Nancy settled down to one partner, Eva, and she seemed to become a part of our lives. We did everything together: the beach, water skiing, tennis, plays, dancing, the opera, and dinner. It was a rare occasion when Eva was not a part of our social scene."

"My gosh. I can't imagine. You mean you didn't...?"

"I didn't suspect a thing. In fact, I sort of liked Eva, but I was sick of their huddled whispering and their physical closeness. Nancy and I argued about it. I tried to entice Nancy to spend time with me alone, even offering trips to Paris and Madrid, but there was always an excuse why she couldn't go. I am still kicking myself for being so stupid."

"Don't say that, Mitch, you are not stupid. You were just blindsided." Nikki takes his hand in hers.

"It was always: *Eva this, Eva that, Eva wants, Eva likes* and on and on. One day I had had enough and put my foot down. I told Nancy I never wanted to see Eva in our condo again. It was either Eva or me. She laughed in my face and said, "You stupid jerk! How long will it take you to realize that I love her? You are just a handy symbol of respectability. Without you, I'd have to come out of the closet and my superiors at work might not understand. My career could suffer."

"I can't believe she would even say such a thing," Nikki commiserates.

"I couldn't either. Career! I said. What about me? She laughed in my face again and said, 'Just try to get Eva out of our lives and you'll find out what suffering means.' After that they were more blatant with their physicality and often I ended up sleeping in the guestroom while Eva spent the night."

"Oh, Mitch!" Nikki felt her heart go out to him. She felt his pain.

"One night I was going to bed in the guest room and I heard Nancy and Eva laughing in our bedroom and thought,

This is ridiculous. I am not going to live like this. I got my camera and snuck into the hallway. I waited by the door until I heard sounds of lovemaking and burst in, turning on the lights as I did and got a picture of them naked on top of the covers in a very compromising position. Nancy jumped up and started throwing things at me and tried to grab the camera. I kept snapping pictures as she came towards me. Eva was cowering on the bed. Nancy was yelling obscenities and calling me names that I am too ashamed to repeat."

Nikki gets up and moves over to sit beside Mitch. "You don't have to continue. Mitch. I am so sorry. I can't imagine how painful that must have been."

"I want to finish. After that scene, I went to stay in a hotel for a while."

"You're still in a hotel?"

"No. I worked things out so that I kept the condo. Things moved so fast. With the pictures as evidence, I told Nancy if she didn't want me to expose her, the property settlement would be my way. She said she would accuse me of abandonment because of all my travel, but she was not very convincing."

"Why would she even want to contest..."

"She didn't. But it is little consolation to know that she ended up with very few of our common assets. I don't worry about her, though. Eva is a prominent anesthesiologist. They'll never hurt for money."

"Mitch, I am so sorry you had to go through all of that. It makes my troubles seem so insignificant. I don't even know if they are real or just a part of my imagination. But I do have to go home and sort things out."

Chapter Twenty

Camping on the Colville River

L eila dozes in the back seat of the plane for a while and when she opens her eyes, notices how quiet it is. She is about to lean forward to ask what the problem is when she realizes that they are on final approach to an impossibly small looking airstrip alongside a river. Rudy has throttled back to idle and is putting the flaps down to their fully extended position. It looks as though they are hanging motionless in the air.

Rudy maneuvers the plane to line up with the airstrip. "Thank goodness for the strong north wind. This strip is pretty small for the Otter, but we can usually plan on a good stiff breeze up here. It might make setting up the tents a bit dicey, but at least it will keep the bugs at bay."

"There's an upside to everything, I guess," Dom smiles.

"Most things, anyway," Rudy glances toward the back seat and his mother.

Once they are on the ground, Rudy taxis the plane to a wide spot at one end of the strip, shuts the engine down and jumps out to place three screw anchors so he can tie the plane down. "This is just a precaution. A plane this heavy shouldn't move around too much, but it would be a real bummer to get stuck here if the plane should be damaged in the wind. None of our satellite phones were available when we left, so we're sort of incommunicado here."

"Why didn't you let me know, Rudy? We could have rented one. You know our policy is to have a *sat* phone on a trip this far away from home base."

"You worry way too much, Mom. What could possibly go wrong? The weather is clear. I know this country like the back of my hand. We've got the toughest plane in the world and the world's best pilot." He smiles.

"Yes, and so was your father. Look what happened to him." Leila puts one hand to her forehead, rubbing her eyes and shaking her head from side to side.

"Oh, Rudy, I just can't let you do this. You have got to stop this foolishness and go back to school. And what's this I hear about you wanting to expand our operation? Don't you have enough to do already? I am still the owner of Pete's Flying Service and have final say in any operational decision—especially one that involves major purchases of new equipment."

"But, Mom, I have it all worked out. I have been talking to the FAA and studying..."

"No, Rudy. We are *not* expanding. In fact, when I get back to Anchorage, I'm going to hire a new chief pilot. You are going back to school, or finding a flying job elsewhere."

Rudy throws his hands up in the air and turns towards the plane, bumping into Dom who has been standing behind him trying to stay out of the conflict.

Dom laughs nervously. "How about setting up the tents and cooking our dinner? I'm starving. And where are those fast birds you promised me?"

"For God's sake, Dom, get a clue," Rudy says. He puts his hands on his hips and opens his mouth as though to continue, then glancing toward the sky, he smiles and his face lights up like a two year old seeing his first Christmas tree.

"Look, Dom, there they are. There's a pair of the falcons. Look at them dive! Wouldn't it be great to be able to fly like that?"

Leila momentarily forgets her anger and watches the peregrine falcons soar and dive. Their screams fill the air with a wild, predatory fury. The thrill of witnessing such a rare happening dims her concerns about anything else. Dom walks towards her, slips his arm around her waist and leads her over to the edge of the strip where a sand dune makes a perfect viewing seat. They lean back on the sand, not taking their eyes off the falcons and Leila rests her head on Dom's shoulder. Her eyes begin to tear up until she can no longer see the birds. She sobs quietly, then intensely, turns towards Dom and buries her face in his shoulder.

"Oh, Dom, What am I going to do?"

"Let it be, Leila. Just let it be. Let's live in the moment, you know that's all we really have anyway; none of us knows what tomorrow will bring. Let's love today."

Leila sniffs and sighs. "I'll try, Dom. I'll try really hard."

Dom and Leila continue to watch the falcons in silence. Leila sniffs once in a while, but eventually puts the memory of her argument with Rudy out of her thoughts. It is very comfortable lying there next to Dom. She can feel the warmth of his body and hear his heart beating. *I have missed this closeness.* The wind dies down a little and Leila recognizes the sound of mosquitoes on the lee side of their bodies.

"Uh, oh, we'd better get the tents set up before the mosquitoes carry us away." Leila rises to her feet and swats at the bugs. She looks toward the plane and sees that Rudy has already set up one tent and is working on the second. "He certainly is quick. Come on let's help him. Or better, yet, you help him and I'll get the stove started and heat up the soup for dinner."

They eat the picnic lunch they had packed: soup, sandwiches and a fresh carrot salad. Leila had not realized how hungry she was.

"Wow, that's the best chicken noodle soup I ever had. I guess food always tastes better outside—even with a few mosquitoes mixed in." Dom wipes his mouth with his sleeve then drinks the last of the soup from his bowl.

"The best is yet to come." Rudy gets up and heads towards the plane.

He walks back with an exaggerated swagger, holding a box above his head with one hand, imitating a waiter serving a fancy dessert. "Ta Da! The world famous fresh strawberry pie from Julie's Café! And," as he sets it down, "our own special whipped topping in a can," pulling the can from his vest pocket.

Dom shakes his head. "You two certainly know how to do it up right. How did you ever manage to get that pie and whipped cream all the way up here in this wilderness?"

"That's the beauty of flying a plane like the Otter," Rudy says. "You can fit a lot of stuff in it. We don't have to put up with freeze-dried food. We can have the real thing. We can have a cooler aboard for things like this and make roughing it a little less rough."

"Remind me never to go camping without a big airplane to haul supplies," Dom laughs.

Leila smiles at Dom's remarks, but persistently ignores Rudy's comments and studiously avoids looking at him. She has been quiet during their meal and after cleaning up the dishes in the stream, she announces, "I'm going to hit the hay."

She walks toward the smaller tent and crawls in, quickly zipping the door up so as not to let any mosquitoes in. She strips down to her underwear and slips into the sleeping bag. It's too warm to sleep in her customary lightweight layer. The sun is still high in the sky; in fact, it will not set at all tonight here above the Arctic Circle. She can hear Dom and Rudy talking and laughing as she opens her book and starts to read.

Sounds become muted and Leila, in a dream-like state, remembers her first trip to the North Slope with Pete. She feels again her wonder at the vastness of the wide-open spaces and remembers Pete's pride in the land of his ancestors. As she drifts off to sleep, she dreams that they are flying above the landscape lush with vegetation. Huge herds of caribou and musk ox wander peacefully. Polar bears and grizzlies lunge across the tundra. She can see their dark eyes. The next moment, she is running with them. Her legs are strong, her breathing relaxed. She looks up and sees the plane she had been in with Pete spinning toward the ground, out of control. "No!" she cries out. She knows Pete is still in the plane and tries to get back in to help him. She tries to jump as it passes by, but her legs are now frozen in place. She can't move them. She tries to scream, "Pull out of the spin!" but no sound comes out. Paralyzed, she watches in horror as he gets closer and closer to the ground and certain death. She breaks free of the paralysis and runs crazily towards the point of impact, screaming, "No, no, no!"

Then she is looking into the wreckage of the plane and sees Pete. But it's not Pete. It's Rudy. "No. Oh, God, don't let him die. Help! Somebody please help!" She continues to scream—without words. She tugs and pulls at Rudy's clothing, trying to get him out of the plane.

She feels someone's hand on her shoulder, shaking it gently. "Leila, wake up. You're having a bad dream."

Dom is sitting next to her on the floor of the tent. Leila, her heart still pounding from the terror of the dream, grabs him and clings like a person drowning. "Oh, Dom, it was terrible. Thank God it was only a dream."

"It's okay, Leila, I'm here. Rudy is asleep in the other tent. I heard you screaming and came to check on you," Dom says as he cradles her in his arms. Leila is still shaken but awakens enough to realize she has only her panties and bra on. She tries to pull away from Dom, but he holds her close.

"Don't worry, Leila. I'll stay with you to chase away any bad dreams." He brushes her dark blond hair from her forehead and strokes her hair and face.

"Relax, now. Go back to sleep. It's late."

Leila lies back pulling the sleeping bag over her naked shoulders and Dom lies down next to her, outside of the bag.

"Shush, now," Dom says as he brushes her closed eyelids with his fingertips. "We're going to be all right."

Leila relaxes. The dream is fading. She feels protected and safe in Dom's arms. The heat of his body and the stillness inside the tent make her sweaty, so she pushes the sleeping bag off from her and snuggles up to Dom. She whispers into his ear, "Thank you for being here."

"You're entirely welcome."

Leila feels relaxed and at the same time, very much awake. Her body is tingling and every point of contact with Dom feels as though it is electrified. Starting at her shoulder, he rubs his hand along her bare arm, then takes hold of her hand and brings it to his lips. He kisses her fingers, then turns her hand over and kisses her palm.

"Oh, Dom, I have missed this so much. I didn't realize until now..."

"Shush, let's just be together."

"I need you, Dom. I want you," Leila says. She presses the length of her body into Dom's and reaches for his mouth with her lips.

She knows that he wants her, too, and is confused when he breaks away. "I need you too, Leila. I want you so much it hurts. But this is not the right time. I want to do it right." He clears his throat. "This isn't the way I planned it, but since the subject came up..." He disengages from Leila and kneels beside her. He takes her hands in his, and says with the voice of a Shakespearean actor, "Leila, will you marry me?"

Leila is caught off guard. The absurdity of their position strikes her as funny all of a sudden, and she laughs aloud. Dom is crestfallen. "I didn't think it was a joke. I'm serious."

This makes Leila laugh even more. Her shoulders rock with laughter and her abdominal muscles begin to hurt from trying to control it. Dom tries to stand up and make a dramatic exit, but cannot stand in the low tent. His head bumps the roof, loosening the stakes holding the tent down. Leila clutches her stomach trying to squelch the laughter.

"Wait, Dom, don't go," Leila says between laughs. She is up on her knees now, too and grabs Dom in a bear hug. "I'm not laughing at you, Dom. I'm laughing for the sheer joy of being with you. Don't you know what a relief this is for me? I'm sorry I insulted you, but it's just that I am only now, too, realizing how much I need you and your lightheartedness. You bring joy into my life, Dom. You make me laugh and that's something I haven't done in years or maybe ever. The thought of being with you from now on makes me want to laugh again. I love you, Dom."

"Then is that a Yes?"

"I think it is. Now will you please go back into Rudy's tent? I wouldn't be able to sleep a wink with your body so close to mine. I'll be okay by myself. I promise."

"All right, my love, but I will be nearby in case you need me."

"I do need you, but that will have to wait."

Leila sleeps without dreaming the rest of the night and awakens to the smell of coffee and the sound of familiar laughter. She smiles, wrapping her arms around herself. *Yes, life is good. Life is very good.* She glances at her watch and sees that it is already eight o'clock. She slips into her clothes, stuffs her sleeping bag and pad into their sacks and crawls out of the tent.

"Hey, it's about time you got up, sleepy head. We've already had breakfast and have the plane packed and ready to go. I've got to be in Deadhorse by nine a.m., so shake a leg, Mom."

"Why did you let me sleep so long? You know business comes first, Rudy. We can't jeopardize our contract with Western Washington."

"Dom told me about your bad dream and your disturbed sleep, so we thought we'd let you catch up on your sleep."

"But, we've got to get going. I can eat later."

"We're doing all right, Mom. Deadhorse is only a half hour from here, so we have plenty of time. You can enjoy your gourmet breakfast. Dom created a mouth-watering frittata. You're lucky we didn't eat it all. I would have, but Dom insisted that we leave some for you. He said something about a special occasion," Rudy winks.

"Dom, you are incorrigible. Why do I put up with you? Have you shared all of the details, or am I left with a modicum of respect from my son?"

"Come on, Leila, I didn't tell him anything you wouldn't have told him yourself. I just thought he would like to know he's going to have to get used to a new father figure."

"Is that what you are, Dom? I thought you would be more like some scary godfather caricature."

Dom punches Rudy in the shoulder. "I'll never get any respect around here. Why do I even try? First your mother laughs her head off at my proposal and then my future step-son calls me a joke." Dom turns away from them in an exaggerated dejected posture. He collapses to his knees and raises his arms in a pleading gesture, mumbling to himself.

"Come on, Dom," Rudy says. "That's enough drama already. You know we love you."

They all laugh as Rudy dishes up Leila's breakfast. Dom walks back to her and gives her an affectionate kiss on the forehead.

Rudy and Dom begin cleaning and packing while Leila eats. As soon as she finishes, they scoop up her dishes and board the plane. The wind has shifted to a southwesterly direction, so they plan to take off to the south.

"The wind isn't as strong as it was yesterday, but since we're light it should be no problem getting airborne from this strip. Just hang on. Here we go." Rudy pushes the throttle forward and the plane accelerates for takeoff.

The flight to Deadhorse is short, as Rudy had promised. Dom is surprised to see the modern industrial complex in this remote Alaskan village. The huge buildings at Prudhoe Bay, the network of roads and the drilling pads seem incongruous after flying for hundreds of miles without seeing so much as a house.

"Wow! Is this for real? I thought I would see polar bears and ice floes, not some Jersey-looking industrial scene. It seems a shame to junk up this pristine wilderness."

"A lot of people feel the same way, Dom. But, you know progress marches on. We need this fuel if we want to continue driving cars or flying airplanes. The oil companies do try to pay their respects to the environment, but..." Rudy shakes his head with an air of resignation. "Well, let's get you over to the terminal. Your flight leaves in an hour and I've got to find my passengers before we load up and head over to Barter Island to pick up the rest of their crew."

Leila and Dom are flying standby, but there are plenty of empty seats and they are given two near the front of the plane. Dom wants to sit at the window, but offers it to Leila.

"No, Dom, you take it," she says. I've seen this scenery before. You'll love seeing the Brooks Range from 30,000 feet."

"Okay, if you insist," he says and eagerly climbs into the window seat.

Dom and Leila hold hands as the pilot taxis onto the runway. The takeoff and climb out are uneventful. Leila turns to the crossword puzzle in the airline magazine while Dom keeps his nose pressed to the window.

"Look, Leila," he says, pointing ahead. "That looks like some mountains but I didn't think they had snow on them yesterday."

"That's not snow, Dom, those are clouds. It looks like the weather system is changing. Lucky we flew through the pass yesterday. We won't have any problem in this jet, though. We'll be well above any weather. Not to worry," Leila says and turns back to her puzzle.

Chapter Twenty-one

Nikki Returns to Caraville

"I won't try to kid myself—or you, Mitch. My husband and I have problems, but maybe we will be able to work them out. I don't know." Nikki tries to sound hopeful.

"For your sake, I hope so, but not for mine."

"Well, I can't promise you anything except that I will be your friend. I don't know exactly what that means at this point, but I am convinced our meeting was not an accident."

"I know it wasn't." Mitch agrees.

"Maybe we're soul mates—whatever that means. I just know that today I found a part of myself that has been buried for a long time. Listening to your story, I found compassion I didn't know I had. I feel a hint of hope that things will be better. Again, I don't know what that means, but time will tell. Just hang in there with me and I will hang in there with you. That's all I can promise." Nikki puts one arm around Mitch's shoulder. With her other hand she turns his face towards hers and looks into his dark brown eyes. "You're a good man, Mitch. Don't ever believe anything else about yourself." Nikki kisses him on the lips.

Their conversation turns to lighter things as they finish their dinner. The waiter tempts them with a tray of decadent desserts, but Nikki says, "No, I don't want to have to run ten miles tomorrow to work it off. But you go ahead, Mitch. You could use a little sweetness in your life."

"You're just trying to fatten me up so I can't keep up with you on your runs." Turning to the waiter, he says, "No, thank you, James, but please bring the check. I think we're done."

"Very well, I hope you enjoyed your dinner and your conversation. It's always a pleasure to serve you. Enjoy the rest of your evening," James says with a wink.

Nikki excuses herself to go to the restroom while Mitch pays the bill. As they leave the restaurant, Nikki is surprised to see that it is still daylight. She had forgotten all about the time and that they had started dinner at five p.m.

"I guess you intend to drive home tonight," Mitch says as they turn down the sidewalk. "May I walk you to your car, Nikki?"

"You probably should since I'm not sure where it is."

"Right."

"Have you called your husband to let him know what's going on?"

"I thought of calling, but I think I'll just let him stew a little longer. He's been such an ass lately, I don't want to get into an argument on the phone and have it color my expectations. I want to think positive thoughts on the way home. I want to believe the best."

"That's usually a good policy, I guess, but not always. Sometimes life does give you lemons."

"We'll just have to get better at making lemonade. There's always a bright side to everything. I love lemonade." Nikki reaches out to take Mitch's hand, unaware that she has done so. It feels natural with Mitch walking by her side. They say nothing else as they walk the seven blocks to the underground parking garage.

Mitch leads the way to her car, saying as they approach it, "See, there it is, safe and sound. Now drive carefully. I want to see you again."

"I need time to think, Mitch. I have to give Gerik a chance. Give me a few days and I'll call. I promise. I'll call you regardless of what happens. But please don't call me at home. Gerik does not need to know anything about you. I'll figure something out. I'll think of a way to get together. Please be patient with me. I want to see you again, too."

As they embrace, Nikki feels her heart go out to Mitch and once again feels his pain and sadness. "You are a real find, Mitch. I'll call. I promise I'll call." Nikki gets into her car.

Mitch stands there waving until she drives out of sight. Nikki sees his forlorn figure and for a moment is tempted to turn around and stay with him but her sense of responsibility wins out and she maneuvers through the city to the expressway and home. Her thoughts jump around as though they are on a trampoline.

What if they really are having an affair? Or what if it is only in my imagination? What did I say to Daphne on the phone? I hope I wasn't too harsh with her. Have I ever forgiven her and Gerik for their affair so many years ago? And hasn't Daphne been a good friend and adviser to me? But Gerik always seems to be angry, especially with Danny. Danny is such a sweet boy. He looks so much like Gerik...and smart...I'm proud that he got that scholarship. I bet the kids would be devastated if we got a divorce. Emma has always been such a good kid: so studious and athletic, such an all around good kid. She's never given me a minute of worry. It's a good thing she is working at summer camp this week. She would pester me with questions non-stop about where I was last night. How will I explain to Gerik why I have been gone overnight?

Nikki puts the car on cruise control and drives at exactly at the speed limit. *I don't want to repeat yesterday's reckless driving.* She vacillates between a desire to turn around and go back to Mitch and a desire to make up with Gerik. *We did have good times when the kids were small. Maybe we can get back to the way we were.* By the time she gets home, she is eager to see Gerik and have a long serious talk with him. She wants to patch it up. She wants to know what is bothering him. Memories of their good times together are foremost in her mind as she pulls into their driveway and presses the garage door opener. She does not notice the car parked nearby on the street. Gerik's car is in the garage and Danny's car, as usual, is gone. *He must be at baseball practice, or at a game.*

As she walks down the hall towards the kitchen admiring the homey atmosphere, she feels safe and secure. The house is quiet and Nikki hears the shower running in their bathroom. *Maybe he'd like a glass of wine.* She opens the special Pedroncelli Cabernet Sauvignon they had been saving for their anniversary and pours two glasses. She sneaks up the stairs and places the two glasses on the dresser before opening the bathroom door. Her shock at seeing the two of them in the shower almost causes her knees to buckle. Daphne is leaning against the wall with her eyes closed, her right leg wrapped around Gerik. Gerik's buttocks are flexed as he presses into her. Nikki silently closes the door and collapses against it. A cold hard rock settles in the pit of her stomach and everything blurs. She stares unseeing at the rumpled bed. Slowly a plan evolves. *They will pay for this. They'll definitely pay!*

Nikki notices two empty wine glasses on headboard. In anger she grabs the two glasses she had brought up and drinks one of them straight down without pausing. Carrying the glasses she walks down the steps like an automaton. She sits resolutely in the overstuffed chair with a view of the stairway, placing the empty glass on a table. She sips the other, barely tasting the expensive anniversary wine. She waits for what seems to be hours. The hatred she feels for both of them is a dark presence, almost as though there is someone else inside of her. *They'll pay for this. They will never get away with it.* Nikki repeats over and over to herself. Finally she sees Gerik at the top of the stairs with a towel around his waist.

He pauses and turns back toward the bedroom, "Hang on, Daph, I'll get us a little more wine. Don't go anywhere."

As he begins to walk down the steps he sees Nikki. His expression goes from the smile of anticipation to fear. His eyes open wide and his jaw drops. He stops. For a moment it looks as though he will turn around and go back to Daphne. Then he clenches his teeth, squares his shoulders and walks towards Nikki like a tomcat posturing for a fight. He asks belligerently, "What are you doing here?"

"I live here. Remember? Or have you forgotten that in one short day?" Nikki glares at him. "You better march up those steps and get some clothes on. And bring that slut back down here with you. We are going to have a talk."

Chapter Twenty-two

Returning From the North Slope

Celeste is at the airport to meet Dom and Leila when they return from Deadhorse. As they load into her car, she assaults them with questions. "Well, how was it? Did you get to see any falcons? What did you think of Deadhorse? Isn't it disgusting, all that industry in such pristine wilderness? I wish I had seen it before all that building."

"It was a great flight, Celeste. I am more and more amazed at how big this state is. Lucky thing I'm not from Texas. I might get a complex or something about being from the second biggest state." He gives Leila a knowing, sideways glance. "But before long I'll be able to rub it in to those cowboys myself."

"What do you mean, Uncle Dom?"

"I've been giving it some serious thought, Kiddo, and I just might check out running my business from Anchorage. I've always wanted to get out of the blasted heat and humidity of the Chicago summers. I just never had a good excuse or a perfect place to settle."

"Well, you *are* full of surprises, Dom," Leila says, "but I will admit I'm glad."

"Wow, listen to Miss Taciturn, will you. She admitted that she likes me."

"That's not exactly what I said," Leila says trying her best to look stern. She turns to Celeste with a huge smile, her eyes lit up like a Christmas tree. "Your uncle proposed to me, Celeste, and in a weak moment I said yes." She glances at Dom, then back to Celeste. "I was worried that he would want me to move back to the Midwest with him, but thank God, he wants to move here. How can things be any better than this?"

"I'm so happy for you, Leila. Hey, maybe we could make it a double wedding. Wouldn't that be fun? One huge party to celebrate all this love!"

"Let's not rush into anything, yet. I've a lot of business decisions to make, and besides, it is going to take me some time to get used to the idea. We only met four months ago. This is a huge step for someone my age. We have a lot of details to work out and…."

"We'll talk soon, Leila. You know, everything always works out for the best. Just wait until Rudy gets home from the Slope."

Leila feels just a little guilty for not mentioning her argument with Rudy to Celeste. She intends to do everything she can to curtail his flying, even if it means firing him. There will probably be more arguments and rough times ahead. Rudy might reject Leila's interference. She resolves to stay determined in her efforts to keep him safe. Her mind is in a rush of thoughts, but when she notices Dom watching her with a smile on his face, she softens and a little flutter races through her heart.

As they pull up to Pete's Flying Service, Celeste says, "Here we are, Leila. Your car is in the hangar. Ana didn't want to leave it outside overnight. Do you want a ride to my apartment, Dom? Or are the two of you going to spend the rest of the day together?"

"What do you say, Leila? Can we do some hiking, or sightseeing or something? I will only be here for a week and don't want to waste all this daylight doing things I could do in Chicago. We haven't done Flattop yet. How about if we hike up there this afternoon, then we can have a celebratory dinner at that place where we met in February?"

"I'll check with Ana, Dom. I feel a little guilty making her work on her days off from her Slope job. But if she doesn't mind, I'm game. Let's make dinner reservations first, though. We'll need them since tourists are overrunning the town. It can get pretty busy around here at dinnertime."

"I'll bet," Dom says. "But probably most people forget to eat until really late. They're probably thinking it's still the middle of the day because of all the sunlight."

"That's true," Leila agrees.

"Okay, then. I'm off to work." Celeste buckles up and drives off.

Dom and Leila are left standing on the ramp. An awkward moment passes and then Dom wraps his arms around Leila. They stand there holding each other and Leila tilts her head up to meet Dom's lips. When she finally comes up for air, Dom says, "Is this for real? Did you really say yes? What have I done to deserve this?"

A customer opens the door to the FBO, bumps into them as he exits and they all stumble to keep their balance. "Oh, sorry!" he says and totters away.

"Let's go and ask her, Leila. Time's a wasting. I want to share the good news. I still can't believe you said yes."

"She said yes to what? And what do you want to ask me?" Ana asks as they walk in.

Dom and Leila look at each other as though to reassure themselves. "You tell her, Leila. I'm sure she would want to hear it from you."

"I know this is rather sudden, Ana, but Dom proposed to me last night, and I accepted. This is all so new to me. I don't quite know how to even talk about it."

"Well, I guess it's fine if that's what you want to do." Ana turns around to go back into the office.

"What's with her?" Dom says, starting in his usual loud voice and getting quieter as he notices Leila raising her finger to her lips.

Leila whispers, "I'll tell you all about it later, but let me go and smooth things over and ask her if she can watch the office for the day. I almost hate to ask her any favors at this point, but spending the day hiking with you is just too tempting. Why don't you go and get my car out of the hangar while I talk to her."

"All right, just don't be too long. I hate to let you out of my sight."

"You clown! I'll never figure out why I like you so much."

Dom walks around to the hanger door as Leila enters the back office with trepidation to face Ana. "Ana, I know this comes as a surprise to you. After all, you don't know Dom. I didn't mean to spring it on you like this. But aren't you happy for me?"

"How could you even think about marrying so soon after Daddy's death? You just met the guy and he's not even an Alaskan. I suppose this means you'll be moving to Chicago. Won't you miss Alaska? And don't you still miss Daddy?" Ana is almost in tears.

"I miss your father so much sometimes I can barely stand. My heart still hurts to think about him. But it's been over three years, Ana. I feel like Dom has brought me back to life. He makes me laugh. Your father would want me to be happy. He was the best husband in the whole world and nobody will ever replace him, but he's not here and he never will be again. I have to go on and start living again."

"Well, just don't expect me to be friends with him. You can do what you want, I guess," She walks out to the counter to greet a customer who had just walked in.

"Ana, don't..." Leila says, but Ana acts like she doesn't hear her.

Leila sits heavily on the sofa across from the desk. She feels ragged, having her emotions yanked from joy to frustration and anger. She leans back and closes her eyes, putting her hands to her temples to massage away the pain. The dark cloud of resignation begins to cover her and she does not hear Dom as he enters the room.

"It's okay, Leila. We can go now. Ana says she will watch the office for the day.

"What..."

"Don't worry. I worked it all out. Let's just leave."

They walk out the front door as Ana is busy talking to a customer and she gives them a brief wave.

"Do you want me to drive, Leila? It looks like you have a headache."

Leila nods and gets into the passenger seat. She is still distraught over Ana's reaction. "Why can't she let it go? Does she expect me to go on moping for the rest of my life? Oh, Dom, she was horrible. She said that she would never be your friend." She pauses to look over at Dom, and then questions him. "What did you ever say to her to get her to watch the office today? I can't imagine her wanting us to spend the day together."

"I have my ways with women," Dom says with a wink. "I even got her to work for you tomorrow. I had her eating out of my hand. I'll tell you all about it someday when we are safely married."

Leila looks at his grinning face and smiles. The cloud of depression lifts and she says, trying to sound exasperated, "I don't know how you do it, Dom, but I find your stupid joking really funny."

"Just point out the way to Flattop, Ma'am, I'm at your service. We already have our hiking clothes on, no need to go home and change. But maybe we could stop and get some sandwiches to eat when we reach the top. Where was that place on the Old Seward Highway you liked so much?"

"There's an even better new place on Northern Lights. It's only a little out of the way. They make the best espresso in town."

"I even know how to find my way to Northern Lights," Dom says. He puts the car in reverse and it jerks backwards as he releases the clutch.

"I guess I should have asked, but have you ever driven a standard transmission before? You're lucky you didn't hit any planes pulling it out of the hangar."

"Luckily, there were none to hit. And yes, of course, I have driven a stick shift. I wasn't born yesterday, you know."

Their banter continues as they drive to the coffee shop. Leila has forgotten about her encounter with Ana. They purchase sandwiches on focaccia bread and lattes to go, and head toward the mountains. The afternoon sun shining on them gives them a golden yellow glow. It makes the inlet appear to be a shimmering blue.

"Look at that! It's the first time I've seen the inlet look blue. Usually it's a steely grey; must be an optical illusion," Leila says.

"Must be my presence, Leila. It's like the song, *Till There Was You*. Dom breaks into song, modifying the words to fit the situation: There was blue on the inlet, but I never saw it shining, no I never saw it at all, 'til there was you."

"What am I going to do with you, Dom?"

"Just take me as I am, Leila. I'm too old to change, anyway."

On reaching the parking lot at the trailhead, Dom and Leila grab their daypacks and take off up the trail. They are out of the trees within minutes and turn to admire the overview of Anchorage.

"We've got to keep moving, Dom. I'm starving and we said we wouldn't eat until we got to the top."

"All right, see if you can keep up with me."

Even though Dom does not exercise regularly, his wiry frame is suited to hiking. He and Leila trot along the trail without stopping until they come to the steep rocky face where they will have to pick their way through the huge boulders.

Leila turns around as they pause to catch their breath. "You're not afraid of heights, are you?"

"Ha, this is child's play. Celeste tells me that four year old kids have made it to the top."

"You're well beyond four years old, and you didn't answer my question. Are you afraid of heights?"

"Now that you mention it, maybe just a little. But with you to hold my hand it should be okay."

"There will be no hand holding here. You have to make it on your own. Just keep your eyes on the terrain in front of you. Don't look down. We'll have plenty of time to admire the view when we get to the top. Flattop is aptly named. The top is perfectly flat and as big as three or four football fields."

"I can't wait. Let's get moving."

There is a light breeze, which keeps them cool during the climb, but on reaching the top, Leila shivers from the sudden increase in wind. A small outcropping of rocks is about fifty yards away and Leila sprints towards it, trying to find a protected spot out of the wind. They find a place to sit and Leila pulls her windbreaker out of her pack and puts it on. Sitting close together to stay warm, they wolf down their sandwiches. The coffee they had poured into insulated cups is still warm. The smell is intoxicating as they open the lids.

"Why did I never know about this before, Leila? This must be heaven."

"If you like this, you're going to love Bird Ridge. Maybe we'll climb that tomorrow. Mid-week we should have the whole place to ourselves. Flattop gets a lot of traffic because it's so easy and so close to town."

"Now that's what I call heaven: a wilderness peak, a beautiful woman and the place all to ourselves. I can feel myself getting aroused already."

"Dom, you are impossible," Leila shivers. "Now would you please look the other way while I change my shirt? I got a little sweaty during the climb and if I don't get out of these damp clothes, I'll never warm up on the way down."

"I know a better way to warm you up."

"Dom, please…"

The descent is slower than the climb. Dom hangs on to every rock as he picks his way down the trail. By the time they get back to the parking area, they have only a half hour before their dinner reservations. They race down O'Malley Road and make it the restaurant a couple of minutes late, with no time to change their clothes. Luckily, there is no dress code at Simon and Seafort's. The mealtime seems to fly by as Dom and Leila talk and joke. Leila doesn't remember what she ate, only that it was delicious. She drops Dom off at Celeste's apartment and hurries home to shower.

"Let's meet at seven a.m. at the City Market for breakfast. You can just walk there from Celeste's. Then we'll get an early start. I want to spend a bit of time at the top of Bird Ridge so we can watch the eagles."

"As long as my legs don't give out! You gave me quite a workout today."

"You'll love it, Dom. You won't even notice your legs you'll be so occupied with the scenery. Bird Ridge is the one place in Alaska where I feel most alive. I don't know what it is, but something about the place energizes me. I never thought about it until today, but I haven't been up there since Pete died. It might have been healing for me to go and reconnect with nature."

"We'll do it together, tomorrow," Dom says. "It must be right, sort of like a new beginning for us both."

"Right. You're always right about such things. See you tomorrow morning."

"Another beautiful day!" Dom says, as he sees Leila walk in to the City Market.

"How did we get so lucky?"

They order warm scones and lattes to eat on the way and then race down the Seward Highway towards Bird Ridge. Leila had packed some snacks and drinks, so when they get to the trailhead, she grabs her small daypack and they're off. The first two hundred yards are paved with a very slight incline and Dom scoffs at the undemanding trail.

"I thought you said it was a challenging climb," he says. "My grandmother could do this—in her wheelchair."

"Just wait. This is only the beginning."

Sure enough, the pavement ends within eight hundred yards, near the outdoor bathroom facilities, and the trail turns to head directly up the hill. It winds through the trees and rocks getting steeper and steeper as they climb. Leila does not let up. Her strong legs feel good and her footing is sure. In about twenty minutes they are in the open, above most of the trees and she stops to survey the scene before them. Dom, gasping for breath, catches up to her complaining, as he gets within earshot, "What are you trying to do, kill me?" Then he turns to see what Leila is looking at. "Wow! That is spectacular. Look at the inlet. It's not quite blue like it was yesterday, but, man, what a view!"

"I told you you'd like it. Just wait until we get to the top."

"If I don't have a heart attack first."

They take a sip of water and Leila heads up the trail again. She slows her pace a little so they can talk. If Dom stops talking for more than a few seconds, she slows even more, sensing that he must be out of breath. He gets his second wind and, with the slower pace, starts to exclaim continuously about the scenery. Fields of wild lupine overwhelm the senses and patches of forget-me-nots along with small white and yellow flowers dot either side of the trail. Before long they reach a rock face and have to slow down, carefully choosing the best route. They see the trail winding along the ridge ahead of them.

"How much farther? Are we almost at the top?" Dom asks.

"We're about half way now. But it gets easier from this point. It levels out a little."

"Well, thank God for small favors."

Leila continues to walk, humming to herself. She spots a patch of chocolate lilies and can't resist pulling a trick on Dom. "Oh, Dom, look, those are chocolate lilies. You have *got to* smell them. They have the most exquisite aroma."

Dom stops and bends down to sniff the small brown flowers. He puts his nose close to the blossom and takes a deep whiff. "Ugh! That smells like shit," he says. "What in the heck...?"

Leila is laughing, "Pete tricked me with that once and I've always wanted to find somebody who didn't know what a terrible odor they had. I got you—for once."

"I never knew that a flower could smell so bad."

"I guess that's what attracts the flies. But, hey, we're almost to the top, Dom. Let's keep going. I am so glad that we haven't seen anybody since that couple we saw heading down. Maybe we will have the place to ourselves."

"Does that mean we can play a little hanky panky?"

"Is that all you ever think of?

"Only when I'm with you."

The ridge is all that it promised to be. Walking along it, Dom can see Bird Creek on one side and Indian Valley on the other. It is wide enough so there is no sense of danger. "Leila, I know what you mean about this place being energizing. I have not felt this alive in years. We should get married up here. I love it."

"We'll see. We'll see."

Leila prepares a picnic spot and they snack on their fruit and nuts and bars, taking time to enjoy every bite. Dom is quiet and Leila is deep in thought. She wishes Pete were here. He had been the first to show her this ridge and they had made love in a secluded area behind a patch of shrubs. She smiles, remembering his tenderness, then notices Dom looking at her with a wistful look on his face.

"I know I'm not him, Leila. But I do love you."

"What do you mean?"

"I recognize that look. I've been there myself, Leila. We can never replace our first loves. I know that. But look at what we have now. I found you and God knows that we are good for each other."

He inches over to where she sits and puts his arms around her. He kisses her forehead, then her nose, her closed eyes, her tear dampened cheeks and finally her lips.

"Oh, Dom. Thank you for being here. Thank you for being you."

After spending three hours exploring the ridge and watching bald eagles soar, Leila says, "We better start down. It's gonna be a lot harder than you think."

"Nah…"

"Really. It's hard on your quads going down. In fact, tomorrow your legs are going to be pretty sore."

"No, I never get sore."

"Just wait."

The trip down is punctuated with exclamations from both of them about the beauty of the place. Both are reluctant to leave and as they near the bottom they look for excuses to linger. Leila picks flowers for a bouquet and Dom collects samples of rocks. At last when they reach tree level, they hurry back to the car.

They are quiet during the drive back to Anchorage. Leila reaches over and holds Dom's hand.

"Let's stop at the airport to check on Ana," Leila says.

"Okay…then what's on tap for tonight, another romantic dinner?"

"We'll see."

As they open the door to Pete's Flying Service, Ana is sobbing. She rushes up to embrace Leila. Between sobs she blurts out, "They don't know where he is, Mama. Rudy is missing! He never checked in at his last reporting point in Bettles. What are we going to do?" She buries her head in Leila's shoulder. "I just know he's dead."

Chapter Twenty-three

Nikki Faces Gerik and Daphne

Nikki's heart is pounding. Her anger bubbles up and takes over. Her hands clench and release, clench and release. She opens her fists and sees deep red indentations on her palms from her fingernails. They hurt. Trying to let go of her tension, she rests her hands, palms up, on her lap. As she does, her arms relax, then her shoulders. *Take a deep breath, Nikki.* She breathes in through her nose and exhales through pursed lips.

A gentle voice sounds in her mind. "Go to that safe place, Elsa, that place where no one can hurt you because you know how special you are."

Now where did that come from? Nikki wonders. The voice was so real, so compelling she knows that someone, somewhere in her past had said it to her. Nikki allows her mind to wander. She remembers a sunny summer day with balloons and party decorations. She remembers crying and feeling left out because she had no presents. She remembers grabbing for a balloon and having it slip from her hands to float off in the wind. She feels the disappointment and sadness. She feels the urge to cry. Her feelings now are as overwhelming as they were that day. She remembers now. It was her sister Leila's birthday party. Then she remembers a comforting arm around her shoulders—a soothing hand stroking her hair. It was Leila's arm: Leila's voice. She was only two years older than Elsa, but she always seemed so much wiser and so much more mature.

Nikki doesn't remember the exact words, but the feeling of being special in spite of the circumstances was a lesson that carried her through many disappointments. When had she forgotten it?

I've got to take care of myself, and the kids. They don't need to know about this. We will just have to go on without him. There is no way we can continue to live in the same house. I must have been living in a dream world, though. How did I not see this before? Or maybe I did and chose to ignore it. I actually feel sorry for them both: Sneaking around, lying, and giving in to their own wants and desires with no thoughts of how it will effect others. How weak! How despicable! I know this has nothing to do with my worthiness or me. Gerik would have cheated on even the most perfect wife. I know that. I've known that all along. But I thought I needed him in order to be whole. I am learning that I am a whole person all by myself. But, oh, God, it hurts. It really hurts. How could they both betray me?

Nikki calms down, has her thoughts controlled and comes up with a workable plan by the time Gerik and Daphne slink down the stairs. She opens her mouth to begin. But Daphne rushes up to her, kneels at her feet and wraps her arms around Nikki's legs. She puts her head on Nikki's lap. She is sobbing.

"Oh, Elsa—Nikki please forgive me! I couldn't help myself. I love him, Nikki, but I love you, too. What can I do to make it up to you?"

Nikki is repulsed. "Well, you can begin by getting up and acting like a decent human being for once. Sit over there and listen. I don't need to hear any more excuses or fake contrition. It makes me sick just to look at you."

"Oh, Nikki, how could you say that after all we've been through?"

"Been through? How much of it has been real? Or has it all been an act so you could get your hands on my husband?" Her voice is louder now and less controlled.

Gerik sits with his feet flat on the floor and his hands on the armrests as though he is about to get up. A movement in the hallway causes him to turn and look. He gasps. Nikki looks up to see Danny leaning against the doorjamb with his hands stuffed in the front pockets of his jeans.

"How long have you been there?" she asks.

"Long enough."

"Now, honey, it's not like it looks. We can explain." Nikki sounds like she is trying to placate a child.

"I'm not a kid anymore, Ma. You don't have to sugarcoat things for me. In fact, I've known about their affair for quite a while. I wanted to tell you, but Dad sort of blackmailed me. He said if I told you he'd take my car away and stop giving me money for college."

"What are you saying? Gerik is that true?"

"Well, I…"

Daphne forces her way into the conversation. "Don't tell her anything, Gerik. She will use it against you."

Danny turns to go up the stairs to his room. "I don't need to listen to this crap. Why don't you grow up for crying out loud? I'm glad I'm going off to school next week. I've got to get out of this sicko atmosphere. All the lying and sneaking around makes me feel like a cheat. I don't want to be a cover-up anymore."

Nikki is desperate to know more from Danny, but he stomps up the stairs and slams the door to his room. She turns towards Gerik, glaring, and says, "So, how long has it been going on? Or did it ever stop?"

Daphne starts to say something, but Nikki holds a hand up towards her and says, "This is between my husband and me. You stay out of it for once and if you can't shut up, you can leave."

Daphne gets up and stands next to Gerik's chair. She puts her hand on the back of his neck and Gerik leans into it, closing his eyes, clearly taking pleasure in the caress.

"Get your hands off my husband! I don't need to see this right now. You can have him soon enough, but it will be under my conditions."

Daphne slinks back to the loveseat.

"Come on, El—Nikki, let's be reasonable," Gerik pleads.

"Reasonable! Reasonable! Is that what you think you've been? Reasonable? It's bad enough to cheat on your wife, but to coerce your son into going along with it and keeping his mouth shut—that is unconscionable. I can't believe any of this. I suppose you even had Emma standing guard while you did your thing. How disgusting!"

"No, it wasn't like that. We were always tactful."

"Oh, that's great, just great. I'm glad you were at least tactful. That makes it so much better." The sarcastic edge in Nikki's voice stops both Gerik and Daphne from saying anymore.

They sit for several minutes glaring at each other. Daphne sits on the edge of the grey loveseat. Nikki stares off towards the back yard through the dining room and notices all of the carefully placed artwork. She admires the polished bamboo floors; their honey coloring compliments the moss green area rug and upholstered chairs around the table. Her award-winning quilt hangs on one wall of the dining room. All the coordinated furnishings and the touches she so lovingly added to make their house a home, a showplace of good taste, have been wasted effort.

You can't make a home with things no matter how beautiful they are. I won't give them up, though. Gerik will have to pay.

Aloud she says, "It doesn't matter how long you've been screwing. The fact is, you've done it. I can make this real easy on you, Gerik, or we can drag everything out into the open. It's your choice. But you really should have thought about your career before you started messing around."

"What do you mean, easy?" Gerik asks.

"I want the house. You continue to pay the mortgage for another year until my business can support it. You can have the summerhouse on the lake. I'll need my car. And a substantial monthly allowance...or if you would rather make it a lump sum and be free of me, we can work out those details. And of course, you would still pay for the kids' college educations."

"Whoa, wait a minute. What are you talking about? I can't afford that."

"What? A big executive like you can't afford to keep his ex-wife in style? Do you want people to think you're cheap? The V.P. of Ellis Manufacturing letting his children live in a dump? Think, Gerik. If we have to go to court, everyone will know the details of your affair and that you blackmailed your own son into silence. How would that look? Give me what I want and I'll tell people we simply had irreconcilable differences and that we both need to move on."

"I need time to think," Gerik says, glancing at Daphne.

"You'll have to think somewhere else. I can barely stand the thought of even being in the same room with you much longer. Why don't you get some things together..."

A ringing telephone interrupts Nikki.

"Aren't you going to get that?" Daphne asks.

"Danny will get it upstairs. Now as I was saying..."

"Hey, Mom, it's Aunt Leila. She sounds pretty stressed. Can you talk to her?"

"Ask her what it's about and tell her I'll call her back. I'm in the middle of something."

"Are you sure you can't talk now?"

"Danny! Just do it!"

"Okay."

Nikki turns back to Gerik who is whispering something into Daphne's ear.

"Would the two of you at least have the common courtesy to continue your lovemaking elsewhere? I've had about all I can take in one day. And you never did tell me how long this has been going on. We better get everything out in the open. I don't want any more surprises."

Gerik begins, "Well, actually it has been since..."

"Gerik!" Daphne pleads. "Please don't! What good would it do? Everything is in the past. Let's just go on from here."

"You'd like that, wouldn't you? You'd like to continue the cover-up and act as though we've been friends all along. Well, you can't have it both ways, Daphne. This is one time you are not going to get everything you want."

Nikki turns back to Gerik, raising her eyebrows, "Well."

"I don't need to tell you anything more. You'll get what you want in the end. I'll just say, it's been a while—since..."

"Gerik, honey, don't! Please don't give her any details. You've been a lifesaver to me. I don't want to see you hurt by her."

Daphne turns to Nikki, eyes blazing, "You never appreciated him like I do. You have never loved him like I do. Just because you got pregnant and he married you out of a sense of honor doesn't mean that he ever loved you. I make him

247

a real man. You just want an obedient robot to make your house look nice."

"Shut up, Daphne. That's enough. Now, get out!" Nikki yells as she gets to her feet. She moves towards Daphne looking as though she is ready to physically throw her out.

Daphne gets up from the loveseat seductively thrusting a hip forward while she looks at Nikki with a contemptuous sneer. "We'll see who wins this one." She stands there challenging Nikki with a defiant look.

"Nobody wins in this kind of situation, Daphne. Can't you see that? Or are you too obsessed with Gerik to have any sense at all?"

Nikki looks like she is ready to throw up. She says forcefully—slowly—so quietly they have to strain to hear her, "Get out of my sight before I throw you out myself."

Chapter Twenty-four

Rudy is Missing

Ana, wrapped in Leila's arms, sobs. "What'll we do, Mama?"

Leila's mind is numb as she tries to remember what Rudy's plans were. Ana's weight against her causes her knees to buckle and she falls against the desk. She leans on it to support herself and her daughter. *It seems like weeks ago when I left him in Deadhorse.*

She tries to say that everything will be all right, but the words refuse to open her mouth. She smoothes Ana's hair and feels herself begin to give in to the sobs rocking Ana's body. She rubs her eyes to squelch the rising tears.

Ana is saying over and over again, "What will we do? Mama, what will we do?"

Dom, at Leila's elbow, puts his arms around both of them. "Come on, girls, let's sit down and figure this out. Let's get all the details first before we jump to conclusions. When did Flight Service call, Ana?"

Ana, her shoulders still heaving, says, "About an hour ago, around four o'clock, I guess."

"Okay, what exactly did they say?" Dom ushers them to the sofa.

"They asked if Otter N423PS had landed and forgotten to close their flight plan. I was too flustered to say anything. My mind was racing a mile a minute. Then it froze. I told them I didn't know anything about their flight plan or when they were due. They told me to let them know if we heard anything from the pilot."

"Did they tell you when they had left Deadhorse?" Dom asks.

"He only said that they had never reported in at Bettles and were now an hour overdue on their flight to Lake Hood Strip."

"How long would it take them to get here from Deadhorse, Leila?"

"Depending on the route, it could take four or five hours. The Otter is a slow airplane. I don't know if the scientists wanted to stop anywhere or get aerial pictures of anything in particular, but Rudy wouldn't plan a landing somewhere en route without allowing for it in his flight plan time. So they must have been coming directly back. Oh, I wish he had a satellite phone with him. I could kick myself for not paying attention to that detail."

"Now, don't go blaming anyone. I'm sure everything will be fine." Dom suddenly remembers Celeste and asks Ana, "Have you called Celeste? Maybe Rudy landed somewhere and called her to let her know where he is."

"He wouldn't do that without calling us, too. But, no, I haven't called her. To tell you the truth, I forgot all about her."

"We'd better call her, Ana. And if she doesn't answer, leave a message or text her to call us," Leila says, "She is his fiancée. She should be informed. And what about Nat, have you let her know that Rudy is missing?"

"No, but what would she care anyway. She's probably off somewhere with her druggie friends."

"Don't say that, Ana. She would want to know. She is his sister."

Dom says, "I'll talk to Celeste, Leila. In fact, why don't we all go over to her house? I'll check to see if she's home and then we can all tell her in person. And maybe, by then, we will have word from Rudy. You can transfer your calls to your cell phone, can't you?"

"Yes," Leila responds.

"Then we can stop on the way and get a pizza from Milano's. No point in going hungry while we wait."

Leila gives him a dirty look. "Is that all you ever think about, Dom? How can you even think of eating at a time like this?"

Ana, her head buried in her hands, cries quietly. "I can't take it. I've got to know what happened. You go along to Celeste's. I don't think I can handle telling her about this. And I certainly don't want to eat."

"But we should be together, Ana. I'm sure everything will turn out just fine. He probably landed somewhere due to weather and is waiting it out. He'll find some way to contact someone. You know Rudy. He is very resourceful."

"But that's just it, Mama; he would already have told someone where he is if he could."

The phone rings and they all jump and then look at each other as though they are paralyzed. No one reaches for the phone until the fifth ring. Finally Dom gets up and answers, "Pete's Flying Service. Yes. Yes...No. A family friend. Yes, okay, just a moment." He covers the receiver with his hand and whispers to Leila, "It's Flight Service. They want to talk to you, Leila."

Leila rises from the sofa and squares her shoulders. Her determination is obvious in the set of her jaw as she takes the phone from Dom. "This is Leila Pletnikof." She pauses to listen, then, "Yes, certainly, that would be good." Another pause and then, "No, I can't tell you about his route of flight. That would have been dependent on the people who chartered. Maybe they have some additional information. Yes, that's right. That sounds right. Yes. It was Western Washington University in Bellingham. Thank you so much." Leila hangs up the phone and sighs. "They've initiated a search. The Rescue Coordination Center at Elmendorf has been notified and the Civil Air Patrol will begin searching within hours. Thank God for all the daylight at this time of year."

Dom jumps into action. "Well, we may as well get started then. Ana, why don't you call and order a couple of pizzas and I'll call Celeste and let her know we're on our way to her house. Leila, go and wash your face."

"Of all the nerve!" Leila is about to make a smart remark but then laughs as she catches sight of herself in the small mirror next to the door. She notices her mascara streaked cheeks. "I look like a raccoon."

Ana looks over at her and starts to laugh, too. Their emotional state is fragile and Dom recognizes their need to let things out. If he can get them to laugh, it might help them cope with the situation, not that it is funny. It might be dreadfully serious, but they are powerless to do anything about it right now. They will need strength and clear thinking to handle whatever comes.

They pile into Leila's car and head towards Milano's. Leila dials Natalia's number and when she hears the answering machine, leaves a quick message. "Nat please call me or Ana as soon as you can." *I don't know what I'm going to do with that girl. Ever since she started hanging around with that gang she hasn't been herself. But I can't think about it now. We've got to find out what happened to Rudy.*

The pizzas are ready when they get to the restaurant, so they rush to Celeste's apartment with the hot boxes. "Here we are, kiddo," Dom says when Celeste opens the door.

"What's the occasion, Uncle Dom?" Celeste tilts her head, questioning.

"Let's get this served up and I'll tell you."

Celeste looks at Ana's red eyes and Leila's worried expression. "Something's happened to Rudy, hasn't it?" Her voice is frantic. "That's why you're all here. I just know it!" She looks at Ana again. "Ana, you've never been in my apartment before. Tell me, what has happened? Is Rudy okay?"

Leila reaches out and takes Celeste's hands in hers, looking at her with sad eyes.

Celeste pulls her hands away and runs her fingers through her dark hair. "What's going on, Leila? Has Rudy been in an accident? I've got to know."

"We don't know either. We just came to tell you that Rudy is overdue on his flight plan. He's already over three hours late. We haven't heard from him and they have begun a search. I'm sure he's just fine. I have to believe that. But it is hard not knowing."

"Well, let's do something." Celeste is unable to contain her nervousness. "Can't we go down to the Civil Air Patrol and find out what they know?"

"Flight Service said that the Rescue Coordination Center (RCC) at Elmendorf has begun a search. They will let us know if anything turns up. You know that airline pilots monitor the emergency frequency and if the Emergency Locator Transmitter (ELT) was activated, they would be able to tell where it is. Of course, Rudy would know that he could

253

contact airline traffic on a center frequency. Maybe he has already tried that."

"But we can't just sit here!" Celeste reaches for her purse and car keys and walks to the open door.

Leila reaches out to hold Celeste's arm. "I know you're concerned, Celeste, but right now we have no choice. Let's just let the professionals do their job. I'm sure we will hear something soon."

"But I feel so helpless."

"I know. I do, too. But, really, right now I'm starving. Dom and I climbed Bird Ridge today and have had only light snacks since breakfast. Doesn't that seem to be a long time ago, Dom?"

"It sure does, but what a trip it was! We want to get married up there, Celeste. The place is awesome. Have you ever seen it?"

"Of course, Rudy and I have done the race to the top. Although that doesn't give you much time to enjoy the scenery. But when we practice for the race, we usually take a little time at the top to look around. It is a special place." She pauses and turns serious. "What could have happened to him, Leila? I know Rudy can be impetuous, but he is serious about flying and is the most cautious pilot I know. Do you think he ran into bad weather?"

Leila frowns. "It did look threatening over the Brooks Range when we flew over yesterday, but I'm sure he wouldn't have taken off in marginal weather. You know the Otter was not current for instrument flight so he would have waited for good VFR. I did check the hourly reports at Deadhorse and Bettles and along his planned route of flight and it looked all right this morning. Maybe he just set it down somewhere to wait it out. I don't know. You're the pilot, Celeste. What would you do if you ran into weather and couldn't climb over it?"

"I'd turn around. Hey, maybe he went back to Deadhorse." Celeste looks hopeful.

"No, they would have that information. There is a Flight Service Station at Deadhorse. And we really don't know if weather was a problem. Maybe he had mechanical issues, although that's not very likely. Not with our maintenance."

"I just can't stand sitting around. Isn't there anything we can do?"

"We could donate some of our airplanes and pilots to add to the Civil Air Patrol Search. I'll get started on coordinating that first thing in the morning."

"You mean he'll have to spend the night out in the wilderness, with injuries or in a precarious position?" Celeste cries, her voice rising. "Can't we take off now?"

"Look, it will be dark here in a couple of hours and even though it really doesn't get dark above the Arctic Circle at this time of year, everybody is exhausted. Ten p.m. is no time to begin a search. Why don't we try to get some sleep after we eat and start out first thing in the morning, if we haven't heard anything by then?"

"How could I sleep, knowing that Rudy is missing?" Celeste says.

They exhaust all possibilities of action before Leila says, "I'm going home to get some sleep. I want to be fresh for tomorrow. All I can do at this point is to pray. Oh, I just thought of this, but maybe I could call the prayer chain at St. Nicholas. They have been known to work miracles."

"Good idea, Leila," Dom says. "Maria always believed in the power of prayer; and, although it didn't do her much good, she often told me of answers that seemed miraculous. It couldn't hurt."

Ana, who has been quiet during the entire conversation, speaks up, "Little good it would do. It's all a waste of time. I've asked God for years for Nat to be free of her drug addiction and there has been no change in her behavior."

"Did you give God a time limit?"

"Well, I..."

"I'm afraid Nat has made her own choices in that matter. No one is forcing her, Ana." Leila, realizing her fatigue, feels herself heading down that slippery slope of despair. But she takes a deep breath and closes her eyes. *No, I won't go there. I have to believe he will be okay For Ana's sake, for Celeste's. They need me to be strong.*

Ana changes the subject. "Have you called Aunt Elsa, Mom?"

"I tried, but Danny said she was busy. I don't know why I try. She doesn't care."

"Oh, but she does."

Dom adds, "Why don't we try again when we know something for sure?"

"Yeah, fine."

"How about driving us back to the hangar so we can pick up Ana's car?"

"Sure, anything you need."

They drive in silence to the airport. Leila's eyes keep closing and she's glad she didn't offer to drive. They get out at the hangar and Dom looks like he is not sure what to do. He hangs back, waiting for directions.

"Dom, why don't you take my car back to Celeste's? We'll meet back here at six o'clock. I'll call a few of our pilots to let them know there's a possibility of a search. And if I hear anything at all, I will be sure to call Celeste. Take good care of her, Dom. She needs you."

"I love you, Leila," Dom says, and then, not knowing what else to say, he hesitates before getting into the car, bumping his head on the doorframe as he does.

None of them get much sleep. As Leila begins to drift off, her dream from a few nights ago enters her thoughts. Her body jerks remembering the terror she felt. She tries to recollect the outcome of the dream, but it eludes her. She struggles to recall all of the details. Maybe there would be some clue that would tell them what happened to Rudy. But it is no good. The details are fuzzy and all she can think of are the feelings of utter hopelessness and the cold fear that had gripped her. She gets out of bed and goes to check on Ana.

Ana is lying on her back, eyes wide open, staring at the ceiling. Her pillow is wet and her blankets are rumpled at the foot of her bed. "Oh, Mama," she says when she sees Leila. "What will we do if he's hurt, or...? How can we stand this? I hate airplanes. I hate this whole place. I hate the mountains. I hate..."

"Shush," Leila says as she sits next to Ana on the bed. "Shush, now. We have to have hope. We don't know that anything bad has happened. Let's just believe things will turn out all right. There could be many explanations as to why he is late." She starts to sing a lullaby she had sung to the children when they were young. "Hush little baby, don't you cry..." Her voice gets quieter and quieter as she tries to control her emotions. Ana has calmed down and Leila lies down next to her. She moves lightly, cautiously, so as not to disturb her; then snuggles close and lies very still, an arm across Ana's chest. She can feel her own heart pounding and wills it to be quiet. She holds herself stiffly, quashing the desire to break into sobs. Tears stream down her face and she whispers, barely audible, "Please, God, let him live."

In what seems to be only minutes later, Leila hears Ana getting out of bed. "What time is it?" she asks.

"It's almost five o'clock. We must have slept. I didn't hear the phone at all, did you?"

"Oh, no, I left my cell phone in my bedroom. I wouldn't have heard it in here," Leila jumps out of bed.

She rushes to her bedroom and notices that she missed two calls. One of them is from Natalia—she will deal with that later. The other is an 800 number, probably Flight Service or the RCC. They called at three-thirty a.m. She calls the number back and wades through an improbably long menu of choices. She is beginning to feel panicky and says aloud, "Why couldn't they have called from a regular phone number? How will I ever get through to an actual person?" She is about to give up when an incoming call interrupts. She answers, "Leila Pletnikof. Yes, yes, that's right. Oh, thank God! Ana, get in here. No, no, I was just telling my daughter to come here. I'm sorry I missed that last part." There is a short pause and then, "Oh, no!"

Leila listens for a long time and then remembers to put the phone on speaker so Ana can hear, too. They both hear the voice saying, "We are sending a helicopter from Deadhorse to the site and will not know anything for sure until they get there. They just left Deadhorse and we should hear something within the hour. I will call as soon as we have any details."

"Thank you so much," Leila says. "We will be standing by the phone." She grabs Ana and twirls her around. "They found him, Ana, they found him!" They are laughing and staggering and bump into the bed, falling on top of it. "Oh, Ana, I just know he's going to be okay."

"What did they say before you put it on speaker?"

"They said that an airline pilot flying overhead heard an ELT and reported it. They were able to pinpoint the position from a satellite. They had not heard any transmissions from the downed aircraft, but that did not necessarily indicate a negative situation." The words tumble out of Leila in a rush.

"But, Mama, if the ELT went off, it must mean they crashed."

"Rudy could have activated it himself, Ana. There is an on/off switch. And it is possible he is in a valley with limited line of sight communications. Oh, my gosh! I've got to call Celeste, and then let's get dressed and go down to the office."

Leila calls Celeste's number and she answers on the first ring. "Well?" she asks.

"They've found him, Celeste. They can't say anything for sure yet, but knowing how strong the Otter is, I know that even if he had to land on the tundra, everything will be okay. We're going down to the office to await their call. They said a helicopter should be at the site within an hour. We'll meet you there."

Possibilities of dire outcomes push at Leila's consciousness. She does not allow them to sway her from thinking positive thoughts. She superstitiously believes that if she thinks something bad it will turn out to be true. She refuses to listen to Ana or Celeste's negative suggestions. She makes a pot of strong coffee and tries to busy herself as they wait for the phone to ring. Then, even though they are expecting it, the ringing phone makes them all jump.

Heart pounding, Leila grabs it. "Pete's Flying Service. Yes, this is Leila Pletnikof." Her face turns white and her knees begin to buckle. Dom, who is standing beside her, grasps her around the waist before she falls and backs her up to a chair, helping her to sit down. She stares off into space and the phone drops from her hand. Memories of Pete's death overwhelm her and her resolve to stay strong and positive loses out.

Dom picks up the phone from Leila's lap and says, "Would you repeat that, please? Wow! What a miracle! Right. Yes. I'll tell them. How long did you say? Fine. Thank you very much. We'll be there. Yes, thank you."

Dom hangs up and faces Celeste and Ana. He swallows and pauses to look out the window as though to gather his thoughts. The silence in the room pushes at them and weighs them down. Everything seems to be happening in slow motion.

Dom clears his throat and starts speaking so quietly they all strain forward to catch his words.

"For God's sake, Dom, speak up! What is it?" Ana yells.

He starts again, "The pilot of a pipeline patrol helicopter found the aircraft on a hillside at the northern edge of the Brooks Range. All five souls aboard survived although two are in critical condition."

"Well, what about Rudy? Is he okay?" Celeste asks.

"They didn't give the names of the ones with critical injuries. They did say the other three had only minor injuries and were able to provide some details about the crash."

Dom turns to Leila and kneels at her feet. "Leila, honey, snap out of it. He's alive. He'll make it. I know he will. Please, don't lose hope now. He's going to be okay."

Leila turns toward Dom as if in a daze, blinks and then leans over to embrace him. Dom pulls her to her feet and they stand together in an embrace. Taking a deep breath Leila says, "If you say so, Dom, if you say so."

He glances at Ana. "They said the medevac plane would be here by seven-thirty."

Celeste stands. "Well, let's get going."

Dom continues without noticing Celeste. "Apparently a medevac crew was in the area for training. Isn't that some miracle? They went along with the helicopter to stabilize the injured at the accident site and are returning to Deadhorse to meet the Learjet."

"Whose jet is that?" Celeste asks.

"He said the North Slope Borough sent their jet over to Deadhorse from Barrow. They'll transfer the patients when the helicopter gets there. So let's head down to the hospital." Dom is all business. He looks at Leila who is still staring off into space. "Come on, Leila. Get a grip."

Leila shakes her head, sighs noisily and clenches her teeth. *No! I can't break down again. They all need me now. I've got to face this head on. No matter what happens, denial won't solve anything.* In a moment she regains her composure. Her thoughts, still whirling, begin to coalesce into an orderly plan. She starts giving orders. "It's just a little after six, so we have over an hour to get to the hospital. Celeste, I know you don't feel like eating, but a little comfort food at a time like this is crucial. You pick up something to bring to the hospital. Ana, you go and find Nat and bring her with you to Prov."

"But..." Ana begins.

"No, buts, just find her and drag her if you must. You know her hangouts. And she did try to call me last night. So maybe she is sober. Tell her I need her there. And you, Dom, come and give me another hug. I need my own type of comfort food right now."

They embrace as Ana and Celeste gather their things and slip out the door. Dom kisses Leila and she hangs on to him as though he is a life raft. They stand together for several moments gaining strength from each other.

"I'm so glad I'm here, Leila. I'll do anything for you; you know that, don't you?"

"Yes, I'm sure God sent you to me. I don't deserve it. But, oh, speaking of God, I've got to call that prayer line. I have a feeling we are going to need all the prayers we can get."

Chapter Twenty-five

Nikki Kicks Gerik Out

Danny bounds down the stairs, rushing up to Nikki, ignoring both Gerik and Daphne, "Mom, Aunt Leila called. Rudy is missing and may have been in an accident. I've got to go to Alaska."

Nikki is caught off guard. She can't quite understand what significance this has to her. She shakes her head as though to clear her thoughts. "What are you saying, Danny?"

"It's Rudy, Mom. They don't know where he is. He might be injured or... I told Aunt Leila I was coming. I told her to hang on, that I would be there as soon as I could."

Danny starts to cry and Nikki puts her arms around him, forgetting for a moment about Gerik and Daphne. Danny is crying. That's all she can comprehend right now.

"Can you call her, please?" Danny, between sobs, pleads with his eyes. "I think she needs to hear your voice."

"I haven't talked to her in years, why would I..."She looks at Danny, "Okay, I'll call. But...what's this about you going to Alaska? You have to start school next week. They expect you to make the practice schedule if you are going to qualify and keep your athletic scholarship. You can't go to Alaska now, no matter what is going on up there."

"But, Ma, Rudy and Aunt Leila need me. Rudy's like my older brother. Actually better than that, he's like my best friend. What would I do if he was hurt? I've gotta go."

"Let me call Leila and find out what's going on before we decide what you're going to do."

"I'm going, no matter what. You can't stop me." Danny storms out of the room, slamming his right fist into his left palm as though punching someone.

"Now look what you've done," Gerik says to Nikki as she walks towards the kitchen.

She turns, furious, exasperated by the whole situation. Her world is being torn apart through no fault of her own and now her adulterous, two-timing husband has the nerve to criticize her.

"Me! Look at what *I've* done? Shouldn't it be the other way around?"

She pauses for effect, not expecting an answer. "I'm going in to the kitchen to call my sister and if your bags are not packed by the time I'm done, I will personally come and pack them. I want you out of here. You can go and stay with that slut for all I care. I just don't want you here."

"Come on, Nikki. You know I can't pack in less than ten minutes."

"Just take what you need for a day or two. You can come back and get the rest of your stuff later."

Gerik mumbles under his breath to Daphne who is still standing near the front door, "I always knew she was unreasonable, just like you told me. But, look, babe, I'll be there as soon as I can. We'll make up for lost time."

Nikki ignores them and stomps into the kitchen, grabs the phone and calls her sister. When she hears a male voice answer she is so upset she almost hangs up, but then says, "I must have the wrong number. I was calling Leila."

"Oh, I'm sorry. This is Leila's phone, but she can't talk right now. Is this her sister? Wait. She says she wants to talk to you. Hang on."

Nikki hears her sister's voice. "Elsa, it that you?"

"It's Nikki. Yes, but who was that who answered?"

"That was Dom."

"Who in the heck is Dom?"

"He's my fiancé. But you didn't call to talk about him."

"No I just called to let you know that Danny will not be coming to Alaska. He has to start school next week and I don't want him to lose out on his athletic scholarship over some silly accident."

"It's not silly, Elsa, it's serious. Rudy was flying back from the North Slope and is…"

"It's Nikki, Leila, not Elsa. If you insist on calling me that, I'll hang up."

"Why do I bother? Look, El, Nikki. I'll call you back later—when I know something for sure."

"And how about asking me how I'm doing? You always just think about yourself. Well it turns out you were probably right all along about Gerik and Daphne. My life is falling apart and you want my son to leave me, too, and give up his scholarship? I can't take any more of this."

Leila starts to cry. "I'm sorry Nikki. I didn't mean to bother you. I just thought you might want to know that Rudy is missing. He might have been in a serious accident. I'm falling apart. I need help. You're my only family except for my kids. You know how hard it is for me to admit I need help. But the next few hours are crucial and I just thought maybe you could pray or something. After all, he is Danny's favorite cousin. They're so close. El, Nikki, please, think of how you would feel if Danny might be fatally injured."

Nikki's shock at hearing that Rudy is missing and might not survive renders her almost speechless. She stutters, "What, when...?"

Leila breaks in. "Listen, I'll call you back when we know something for sure. And I hope it works out with Gerik. I always hoped it would. You deserve the best."

Nikki is crying now, too. Her problems are huge, but not life threatening like her sister's. Even in her distraught state, empathy rises to the surface. "Oh, Leila, I'm sorry. It's just that my nerves are almost shot. My head feels like it's in a vise and my heart is cut into pieces. But Leila, oh, Leila, I'm so sorry about Rudy. I'll pray, of course, I'll pray. I know he'll be okay. Things like this don't happen to someone as good as he is."

"I've got to go now, Nikki, the FAA might be calling any minute. I need to be available. I'll call back soon. Thanks for listening. I love you, Nikki. Bye."

Nikki holds the phone for a long time, standing there with her eyes closed. *She said she loves me. I don't remember her ever saying that before.* Nikki smiles as she remembers the voice she heard before the nasty encounter with Gerik. *I am worthwhile. I am special. Nobody can hurt me in that safe place where I know who I am.*

Nikki walks up the stairs slowly, with confidence. Gerik is throwing things into a suitcase. He tenses when Nikki walks into the room.

"Relax, Gerik. Take your time. Just as long as you're gone before I go to bed. I think I'll go downstairs and open that $1500 bottle of Chateau Lafit-Rothschild. I deserve a treat today, don't you think? I may even polish off the entire bottle, unless Danny wants to share."

She walks down the hall to knock on Danny's door. He opens it a crack and peeks out. Nikki pushes into the room and grabs him in a protective embrace. "You better start packing too, Danny. We're heading for Alaska tomorrow."

Chapter Twenty-six

On the Way to the Hospital

D om and Leila get into the car for the short drive to the hospital. Dom says he will drive. Leila calls the prayer line at St. Nicholas Church and leaves a message on the answering machine, confident that it will be passed on. When Dom asks her if she needs anything from home, Leila snaps, "Are you kidding? What would I need at a time like this?"

"Well, you don't have to bite my head off. I just wondered." Dom is contrite. "It's just that we have a lot of time and I wondered what we would do once we got to the hospital. The mede-vac flight won't arrive in Anchorage for another hour and a half and the hospital can be a depressing place to hang out."

"I don't know. I just want to be sure to be there when Rudy arrives. I don't know if he will need surgery or..." Her voice trails off and she begins to cry.

"Come on, Leila. We'll get through this. The important thing is he survived. We know that. They've got wonderful doctors here in Anchorage. We will just have to trust. Rudy will need you to be strong. The girls need that too. And it is possible that Rudy is one that has only minor injuries. Did you ever think of that?"

Leila brightens a little and says, "You're right, Dom. No reason to expect the worst when we don't know for sure what happened."

They ride in silence for a few minutes and turn on to Tudor Road in time to see an ambulance rush by with siren blaring and lights flashing.

"I hope that doesn't mean an accident up ahead. Traffic on Tudor is usually bad, but an accident could really snarl it up," Leila says.

Brake lights go on in front of them and within a couple hundred yards, they have come to a complete stop. "Too late," Dom says. "Looks like a big pile-up. We might be here a while."

"Oh, why did we ever take Tudor Road?" Leila cries. "We'll never get there in time."

"Calm down, Leila, calm down. We have plenty of time. Maybe we could make some phone calls while we're stuck here. Do you have anyone to watch the office today?"

"No, I never thought of that in my rush to get away. Thanks for reminding me. I guess I could call our temporary bookkeeper, Donna, to come in and open up."

She calls Donna and asks her to cover the office for the day. She gives her only the briefest details, saying, "There has been as incident involving the Otter. Rudy and the passengers are on their way to Anchorage now. I'll fill you in on details later. Thank you so much, Donna, you are a lifesaver. Yes, I'll call."

Leila covers her eyes with her left hand and massages her temples. Her heart is pounding and she can feel the blood pulsing behind her eyes. She notices a sour feeling in her stomach and feels as though she is on the verge of being sick.

Dom looks at her and hesitates before saying, "Can I tell you a story, Leila?"

"Sure, go ahead," Leila responds, "But please, don't make it one of your stupid jokes."

Dom looks at her with a feigned indignant look. "Now you've hurt my feelings. Would I do anything like that?"

Leila smiles tolerantly. "I don't know how you do it, but you are like medicine for me. You bug the heck out of me, but you do manage to get me out of myself. Thanks, Dom. Go ahead with your story."

"This is not my typical type of story, I'll have you know, but I want to tell you about my first summer in my Uncle's pizza restaurant in the suburbs. In fact, it was the town where you grew up, Caraville. I was a city boy, you know. Never had been out of the city before, and when I got to the hick town—excuse me—Caraville, I was properly unimpressed. I looked around for places of action and, wow, Dullsville is what I thought."

"I didn't think Caraville was all that dull. I kind of liked it."

"But to a city boy, it was pretty hick-like."

Leila shrugs. "Point taken. Go on."

"Anyway, I eventually found some action and let me tell you, it was pretty hot and heavy there for awhile."

"Come on, Dom. I really don't want to hear about your escapades. What does this have to do with anything, and why tell me right now? I've got enough on my plate."

"Well, it a confession of sorts. This just seems like a good time for confessions."

"Go ahead, then."

Dom hesitates before continuing. "Like I said, it was hot and heavy. Things began to look up when I found some action."

"Don't tell me. You met Daphne, right?"

"How did you know?"

"Well, let's just say, she had a reputation for getting around."

"She came into my uncle's place one night and put a move on me. I fell for it. She was a real looker, and I was young and full of hormones. How can I say this without sounding crude? Anyway, we had a fling that I still dream about, even after my many years with Maria. She really knew how to please. I guess you could say she was experienced."

"Please, Dom! I don't need to hear this."

"I'm sorry, Leila, I didn't mean to go there, I guess I just wanted to get it off my chest. I've always felt guilty about it and you're the first person I have ever told about this. I just never knew how to get it out in the open. I especially felt guilty when I found out that she had a steady boyfriend, and I'll never forget the name, it was Gerik—an unusual name, so I remembered it."

"How did you find that out?"

"He came into the pizza joint one night, all bent out of shape. He was a little drunk and he was ranting and yelling and threatening to kill the bastard who was messing with his girl, Daphne. He said someone told him about us making out in the kitchen."

"So what did you do, Dom?"

"I backed off and laid low and when Daphne came in again to hit on me, I told her I couldn't go with her, that I was moving back to Chicago. But, man, could she pout! She made me feel like such a heel for rejecting her. I couldn't resist one last time together. I'm lucky, though, that I wasn't killed that night. Gerik found us at the beach where we had gone and he dragged her off, half-naked, saying if he ever saw me again, I wouldn't live to talk about it. And if I knew what was good for me, I would tell no one that I even knew her."

"What was her reaction to being dragged off?"

"I was so afraid for my own self; I hardly had time to care about what she thought. But, I did notice that she was sort of clinging to him, though, and looked like she would just continue with him what we had been doing. I realized then that it was not me that she was attracted to. It was the fact that I was of the opposite sex. I felt used."

"Dom, what does this have to do with anything?"

"I just wanted you to know all about me before you say yes to spending the rest of your life with me. I want everything to be out in the open. I have not always been lily white and chaste. It's the one thing I'm ashamed of."

"Well, it happens that I do know Daphne and her methods. It has to be the same person. How many blond Daphnes can there be in Caraville who was the part time girlfriend of my brother-in-law Gerik?"

"He's your brother-in-law?" Dom is incredulous.

"Yes, although I told Elsa not to marry the cheating fool."

"I guess there's more to this story than meets the eye. I thought it was just my story."

"It is a small world. Yes, it must have been that time when Elsa was off at college and she was engaged to Gerik. She found out that he was having an affair with Daphne and went off the deep end. They somehow worked it out, even though I strongly advised her to stay away from him. But she has always been stubborn. It was probably my fault that she ran back to him. I shouldn't have ever said anything to her. I pushed her into his arms. But maybe it's all worked out okay. I don't know. I never talk to her anymore. When she returned my call last night she was only worried about me calling her by her new name, Nikki. She's so self-centered. We have nothing in common."

"Is she your only sibling?"

"Yes, there's just the two of us. And since Mom died, I haven't been back to Caraville. But I can't say that I miss it, or her."

"Leila, how can you say that? She's your only sister. Where is your family loyalty?"

"Rudy, Ana and Nat are my family now. They are the ones who matter to me. Oh, I wish this traffic would start moving. How will we ever get to the hospital in time?"

"I think it is starting to move a little."

Chapter Twenty-seven

Nikki Talks to the Kids

Nikki strolls to the wine cellar—a small, refrigerated room attached to the garage—and searches for that special bottle they had splurged on for their twentieth anniversary coming up next year.

If the kids got hold of it, I'll kill them. She gets up on the step stool and spots the bottle tucked away on a high shelf. *Aah, Chateau Lafit Bordeaux. What a treat!*

Taking the bottle to the kitchen, she opens it ceremoniously. *I'll let it breathe while I go and check on flights to Anchorage. On second thought, I'd better take it with me.* She takes the opened bottle and two glasses up to her office and pours a tiny bit into one of them. Gerik is noisily opening drawers and throwing toiletries into his suitcase. Nikki takes the wineglass in both hands and inhales the aroma. *This is going to be good; the bouquet is intoxicating all by itself.* Raising the glass in a mock toast, she says under her breath, "Here's to you, you two-timing, sneaky cheat. Throwing away almost twenty years for that shallow, conniving—no, I won't go there. I'm just going to enjoy the wine and the anticipation of freedom." She takes a small sip and lets it roll around on her tongue. New complexities assault her senses as it does. Swallowing reluctantly, Nikki finds the resulting finish even better than the freshness on the tongue or the bouquet and closes her eyes to enjoy the momentary luxury. "Wow! This is worth every penny we spent on it. It's undoubtedly the best wine I have ever tasted." Nikki puts the glass down. *I'd better get to work if I want to find a flight to Anchorage tomorrow.* She turns to the computer and looks first at the cheap flight websites. There are no last minute deals at this time of year. Alaska is a popular tourist destination and flights are very full. North Country Tours, a charter airline, offers group rate flights from Chicago to Anchorage in the summer. She is lucky to find two seats on their flight leaving O'Hare tomorrow. As she is about to hit the button to purchase the tickets, Danny interrupts her. Sheepishly hanging his head and shuffling as though kicking an imaginary tiny ball, he clears his throat to get Nikki's attention. Nikki jumps, surprised to see him there.

"Look, Ma, I'm sorry about what I said earlier. It's just that I really need to go and see Rudy. He's always been my role model, especially since Dad has been acting like such a jerk." He pauses. "Did you really say *we're* going to Alaska?"

"Yes, in fact, I'm trying to book reservations right now."

"I'll be glad to get out of here and away from all this drama. I can't believe him sneaking around like that."

Nikki is conflicted. On one hand, she wants to side with Danny and talk about what an ass Gerik is; but on the other hand, she doesn't want to cause any more harm in the relationship between Danny and his father. She shakes her head, silently sympathizing with her son.

"I discovered Dad's affair a while after Rudy lost his dad in that accident. You know, I always felt like I had gotten a worse deal than him. He was so broken up over his dad's death, but at least Uncle Pete was still his dad. Rudy's memory of him is untarnished. And as hard as that must be, at least he has the good memories, instead of... They were always really close. I remember envying him whenever I visited. Uncle Pete was an all right guy. And Rudy..."

Danny's eyes tear up and he looks like is about to cry again. Nikki smiles at him and says, "I have a plan..."

Danny interjects, "but, I really came in here to apologize. I remember how devastated I was when I first found out about Dad and Daffy so I realize that you must be going through hell about now. I'm sorry for yelling at you. I don't want to be disrespectful, but I wanted to tell you how much Rudy means to me. He's more than a cousin, or even an older brother. I need to be there to tell him to hang on."

"Well, if you'll let me get a word in edgewise, I'll tell you what I have planned." She pauses, "What was that you just said? Did you call her Daffy?" Nikki laughs.

"Emma and I have always called her that. I think it started when Emma was learning how to talk and couldn't say Daphne and it just kind of stuck. I never called her that to her face, but it did strike me as being funny and in some ways, appropriate."

"You are bordering on total disrespect, Danny. But please, now, just let me get back to the computer before the tickets I found are gone. They were the last two seats on a flight to Anchorage. Hang on."

"Really, Anchorage! You're getting *us* tickets to Anchorage?"

"Haven't you been listening? Yes, that's the plan. I hope the tickets are still available." She looks at the computer screen. "Oh, good! There they are! Now, no more questions until I get them purchased."

Nikki types in the required information and then relaxes back in her chair. "There. I've done it. We both get middle seats way in the back, but it's better than nothing."

"So, why did you decide to go, too?"

"Well, your Aunt Leila could probably use some home-making and cooking help about now. She never was much of a cook. I don't know any of the details of Rudy's accident, and maybe by the time we get there the crisis will be over. But I'm sure she could still use some moral support after such a traumatic experience."

"Cool! So when do we leave?"

"The flight leaves O'Hare at five p.m. tomorrow and gets in to Anchorage about eight-thirty. The afternoon departure will give us some time to get ready and take care of stuff before we leave. Hey, I just opened this Bordeaux. How about having a glass with me, to celebrate?"

"Really? You'd let me drink this expensive wine?"

"Of course. I know this isn't your first alcohol. It's just the first as the man of the house. It's appropriate that it's a good wine."

"I heard you and Dad discussing how expensive it was. Wasn't it for your twentieth anniversary?"

"Well, that's not going to happen, so I want to celebrate having things out in the open and new beginnings. But I don't want you to get used to having such fine wine—until you can afford to buy it yourself."

Nikki pours a small amount of the expensive Bordeaux into the crystal wine glasses. She hands one to Danny and raises the other in a toast. "Here's to Rudy's health."

Danny lifts the glass to his mouth, but Nikki stops him, saying, "Wait, you've got to do this properly. Don't just slug it down. Lift the glass to your nose. Take a deep whiff. What does it remind you of? Is it flowery? Does it smell like fruit? Can you detect any earthy aromas?"

"I don't know. It just smells like wine to me."

"Okay. So next, you take a small sip and let it sit on the tip of your tongue, then purse your lips and inhale, letting the wine burble over your tongue. Next, swirl it around your mouth. As it touches different parts of your mouth, notice how it tastes..."

"Come on, Mom, can't I just drink it and enjoy it in my own way?"

"All right, I just wanted to make sure you enjoy it as much as possible."

Danny takes a small sip, swallows and rolls his eyes. "Wow, that is good! It's smooth. There is no comparison to the stuff Esther and I snuck from her parents' wine rack."

"Danny! You shock me. You went around sneaking wine from your girlfriend's parents?"

"Only once. Well maybe more than once, but we were always tactful, just like Dad," he smiles.

"Tactful? You were listening to the whole sordid conversation, weren't you? I'm sorry you had to hear all of it. I can't believe the nerve..." Nikki breaks off, realizing it's her son she's talking to. "Tactful, huh? As if that makes everything okay, but it does sort of strike me as funny. Do people really say that sort of thing, or believe it? How ridiculous!"

Danny doesn't know what to say or do. He looks like he would rather be somewhere else. He drinks more of the wine, appearing to enjoy it. Nikki sips thoughtfully. Without warning, the tension of the evening's experience hits her between the eyes. She feels like laughing and crying at the same time.

They both finish their first glass and Nikki pours another for each of them.

"Remember to sip slowly, Danny. That small glass you just slugged down was worth approximately one month's groceries."

He sips until the glass is almost empty.

"I guess I could stand to eat a little less if I could drink wine like this. It's—what can I say—delicious. No, that sounds too weak. It's…"

"Like the nectar of the Gods," Nikki says, laughing. "Listen to us. I think we're getting a wee bit drunk." That strikes her as funny and she begins to laugh. "Nectar. Whoever came up with that expression?"

Danny joins in her laughter. Every time they look at each other, their laughter builds until tears are streaming from Nikki's eyes. Her laughter unexpectedly turns to sobbing.

Danny walks to his mother and puts an arm around her shaking shoulders. "That's okay, Mom, you've got to cry." He pauses. "Hey, maybe we could go and get something to eat. Aren't you supposed to enjoy good food with good wine?"

"That's right. You probably have not had dinner and two glasses of wine on an empty stomach, even for a guy your size, can be a bit much." But, man, this stuff is good. Would you care for another?"

"That sounds great." Danny holds his glass out. "Hey, I just thought of this, but what about Emma? Do you think she would want to come to Alaska?"

"No, she's busy with that summer camp job and she stays there Monday through Thursday. Uh, oh, that means she'll be coming home tonight. What time is it?"

"It's nine o'clock."

Almost as though on cue, they hear the sound of Emma opening the front door. "Is anybody home?"

Nikki and Danny look at each other like little kids caught with their hands in the cookie jar. Before they have a chance to say anything to each other, Emma bursts into the room.

"Hey, what's going on?" She looks questioningly from Nikki to Danny and back again.

Nikki takes a deep breath. "Danny, run and get another glass. I think Emma should have a little taste of our anniversary wine."

Chapter Twenty-eight

Waiting at the Hospital

The first thing Leila notices on entering the emergency room is the calm and quiet atmosphere. She expected it to be frantic like the scenes on television with doctors and nurses rushing around, shouting orders and moving equipment. There is one nurse standing by Rudy who looks like he's sleeping, except that he has an oxygen mask over his face. Leila and Celeste head towards him, both frantic to touch him to assure themselves he is alive, but the doctor cuts them off and ushers them to chairs next to the door.

"Mrs. Pletnikof, you need to fill out this insurance paperwork so we can begin to treat your son." The doctor pushes a clipboard in front of Leila.

"Can't you tell me what his injuries are?"

"He is in stable condition right now. The medevac nurses did an excellent job of stabilizing both the patients on the way to Anchorage. But your son will need surgery to find the cause of internal bleeding. If it is a ruptured spleen time is of the essence. He also has several broken bones that may need to be pinned. But most serious appears to be the head injury. We won't know the extent of it until we do some testing.

Another concern is the crushed thoracic cavity. It could be that his sternum is pressing against his vagus nerve causing an erratic heartbeat from time to time."

"I don't know what all of that means, but, go ahead, do whatever you need to do. Please, hurry."

"He is just lucky there was a fast plane standing by on the North Slope "

Leila fills out the forms barely reading them. "Here, I think that's all you need."

The doctor continues, "We have the best team of specialists in Anchorage on the way. Luckily, both our top-notch orthopedic and general surgeons are on call today. Your son is in good hands."

"How long will it be?" Celeste asks.

"It might be as long as four or five hours. We will try to keep you posted if it goes much longer than that."

The doctor turns to leave the room, stopping for a moment to look at the monitoring equipment next to Rudy.

A nurse appears and takes Leila by the arm, ushering her to a nearby room. Celeste follows. The room is small with two loveseats and three over-stuffed chairs in subtle shades of pink, grey and lavender. Lighting is subdued. Claustrophobia takes Leila's breath away as she enters the room, but soon the quiet music calms her nerves.

"You can wait in this private room. Your son will be taken to OR three which is just down the hall."

"My daughters will be here soon. Can they wait here, too?" Leila asks.

"Yes, that's fine. Just make sure if you all leave this room you let the receptionist at the front desk know where you are going so we can reach you. And, one more thing—does your son have an organ donor card?"

Leila gasps. Her mind immediately jumps to conclusions about the reasons for this necessity. She is speechless.

"It's a routine request, Ma'am. We ask for it anytime someone goes into surgery."

"But..." Leila stammers.

"Yes, he does," Celeste offers. "I was with him when he renewed his driver's license and he checked the box that asks if you want to be identified as an organ donor." She turns to the nurse and says, "I'll check in his wallet. It must be in this bag of his belongings." Celeste rummages through the bag and locates the driver's license. "Here."

"Thank you," the nurse says and leaves.

"Oh, my God!" Leila sobs.

A couple minutes later Dom enters the small waiting room followed by Ana and Nat. "Look who I found wandering around."

Sister Joan, the hospital Chaplain, slips into the room behind them unobtrusively and stands to one side while Leila greets her daughters.

"Oh, Ana, I'm so glad you found her. Nat, it's good to have you here." She embraces them both in a three-way hug.

Natalia's sunken eyes are brimming with tears, her sallow complexion moist with perspiration. Tremors move in waves through her body. Obviously, Ana had filled her in on as many details as she could on the way to the hospital.

She says, "He's not going to die, is he? It's not fair. I should be the one on the operating table. He's never done anything to deserve this. I'm the shit-head around here."

"Now, Nat, don't. Don't do that to yourself," Leila says.

"It's true. I've always been a failure and a loser. I'm such a screw-up." She turns and as she notices Sister Joan, shrugs her shoulders, looks up towards the ceiling and closes her eyes. Tears are squeezing out of the corners of her eyes.

"But, I promise, God, if only you let him live, I'll straighten up. I'll never do drugs again. I promise. I can't live with the thought of Rudy dying."

Leila wraps her arms around Nat and holds her. Nat is as tall as Leila, but much thinner. Her bony shoulders shake with sobs. Leila strokes her dirty hair and pats her back as though she is patting an infant. "Oh, baby, my little baby. He's going to be fine. We just have to believe that."

They settle into a silent waiting. Dom clears his throat and leans forward as though to start talking, but Celeste gives him a stern look and he sits back in his chair. Sister Joan sits with them yet her presence is all but invisible. She has taken a small book out of her pocket and reads for a few moments then closes her eyes and bows her head. Her hands rest easily on her lap, palms up, fingers relaxed. She is the image of contemplation. The peace surrounding her permeates the rest of the room and everyone in it. Their breathing gradually becomes synchronized and relaxed.

In a small voice, barely louder than the breathing, Nat begins, "Rudy was always so good to me. I remember when I was in second grade; every day after school he would help me with my reading. Sometimes I just wanted to play, but he would get my reading book out and make it into a game. I loved reading because he was spending time with me. I looked up to him—idolized him. He was everything I could want in a brother. Not that we didn't have our fights. I remember how he would yell at me when I was in high school. I would call him, so drunk I could hardly stand up. But he would always come and give me a ride home no matter how late. He begged me to stop drinking, and made me feel guilty. I hated him for that and yet loved his attention all the same."

The others in the room are silent, almost holding their breath, sensing Nat's need to talk. She had always been so withdrawn and angry. Leila often felt like she was walking on eggshells around her and was afraid to say anything for fear that she would blow up and do something drastic. So now she lets her talk, without interruption.

Nat continues. "For the past year or so, he always seemed to find me when I was at my lowest. I did nothing to encourage his attention; in fact I pushed him away and told him I never wanted to see him again. How could I have said that? But he always showed up—somehow when I needed someone to protect me from myself. Just last month—oh, Rudy—you can't die!"

"He's not going to die, Nat," Leila says, patting Nat's hand. "We all loved I mean, love him too much."

Celeste interrupts, "Maybe we could say some prayers, or something."

Leila glares at Celeste. "What do you think I have been doing, Celeste?" she says icily.

"I just meant maybe we could say something out loud... together."

Sister Joan offers her opened prayer book diffidently to Dom who is sitting next to her on one of the loveseats. "This is one of my favorite psalms. Would you like to read it aloud, Dom?"

"I guess—if it's okay with everyone else." They all nod silently.

Dom clears his throat and begins to read. "You who live in the shelter of the Most High and abide under the shadow of the Almighty, who say, 'The Lord is my safe retreat, my God in whom I trust'; he himself will snatch you away from the fowler's snare or raging tempest. He will cover you with his pinions, and you shall find safety beneath his wings; you shall not fear the hunters' trap by night nor the arrow that flies by day. For you, the Lord, is a safe retreat; you have made the most high your refuge."

Dom pauses before reading the next part and reads it slowly with a catch in his voice. "No disaster shall befall you; no calamity shall come upon your home. For he has charged his angels to guard you wherever you go, to lift you on their hands for fear you should strike your foot against a stone."

"That's beautiful, Uncle Dom."

"It gets better, listen. 'Because his love is set on me, I will deliver him; I will lift him beyond danger, for he knows me by my name. I will be with him in time of trouble; I will rescue him and bring him to honor. I will satisfy him with long life to enjoy the fullness of my salvation.' That's Psalm 91."

Again there is silence in the room. Dom leaves the book open on his lap, lifts it from time to time to read a few words, smiles and then puts it down again. He laughs to himself and then says, "Hey, I didn't know there was something about me in here. Listen. 'O Lord, it is good to give you thanks, to sing psalms to your name, O Most High, to declare your love in the morning and your constancy every night, to the music of a ten-stringed lute, to the sounding chords of the harmonica.'"

"It doesn't say that, does it?" Celeste laughs.

"Sure, here, see for yourself." Dom hands her the book.

Celeste glances at the page, and then lifts the book as though to throw it at Dom. "You joker! Can't you ever be serious?"

"I know things are serious here, but do we have to be so somber? How about a story to pass the time?"

"Oh, Dom, please! I don't think I could take another story like your last one."

"No, no. This one will be at least PG13. We do have youngsters present."

"Uncle Dom!"

Nat looks at Dom cynically, "I don't think you could tell anything I haven't seen or maybe even experienced. You might say I've been around the block."

Leila shakes her head with lips pressed together. "Go ahead, Dom. This room could use a little lightening."

Dom stands up and faces the others in the room. Like a comedian who has just taken the stage, he struts back and forth, hands in his back pockets. He squints one eye and looks across the room as though he is seeing something far off in the distance. He starts slowly in a Jimmy Stewart type of drawl.

"It's like this, you see. My old buddy Roy Rogers got himself a new pair of boots. He was mighty proud of them boots. He had them all nicely broke in and wore them everywhere—even with his 'Sunday-go-to- meetin' clothes. He polished them every night."

Celeste rolls her eyes. She has heard this one before, but everyone else is listening to Dom, wrapped up in his storytelling.

Dom continues. "One morning he told Dale that he had to ride the fence line and would be out with the hired hand all day—maybe even overnight. And off he went, wearing his new boots, of course. They were far from the ranch house at sunset and decided to spend the night camped out under the stars. They made a fire and sat around, eating their beans and exchanging stories. Then he got his bedroll out and put his dearly loved new boots at its foot. He slept like a log and in the morning when he got up and reached for his boots, they were gone. Gone! 'Well, I'll be!' he said, 'Gus, what did you do with my new boots?'

Gus said, 'I ain't touched 'em. Musta been that ol' mountain lion I heard in the night.'

287

Roy grabbed his gun and, barefooted, started tracking that dang cat. About a hundred yards from the campsite he saw the boots half buried in the sand of a dry riverbed. He put them on and stomped back to get his horse. 'I'll get that damned cat if it's the last thing I do,' he vowed. Without a word to Gus he saddled his horse and rode off, tracking the beast.

Gus rode directly to the ranch house and told Dale he didn't know when Roy would be home; he was after a mountain lion that had destroyed his new boots.

For three days and nights Roy tracked that mountain lion. Many times when he thought he had lost him in the rocks, he would spot him and take off again. At long last, he got the lion trapped in a blind canyon and shot him. He approached the motionless cat and at point blank range, shot him again for good measure. He draped the lion over the back of his saddle and took off for the ranch house. He aimed to skin him and make a fine rug out of it so he could walk over it every day.

In the meantime, Dale had been worried sick over his lengthy trek. She wondered what could have happened to him. Most of the day she would look out towards the horizon to the west, watching. Finally one day she spotted him riding his horse toward the house. She got the binoculars out and saw that he had a huge mountain lion draped over the back of his horse.

As he got closer Dale sang, 'Pardon me Roy, is that the cat that chewed your new shoes?'"

A collective groan sounds in the small room. "Uncle Dom! You promised never to tell that joke again in my presence. But I must say, it did brighten up the room a bit."

"I'll have to remember that one for some of our long bus rides, although, I don't know if I could do it justice.

I couldn't quite get the accent like you do, Dom," Danny laughs.

Ana pipes in, "Hey, whatever happened to the snacks you were supposed to bring, Celeste? I'm starving."

"I have them right here, some bagels from the Bagel Stop and various spreads. Have at it." She looks at Sister Joan and asks, "Is it okay to eat in here?"

"I don't see why not." Sister Joan says. "How about if I go and get some drinks? What would you all like?"

"That's not necessary, Sister," Leila says. But everyone else has already started giving her their orders and she does not hear Leila above their voices. When she comes back with the coffee and sodas they all eat without speaking until Dom breaks the silence with a few more jokes. They all groan and complain with each new punch line, but are captivated by his story telling ability.

Leila looks at her watch. "It's been almost four hours already. I wonder if we can find out anything new?"

Sister Joan says, "Let me check with the OR scheduler and if I learn anything, I'll come and tell you. Otherwise, I am going to the chapel for daily mass. Would any of you like to join me? It starts in fifteen minutes. The surgeon did say it would be five hours, so you would have plenty of time. And what better place to be than the chapel?"

"I'll pass," Dom says.

Leila, to her own surprise, says, "Yes, Sister, I'll join you," and walks out of the room with Sister Joan before waiting for anyone else to respond.

They look at each other in stunned silence. Ana says, "She hasn't been to church since Daddy died."

"We all have our own way of dealing with things, Ana," Dom says. "Maybe this is just the right time for her to acknowledge a Higher Power."

Not long after, Leila returns to the waiting room subdued and thoughtful. She smiles at Dom as she enters and sits without saying a word.

Minutes later they hear a knock on the door. It opens a crack. "Is this the Pletnikof family?" a voice asks.

Chapter Twenty-nine

Nikki Flies to Alaska

Danny gets up, looking relieved to be out of the room and the scene he expects. He knows Emma worships her father and will not believe he has done anything wrong. As he leaves Nikki's office he bumps into Gerik in the hallway. Gerik is struggling with a large rolling suitcase, a laptop computer and another shoulder bag.

"Sorry, Dad. Can I help you with that?"

"No, I've got it. And watch where you're going would you?"

"I said I'm sorry."

"You certainly are, you and your mother, too."

"Dad..." Danny says, incredulous at the mean tone in his dad's voice. Tears spring to his eyes and he turns and rushes down the stairs to the kitchen. He reaches into the glass-fronted cupboard for a wine glass. Upset and distracted, he knocks it into another and a whole row of closely spaced glasses falls with a splintering sound.

"Oh, man, now look what I did!" He sinks onto the barstool by the counter and stares off pressing his lips together. "What is Mom going to do?"

He grabs a glass from another cupboard—the everyday ones—and sprints up to Nikki's office to hand it to her.

"I'll be right back," he says without interrupting their conversation. They don't seem to notice that he was even in the room.

In the kitchen Danny methodically cleans up the broken glass, taking his time. He does not want to hear Emma's outburst.

When Danny first walks out of the room, Nikki and Emma both start talking at once.

"What's happening?" Emma asks.

"I don't know how to tell you, Emma." Nikki is sobered by the reality of telling her daughter the story.

Emma, hearing the scuffle in the hallway turns to see her dad with the suitcases. "Hey, where is Dad going?"

"Your father and I have had some differences, Emma. We both thought it best if he stayed somewhere else for a time."

Emma rises from her chair and starts to go after Gerik.

"Wait, Emma. Let him go. I'll explain everything."

"Why does he have to leave? Why isn't it you who is going away?"

"Emma, look, right now I'm just trying to get over two shocking experiences. I can't explain everything. I need time to think things through. I know how much you admire your father and I admire that about you. You two have always had a great father/daughter relationship. I won't say anything to get between you two, but I will say that I have been hurt— betrayed—very deeply. I'll let your father tell you the details if he wants to. But after what I've learned, I just can't go on with him. I need space."

"What could he have done that would be so awful? And isn't stuff like this always two sided? What did you do to him? Why would you throw him out of the house?"

Emma is getting wound up. She stands up and looks out the window to see Gerik back out of the garage and speed away. "Where will he go?"

"I don't know. He might stay at the lake house for a while, or with a friend."

"Well, I'll go and stay with him, then. I don't want to stay here with you."

Emma takes out her cell phone and says, "I'm going to call him and ask him to come back and pick me up. We can stay at the lake house together."

"I wouldn't do that, Emma. I don't believe he was thinking rationally when he left."

"Well, who would be after being kicked out?" She presses the speed dial number for her dad's cell phone.

Nikki grabs the phone from her and ends the call. "I don't think he would want to talk to you right now, Emma. He is on his way to Daphne's house. I didn't want to tell you, but they're having an affair."

"You're lying! Dad would never do that."

"Oh, Emma, I wish it were not the truth. But, I'm sorry, it is."

"Well, you must have driven him to it. You and your stupid quilt business and your physical fitness crusade. You are changing so much I never know what to expect when I come home from camp every weekend. No wonder he…"

Nikki rises to her feet and stands in front of Emma, glowering. She has difficulty restraining herself from slapping Emma. "Emma, it would be best if you would give some thought to what you say before blurting out something hurtful." She clenches her teeth and narrows her eyes. "I'm trying to make the best of a difficult situation and now I have my sister to worry about, too."

"What do you mean? When have you ever cared about your sister?"

"Things have changed. Leila just called and said that Rudy has been in an accident and he is in critical condition. Danny and I are leaving for Anchorage tomorrow afternoon."

"Wow! Just like that! You're going to Alaska?"

"My sister needs me and Rudy needs his cousin to be there for him. I was going to ask if you would like to come, too, but it sounds like you would rather stay here with your dad."

Emma's demeanor changes in a matter of seconds as Nikki watches. "No," she says, "actually, I would like to come, but I don't know how I could get out of my job. But, really, if I could get someone to take my place, would you let me come, too?"

Nikki is nonplussed by Emma's sudden transformation. To have more time to think, she says, "I can't get you a ticket for tomorrow, but maybe the next day would work, if you are serious."

Danny walks into the room without talking and sits next to Emma. She turns to him with a look of sympathy. "Rudy's gonna be all right, Dan. But it's great you're going up to see him."

"Hey, Mom and I were just having a glass of wine. Maybe you should have a taste before it's all gone."

Emma looks at both her mother and brother with raised eyebrows. She has many questions, but suppresses them for the time being. Her mother offers her a small sample of the expensive wine. Emma takes it and grins at Danny with a knowing look. They would never tell their mother, but they had talked about sampling this very bottle before Danny went away to college. They had no idea how expensive it was. They just knew it was special.

The conversation turns to Rudy's accident and the details of their flight. Nikki checks availability of flights for the following day just in case Emma manages to get the time off.

Nikki leaves Danny and Emma in her office while she goes to the kitchen to fix some snacks. She hopes that Danny will tell Emma enough about what happened so she will be sympathetic, but not too much. She doesn't want her turning against her father. "Come on down, kids," Nikki calls when the snacks are ready.

The table is set with the fine china and cloth napkins. Nikki dishes up the Greek pizza she had made from scratch. Small bowls of watermelon balls are at each place setting and Nikki has opened another bottle of wine. A crystal wine glass is by each plate and Danny gasps as he realizes that his mother must have seen the broken ones.

"I can explain, Mom. And I promise, I'll buy you new ones. I didn't mean to do it, it was an accident."

"Don't worry about a few broken glasses, Danny. They are only things. You two are much more important and you are here with me. That's all that matters."

She grabs each of them and wraps her arms around their shoulders.

"I love you both," she says. "You are worth more than anything to me."

As they eat, each of them hesitates to bring up any subject that will spoil the tenuous tranquility. There are only occasional murmurings of appreciation for Nikki's culinary expertise.

"Boy, I'm going to miss Mom's cooking when I go back to school," Danny says.

"So you're going? I thought you were going to Alaska," Emma says.

"I've been giving it some thought, and if it's okay with you, Mom, I'd like to return to Chicago on Tuesday so I can still be in Urbana for the start of training. I'll need to hustle to get everything packed, but it's not that far. I can come home on weekends and get the rest of my stuff later."

"That will only give you two and a half days in Alaska, but if that's what you want to do, we'll make it happen. But maybe Rudy will be well on his way to recovery by then anyway."

Nikki allows them each a small glass of wine with their meals and then shoos them out of the kitchen so she can clean up by herself. She enjoys cleaning and polishing her things and putting them away in their proper places. Nikki finishes the bottle of wine as she cleans up. When everything is put away, she dims the lights and admires their soft glow on the granite. Then she makes her way to her bedroom, hanging on to the railing for support as she weaves up the stairs.

"What a day this has been," she says as she smoothes the sheets, ready to collapse onto the bed. Then, remembering Gerik and Daphne in the shower together, she rips the sheets from the bed in a fit of anger, runs down the stairs and throws them into the garbage can. She returns and fixes the bed with the pale green Egyptian cotton sheets. "There, that's better," Nikki says as she lies down. She falls asleep as soon as her head hits the pillow.

Sleeping soundly for only a few hours, Nikki awakens drenched in sweat. In her dream Gerik and Daphne run along a beach, naked, then plunge into the water and merge into one. Their arms are wrapped around each other and their faces are touching. Nikki can see under the water and sees that Daphne is wrapped around Gerik like she is sitting on his lap facing him. She notices a big wave hovering over them and laughs to think that they will drown in its wake. Just as the wave is about to engulf them, she gasps. *It's not Gerik she's hanging on to; it's Mitch.*

"No, you can't have him, too," Nikki yells. She tries to run but she is tangled in the beach towel and can't move. "You bitch; you're not going to get him."

She awakens just as the wave crashes over their heads and Mitch is ripped from Daphne's arms to sinks to the bottom. "Oh, God! What am I going to do? She will get him, too. I know she will. I hate her."

Nikki tosses and turns the rest of the night. Several times she reaches for the phone to call Mitch hoping to hear his soothing voice, but can't bring herself to admit she needs help. *After all, I hardly know Mitch. Why would he care about my problems? I'll make it through this—alone.*

The next morning Nikki wakes to hear Emma shouting to Danny from the kitchen. "Woo hoo! They found someone to take my place for a week. I can go."

"Cool. Wait 'til Mom wakes up. I hope she can get you a ticket for tomorrow."

Nikki has a lot of phone calls to make and emails to send before leaving and noon comes much too quickly. She rides the two-thirty shuttle van from downtown Caraville to O'Hare so parking will not be a problem. She is not sure how long she will stay in Alaska.

She purchases a ticket for Emma for the following day and asks Jill, her sister-in-law, to drive Emma to the airport. "I'll already be there, so I'll pick her up in Anchorage."

"You're going to visit your sister?" Jill is incredulous.

"It's a long story, but Rudy was in an accident. I've got to go." Nikki does not mention anything about Gerik; there will be time for that later. Jill's relationship with Gerik is not the greatest, but he is her brother. So Nikki lets it ride for now.

Nikki is a bundle of nerves as they ride to the airport. She has never liked flying. It makes her sick and she had no time to get medicine for motion sickness. *Maybe I can get some at the airport.* As usual, the lines for check-in are long. Danny seems to take it all in stride. He has traveled to Alaska many times and always engages the flight attendants in conversation and loves hearing stories about their layovers. It seems like such an exciting life.

Nikki, on the other hand, closes in on herself and tries to ignore everyone. The ticket agent is friendly and asks Nikki if she is going on a tour when she gets to Alaska.

Nikki answers her tersely. "I don't know that that is any of your business."

"Hey, Mom, she was just trying to be friendly." Danny turns to the agent saying, "We're going up to see my cousin Rudy who was in an airplane accident. He's the chief pilot of Pete's Flying Service on Lake Hood."

"Danny! She doesn't want to hear all of that. Look at the line behind us. Let's get moving."

The agent hands Nikki and Danny their boarding passes and says, "I hope everything goes well with your cousin. I'll send up a prayer for him. Have a nice flight."

As they make their way through security and to the gate, Nikki is tense but Danny seems to enjoy the hustle and bustle of the airport terminal. They rush to get to the gate before the published boarding time and when they get there, a sign says that boarding will begin at six-twenty.

"I thought the departure time was five p.m. What's with this?" Nikki asks no one in particular.

She approaches the agent at the counter and demands to know what is causing the delay. The agent apologizes. "I guess you didn't hear the announcement. The airplane will be arriving late and needs a routine inspection before departing again. We will try to make it a quick turn and be off as soon as possible."

Nikki looks at the agent as though she is personally responsible for the delay and she sniffs as she turns her head. In a voice everyone in the gate area can hear, she says, "I guess that's the kind of service you get from a low-cost carrier. I never should have booked with North Country Tours. I can tell you, this will be the last time I do so."

Danny moves away from her and sits down facing the windows. He watches the airplanes taxiing and when Nikki sits down next to him, he pretends he doesn't know her.

Nikki takes a book from her bag and starts to read. After several attempts to concentrate she puts it down. Her irritation and uneasiness about flying make it impossible for her to focus. "I don't know why I'm doing this. I don't think my sister will appreciate how much I'm giving up for her. She always has been self-centered."

Danny says nothing. He has learned when his mother is in one of these moods, it is best to keep quiet. Maybe she'll feel better after a nap on the plane.

By the time they finally board Nikki is a nervous wreck. She had forgotten to look for airsickness medicine in spite of having had plenty of time to do so.

The seats are squeezed so close together on the Boeing 757 that Nikki's knees touch the seat in front of her. When the pilot announces the proposed flight time—longer than usual because of headwinds—she groans. "This is definitely not going to be a pleasant experience."

And, needless to say, for Nikki, the flight is miserable. She arrives in Anchorage exhausted, irritable, hungry and nauseous. Her good intentions of going there to help her sister are buried deep beneath the effects of the past two days' ordeal. As she exits the secure area Nikki looks around, hoping to see Leila and be relieved of some of her carry-on luggage. "Well, it's just like her to be late," She grumbles. As she heads toward baggage claim, she spots Leila talking on her cell phone and makes her way toward her sister, bracing herself for the encounter.

Chapter Thirty

Nikki and Leila Meet

Leila rushes across town from the hospital to meet Elsa's flight from Chicago. She had checked on the arrival time and gets there with little time to spare. She stands by the top of the stairs where deplaning passengers exit security. Her phone rings just as she sees a large group of tourists heading her way. She moves away from the stairway so she can hear. It is Ana calling to check up on her. Leila asks if Rudy has regained consciousness. He hasn't.

She sees a woman with dark auburn hair who looks a lot like Elsa walking with purpose. *That can't be her. She's so thin and shapely. She looks like a model.* When she sees her nephew Danny walking next to the stylish woman, Leila realizes that it is indeed Elsa. It is a relief to see her sister. She hugs her like a drowning person clinging to a log, but feels like she is hugging a mannequin. "How was your trip, Elsa?"

"Well, I'm here, aren't I? By the way it's Nikki, not Elsa. I told you that. Can't you remember anything? And how come it's so bright out? It's almost midnight."

"Oh, for crying out loud, Elsa, we haven't seen each other for years and all you can talk about is the amount of daylight we have in June."

"Well, I have my own problems to deal with right now that you don't seem to give a damn about. But, as a matter of fact—since you asked—I'm exhausted. I haven't slept well for days and I've been cramped up in that tin can of an airplane for five and a half hours. It doesn't help that we were two hours late getting out of Chicago. I can't understand how anyone would want to fly one of those contraptions: Babies crying, people gawking at the scenery, shoving and pushing to get a better view. Then just as I was about to fall asleep, the stupid pilot would make an announcement pointing out some obscure mountain or glacier. It all looks like a pile of rock to me."

Leila's shoulders sag and tears burn her eyes. *Why did I let Dom talk me into asking her to come? I don't need this. I can barely get through the day as it is. How on earth am I going deal with this animosity between us? I hoped maybe she had changed.*

Leila's knees buckle. She wants nothing more than to curl up in a ball and pull a blanket over her head. She notices Danny hanging back, trying to avoid the conflict. "Oh, Danny, it's so good to see you. I'm sure Rudy will perk up just to know you're here."

"Can we go right to the hospital, Aunt Leila?"

"We'll stop by and you can meet my fiancé and talk to the girls, but I'm afraid Rudy is not able to have more than one person in his room at a time. We've been taking shifts. He's still in intensive care. I'll fill you in on all the details when we get out of this airport."

Leila says nothing to her sister, but turns and strides toward the baggage claim level.

Nikki, rushing to keep up says, "Aren't you going to help me with my carry-ons?" Then in a conciliatory tone, "I brought Rudy's favorite jam along: raspberry-rhubarb.

Maybe we can bring some to the hospital tomorrow morning."

"He can't eat it now. He can hardly breathe on his own. He hasn't spoken since he got to the hospital and the drugs they're giving him for pain are turning him into a zombie. At least he and Nat now have something in common." Leila shakes her head. "I'm a mess, Elsa—Nikki. I never thought I'd say I need you, but my life is falling apart and I can't hold it together. If Rudy dies, I may as well die, too. I hate this stupid place."

Nikki looks at Leila, open mouthed, wide eyed.

"I hate it, El-Nikki. I hate the mountains, the wide-open spaces, the remoteness of it all. I even hate the stupid airplanes. Why did I ever move here and leave the civilization of the Midwest?" Leila's angry outburst leaves her feeling exposed and vulnerable. She does not dare to hope that her sister will sympathize.

For once, Nikki is at a loss for words. She swallows, feeling a momentary twinge of pity for her sister, but the years of fighting, bickering and competing have worn deep grooves in her emotional responses. She can't help herself. In the same old tone she used as a teenager she says, "Well, I told you not to move to Alaska."

Leila feels like throwing up. She stops walking and spotting a row of chairs, sits down, unable to take another step. People are rushing by, talking, laughing, holding each other's hands and smiling. Leila notices none of that. The darkness that had enveloped her when Pete died settles over her again, but instead of the cold, hard resolve she had felt then, she now feels helpless—hopeless. *I can't do it anymore. I can't take another blow. I just can't...* and she bursts out crying. Between sobs she speaks haltingly. "He's going to die, I know he is. I don't want to go on. I am not strong enough for this. What will I do?"

Danny sits next to his aunt and puts a consoling arm around her shoulder. "He is not going to die, Aunt Leila. I'm here. I'll help him. He always helped me out of scrapes. Now it's my turn to help him. Let's go to the hospital. Let me take a turn in his room. I'll tell him to straighten up and get better."

Danny notices his mother standing above them, hands on her hips. He whispers into Leila's ear, "Give my mom some time, Aunt Leila. She's had a terrible blow herself. She'll come around. She really wanted to come and help you out. Let her get a good night's sleep. And, hey, Emma is coming tomorrow. Won't it be great for her and Natalia to spend some time together?"

"Nat...well that's another story." Leila feels the hopelessness assail her again as she thinks about Nat and her drug use. She doesn't want to burden Danny with that right now so she shakes off the depressing thoughts and smiles at Danny. "But thank you, Danny for trying to perk me up. I need a little of your youthful energy and hope about now. Thank you for coming."

Danny squeezes her hand.

Leila continues, "I think we'll drop your mom off at the house so she can get some sleep and then I'll take you over to the hospital. If you want to spend the night there with me we can give the others a break from their vigil. You can catch a nap in the waiting room. It's pretty quiet there at night."

They get up and continue to the luggage carousel to pick up Nikki's two large suitcases. Danny has only a small carry-on backpack. Nikki is quiet while Danny explains their plan to her as they walk to the car.

Chapter Thirty-one

Nikki at Leila's House

*M*e *and my big mouth!* Nikki feels remorse and berates herself for her lack of sympathy, but it is difficult for her to hide her irritation and to let go of her feelings of betrayal. Gerik's infidelity flashes across her mind again and again. She wants to strike out at someone—anyone. Leila just happens to be an easy target and one she is accustomed to badgering.

It's not her fault, though, God, what she must be going through! I don't want to make it worse, so I'll just keep my mouth shut until I feel a little better. A nice soft bed would feel good about now.

Nikki climbs into the back seat and leans her head against the window. She puts her feet up on the seat and closes her eyes. In the few minutes it takes to get to Leila's house she falls asleep.

"Here we are, Mom," Danny says as Leila pulls into the driveway.

Nikki feels the car come to a stop and opens her eyes. "What? Where are we?" She is disoriented and unstable as she unbuckles her seatbelt and gets out of the car. In the twilight she notices the dark and sleek contemporary architecture of the house whose large windows almost cover the entire front. Light colored delphiniums lean against it, waving in the breeze. A sweet odor along the walkway reminds her of the nicotiana in her own garden, but it is sweeter and spicier.

"What is that smell?" she asks.

"Oh, that's the stock Ana planted. It's not very attractive, but it sure smells good. Ana's the gardener around here. I don't have time for it," Leila adds.

They enter the house through the front door. Danny lugs the heavy suitcases behind them and takes a deep breath as he looks around the expansive entry with dark slate flooring. He sighs and says, "It's good to be here, Aunt Leila. It feels like coming home."

Nikki glares at him. *What an ungrateful child! He prefers this stark and modern—cold—place to my award-winning decorating, my tasteful, warm and homey...*

Danny interrupts her thoughts, "Well, what do you think, Mom? This is the first time you've been here. Isn't it great?"

"It's nice, Danny—Leila. But right now, I just want to find a bed. I'll look around in the morning."

Leila leads her down a long hallway whose walls are filled with pictures. She notices many with Pete's smiling face standing next to uninteresting looking airplanes. Stopping when she notices a close-up of Rudy as a youngster sitting in the back seat of a small plane, she smiles. *He must be sitting on cushions.* His expression is a mixture of delight and fear and excitement. With wide eyes and open mouth, he points toward the front of the plane with one upraised finger.

Leila sees what Elsa is looking at and says, "Isn't that a great picture? It captures Rudy's love of flying. It was the first time Pete took him up in the Super Cub with his new booster seat so he could see out the front window. They loved flying together so much." Leila's voice catches and she turns and heads down the hallway to the guest room.

"Here's your room, El-Nikki. Make yourself at home. You should find everything you need for a shower in your bathroom. If you're hungry, just rummage around in the kitchen. Danny and I want to head right back to the hospital."

"Thank you, Leila."

Leila stiffens and gives Nikki a perfunctory hug. "Thank you for coming," she says and leaves her sister standing there with her hands at her sides.

Chapter Thirty-two

Leila and Danny go to the Hospital

"Come on, Danny. Let's go and see Rudy. I'm sure Ana, Nat and Dom will be exhausted and in need of a break. We've been at the hospital almost non-stop since the accident. When was it? Only two days ago? It seems like an eternity. I can't remember what normal life feels like."

"So what happened, Aunt Leila?"

"Rudy was on a charter flight from Deadhorse to Anchorage with a couple of stops en route. He had four passengers. They had just landed at an airstrip on the northern edge of the Brooks Range and intended to continue on to another stop between Bettles and Rampart and then to Anchorage."

Talking about the accident makes Leila feel better. It takes her mind from the immediate reality of Rudy in critical condition. She finds she can talk about it dispassionately—as though she is reporting a news story.

"Is that where the accident happened?" Danny asks.

"Yes. Fortunately the three passengers in the back had only minor injuries. They reported to investigators that Rudy had decided to return to Deadhorse because of the marginal weather ahead of them. One passenger said they took off to the south and had to turn around to head back to Deadhorse. There were clouds obscuring the hills, although the visibility looked good to him. They had almost completed the hundred and eighty degree turn when the plane slammed into the hillside without warning. He said it seemed to be in slow motion and they were sliding along. He could see Rudy's hands moving controls and switches and then the right wing tip hit something and the plane turned abruptly. He thought it was going to cartwheel, but said it teetered before crashing down in an upright position."

"Wow! How did the passenger manage to keep his wits about him and observe all that? It must have happened pretty fast."

"Rudy's passengers were all research scientists from Western Washington University. They're pretty sharp guys. They've chartered with us every summer for the last seven years. They're used to flying around in small planes and their powers of observation are keen. I don't think an untrained passenger would have had any idea of what was happening."

"Well, that's a plus, I guess."

"It certainly was. Rudy and his front seat passenger were both unconscious and the passengers in back were shaken up but not seriously injured. They assessed the situation and saw that Rudy had turned off the fuel, so there was no immediate danger of fire. Then they unbuckled and checked on Rudy and their partner. They didn't want to move them in case they had spinal cord injuries."

"That was smart."

"Yes, it was, and probably prevented further injuries."

"So how were they picked up and how did he get to Anchorage?"

Leila has pulled into the parking garage and is searching for a spot. "Look, we're here at the hospital now. Let's hurry in to see how Rudy is doing. How about if I let Ana fill you in on the rest of the story?"

Leila rushes down the hallway towards intensive care. Danny almost runs to keep up with her. The familiar waiting room is dark and Leila sees Dom leaning back in one of the chairs with his eyes closed, mouth open and snoring. Celeste is lying on her back on one of the loveseats with her eyes open, staring at the ceiling.

"Where are Ana and Nat?" Leila whispers, not wanting to awaken Dom.

"Ana is in sitting with Rudy and Nat took off about an hour ago. She said she was getting antsy just sitting around."

Celeste notices Danny standing there and says, "You must be Danny. I can see the family resemblance. I'm Celeste, Rudy's fiancée. I've heard a lot about you. Rudy really admires you. He says you're going to be the next John Elway."

"Actually, it's the other way around, Celeste. Rudy is my hero. He's always teaching me things. Whenever I visit Alaska I am amazed at how much he knows about everything."

"Yes, he is one of a kind. But he says you're a fabulous pitcher and have an athletic scholarship for both football and baseball. That's impressive! You must have brains, too, I'm sure."

Danny turns to Leila, "Aunt Leila, can I go in and see Rudy? I want to let him know I'm here."

"His doctors said only one person at a time, Danny. He is still in ICU. Let me go and check with Ana to see what has been happening."

Celeste chimes in, "It was just a few minutes ago the nurse in charge came in and reported some small changes. She said his vitals are becoming steadier. His EKG is normal now, although his blood pressure is still very high. She said he was still unconscious, but apparently that's normal for the intensity of head injury he suffered and the five hours of surgery he went through. In the morning, Dr. Bingham—his neurologist—is going to do more testing."

Leila heads toward the waiting room door to check up on Rudy. "I'll be right back, Danny, hang tight."

Danny has so many questions; he stutters as he tries to drag information out of Celeste. "How... what was...Is he going to make it, Celeste? How much...? When did he leave Anchorage? How did he get to the hospital? Why weren't you with him? Wasn't—isn't he the best pilot in the world?"

"Oh, Danny, I don't have any answers. I don't know how or when he will recover. I'll be glad just to have him open his eyes and smile at me. It's agony to hold his hand and not have him respond. He looks so helpless...all those tubes and wires. I can't stand it, Danny. The doctors are so close-mouthed; it seems like they're trying to hide something."

"They probably don't know any more than you know. They're not miracle workers. All they can do is patch us up and hope our spirit is willing to recover. Hey, maybe that's it. Maybe Rudy is so ashamed for making a mistake he doesn't want to recover."

"Oh, no! That can't be. He didn't make any mistakes. He knew that terrain like the back of his hand. He knew the airplane as well as he knows how to walk. To him, flying is like breathing. But...what if what you say is true? Maybe subconsciously he is feeling guilty for crashing and doesn't want to face his mother—and me."

"That's why I have to talk some sense into him. I've got to get in there and see him."

Danny gets up and walks toward the Intensive Care Unit. As he exits the waiting room, he bumps into Ana. He notices tears welling up in her eyes. Her cheeks are red.

"Danny, I am so glad to see you. Thank you for coming."

"Well, where else would I be when my favorite cousin needs me? I'm going to go in there and kick his butt and tell him to shape up. This is no time for him to be pulling our leg with one of his tricks."

"It's no trick, Danny. It's serious. Just a few minutes ago he stopped breathing and everyone was rushing around. It was terrible. Maybe you should come back to the house with me and get a good night's rest and come back tomorrow."

"How could I do that when he needs me?"

"Well, I'm going back to Mom's house. I've got to drop Dom off at Celeste's and then go and get some sleep. Dom is leaving for Chicago tomorrow night and I have to go back to the North Slope the next day, or I'll lose my job. I'm glad you're here to take over for a while."

"I'm only staying for a couple of days, Ana, so I have to stay at the hospital tonight and see Rudy as soon as I can."

"Relax, Danny. You'll be able to see Rudy shortly. Say, why do you have to go back so soon?"

"I have to report for fall training in Urbana on Friday. But Emma is coming tomorrow and my mom can stay as long as she needs to. She and Dad...well, now is not the time to go into that."

"Look, I'll walk you down to the nurses' station. Maybe if we explain who you are she will let you go in and see him for a while."

They walk arm in arm down the hallway. The antiseptic smells of the hospital assault Danny's nose. The subdued sound of equipment humming belies the seriousness of what happens here in this place fraught with the struggles of life and death.

The head nurse allows Danny into Rudy's room, but says, "Five minutes, young man—that's all I can allow."

Ana gives Danny a hug and turns back towards the waiting room. "Good luck, Danny. See you tomorrow. I'll bring your mom back with me in the morning."

Chapter Thirty-three

Nikki and Ana

Nikki walks into the kitchen as soon as Leila and Danny pull out of the driveway. *What I really need is some wine. I wonder if my straight-laced sister has any that's drinkable.*

Nikki rummages through the cupboards and spies a small, refrigerated wine cellar in the walk-in pantry. *Ah, a decent Chardonnay. This will do.* Nikki searches through the drawers for a corkscrew. She finds one and spots the wine glasses in a cupboard next to the refrigerator. Then, wine in hand, she walks into the living room. She places the glass on a table next to the sofa. The table looks like a slice of a huge cedar log. The top has irregular edges and is covered with beveled glass cut into an interesting shape matching the irregularities of the cedar. *Interesting.* Taking a sip, she becomes aware of hunger pangs gnawing at her stomach.

She returns to kitchen and searches through the refrigerator and pantry for anything edible. *Not much in the way of food. I wonder how my sister survives. No wonder she's as skinny as a rail.*

She spots a container of vegetable soup and decides to warm that while she searches for bread. In the freezer she finds a loaf of crusty Italian bread. *Well, this might make the soup a little more palatable.*

Nikki thaws the bread in the microwave then turns back to the stove. The aroma wakes up her taste buds. *Is that ginger I smell?* At last she sits down to enjoy a meal in solitude. Surprised at the quality of the soup, she eats one bowl of it before returning to the living room for her wine. *Wow, this is excellent! I guess Leila has improved in her appreciation of fine food and wine.* She serves another bowl and savors every spoonful, trying to analyze the ingredients and flavorings.

Finished, fatigue from the events of the last two days hits her. She heads for the living room and collapses into the comfortable, overstuffed sofa, closing her eyes. Warmth surrounds her. She feels safe. Nothing can hurt her here. Thoughts of Gerik's infidelity, Daphne's betrayal, Granite's rejection and Mitch's revelations are buried deep. They are as far away as the Midwest she left so eagerly. She stretches out on the sofa and drifts off to sleep.

Nikki dreams she is in a tropical paradise. A small lagoon surrounded by lush foliage and orchids is before her. She decides to go for a swim, looks around to verify that she is alone and undresses. Naked, she enters the water. It is refreshing and comfortable. She lies back and floats effortlessly in its embrace. She notices a familiar smell as she inhales the moist air. What is it? It's almost like cinnamon, but...she notices someone swimming next to her. Whoever it is is moving with strong, sure strokes. She can see that the swimmer is headed toward a door in the jungle and will get the treasure beyond it. Nikki realizes she now wants whatever it is behind the door more than anything she has ever wanted before. *I have to get there first. I can't let anyone take it from me. It's supposed to be mine.*

She starts swimming as fast as she can, but her splashing strokes are ineffective. She is simply treading water and getting frustrated. The swimmer is getting closer and closer to the shore and the beckoning door in the jungle. Nikki screams, *No, you can't have it. It's mine.* Then as the swimmer steps onto the shore and walks towards the door, Nikki sees that it is her sister, Leila. *No, dammit! Leila, you always win. I won't let you win this time. You can't have it.* Leila turns before she opens the door and looks at Nikki splashing in the water. Her nostrils flare and her mouth is twisted into a grimace. She squints menacingly and opens her mouth to speak. Nikki can't understand what she is saying and strains to catch a word or two. She hears the door open and heavy steps clomp across a hard surface.

Nikki kicks as hard as she can and makes it to the shore. "Let me have it, Leila." The room behind the door is dark and Nikki struggles to open her eyes wider. With great effort she opens them. Leila is sitting on the edge of the sofa next to her.

"How did you get here so fast, Leila?" Nikki asks.

"It's me, Ana, Aunt Elsa. You must have been dreaming," Ana says as she leans towards Nikki.

"So you're changing your name now, too?" Nikki says, still in her dream.

"No, it's me, Ana—Anastasia—Leila's daughter. Mom is at the hospital with Rudy."

"Why do you always have to have the upper hand? Can't you just once let me have first choice at something? You always win. But, I'm going to get it this time. And, besides, I told you my name is Nikki now. Can't you show me a little respect?"

Ana tries to snap her out of her dream. She attempts to convince Nikki that she is Leila's daughter. She knows something of the rift between her mother and aunt, but has never been told the whole story. The anger in Nikki's voice surprises her.

"Look, Aunt El-Nikki, what you're dreaming has nothing to do with me. I'm Ana, your niece. I don't know what got between you and my mom, but please wake up. She really needs you now. She always tries to handle everything herself and never admits needing anything."

Nikki struggles to make sense of what she is hearing.

Ana continues. "My mom called you out of desperation. I was there when she talked to you and she was working so hard to keep from breaking down I thought she would tear apart at the seams."

The urgency in Ana's voice penetrates Nikki's consciousness and she realizes where she is. She tries to sit up to give her niece a hug. "I'm sorry, Ana, but you look so much like Leila when she was a teenager. That single braid down your back looks just like hers and the blond wisps of hair around your face...which is exactly like hers...your hazel eyes...everything. I thought you were her." Nikki pauses to collect her thoughts. "I was dreaming that we were racing towards a treasure in the jungle and just seeing you and thinking it was her made me..."

"That's all right, Aunt El-Nikki. I'm just glad you're here...and finally awake. Mom is so desperate for comfort and hope that she is grasping at anyone or anything that might give her a glimmer of light. I know she always seems so much in control, but deep down, she is more sensitive than anyone I know." Ana pauses and looks at her aunt. "Are you fully awake now?"

"Sort of."

"Well, just to give you an idea of her sensitivity, can you stand to hear a little story?"

"Fine. Go ahead."

"I remember one day when I when I was in tenth grade I got home from school and saw her kneeling in the garden with tears in her eyes. She was trying to prop up a flower with a broken stem, using some tape and a small stick. I heard her whispering, 'You can make it. Just try a little harder.' She would have been embarrassed to think anyone saw her being so tender. But she definitely has a soft side. After Daddy died, though, she looked and felt like she had a shell of concrete around her. Now with Rudy..." Ana looks at the floor and cannot continue.

Nikki slumps down in the sofa and tries to feel some sympathy, but her emotions have been working overtime. Her store of compassion is depleted. "Well, that's not my. . . No, wait just a minute. Let me start over." She closes her eyes and memories of feeling inept and ugly assail her. The picture of Gerik and Daphne in the shower makes her stomach tighten and a bitter taste in her mouth makes her feel as though she will vomit. She clenches her teeth as she remembers Leila's put-downs. She shakes her head as though to clear it and a new thought enters her mind. *I'm not the only one who has suffered loss. Poor Leila! First her husband dies in such a traumatic accident and now her son might not make it. She never did anything to deserve this. We may not have been the best of friends, but we are sisters and she needs me. Maybe if I help her through this, she will help me to put my life back together.*

"Look, Ana, I know your mother and I have not always been close. Maybe that's an understatement, but I don't know who she is anymore, if I ever did. Our relationship hasn't grown or developed beyond what it was in high school. Isn't that pathetic? But we all can change and grow, can't we?"

Ana nods.

"I haven't been a very good aunt, either, have I? But here we are now. I'm tired of living in denial and in the past. I'm ready to change. I don't know where to start. I need to know how I can help."

Ana picks at a loose thread on her shirt and blinks tears away. When she left the hospital, there had been no change in Rudy's condition. His recovery would be slow and the doctors gave no indication of how complete it would be. Hopelessness pushes at her like a cattle prod. "Aunt El Nikki, I really appreciate you coming here. Look, can I call you Aunt Elsa? Aunt Nikki just doesn't seem right to me."

"Nikki is my name now, sweetie. I am a different person than I was a year ago when I changed it. So many things have happened and as Nikki I am free to acknowledge the real me. Please, just call me Nikki. You can drop the Aunt part. Pretend I'm someone you just met, because essentially I am."

"You sure look a lot different than you used to. I remember you as a soft, plain looking motherly type."

"Really? Is that how I came across?"

"No, that's not what I meant; it came out all wrong. But, wow, you certainly are stylish now. Your hair is so cool. I wish my mom would do something to change hers."

"That's just surface stuff, Ana. The real change in me is inside. Your mother has always been self-assured and competent at everything. I am just beginning to have a sense of my own strength. Who knows why I was such a dependent, insecure woman with no sense of my own self-worth. I was quite pitiable. I had to knock others down so I could feel like I was better than them."

"Oh, Nikki, you never acted that way to me. You were always encouraging when I decided to pursue a career as a chef. I remember calling you for advice because my mom always said how gifted you were in the kitchen—at everything having to do with homemaking. She's always envied you."

"How absurd! Why would anyone, especially Leila, envy me?"

"You're both incredibly gifted, Nikki. Maybe it's time for you to work together. Rudy needs you both."

"You're gifted, too, Ana. That vegetable soup in the refrigerator was delicious. You didn't say you made it, but I'm sure you did. The freshness of the vegetables and the way the flavors blend together without losing their individual character is wonderful. And the spices—wow! I couldn't identify all of them, but the ginger sure complements the carrots. You must be really popular up on the slope."

"Yeah, they all love me. They say the way to a man's heart is through his stomach. But, I'm in no rush to get too involved with anyone just yet. I'm only twenty-two. My goal is to get a real job as a chef. The North Slope is good experience, but it doesn't give me a chance to practice the gourmet dishes I mastered in the culinary arts program at the university. And I hate being gone for two weeks out of every month."

"Do you have any prospects?"

"As a matter of fact, I had an interview lined up at the new French restaurant in mid-town, but then Rudy…"

"I'm so sorry, Ana. This has to be hard on you."

"Yes, but not half as hard as it is on Mom. She and Rudy have drawn so close to each other since Daddy died. At times it seemed that he was the adult and she was the child. If he doesn't make it…"

Nikki interrupts saying, "Don't say that, Ana. Of course he'll make it. But now, what can I do to help?"

"I have to go back to the slope the day after tomorrow and my mom will need someone to see that she eats once in a while. She'll need a break from her vigil at the hospital. And just having another presence in the house will help her not to feel so lonely. Dom said he has to return to Chicago tomorrow. He'll only be gone a few days, but my Mom is leaning on him so much—did you know they were engaged? She would be all alone with both of us gone. Of course there's always Natalia, but we never know when she will go off on a binge again. And Celeste is a basket case herself."

"I'm not really following all of this. Who is Dom—and Celeste? But, whatever. I'll be here for as long as I'm needed."

Ana gets up and wraps her long arms around Nikki. She lays her head on her shoulder and a sob escapes her.

"Thank you for being here, Nikki. I just know your presence will help us all. I'm so glad you came. And I think Danny will be able to get through to Rudy. They're two of a kind. Rudy always loved showing off for him when he visited. Maybe he'll show off now and recover in record time."

Nikki tries to stifle a yawn, and fails.

Ana looks at her watch and says, "Wow, how did it get to be so late? You'd better get to sleep, Nikki. It's almost four a.m. Chicago time. Don't worry about getting up in the morning. Mom will be at the hospital most of the day and I can give you a ride down there whenever you get up."

Nikki rises from the sofa and heads toward the guest room.

"I guess my mom showed you where everything is. Just make yourself at home. I hope the daylight doesn't bother you."

"Nothing will bother me at this point. I feel as though I'm doing something useful. Just let me get a good night's sleep and I'll be ready for anything—even Leila."

Ana smiles as Nikki continues.

"I'm glad we had this conversation, Ana, and I'm really glad I came. In spite of all the reasons I'm here, or maybe because of them, I am hopeful that all will be well."

Chapter Thirty-four

Danny Visits Rudy

Danny's hand touches the handle of the door to the Intensive Care Unit but he doesn't turn it. He stands there for a long time, frozen. Finally, the door opens and Leila appears like a ghost right before him.

"You can go in now, Danny. But don't..."

"I know, Aunt Leila. The nurse said only five minutes."

"I'll be in the waiting room."

"Okay."

Danny takes one step into the darkened room and gasps. Nothing can prepare one for visiting the ICU. The last time he saw Rudy they had been waterskiing at Big Lake and Rudy in his wet suit was the picture of strength and vitality. His wide grin and shining black hair...Danny clutches his chest and falls to his knees.

"No..."

He hadn't noticed the nurse by the far wall.

"Are you all right, young man?" she asks.

"This isn't my cousin. There must be some mistake."

Danny looks around at all the equipment in the room. It all seems to be attached to Rudy. Wires and tubes and beeping monitors make him look so small and helpless.

"You've only got five minutes in this room. You can spend it there by the door, on your knees, or you can come and give your cousin some encouraging words. He can hear you, you know. What he needs right now is…"

"I know."

Danny straightens up immediately, rising to his feet. He approaches Rudy, looking away from all the wires, tubes and equipment. He places his hand on Rudy's shoulder.

"Hey, cuz, what in the heck are you doing in this get-up?" He pinches his lips together and takes a deep breath. "I'm here for you, buddy. Everyone is pulling for you. Wow, you've got a knockout of a fiancée. How did you get so lucky? She's out there saying rosaries for you. Well, not actually rosaries, but I'm sure she's praying in her own way." Danny chuckles, and then grows serious again.

"Look, man, you've got to try a little harder. Remember when we were fishing on the Copper River and I got too close to the fast current and was about to lose my balance and be swept off? I was terrified. I froze up and just about lost it. Remember how you yelled for me to stay calm, focus on my footing and lean into the shore and take that leap of faith toward safety? That's what you've got to do now, Bud. Come back to the shore. I'll even give you a hand." He reaches toward Rudy's hand lying limp on the sheet.

"Come on, Rudy. Try a little harder. We don't care how you got here—or if you did anything wrong, or anything. We just want you to open your eyes and smile at us and let us know you'll be okay. You can take a rest if you want to, but I'm telling you, man. You'd better be up and about tomorrow when I come back. I can't stay here forever."

Rudy just lies there inert. It doesn't look like he heard anything. Danny glances at the clock. He only has one minute left before the nurse will shoo him out of the room. He strokes the small patch of skin on Rudy's hand that is not covered with bandages. He whispers, "I love you, Rudy. We all love you. We're going to pull you through this. Trust me."

Danny turns and leaves the room as fast as he can. He collapses into a chair just outside the door. He covers his face with his hands, shoulders heaving, sobbing uncontrollably. "Oh, man, what if he doesn't make it? God, please…please help him. We want him back," he whispers.

He sees Leila's feet through his outspread fingers. Her hand is on his shoulder. He rises to be enfolded by her embrace.

"Oh, Aunt Leila…"

"Shush, Danny. Shush. I know."

Chapter Thirty-five

Nikki and Leila Finally Talk

The night, for both Nikki and Leila, drags on like the seemingly endless nights of an Alaskan winter. After her conversation with Ana, Nikki falls asleep and doesn't move for two or three hours. At the hospital, Leila dozes off and on in the waiting room. Dom and Ana leave, so only Leila, Celeste and Danny are there to take turns in Rudy's room.

Poor Celeste, Leila thinks as she drifts off to sleep. *The bond she and Rudy have is so like mine and Pete's. They complement each other—just like Pete and me—but now, there's Dom. He certainly is not someone I would have chosen, but I have to admit, he does have his good qualities. Somehow, he's always making me laugh. I've needed that. But poor Elsa, or Nikki as she calls herself now; she's always had a chip on her shoulder. I don't know if we'll ever patch things up or if we'll know where we ever went wrong. We're just so different. But I do need her now. I need her homemaking, comforting, stabilizing presence. I need to tell her that. I need to tell her how much I appreciate her gifts.*

Nikki, after three hours of sound sleep, tosses and turns and tries to get back to sleep. She finally gives up and gets out of bed. She paces the floor and tries to figure out why she is here in Alaska. She tries to ignore her problems at home. *Poor Leila, I never realized before how it must have been for her to lose a husband so unexpectedly. How has she been able to go on living? Now I have a bit of a clue how it feels to lose someone. I feel like I may as well cash it in. How can I have been such a failure? I could be to blame for the mess I'm in, but Leila never did anything to deserve her problems.*

The sun is high in the sky at five a.m. as Nikki wanders through the house. She doesn't enter Leila's bedroom, but goes into another room, which is set up like an artist's studio. She wonders who the painter is. *It must be either Leila or Ana. Rudy couldn't be this talented—but then again, he is a surprising young man. Who knows? Maybe he can paint.*

Nikki appraises a partially finished portrait of a girl. She doesn't know if it is a portrait of a real, living person, or if it's from the artist's imagination. *It's good though. It could stand next to Daphne's paintings favorably.* At the thought of Daphne, Nikki clenches her teeth, but blocks out the images of her betrayal. *I'm going to focus on Leila and Rudy.*

The portrait is done in blue tones with dark shadows covering most of the canvas. The subject seems to appear out of the darkness almost like an apparition. Her dark eyes stare vacantly at something off to her right. The artist captures the essence of a person lost, yet desiring—what—she doesn't know. A small printed card on the easel says, "Natalia, Searching for Self."

Wow. This is most amazing. It is heartbreaking. If this is how Natalia is now, I don't know how Leila can stand it. I kind of gathered that she had some problems with drugs, but is she really this bad off?

Nikki hears a sound behind her and turns to see Ana standing at the door.

"Aunt El-Nikki, I'm surprised to see you up so early. Did the sunlight bother you?"

"No, I guess there are just so many things on my mind I couldn't sleep."

Pointing at the easel, Nikki says, "This portrait is amazing. Is this yours or your mother's work? It's brilliant."

"It's Mom's. She only took up painting about five years ago. She was in a support group of parents with children addicted to drugs and painting was one of the ways the facilitator recommended to deal with all the frustrations of the situation. Art therapy they call it. Mom was at her wit's end with Natalia's addiction."

"I never knew she could paint. But I guess there are a lot of things I don't know about her."

"She showed real talent right from the start and Dad was so supportive. He came from a long line of artists, although they mostly worked with natural elements like ivory and furs. Some of his grandmother's sketches are in the Anchorage Art Museum. Dad didn't inherit that creative gene, though, so he was thrilled that Mom was so good at it."

"She certainly is. Is this a recent portrait? It doesn't look quite finished."

"No, it's not. Mom hasn't picked up a brush since Daddy died. She's been like a zombie walking around half-alive. Rudy has tried to get her back into painting; it was so good for her. It was therapeutic. But now that he..." Ana stops, closes her eyes and shakes her head from side to side. "I can't say it; I can't stand to even mention how serious his condition is. What if he doesn't make it? "

"Look, he's going to be fine. We have to be positive. We have to believe. Don't let me hear you saying anything negative—especially around your mother."

"But she has been living in denial ever since Daddy died. She has to face up to the facts."

"We don't know what is going to happen, Ana. The doctors have done their best and now we have to support Rudy with our positive thoughts and prayers. His spirit can sense the light and healing love we are sending."

"I don't know. It's just so hard to believe, after the way Daddy died." Ana walks to the window and stares at the Chugach Mountains. Her eyes lose focus, tears sting her cheeks as they run down and her breathing is shallow. She leans against the window frame looking as though she will collapse under the weight on her shoulders. Nikki walks over to stand beside her. She wraps an arm around her waist and in return, Ana puts her head on Nikki's shoulder. They stand there for several minutes without talking.

Ana takes a deep breath and turns to face her aunt. "Thank you. Now, how about if I fix you a cup of coffee and some breakfast?"

"That would be wonderful. I didn't realize until now, but I am famished. Airline food leaves a little bit to be desired and the fabulous soup I ate last night only whetted my appetite."

As they walk towards the kitchen, Ana says, "You can watch me if you want, but no helping. I like to work alone. Or if you'd rather, you can go out on the deck to enjoy the morning sunshine and the view. I'll bring your coffee out as soon as it's done. How do you like it? Or would you prefer a latte?"

"A latte would be perfect. What did I do to deserve the royal treatment?"

"Well, it's not everyday my aunt comes to visit. I want to show off a little."

"Ana, you're a wonderful niece. I'm only sorry I have not gotten to know you before this."

Ana shrugs and turns toward the kitchen. Nikki follows her to admire it in the light of day. The stainless steel counters and work spaces, commercial cook-top in the center with a polished copper hood hanging over it and the double wide refrigerator-freezer look like they were installed with a skilled chef in mind. Knowing Leila's lack of ability or interest in that area, Nikki asks, "Why does your mother have such a fancy, professional looking kitchen? She's never been one for fussing over meals."

"When they built this house two years before Daddy died, I was still in high school but since I was enrolled in culinary classes at the University, I begged to have it built with entertaining in mind. I studied for months to come up with the perfect design and still have it look like a home and not a restaurant kitchen."

Nikki spots the professional espresso maker on the counter and points at it. "That espresso maker looks like it has had some use."

"Yes, Mom does appreciate fine coffee. In fact; she is a bit of a coffee snob. It was my gift to them when I graduated from culinary school. Of course, I get to use it whenever I'm here. Since I work on the Slope and am only in town half the time, it's just easier to stay here. Mom has needed company since Daddy died. Of course, now that Dom will be moving in, I guess I'll have to find a place of my own."

"Dom is moving in?"

"Well, yes, as soon as they're married. But who knows when that might be—now." Ana turns toward the refrigerator, grabs eggs, shallots, mushrooms, breakfast sausage and some other items and starts piling them on the counter.

Nikki admires her efficient movements and would like to stay to watch but senses Ana would rather be left alone. She turns and walks through the living room, slides the glass door open and steps out onto the deck. It spans the entire house on the downhill side and Nikki gasps at the panoramic view. A mountain range across a grey colored bay has some snow covered peaks. One of the mountains has the distinctive cone shape of a volcano. *I'll have to find out what that is.*

Closer, a small group of tall buildings is sparkling in the sun. *That must be downtown Anchorage.* Looking back toward the water she wonders why it is so dirty. *They must have some indus-try around here to make it all grey and ugly looking.*

Nikki collapses into the gliding rocker. She tries to get her bearings but at this latitude in June, the sun is above the horizon most of the day. It's hard to tell directions from the sun. The breeze is soft and warm on her face. Even dressed in her light pajamas she is comfortable. She closes her eyes and leans back into the cushion. She gets a whiff of coffee brewing as it wafts across the deck and for a moment, Nikki forgets where she is. The memory of a camping trip with Leila and her parents is so real she feels like an eight year old again.

It was a lazy summer morning by a crystal clear lake in Northern Wisconsin. She lay in her sleeping bag listening to the quiet murmuring of her parents at the picnic table right next to the tent. The smell of coffee perking on the camp stove was intoxicating. *I wish I could have some. It smells so good.* She opened her eyes and saw Leila sleeping on a cot next to hers. She unzipped her sleeping bag and tiptoed to Leila's cot. She intended to tickle Leila's nose, but just then Leila turned and Nikki lost her balance and fell on the edge of the cot, causing it to topple. They ended up on the floor of the tent rolling in laughter.

Nikki smiles as she remembers how much fun they had on that camping trip. The sound of Ana opening the door wakes her from her reverie.

"Here's your latte and hey, look who's here."

Leila walks onto the deck and kneels beside Nikki. Nikki leans forward to embrace her.

"Thank you for coming El-Nikki. I never thought I'd say this, but I need you—desperately."

"I need you too, Leila. And that's something I thought I'd never say. But maybe it's time we started acting like real sisters again. We have a lot of catching up to do, but first things first. How is Rudy?"

"He's the same, I guess. Nothing changed during the night and later today the neurologist is going to run a follow-up CT. I just needed to come home for a bit to take a shower and get away from the terrible atmosphere. That place makes me feel like I am being strangled. I don't know how anyone gets well in a hospital."

Leila gets up and pulls a chair closer to Nikki's. They sit facing each other.

"I've never had to spend much time in a hospital, thank God. Danny and Emma are so healthy. The only time I ever had any exposure to a hospital was when Emma had her tonsils removed. That was bad enough. How are you able to handle it, Leila?"

"I have to be there for Rudy. I feel guilty leaving even for a couple of hours. What if something happens and he needs me? But I'll tell you, Dom has been a lifesaver. He's such a good uncle to Celeste. She and Rudy are engaged, you know. And Dom and I plan to be married. He proposed to me on the way up to Deadhorse. That seems like years ago. I can't believe it's only been five days."

Leila stares out at the vista, remembering the chain of events of the past few days: camping, watching the falcons, returning to Anchorage, and hiking on Bird Ridge. The image of Ana's face when she told her about Rudy being lost pops into Leila's mind and the memory is devastating. The pain and fear painted there are exactly what she feels right now. It is almost too much to bear. Her shoulders droop and tears spring into her eyes.

Nikki notices Leila's look of desolation. "Oh, Leila, what can I do to help? I feel so useless."

"Just having you here is enough. Right now I need to know I have a home to run to when I am overwhelmed. Dom is leaving today and will be gone for three days. He has some business in Chicago he couldn't postpone and I'll be rattling around here by myself. Ana is going to the Slope for a week and Celeste needs a mothering figure. Natalia has relapsed so many times; I know I can't depend on her for anything. I've tried to be strong, but this is beyond me."

Ana opens the sliding glass door a few inches and announces, "I'll have breakfast ready in fifteen minutes. Do you want it out here or in the dining room?"

"Out here will be fine, Ana."

Leila turns back to Nikki and says, "It's such a beautiful morning. It's a rare day when we can eat on the deck without being eaten alive by mosquitoes."

Nikki sips her latte and nods as Ana closes the door. "Isn't she great?"

"She certainly is. I'm so fortunate to have such a talented daughter. I think she takes after you."

"You're just saying that. What talents do I have?"

"Nikki, be serious. I've always envied your abilities to bake and cook and entertain. Your home looks like it came out of a magazine and for you it all seems so effortless. I've watched how you so graciously make people feel welcomed and loved. I've tried to copy your creativity in your quilting, but..."

"Leila, your artistic talent puts mine to shame. I saw your portrait of Natalia. It's splendid—no, splendid is not quite adequate. It's...art with a capital A."

"But your homemaking ought to win awards. It's the stuff that matters. How did Gerik ever get so lucky? I hope he appreciates you."

Now it is Nikki's turn to stare off into the distance. Her face distorts in pain. She tries to control the quivering of her chin. Her grimace of hurt feeling turns to one of anger. She clenches her fists and every muscle in her body feels as though it is coiled and ready to spring. The chair beneath her feels as hard and cold as a steel plate. She rocks back and forth as though she is in a race.

"Oh, Leila, everything is a mess. I'm a mess. It all seems like such a waste. The whole lot of our marriage has been a sham."

Leila's mouth falls open, "Nikki, what...?"

"Gerik has been cheating on me...for a long time. I came home last week to find him and Daphne together in the shower. I hate him. I hate her." Nikki feels the rage building again. "We had it out that night. You can't believe the hurtful things we said and Danny heard it all. It turns out he knew all along that his dad and Daphne were having an affair. Isn't that a nice turn of events?"

A part of Leila wants to say, *"didn't I tell you?"* But she waits for Nikki to continue.

"I can't go into it now. I need time to think."

"But, Danny, how...?"

"I don't know and I haven't had time to confront him. We got your call the night I threw Gerik out and I haven't had time to think about anything else."

"You threw him out? Good for you."

"Daphne's true colors finally came out. I just can't believe what a conniving, devious, lying bitch she has been. You should have seen her hanging on him. It makes me sick to think about it."

"Did you tell him you were coming to Alaska?"

"No, but I'm sure Emma will. She has always been daddy's girl. She's mad at me for throwing him out. But it wasn't as though he didn't want to leave. I think he was only too eager to rush to Daphne's bed. But I have to let that go for now. I don't want to face anything until I go back and I don't intend to do that until Rudy is better."

"How did you and Danny get here so fast?"

"We were able to get seats on a vacation charter airline the day after you called. Emma is coming too, but I wasn't able to get her reservations on our flight yesterday. She's coming today. It wasn't the best service, but we survived. And Leila, I am so glad to be here. Honest. I feel like I can actually talk to you now. It's just too bad that what we need to talk about is so serious."

"That's what family is for."

Ana opens the door wide, steps onto the deck carrying a serving tray and sets it down on the table. She returns to the dining room and brings another identical tray. On each is loaded a fruit platter arranged with sliced peaches, melon, raspberries, strawberries and bananas garnished with fresh mint. There is also thick sliced and toasted crusty bread with butter melting into it, various crystal dishes with jams, ketchup and more butter, a dish covered with a silver dome, a steaming latte, and a white cloth napkin. She uncovers the hot dishes.

"Breakfast is served, Madams. Bon Appetite!"

"Wow! That is almost too beautiful to eat," Nikki says, rising to take her place at the table. She puts her face over an omelet and inhales its luscious aroma. "It smells heavenly."

"I hope you like mushrooms. I gathered them yesterday for soup, but stole a few for the omelets. They go so well with the Gouda, shallots and spinach. The potatoes are Alaskan— sorry they are not this year's crop, but you will appreciate their flavor, I'm sure. I know they grow Yukon Gold potatoes

335

in other parts of the country, but something in the soil here in Alaska gives them a wonderful, unique flavor. They almost melt away in your mouth. And…the caribou breakfast sausage is from Rudy's last hunting trip."

Leila takes a bite of the omelet and closes her eyes, obviously enjoying the light texture and rich flavor.

"Ana, you are hired. You can do my cooking from now on. I've never been able to master a fluffy omelet. How do you do it?"

"If you hang around I might show you some of my secrets."

Nikki and Leila eat in silence for a few minutes. Leila pushes the food around on her plate, taking an occasional bite, whereas Nikki digs in and savors every bite. Leila has never appreciated fine food and Rudy's condition has caused her normally puny appetite to shrink even more.

With her mouth full, Nikki mumbles to Leila, "Hey, aren't you going to eat? This is outstanding. Ana is a genius."

"I just don't feel much like eating. My stomach is in turmoil."

"Maybe you should go and take a little nap. I'll listen for the phone and let you know if they call." She pauses. "When do you want to go back to the hospital? And do you want me to come with you?"

"That would be fine." Leila says in a monotone. She looks preoccupied and Nikki senses that she is reliving the last few days of anxiety. Leila's expression makes Nikki want to hold her until the pain goes away. She gets up and walks over to grab Leila's hands and pulls her up from the chair. They stand there embracing each other for several minutes. Leila's shoulders begin to shake. Her pain pierces Nikki's heart and she begins to sob, too.

"This is too hard," Leila whispers.

"I know, LaLa, I know. I can't fix it for you, but I can be here with you. We can be here for each other."

"Would you say a prayer for Rudy, please?"

"Of course I will. I'm a little out of practice, but I don't think God cares. I think God already knows about our pain."

"You're right. I'm sure God knows, but I just want to be sure He knows I can't live if Rudy doesn't make it."

"He's going to make it. I know he is."

Ana rushes onto the deck with a phone in her hand. "They want you to get back to the hospital right away, Mom. It sounds urgent."

Chapter Thirty-six

Back to the Hospital

Leila pushes herself away from Nikki, turns and rushes toward the garage without saying a word. Nikki trailing her says, "I'm going with you, LaLa." Without realizing it Nikki has again reverted to the name she used for Leila when she was a toddler. "You're not going to block me out this time."

Leila stops and turns around. Nikki, right on her heels, bumps into her. Leila puts her hands on Nikki's shoulders, looks into her eyes and smiles.

"Thanks for reminding me of that name. I always loved it when you called me that. It made me feel like such a big sister." She adds, "Of course you can come with me. You're my little baby sister."

"Just let me throw on a shirt and pants, instead of these pajamas. I'll be out in a minute." Grabbing the first things she sees at the top of her suitcase, Nikki slips on a pair of tan capris and a rust brown sleeveless shirt. While buttoning it, she rushes to meet Leila who is backing out of the garage. They do not talk during the drive to the hospital.

Leila's hands grip the steering wheel so tightly they begin to go numb.

Nikki notices traffic lights turning red as they speed through intersections with the traffic seeming to clear out of the way at Leila's approach. She almost feels as though they have flashing lights and a siren on top of their car.

They turn on to Lake Otis Parkway, squealing the tires and throwing gravel. As they are crossing Tudor Road, the yellow light turns red. A car to the east of the intersection barely misses them as it accelerates forward the instant the light changes.

Nikki can't help but scream at the near miss. "Leila, slow down, you're going to kill us both."

Just then they both hear a siren and see a police car behind them signaling to pull over.

"Oh, now what? Can't he see we're in a hurry?"

"Of course he can. That's why he's pulling us over."

Leila pulls into a parking lot. She reaches for her purse and realizes she left it at home in her haste to get to the hospital.

"Now what am I going to do?"

Nikki, trying to calm her down, says, "Let me do the talking."

The policeman walks up to the driver's side of the car and Leila rolls down her window. Tears are streaming down her face and she grabs a strand of her long blond hair, twisting it around and around her index finger.

"Please, officer…"

"Not so fast, young lady. Where's the big rush? Do you realize you were going fifty miles an hour in a thirty-five zone? I've been on your tail since O'Malley Road and you almost ran two red lights."

"Please…my son…" Leila pleads.

Nikki puts her hand on Leila's arm and looks up at the police officer, "Sir, please let me explain. My sister just got news from the hospital that her son might…he's critical and she needs to get there as fast as possible. Would it be okay if I drove the rest of the way? We are so close. You can follow us the rest of the way and give her a ticket if you have to, but please, let us go. Her daughter said it's urgent."

The officer scratches his beard, thinking. "Well, all right, change seats quickly and I'll give you a police escort the rest of the way. Is he in the ER at Providence?"

"I think he's in the ICU, but I've never been to the hospital. I'm from out of town, but I do know it's Providence."

"Well, let's get a move on."

He runs back to his patrol car, pulls in front of Nikki and Leila and motions for them to follow. They pull out on to Lake Otis behind the flashing lights and siren of the police car and travel the rest of the way to the hospital in a few minutes.

Nikki parks in the emergency room lot and she and Leila rush in with the police officer following. Once he is assured that Leila's son is, indeed, in the hospital, he takes Nikki's arm and pulls her aside. "Tell your sister I'm letting her go this time. I can see she doesn't need any further aggravation right now. But I'm telling you, don't let her drive in this condition, or it might be more than her son who's in critical condition."

"Thank you so much officer. You're a godsend."

"Don't mention it—and best of luck to you all."

"I think we're going to need a lot more than luck." Due to her brief conversation with the policeman, Nikki does not know where Leila has gone and never having been to the hospital before she feels disoriented and panicky.

She starts down a hallway in the direction she thought Leila went but a nurse stops her. "Where do you think you're going? That's off limits except for family members."

"Well, I'm family."

"Who is the patient?"

"It's Rudy..." Nikki starts and for a moment cannot remember the last name. "Listen, I've got to get to my sister Leila."

"I thought you said the patient's name was Rudy."

"It is. Leila is my sister, his mother. Can't you tell me where they are?"

Nikki is on the verge of tears.

The nurse is unsympathetic and blocks the hallway in the direction Nikki assumes is the right way.

A familiar voice behind her makes her turn around. Danny is approaching from a wide hallway in the opposite direction. When she sees him her knees almost buckle and give way, but she stiffens and stretches her arms out toward him. "Danny!"

"Mom, I'm so glad you're here. Come on, it's down this way. Aunt Leila is going to need you."

"What is it, Danny? What's happened?"

"You'll see. Just—let's hurry before..."

Chapter Thirty-seven

Rudy in Surgery

Nikki finds Leila in the hallway outside of a small critical care unit. A thin, dark haired man is holding her in his arms as though she will fall over if he lets go. His face is buried in her hair.

"Oh, Dom, what is it going to be next? How much more can we—and he—take?"

"Come on, Leila, let's go and sit in the waiting room. Celeste is still here, but she was napping when I got back this morning. I think she was up most of the night, poor kid. So when they came to inform us about the emergency surgery I couldn't bear to wake her." Dom looks up to see Danny and Nikki hurrying towards him and Leila. "Look! Here's Danny now, and this must be your sister."

Nikki holds out her hand to Dom but he brushes it aside and gives her a hug instead. Too stunned to resist, she is speechless.

"I thought you were the talkative one," Dom says.

"Well, I…"

"I must say there is a family resemblance. I didn't know a small town like Caraville could produce two such beauties."

"How do you…Oh, I guess you must be…"

"Please excuse my bad manners. I didn't introduce myself. My name is Dominic Perfetti, soon to be your brother-in-law. Call me Dom."

The four of them walk the few steps toward the private waiting room. Celeste opens the door as they approach. "What's going on, Uncle Dom?"

"They've taken Rudy to surgery. They said something about the advanced CT scan showing some bleeding that didn't appear on earlier scans. Don't worry, kiddo, he is in good hands."

"Is he already in the operating room?"

"Yes, the surgeon has a full schedule today and wanted to get him in before he started on his other patients. He said to expect at least three hours." Dom does not share the fact that the doctors told him Rudy suffered a seizure and they needed to operate quickly to preclude further complications. "Hey, how about getting some breakfast while we wait?" Dom asks.

"We just had breakfast at home, Dom. I don't think I could eat another thing right now," Leila says.

"I'll join you, Dom." Danny and Celeste say in unison, then turn to each other and laugh. The laughter releases their tension for a moment and the three of them turn and walk towards the cafeteria hand in hand.

Dom turns to say, "See you later."

Leila and Nikki are left standing in the hallway near the small private waiting room.

"Well, Sis, it looks like we've got some time on our hands. What time is it now?"

"It's seven forty-five and Dom said they took Rudy to surgery at seven so he won't be out until ten at the earliest."

"Is there a chapel around here somewhere?" Nikki asks. "You said you wanted me to say some prayers."

"Yes, that's a good idea. I'll walk you down there and then come back and try to rest a little."

Leila stops to let the nurse in charge know she's going to the chapel and will be away for a short time. She then leads the way across the hospital to the small chapel.

"Why don't you stay with me for a while? If no one is there I'm sure we can talk a bit."

"I can't stay there. I tried to go to mass, but it brings back too many bad memories. I haven't had much to do with church since Pete died. Oh, Father Ignaty helped me a lot right afterwards, but later I couldn't bear to go alone and besides, it really wasn't my faith anyway. Pete was Russian Orthodox and we attended regularly when he was alive."

"I never knew he was Russian Orthodox."

"His grandmother saw to it that all her grandchildren got the proper indoctrination. Pete loved her so much he went, I think, mostly for her."

As they walk in, Nikki heads right up the center aisle toward the front. A few people are seated throughout the small chapel. Leila grabs Nikki's arm to tell her that she doesn't want to share the space with anyone, when a side door opens and a priest in long vestments enters carrying a large book, which he reverently places on the altar. All the people stand and begin to sing.

"Let's get out of here," Leila whispers.

"No," Nikki whispers back. "Mass is starting. This might be just the perfect way to offer our prayers."

"Well, I'm not staying." Leila is eager to get away.

"You can leave if you want, but I'm staying."

The singing stops as abruptly as it started. Leila now feels awkward standing there holding her sister's arm, but she is frozen. Several people frown at them.

"The Lord be with you!"

The priest is looking right at the sisters and Leila thinks the priest is addressing her. She starts to say thank you when she hears the people near her respond, "And with your spirit."

"We can't leave now, LaLa. Come on, humor me for once." Nikki's face is close to Leila's ear.

Leila sees that the people are now seated. She is still holding on to Nikki's arm but drops it and turns. Nikki puts her arm around Leila's waist and pulls her towards the closest unoccupied seats. They sit down.

The words of the people who get up to read and the voice of the priest as he says the prayers are like a distant hum to Leila. Her mind is in turmoil from the events of the last few hours. *I never had a chance to give Rudy a hug before they took him off to surgery. What if...? Oh, God!* It reminds her of not saying goodbye to Pete when he left the office before his crash and she is filled with sorrow. *How can you, God, if you are real, let something like this happen?*

She notices Nikki standing, kneeling, sitting and responding to prayers, but it is like watching a movie in a foreign language. It's not real. Leila's reality is anguish and fear. She kneels and rests her folded arms on the unoccupied chair in front of her. She buries her face in the crook of her elbow and cries quietly. *I don't believe you're there, God. You dupe these people into some sort of stupor, promising happiness, promising—I don't know what, but it's all a lie. What have you given me but pain? I can't believe in a God like that. I won't believe in a God who sends punishment. You don't even care. And here I am addressing you as though you exist. I've got to get out of here. This is insane.*

She is about to get up and leave when she hears a voice full of compassion and love speaking close to her ear. "All is well."

Leila opens her eyes and turns her head sharply to the right to see who was speaking but no one is there. She looks to her left. It's only Nikki.

"What did you say, Nikki?"

"I didn't say anything."

"But, I..."

"Shush. I want to hear this." Nikki turns back towards the priest who is talking from the ambo.

Leila hears the drone of his words but their meaning is lost. He may as well be speaking Swahili. She stares, eyes wide open now, at the modern looking metal sculpture of a dove. About three feet tall and four or five feet across, it appears to be in flight. *I wonder how they did that.* The polished silvery metal reflects the light and as Leila stares it seems to vibrate and glisten with life, almost as though it is breathing. *I must be losing my mind.*

Leila tears her eyes away from the sculpture with difficulty. She studies the religious paintings on the walls, the grey and brown patterned rug on the floor, the burgundy cushioned chairs, the priest in his green vestments, the altar, the enormous urn full of unrecognizable flowers on the floor in front of the altar, the crucifix. Everything seems to have a light shining from within. She looks at Nikki sitting to her left and notices her flawless complexion, her high cheekbones, the way her hair brushes her neck so smoothly. *How have I never noticed her beauty before?*

The dust motes floating in the sunlight streaming in from the skylight seem to be dancing in rhythm and have a life of their own. Peace and contentment flow over her like a warm river. Such feelings have been so lacking in her life she cannot name them. She only knows it feels good.

Her mind, just moments ago so full of fear and anguish, is suddenly calm. The pain in her heart is still there, but it is sweet, like the thrill of being lifted up by a huge powerful wave. *What just happened?* At first she wonders, but then begins to accept that something has changed and she doesn't need to understand what it is. She notices every breath she takes and can feel the tingling of oxygen reaching even to her fingertips. Her body feels warm, like being wrapped in a soft blanket and cradled in someone's arms. Inside she has calmness and an assurance that Rudy will be fine. She sits there basking in refulgence. *I feel so grounded, yet light. I feel so alert, yet dreamlike. I am energized, yet peaceful. How can this be?* Her euphoria continues until she realizes that everyone has left the chapel except Nikki and her. Nikki is peering at her with concern.

"Are you okay, Leila? You looked like you were in a trance. What is going on?"

"Nikki, you wouldn't believe me if I told you."

The side door opens again and the priest, now dressed in black slacks and shirt with a Roman collar enters the darkened chapel. He walks between the rows of chairs where Leila and Nikki are seated and sits down next to Leila.

"You must be Leila Pletnikoff. Would you like to come to my office and talk about what just happened?"

"What are you, psychic? How did you know about...?"

"Please, we'll have more privacy there. Is this your sister? She can come with us if you'd like."

"No," Nikki says. "I want to get back to the kids. They must be done with breakfast by now and are wondering where we are."

She stands and starts to walk out, then realizes she doesn't know which way the room is where Danny, Celeste and Dom are waiting.

"How do I get back there?"

"Turn right out of the chapel and then right again down the wide hallway where you'll see signs for the ER. Follow those and "Family Waiting" will be on your right, just before you get there." Father Steven leads Leila into his office, which is right next to the chapel. They sit at right angles to each other in matching upholstered chairs. Leila sinks back into the softness of her chair. The cushy fabric feels as though it is caressing and comforting her.

"You know, if you had talked to me a half hour ago, I probably would have told you to go to hell. Sorry for the language, but I was very angry and feeling betrayed. But I believe God spoke to me there in the chapel during mass and I want to know more. By the way, how did you know my name?"

"Well, I just came from the operating room where your son..."

"So then you know that he's going to be fine."

"Actually, what I wanted to tell you is that I was called to the operating room right after mass to administer last rites. Rudy had died on the operating table, and you won't be..."

"He died? No! You're lying. No! I don't believe you. God assured me he was going to be okay. Why are you doing this to me?" Leila, on the verge of hysteria, screams. Father Steven tries to put a hand on her shoulder but she pulls away and yells. "Don't touch me! You're just like the god you pretend to follow. You're cruel. You're inhuman. You're sadistic. Why do you insist on torturing me? Why would you tell me that Rudy died?"

Sister Joan has slipped into the room. She stands next to Leila and brushes Leila's hair back from her forehead.

"Tell me he's lying, Sister, please. Tell me Rudy is fine."

"That's just what he was trying to say, Leila. Rudy did indeed die on the operating table. But when they called Father Steven in to anoint him, the moment he touched him with the sacred oil, Rudy's vitals returned to normal. His EKG and EEG resumed their normal patterns. They were almost done with the operation, since things were much less serious than the CT scan had indicated. It's a mystery as to why his vitals plummeted at that point. It may have had something to do with the anesthesia. I don't know. In any case, they were able to wrap things up quickly. He is in the recovery room right now. You can go in and see him in about a half hour, although he won't be awake from the sedation for several hours."

"I've got to get back there," Leila says and stands to leave. As she reaches the door she feels guilty for her outburst. She turns back. "Father Steven, I am so sorry for yelling at you. It was just such a shock. I thought you asked me to come and talk to you about my experience in the chapel—although I wondered how you could know—so when you talked about Rudy, I flipped out."

"What did happen to you in the chapel? Would you like to share?"

"I don't have time right now, but I would like to come back sometime and talk to you about it. It was a profound experience. Even now, after getting so upset, I feel a peace and assurance so unlike anything I've ever felt before. It's more than a feeling though. It's like I've been given a new mind. Things look different. But I'm going to need some time to process it."

"I'm always here, Leila. You can come and talk to me anytime. And I'll be praying for you and your family. In God's hands, all will be well."

"Thank you, Father. I'll be back."

Leila hurries down the corridor to the waiting area humming the melody of 'Ode to Joy'. She repeats the same phrase over and over, "Rudy will be fine, I know it. Rudy will recover. Rudy will be fine. I know that all is well and all will be."

Nikki, Dom, Celeste and Danny look towards the door with worried expressions as Leila enters. When they see her serene face and hear the last strains of Ode to Joy they glance at each other with raised eyebrows.

"Leila, you look like you've just won a million dollars. What happened?" Dom asks. "Do you have any news from the doctors?"

"Not directly, but Sister Joan told me Rudy is in the recovery room now and we can see him shortly."

"How did Sister Joan know?" Dom asks.

Chapter Thirty-eight

Rudy in Recovery

Leila takes a deep breath and starts, "It's a long story, Dom. Now I don't want to make the same mistake Father Steven did when he told me what happened, so I will choose my words carefully."

"What do you mean by that?" Celeste asks.

"Well, Rudy is fine right now. His surgery went well. Apparently the problem was less severe than the tests had indicated. But for some reason, during the surgery, his vitals deteriorated and the priest was called to administer last rites."

"Oh, my God! You mean he died?" Danny asks.

"Yes, technically, but he's fine, Danny. Really, he is. Father Steven told me that as soon as he anointed Rudy with the sacred oil his heart restarted and his blood pressure—everything—returned to normal."

"It's a miracle," Dom says.

"I guess! Rudy is not out of the woods yet, but Sister Joan told me the surgeon said Rudy must have someone looking out for him. He's never seen such a quick turnaround on the operating table before. He expects a full recovery."

"I can't believe it," Celeste pipes in. "I've never heard of anything so incredible."

Leila gives her a sympathetic smile. "I know it does seem a little far-fetched, but I believe our prayers and love for Rudy have had an effect. I know I haven't been much of a praying person, but…"

"Well, nobody could doubt the love you have for Rudy—and for all of your kids, Leila." Dom pats her shoulder.

"That's true. I do love them all even though Natalia brings me such heartache at times."

"Hey, maybe we could have Father Steven anoint her. She's in need of healing."

"That's a wonderful idea, Danny," Nikki says. "What do you think, Leila?"

"That would be a huge miracle, but I guess bigger things have happened." Leila goes on, "But it almost seems more than I could hope for. You don't know how many times she has fallen off the wagon. For a person as young as she is, she's been through hell and dragged us all along with her. I've had very little hope that she could be healed, but now I am ready to accept whatever happens and love her exactly where she is. Underneath all her troubles she is a beautiful, talented, loving young woman. I choose right now to focus on that."

"You know, Emma is arriving in Anchorage this afternoon. I don't think I told you, Leila, but she works at a camp for kids with drug problems. Her supervisors say she is quite gifted in meeting these kids head-on and telling it like it is. Maybe she can talk to Natalia. They used to have some things in common when they were younger. Emma always told me stories after her visits to Alaska about their shenanigans."

"They do have a bond. I think she's closer to Emma than she is to her own sister, even though she doesn't see her very often."

Dom looks at his watch and jumps up with a gasp. "I've got to get going. My flight leaves in an hour and a half.

Where has the time gone? Can you drive me, Danny? Then maybe you can hang around the airport and wait for your sister."

"I want to see Rudy before…"

Nikki squints at her son and with pursed lips says, "Danny…"

"Okay, you're right. I'm the best one to do it and to pick up Emma, too." He turns towards Leila and gives her a hug. "Tell Rudy not to go anywhere. I'll be back as soon as I can."

"I'll be sure to tell him that."

A nurse sticks her head in through the open door. "You can visit your son now if you'd like. He's in Critical Care Number Three."

"Thanks," Leila says as she heads towards the door. "Oh, Celeste, would you call Ana and tell her the good news? She'll be worried sick."

As she passes by Dom, he grabs her and holds her tight, saying, "I'll be back, my love, as fast as I can—in the blink of an eye."

Celeste follows Leila into the hallway toward Rudy's room. "I'm coming, too."

"I'm not sure if that's all right with the doctors."

"Well, I am his fiancée. I want to be there when he first opens his eyes." Celeste pushes her way past Leila.

Leila squares her shoulders and sniffs. *But he's my son.* She reaches out her hand to block Celeste, but stops. *She's right. I never even thought before of the suffering she must be going through. She's so young and she loves Rudy so much. He's going to need her much more in the coming days than he will need me. I've got to let him go. God, it's so hard; just when I know he's going to be okay I have to give him up again.* "You're right, Celeste," Leila murmurs, touching her arm. "You go on in. It's best that Rudy sees you first. Then I'll ask the nurse if both of us can be with him at the same time."

"Thank you, Leila." That's all she manages to say before choking up.

"Be strong for him, Celeste. Smile. He's going to be fine."

Celeste gives Leila a quick hug and walks into the room where Rudy lies. Nothing has changed since the last time she saw him other than new bandages on his head. He is still connected to monitoring equipment by lines and hoses. Beeping sounds are louder than ever and he lies there on his back, pale and helpless. Celeste stands near the head of the bed and rests her hand on Rudy's chest, feeling his steady heartbeats. "Oh, Rudy, Rudy. I love you so much."

She bends over to kiss his cheek and holds her face next to his. His breath on her ear tickles and as she raises her hand it gets tangled in one of the cords and pulls it free.

"Oh, no! What have I done?" Celeste looks around, afraid. "Have I ripped out something vital?"

The nurse is at the bedside in an instant. She picks up the dangling end of the cord and smiles reassuringly. "This is to measure the oxygen saturation levels, honey. It's not critical and besides, he doesn't need this connected anymore anyway. His oxygen levels are fine, but please, watch where you put your hands. You wouldn't want to pull his IV out. Be careful."

"Oh, I will. I'll be careful," Celeste says.

Celeste moves away from the wires and hoses. She pulls a chair over to the side of the bed and sits there, eyes intent on Rudy's face. She strokes his fingers and his bruised chin. She traces the outline of his lips with her index finger. She gently touches his eyelids and runs her finger down to the tip of his nose. She is humming softly. Normally, when she is with Rudy, she hums or sings a song they heard on their first date, but when she is focused or nervous she sings lullabies or songs from summer camp. Rudy used to tease her about her song selections. Whenever he heard her humming Camp Town Races he'd say, "You must have a lot on your mind. What are you worried about?" Now, in the quiet of the hospital room she hums it furiously: D*oo-dah, doo-dah, oh doo-dah day.*

"I'm sure that will get him to wake up," Leila says as she enters the room. "Maybe if we sang it a little out of tune he wouldn't be able to stand it and he'd get up to silence us." Leila laughs.

Celeste raises her hand as though to slap Leila. She glares at her. She half rises from her chair then with a shrug of her shoulders she turns back to study Rudy's face.

Leila stops near the door. *Wow, I'd better back off. Looks like she wants to kick me out of here, not that I could blame her, but it's like walking a tightrope. I'd better be careful about what I say. We're going to have to pull together for Rudy's sake.*

Celeste ignores Leila and focuses on Rudy with such intensity it looks as though she thinks she can will him to open his eyes. She whispers, barely loud enough for Leila to hear, "Please, Rudy, please open your eyes. Please, just for me."

Rudy moves his head from side to side, wrinkles his nose and struggles to open his eyes. One eye opens briefly, then closes again.

"Hey, Mom, he opened his eyes."

Celeste and Leila stare at his bruised face, each holding her breath.

Chapter Thirty-nine

Danny at the Airport

As they walk towards the parking structure, Danny tries to make conversation with Dom. "So, how did you meet my Aunt Leila, Dom?"

"Celeste introduced us last winter when I came to Anchorage to see the start of the Iditarod." On any other day, Dom would have gone on, giving all the details of their meeting: their winter camping trip to Lake Clark, the ice boating, the trip to the North Slope, his proposal. Under normal circumstances one question would be enough to launch an hour-long monologue. But today he apparently doesn't feel like talking.

They continue walking towards the parking area. Danny presses. "You mean you only met her a few months ago?"

"Yeah."

"She's some lady, isn't she?"

"She sure is," Dom agrees.

They enter the parking structure and spot Celeste's car squeezed into a narrow space next to the wall.

"Is it okay if I drive, Dom?" Danny asks.

"Why not? I can tell you where to go. Celeste's apartment is off Wisconsin, so you can take Thirty-sixth Avenue across town. But first, would you back up so I can get in?"

"Sure."

In the car, as Dom fastens his seatbelt, Danny continues the conversation. "Does Rudy live there with her?"

"Who?"

"Celeste."

"Mostly, but he has his own apartment."

As Danny drives, following Dom's instructions, he asks several more questions, but getting only one-word answers, he gives up.

Danny observes Dom staring out the window as though he is in a daze. Then, without prompting, Dom asks, "Do you have a steady girlfriend, kid?"

Danny raises his eyebrows...eyes wide open. "You talking to me?"

"Yeah. I asked you if you had a girlfriend."

"I do, but nothing too serious."

"Well, someday you will and then you'll understand. It hits you all of a sudden. It's like chemistry. You just know."

"That's great. I'm glad for you and my Aunt Leila."

"I already miss her and just want to hold her and protect her from any hurt. She's suffered so much."

"I know."

"But, the way she's handling this crisis really shows how strong she is. She reminds me of...oh, never mind."

"How long will you be gone?"

"Just for a few days, and I tell ya, when I come back I'm not leaving her ever again. She's one special lady. We make such a good pair. Her smile and her laugh go right to my heart. I can't help myself from joking with her just to hear the uplifting sound of her laughter. She's so much fun to be with."

"I think you bring that out in her, Dom. She was always so serious before."

They travel the remaining distance in silence. Their stop at Celeste's apartment is only long enough for Dom to grab a few things.

As Danny drives up the departure ramp, Dom says, "No need to wait for me, Danny. You can't go beyond security, anyway."

Danny looks hurt, but doesn't say anything. He stops to let Dom out and mumbles, "Have a good trip, Dom." Driving away from the terminal, he glances at his watch. "I still have two hours to kill before Emma gets here. No time to go back to the hospital. I may as well go over to Lake Hood to watch the floatplanes for a while." He heads toward a park on the north side of the lake.

"Oh, hey, there's Pete's Flying Service. Why don't I stop in and give them a report on Rudy?" As he pulls up to the office, a group of five or six crowds around the dock where a floatplane is parked. The small office is packed with at least a dozen more customers.

Danny makes his way to the woman behind the counter and says, "I thought you might like a report on Rudy's condition."

She frowns and touches her forehead with shaky fingers, "Not now. Can't you see I'm busy?"

Danny stalks to the small sofa by the window, muttering, "Boy, you'd think she would at least be interested in how he is doing. What's her problem?" He sits staring out at the lake where a stream of floatplanes taxis by before he turns to watch the process of checking in the customers, weighing them and their equipment, filling out forms and accepting payment. The woman moves in slow motion. He gets his phone out and calls his mother. "How's Rudy? Any changes?"

"I don't know, Danny. Your Aunt Leila and Celeste went into his room right after you left and they haven't come out yet. Ana is here with me. Maybe I can have her go and check. I'll call you right back."

Danny paces back and forth as well as he can in the crowded room. He makes his right hand into a fist and slams it into his left palm again and again. In his pacing he stumbles over a duffle bag lying on the floor, loses his balance and bumps into one of the waiting passengers. He moves back to the sofa and slumps down out of the way.

Several pictures and framed newspaper clippings are on the wall opposite the counter. Danny cranes his neck as he stands again to get a view of them, but the crowd blocks most of the pictures. To see them all, he would need to push some people out of the way, but his hands hang by his sides. He shuffles through the crowd like an awkward thirteen-year-old boy in a body too big for him.

Eventually the customers leave to walk toward the large floatplane at the dock. Danny is left alone with the scheduler who keeps her head down, busy with paperwork. Danny approaches the counter and clears his throat to get her attention. He gets a call just as the woman looks up. Danny answers, expecting his mother. "Yes, how is he?"

"Hi, Danny, this is Ana. I just was in Rudy's room and he had his eyes open and was talking to Celeste. I could hardly hear him because he was whispering but when he saw me, he smiled—sort of. He's better, Danny. He's awake. I was almost afraid to hope but now I know he's going to live."

The woman behind the counter waits for him to end his call, looking up at him while tapping a pencil on her desk.

Danny holds his hand up. "Hey, Ana, slow down, would you? Did you actually talk to him? Did the doctors or nurses say anything? When is he going to be up and around? When can I see him?"

"Now you slow down. I don't know any of that. The nurse pushed me out of the room as soon as she saw me and I came to give you a call."

"Thanks. Look, I've got to pick up Emma in about an hour. I'll check with you then." He pauses. "Or we may as well just come right back to the hospital."

"Yeah, that would be good. I have to leave for the North Slope this afternoon so I won't see you, but maybe Nat will show up. She ran off after that first night and we haven't heard from her. I hope she isn't off somewhere getting high again. Mom has had just about all she can take."

"Thanks again, Ana. Gotta go, though. I want to fill in the people here at Pete's Flying Service." He ends the call.

The woman is still looking up at Danny with raised eyebrows.

"Rudy is awake and talking. It looks like he's going to make a full recovery, Ma'am. We were worried, though when they took him to surgery this morning. Apparently he had some bleeding in his brain."

The woman squints at him quizzically as though she has no idea what he's talking about. "Who on earth are you and why are you telling me all of this?"

"Oh, I'm sorry, ma'am. I am Rudy's cousin, Danny. I came up to Alaska when I heard that Rudy was in a crash. But I can only stay a few days. I have to get back to school."

The plump, grey-haired woman dressed in denim pants and a t-shirt with a picture of a floatplane on the front stands, places her hands on the counter top and looks Danny in the eye. "Young man, I know nothing about what you are telling me. I just came in this morning to take over for Donna. She had a doctor's appointment and just gave me enough information to turn the computer on and basically take payment from clients who were already scheduled. I have my hands full here. Can't you see?"

"I'm sorry. I just thought someone would want to know about Rudy."

"Well, I'm not the one."

Then in a conciliatory tone, "Donna will be here in less than an hour. Maybe you could fill her in on whatever news you have."

Danny has had enough. "What? Are you deaf and blind? What kind of Neanderthal would not have heard of Rudy's crash? It must have been all over the news. I'm sure everyone in Anchorage has heard. How could such an insensitive bitch even..."

The woman looks past Danny toward the open door. A young couple walks in holding hands.

"Can I help you?" The woman asks, her face red and a forced smile pasted on her lips.

Danny turns, bumping into the short young woman behind him. Without apologizing he storms out to the car.

Chapter Forty

Danny Meets Emma at the Airport

D anny drives the short distance to the airport terminal and pulls into the parking garage. He glances at his watch. Emma's flight will be arriving in a half hour. As he enters the lower level of the terminal, he is drawn by the smell of hamburgers cooking on a grill. His stomach growls. There is no line at the counter and he orders a hamburger—everything on it—with a large order of fries. In less than two minutes he eats everything in the basket. He pats his stomach. "That's much better!" His hunger satisfied, he makes his way to the upper level and drops into a chair near the security exit. He leans his head back against the wall and closes his eyes.

Emma spots him sleeping as she drags her roll-aboard along the tiled floor. She leans over to put her mouth close to his ear.

"Hey, Danny, what's up?"

Danny opens his eyes to see Emma's face inches from his. "What are you doing here?" Danny asks. Awakened from a deep sleep, he is disoriented.

"Hey, I'm your sister, remember? I'm here to see our cousin."

"Well, back off. Let me have some space. You didn't have to wake me so rudely."

"It's nice to see you, too." Emma straightens up. She turns away and bites her lower lip as a tear trickles down her cheek.

Danny, now fully awake, stands and gives her a brotherly hug.

She tries to pull away.

"I'm sorry, Em. But you know I don't like to be woken up suddenly." He reaches for her suitcase and puts an arm around her shoulder to lead her toward the baggage claim level.

"We should get right back to the hospital. I can fill you in on the way. Do you have any other luggage?"

"No, this is it. I'm only going to be here for ten days."

They walk to the parking garage and find Celeste's car.

"Tell me what's going on. Is Rudy awake? How bad are his injuries? It was hard to get any information out of Mom. It seemed like she was just coming up here to get away, like she doesn't really care about Rudy or Leila or anything. How is she getting along with Aunt Leila? Are they talking?"

"I don't know, for crying out loud. I've been at the hospital non-stop since I got here and the only people I've talked to are Celeste, that's Rudy's fiancée, and her uncle Dominic. Well, Ana was there for a while, and Aunt Leila, but she's a basket case."

"How will I ever keep track of all these characters? I hardly know Ana anymore and what about Natalia? Where is she?"

"I haven't seen her since I got here. I guess she showed up at the hospital when they first brought Rudy in, but Ana

363

says she took off and hasn't heard from her in a couple of days. You know she's been using drugs, don't you?"

"No. I had no idea."

"Maybe you can help her somehow. Isn't that what you do at that camp where you work?"

"Yeah, Danny, but she's family. How could I approach her?"

"You'll think of something. But, first things first. We've got to find out how Rudy is doing. I talked to Ana just a half hour ago and she said he's conscious and talking. She doesn't know much more than that."

"Speaking of first things, I'm going to have to apologize to Mom. I guess I sort of blew up when she kicked Daddy out of the house. I thought it was all her fault. But I called Daddy at Daphne's house before I left to see if he wanted me to stop by and see him and he brushed me off like I was a stranger. I could hear Daphne's voice in the background—well quite close, actually—and she was telling him to get rid of whoever it was. I felt sick. I still can't believe that he is cheating on Mom."

"It makes me sick, too, Em. I am kicking myself for not saying something sooner. Maybe it wouldn't have gone so far. I'll never forget that day, though, when I came home and heard Dad and Daphne in the bedroom."

"Oh, my God, I didn't know."

"Really? At first I thought it was kind of odd that Mom and Dad would be messing around during the day. I tried to be quiet so they wouldn't know I was at home. I went to change into my baseball uniform and was hoping to sneak out before they knew I had been there, but when I came out of my room, there was Daphne coming out of the master bedroom. She rushed off without saying a word. Then Dad saw me and made me promise not to say anything. He made all kinds of excuses and said if Mom ever found out he was afraid to think of what would happen. He told me if she did find out he would cut off my college expenses and I would be on my own to pay for my car and tuition and everything. I couldn't let that happen."

"I didn't know any of this until the other day. How long have you known?"

"It's been about a year. It was just before I went off to college last summer."

"How awful. How could you keep that secret?"

"Well, most of the time I was so busy with practice and games and classes I didn't have time to think about it. And I honestly thought it was just a one-time thing. I think I've learned my lesson, though. Things do not get better if they are swept under the rug. How stupid I was."

"But you were blackmailed."

"And that's a terrible way to live. I'd rather get things out in the open and deal with them than have all that undercurrent of tension. Coming up here has been a real eye-opener."

"How's that?"

"Seeing Rudy hanging on to life by a thread and not knowing if he's even going to be here tomorrow has made me realize that I want to be real and open and honest."

Emma nods, agreeing.

Danny continues. "I want to let people know I love them and apologize when I hurt them. In fact, I'm sorry, Em, for how I snapped at you. I guess I've been a little on edge. You're the best sister a guy could have. Really. I think it's cool what you do. I actually brag about you to the guys on the team. Now, don't let this go to your head, but..." Danny looks down at the floor and then back at Emma, "your work at Right Way Camp makes me proud."

"Oh, you're just saying that. But I'll accept it. Coming from you I think that's the best compliment I ever got."

Chapter Forty-one

Turning Point

R udy's eyes flutter several times. Celeste leans over him and reaches out to touch his arm.

"We're here, Rudy."

Leila presses against Celeste, close to the bed. "You're through the worst of it now, Rudy. You're going to be fine."

He opens his eyes and looks first at Celeste, then at his mother. He opens his mouth as if to say something, but only moans. A pained expression crosses his face.

"Do you need anything? More pain medication?"

He shakes his head no.

"You don't need to talk now. Just rest. We'll talk later. You and Celeste need some time together. I'll be right next-door. I'm not going anywhere."

Leila walks back to the waiting room looking as though she is carrying a heavy backpack. Her feet drag, with each step a major effort.

Nikki and Ana both rise to greet her as she opens the door.

"You look like death warmed over. What is it? Is Rudy okay?" Nikki asks, giving her a quick hug.

"Well, the vigil is over, but somehow I feel like the hard part is just beginning."

"Have you talked to the doctor yet?"

"No, but the nurse said his vitals are good and stable. For a patient who had surgery such a short time ago, he's doing amazingly well."

"But you don't know his prognosis for a total recovery?"

"No, nobody is saying anything for sure yet," Leila says, too drained to say more.

"You seemed so certain after your experience in the chapel. Didn't Sister 'What's-her-name' say his recovery was assured? Why the change?" Nikki presses.

"I don't know. It just seems that I've been holding everything together and now that I don't have to, I'm suddenly exhausted." Leila shakes her head. "I just want to go home and sleep and not wake up for a week."

"Well, why don't you?" Ana interposes. "Aunt Nikki will be here to take over for a while. I have to leave soon, but Danny and Emma should be here any minute as well."

"That's true. I can take over. Go home and rest. I'll call if anything happens."

Leila allows herself to be talked into resting at home. "But I want to see Emma first. I'll leave after she and Danny get here. It's been four years since I last saw her. She must have grown into a beautiful young woman by now."

"She has. And she is so responsible for an eighteen-year-old. Her work with those kids at camp is amazing. Her supervisor says she is such a gifted counselor. He has watched her work with the most difficult cases of teenage addicts and he told me even he could not have done as well. I think it has something to do with her age and her ability to talk their language."

"I do hope she can connect with Natalia—if she ever shows up, that is. I've felt that she is so lost…"

Leila begins to sink into despair, her body folding in upon itself. Her shoulders droop. Her face sags. Her hands hang limp at her sides. As her knees almost cave in, Nikki reaches out to put an arm around her.

"She's going to be fine. Have faith. Emma will be able to reach her. You'll see. Emma will help. I know she will."

"What will I help with, Mom?" Emma asks as she and Danny enter the room in time to overhear Nikki's last statement.

"Oh, Emma, I'm so glad to see you. Tell your Aunt Leila what miracles you've worked with addicts. Tell her how you'll be able to help Natalia shake her drug habit."

Emma's cheeks flush and she looks down. "I'm just an ordinary kid, Aunt Leila. I can try, that's all I can say. But I do love my cousin and if anything can help, it's love. Love is always the answer."

"That's an awful lot of wisdom coming from someone so young, but then again you've had a good example to follow. I've always admired your mother's compassionate, caring heart." She glances at Nikki, her expression impossible to read. "I couldn't understand, though, why she was so hard on me."

"Don't say that. It's not like I meant to be mean to you. I just felt like I was reciprocating your coldness. But let's put that behind us. We have to go forward from here and it looks like we will need each other's strengths to deal with what's ahead."

Ana looks at her watch and stands up. "Look, guys, I have to get going. I don't know if Danny told you, Emma, but I have to leave for my job on the Slope today. I've put it off as long as I can, but they will find a replacement if I don't show up."

"I'd like to spend more time with you, but you've got to do what you've got to do. But, before you go what can you tell me about Nat?"

"When's the last time you saw her?"

"It's been four years, I think. We were both freshmen. That's the last time I visited Alaska."

"Was she using then?"

Emma's face reddens. She swallows, squares her shoulders and juts her chin out like a person facing a firing squad.

"I've never told this to anyone before, so I guess it's time for the truth. Last time I was here Nat and I went to some pretty wild parties. I thought it was so cool to be able to stay up all night and never have it get dark. Nat was always pushing me to try new things. First we drank a little beer, but that always made me sick to my stomach."

"Emma! Why didn't you ever tell me?" Nikki glares at her daughter.

"How could I, especially since shortly after that, I started volunteering at the Right Way Camp? Anyway, one night we were at a beach along the inlet just off the coastal trail. Everyone there was drinking beer, but I didn't have any because I didn't want to get sick."

"That was good."

"Well, yes and no. Some kids were smoking, but cigarettes always made me cough, so I moved away from them. Then Nat came up to me and urged me to try some marijuana. 'Just take a couple of drags' she said, 'it feels really good.' "

Leila breaks in. "How could she? How could you?"

"Please let me finish, before I lose my nerve. So, when she handed it to me I choked down a couple of puffs. I coughed a little but after that my throat relaxed. I took more and more and soon Nat and I were hugging and laughing. I felt so good. We looked around and everyone was—well, I don't need to go into any more details—you get the idea. But at the time I thought it was just fun."

Danny had been listening, becoming more and more somber. "Was that the only time?"

"I wish I could say it was. But the whole month I was here we partied as often as we could. It was addictive. I loved the feeling of being alive and feeling attractive. But now I could kick myself because Nat and I promised each other that we would never tell."

"No, honey, Nat's addiction is not your fault. She would have gone down that road even if you had never visited that summer."

"But I was able to put it behind me once I went back to Wisconsin. I never even thought about it, or craved it or anything. In fact, once I got back home it all seemed like a silly dream."

"Of course, it would."

"I called Nat a few times after I got home, but we couldn't talk about it on the phone. Somebody might have been listening. I meant to stay in contact with her, but I got so busy with school and the volunteer work that I just let her slip away."

"Don't blame yourself. We all make our own choices, although with addiction I don't know how much freedom of choice one actually has."

Leila pauses and Nikki pipes in, "I hate to even suggest this, but maybe that experience is why you can relate so well to the students at camp."

"That thought did occur to me. But I still feel like I betrayed Nat by not even checking in with her or caring enough to ask how she was doing. Distance should not make such a difference."

Nikki and Leila look at each other and speak at the same time, "But it does."

"I guess it does, but I'm here now and if you want me to try to reach Natalia, I'll give it my best shot. And if that doesn't work, she can always come down to Right Way Camp for a residency. She's a little old for the program where I work, but I can pull some strings. It really works, Aunt Leila."

"I'll give it some thought, but right now, I need a good soak in the hot tub and a week's worth of sleep. I'm making a bee line for home." She gives Emma a hug. "Thank you for coming. I have a feeling you're going to be a lifesaver. I feel so safe and secure surrounded by family. You are all a real blessing to me." Leila gives hugs all around. "Thank you all for being here. Now Ana, you better hit the road if you're going to catch your flight."

Chapter Forty-two

Nikki and the Kids

When Leila and Ana are gone, Nikki, Danny and Emma sit in silence, avoiding each other's eyes. After several minutes Nikki clears her throat and starts talking in a low voice. "I know you both love your dad, but after such a betrayal, I can no longer live with him."

"But what will you do?"

"I don't have it all figured out yet. Things are changing so fast I can hardly hang on, but I have had a little time to think about it."

"What does that mean?"

"It's too soon to tell. Your dad and I will discuss things when I get home. This cooling off period will be good for us."

Emma looks at her mother and sighs. "I'm so sorry I overreacted and accused you of driving Daddy away. From what I overheard, I'm sure he was not without fault. He's really hooked on Daphne, isn't he?"

Nikki hates to even think of the two of them together, and her eyes begin to tear up. "Sometimes you have to separate yourself from painful situations. I am much stronger now than I used to be. Still, I don't think I can bear to have their relationship thrown in my face every time I turn around. You don't need to know all the details, although I don't think your father has been honest with me for a long time. But I don't want to turn you against him."

"Well, he's been a slime ball sneaking around like he has. And I can't believe he tried to blackmail me—actually did for a while."

"Do you know anything about this, Emma?"

"Yeah, Danny filled me in. It's disgusting."

"I don't need to make any decisions today or even this week. I'm going to see Leila and Rudy through their ordeal and then I will deal with my problems."

Celeste knocks on the door and enters without waiting for an answer.

"I thought you might like a report on Rudy."

Danny jumps up. "Yes, of course. When can I see him?"

Nodding toward Emma, Celeste asks, "Aren't you going to introduce me to your sister?"

"Oh, yeah, sorry. Celeste this is Emma. Emma—Celeste."

"Nice to meet you. Danny says you and Rudy are engaged."

Celeste's lower lip quivers. "Yes, we are, but who knows what will happen now?"

"It must be hard. So, how is he?"

"He's resting. We talked for quite a while. He was a little confused; he doesn't remember much about the events leading up to the crash. He says he feels so guilty for letting everyone down."

"But it's not his fault."

"Yeah, well, accidents do happen. Even though Rudy's one of the best pilots I've ever flown with he's always relied on luck to pull him out of tight situations and this time his luck ran out. Now he says he never wants to fly again. I don't know how I feel about that because it was flying that brought us together."

"Doesn't he love it just like Uncle Pete did?"

"Yeah, he does, or did. I can't imagine a life without airplanes or flying. It would be like cutting off one of my limbs. But how would it be for me to fly and leave him on the ground? It just wouldn't work for very long." Celeste shakes her head, her lips compressed in a straight line, her eyes shining with tears.

"Maybe he'll come around. Give him some time," Nikki adds.

"You're right. I guess now is not the time to be thinking about that. He needs to focus on recovery and getting back on his feet. By the way, the doctor visited a few minutes ago and said that he is doing very well   considering. They expect a full recovery."

"Thank God."

"He's talking about prescribing physical therapy for the hip that's pinned together. It will start slowly, but he wants Rudy up and moving as soon as possible. Later today they plan on doing some cognitive tests to ascertain any brain injury. So far they've determined that there is no nerve damage. Thank goodness for his toughness."

"Yeah, I think he inherited his vigor and mental strength from both the Pedersons and the Pletnikoffs. I know his mom has plenty of both." Nikki adds, "I think she even took my share."

Emma smiles at Nikki. "No, Mom, you've got your own strengths. Your race walking leaves me in the dust."

"And you showed tremendous strength in dealing with the Daphne situation." Danny puts a hand on his mother's shoulder.

Celeste opens her mouth as though to ask a question but thinks better of it when Emma gives her a stern look and shakes her head.

"Well, I'd better get back to Rudy. He's awake more of the time now, but he's still a little dopey. I'll see if he's up to talking to you, Danny."

"Let me know as soon as you find out, would you? You know I'm leaving on the red-eye tomorrow morning. I have to get down to Urbana for training by the day after tomorrow. Otherwise I'll be kicked off the team."

"I'll ask the nurse, but I think Rudy will be out of intensive care and in a regular room soon. Then anyone can visit. I'm sure he will want to see you."

"Just tell him he better get off his duff soon. Next time I visit Alaska I expect to race him up Bird Ridge." Danny pauses. "On second thought, no, don't say anything. I'll tell him myself."

"You might try a little sympathy, Danny, after all he's been through." Nikki can't resist giving some motherly advice.

"He can handle it. He's always liked challenges."

"You're right about that. He thrives on difficulty. Maybe that's why we get along so well." Celeste smiles as she leaves to return to Rudy's room.

As the door closes behind Celeste, silence enshrouds them like a heavy quilt. Nikki, Danny and Emma all appear to be lost in thought. Nikki closes her eyes and images of Gerik and Daphne slap at her like a driving rain. The closeness of the room presses in on her. She rises from her chair. "I can't stand it. I need some space and some fresh air."

With relief Danny and Emma watch her leave. Emma starts, "I don't know what to think. How could Daddy be so crude and childish? Do you think Mom did anything to drive him away?"

"It's hard for me to imagine anyone that old being so caught up in sex. But maybe he wasn't getting any at home and..."

"But," Emma hastily interjects, "you said he and Daphne were messing around in our own house. I still can't believe that."

"Yeah, well, Mom was traveling a lot in the last few years. She was pretty involved in her quilting design business. Maybe Dad couldn't wait for her."

"I want to get the whole story. I'm sure there's more to it than either of us knows."

Nikki's phone rings. Both Danny and Emma look at it, then at each other. "Should we answer?"

"Of course, it might be Aunt Leila."

Emma picks up the phone. "Hello."

"Oh, Nikki, it's Mitch. I'm so glad you answered. I know you told me not to call you, but after that night in Chicago, I just had to talk to you again. I've realized how much I need..."

"Wait a minute. I'm not Nikki. I'm her daughter, Emma. Who are you and what do you want with my mother?"

"Oh, no, I, ah...Is this a bad time?"

"That would be an understatement. I don't know who you are but my mother is definitely not available to give advice to anybody right now with all the problems our family is going through. I don't think you should call again unless you are ready to explain yourself to me." Emma hangs up and slams the phone down on the table where it lay before it rang.

From the door Nikki pokes her head into the room and asks, "Who was that? I heard you talking on the phone."

"That's a good question. Who *was* that?" Emma glares at her mother. "Who *exactly* is Mitch?"

Nikki feels warmth rising from her chest. Her neck reddens. Her cheeks flush. A hazy memory of being pressed close to a man, dancing, rouses her. Thoughts of the story he shared launch feelings of sympathy. She needs to protect him. But how can she explain to her own children without sounding deceitful?

"Well, I'm waiting." Emma folds her arms across her chest.

"I don't think I can explain to your satisfaction right now. It's a long story." Nikki stalls.

"How can you expect me to be on your side when it sounds like you've been having your own fling?"

Danny shifts uncomfortably in his chair. He studies the plaque on the wall as though it is a novel piece of art he's never seen before. He avoids looking at either Nikki or Emma.

Nikki leans back in her armchair, rests her head and closes her eyes. Her hands cover her face. She takes a deep breath. Without uncovering her face she begins. "Your dad and I have not gotten along for some time. I think you both knew there were problems between us. I tried to ignore them and focused more on my business and started working out. I thought maybe if I made myself more interesting and attractive he would…"

"That's old news. I want to hear about Mitch."

"It's not what you think."

Danny blurts, "Give her a break, would you? You think if you keep hounding her she'll want to share anything with you?"

"You are all idiots. No wonder this family is in such a mess. I don't blame Daddy at all. If this is the type of behavior he faces at home…I feel like leaving myself."

"What good would that do?" Danny confronts her head on. "Wouldn't that be just like what we've all been doing?

Running from our problems and burying our heads in the sand?" Danny looks from his mother to Emma and then back. They are so much alike. Emma is a taller, younger version of Nikki, but their personalities are so different. Emma always seems so tough and ready to take on the world. Nikki is always trying to please. He goes to stand beside her and lays a protective hand on her shoulder.

Emma looks away. "I don't want to bury things, Danny, but I do want to know the truth about what has happened. Sometimes facing the reality of a situation is the only way through it."

"You're right. Of course you know a lot of this stuff from working with addicts, but you need to apply it to yourself, too."

"Look, kids. Just let me say that I love you both so much and am so proud of you. I'll tell you everything. I don't want secrets between us. But will you let me do it in my own way, in my own time?"

"Okay, I guess. But can you at least tell me who this Mitch is and what he wants from you?"

"Come and sit next to me, Emma. I know you're no longer a little girl, but you will always be my baby." Nikki pats the chair beside her.

"Oh, Mom." Emma raises her eyes to the ceiling. Dragging her feet, she goes to sit down stiffly next to her mother.

"Please try to see things through my eyes. I know I've been distracted and distant in the last few months."

"You could say that."

"Well, last week I met a man when I was on a business trip to Chicago." *That's fudging a little but it is close enough to the truth* "We had dinner together and he somehow ended up telling me about his nasty divorce. It was rather awkward to listen to. But I was able to give him some encouragement and he said he wanted to talk to me again." Nikki's heart pounds as she tries to keep her voice even and reserved.

"That's it?"

"Yes, I had never seen him before. Don't know if I will ever see him again. It was just one of those chance things."

"How did he get your phone number?"

"Emma! Isn't that enough for now?" Danny sounds desperate to have peace in the room.

"I gave him my name and where I live. Why shouldn't I? He knew about my quilting business. He must have been able to figure out how to get my number. He's a smart man."

Emma is silent. Her interior struggle is evident: She taps her foot, purses her lips and wraps her arms around herself. Danny catches her eye and smiles with a pleading look. Emma stiffens. She hears Nikki's sudden intake of breath. As she turns to face her mother, she sees the same pleading, pinched smile on her face.

"Emma...please."

Emma tries to sit upright to square her shoulders but loses her balance and falls back in the chair, resting against her mother, her head on Nikki's chest. The even rhythm of Nikki's heartbeat soothes her. She relaxes, eventually returning the embrace. Her long legs hang off the edge of the chair and her contorted body looks uncomfortable, but her face is serene. Nikki strokes her hair.

"I love you, Mom. Just give me time to deal with this whole thing. My world feels like it's coming apart."

"I know. I feel the same way. But there is no need to rush into anything. We have time. I'm seeing things more clearly every day. They say time heals all wounds. Maybe the same can be said about distance."

"It didn't much help my relationship with Natalia."

"That's a different story and one you will put right once you meet with her. But I'm just saying this separation from your dad has been good for me. It's given me a different perspective—somewhat. One thing I know for sure is that you kids are important to me. You're my life. I don't want to do anything to jeopardize that."

"Well, don't make Daddy out to be an ogre. He's been one of my greatest promoters. Without his influence and support I never would have gotten a job at the Camp. He helped me through many tough times in my first year there. He believes in me."

"I do too, Emma. But I know how close you and your dad have always been. I don't want that to ever change. This problem is between your dad and me. It has nothing to do with you. We will both always love you."

The door opens and Celeste sticks her head in. "Rudy wants to talk to you, Danny. You better hurry. He doesn't stay alert for very long. He's still right down the hall. Come on." She closes the door and hurries back to Rudy's room.

Chapter Forty-three

Danny Talks to Rudy

D anny jumps up, eagerly leaving the room while Nikki and Emma to continue their discussion. As he opens the door, Celeste and Rudy are kissing. Celeste's hand hovers over Rudy's broken hip in a protective, loving way, caressing his wound with the lightness of a butterfly's wing. Her fingers touch, one by one, as though fingering the beads of a rosary. Danny clears his throat. "Hey Cuz, how are you doing?"

Rudy looks around Celeste with a weak smile. "Whoa, am I ever glad to see you."

"Same here."

"What brings you to Alaska?"

"Isn't that obvious? You had to go and get yourself smashed up just to see me? I would have come if you had just asked."

"Well, you know. I'd go to any extreme for a..." Rudy's face contorts in pain as a spasm shoots through his body when he tries to move his hips to turn in the bed. "Oh, sorry."

"Don't try to move. I'll come closer." He moves to Rudy's bedside and grabs his hand. "I'm sorry. I shouldn't be joking at a time like this."

"Is there a better time?"

"What I mean is, I'm just so glad to see you awake and alert—well, sort of alert. I guess as alert as a retard can…"

"Come on, be nice. Remember, he's just come out of a coma. I don't think he's ready to take much ribbing." Celeste moves closer to Rudy's head as though to protect him from hearing anything bad.

"He's a tough cookie. That's why he's going to be racing me up Bird Ridge next summer. That's why he's going to walk out of here before too long and hop into an airplane to show you how to really fly."

Rudy grimaces and closes his eyes. "I don't know, buddy. I'm not sure where I'm going from here. I just need to rest right now. Can you get the nurse? I think I could use some…" His voice fades. He turns his face toward the wall, away from Danny.

Danny can't understand what he is saying and asks, "Is he asleep?"

Celeste puts a finger to her lips, faces Danny and whispers, barely making a sound. "He's been doing this all morning. He'll be wide-awake and alert and suddenly he falls into a restless sleep. The nurse says it's a normal stage of recovery. Besides, all the painkillers they're giving him make him groggy. Wait a few minutes. He'll be up again soon."

"Has he told you anything about the crash?"

Celeste motions to Danny to move closer to the door. "We have to be quiet. They say he can still hear even if he appears to be asleep. He doesn't want to talk about it. He keeps saying 'How stupid I am.' I think he's depressed."

Danny leans towards Celeste until their faces are inches from each other and whispers back, "Who wouldn't be in this place?"

"I mean about the accident. He blames himself. He doesn't want to face anyone, his mother especially."

"But he's got to get back in the pilot seat. He can't just give up on life. That's not the cousin I know."

"This might not be the time to push it. Maybe it's too soon."

"Well, I don't have much time here and I don't want to leave with him feeling all sorry for himself."

"Just be gentle. That's all I'm saying." Celeste gives Danny a warning look.

"I will."

"Hey, Danny! What are you doing, putting a move on my fiancée? I close my eyes for one minute and look what happens."

They turn to face Rudy and smile.

"As long as you're just lying around, I've got to do something."

"Well, back off if you know what's good for you," Rudy says with a smile in his voice.

"Okay, I'll back off if you tell me what this is all about. Celeste says you're ready to hang up your flying goggles. Come on, get real."

Celeste scrunches her face, giving Danny the evil eye, but says nothing.

Rudy's face goes blank. Even though his position in the bed has not changed, something of his aspect—a flatness or lack of affect—speaks loudly of his dejection. It is clear he does not want to talk about this right now.

Danny's tone changes, becoming gentler. He starts, "Remember that day when we were sort of lost in the woods up near Gulkana? When we got the jeep stuck?"

Rudy smiles, "That was a long time ago."

"I'll never forget how scared I was. No food or water, how stupid of us! We were, like, so unprepared."

"Yeah, that's for sure."

Danny continues. "How come hindsight is always so good? We certainly learned a lot from that experience, didn't we? But the thing I remember the most about it was your determination and total confidence."

"That was just false bravado, you know."

"I realized that after we got back to Anchorage, but at the time I thought you were the greatest, most competent, most innovative person in the world. The way you kept my spirits up when I just wanted to lie down and cry was so mature. I hung onto that confidence of yours like it was a lifeline."

Rudy closes his eyes, remembering. "I was pretty scared, too. I remember kicking myself for getting us into that situation."

"But the point is, you did get us out of it. Sure you made a mistake, a stupid mistake, but you didn't give up and let us die out there in the woods. You knew our lives depended on your staying calm and figuring out how to get us out of it."

"But we never should have been there in the first place." Rudy scowls.

"Stay with me, buddy. Don't focus on the mistake. That's over and done. It's happened. We can't go back and undo it. What we have to do now is look towards the future."

"This isn't the same." Rudy looks at Danny with determination.

"Yes it is. Only it's your life we're talking about. Your life depends on you showing some grit and getting better. You can't just lie back and let life happen to you. That's not you, Rudy. You always grab life by the horns and hang on for the thrill. That's the cousin I know."

Rudy closes his eyes again. They watch the progression of expressions on his face go from consternation to sadness to shame and finally to anger. He looks like someone responding to a movie in high speed.

"You have no idea what you're talking about. You weren't there. How could you know how stupid I was?"

"You're right, I can't. But I can see how stupid you're acting now. Maybe you can tell me exactly what you remember and how you've figured out it was your fault."

Rudy is silent for a long time. Danny and Celeste think he must have fallen asleep again, but he starts to whisper. "The weather was getting worse. We had landed at that strip north of Galbraith and the guys picked up the equipment they had left there. They were eager to get home."

"But you said no, right?" Celeste asks.

"Yeah, I said we had to go back to Deadhorse and wait for the weather to improve. The clouds were getting lower. Rain and mist...I don't know why we didn't just make camp there and wait it out."

Danny is holding his breath. He doesn't want to miss a thing.

"Usually those guys are so good about respecting my flying decisions. But one of them was grumbling about having to spend another day on the North Slope. I guess I let that distract me and I didn't notice the wind shift until we were almost ready to lift off. Then it was too late, the end of the airstrip was too close to abort."

"So you took off downwind?"

"It wasn't much of a wind. It shouldn't have made any difference once we were airborne."

"How could you not notice something that basic?" Celeste blurts out.

Rudy winces. Celeste's hand flies to her mouth to try to cover up her blunder.

"Now you be nice, Celeste." Danny looks at her, worried. "I'm so sorry, Rudy. Don't pay attention to me. It's not like I've never made that mistake. We all have. I'm sure that's not what caused the accident."

But Rudy has withdrawn into his drug-induced lethargy. He sighs with resignation and the corners of his mouth turn down. A tear trickles down his cheek. He gives a little shake of his head. He is not yet ready to face the last few minutes of his disastrous flight.

A nurse enters the room ending any attempts at further conversation. "Would you leave us alone for a couple min utes? I need to check on some things to see if we can get him ready to move up to the fourth floor."

Celeste and Danny move toward the door.

"Thanks. I'll let you know when you can come back in."

As soon as the door closes behind them, Danny grabs Celeste's shoulder, ready to berate her for her huge gaffe, but her devastated face stops him.

"I've blown it, haven't I? How could I be so stupid? Just when he was ready to talk about it, I had to go and accuse him of incompetence. Can he ever forgive me?"

"No, it's my fault. I think I was pushing him too hard to get him to remember. I wanted the whole story."

They walk towards the waiting room, Danny supporting Celeste by the arm. When they enter the room, both Nikki and Emma's eyebrows rise in questioning looks.

"How is he?"

"Rudy's fine. It's Celeste I'm worried about."

"What?"

Celeste slumps on to the loveseat. She stares without expression at the door. "We don't need to talk about it now."

The silence is almost unbearable. Danny's muscles look tense. His fists are tight. Nikki watches his struggle as he rolls his shoulders and head around. The next moment he is clenching his fists again. Nikki wishes she had some fabric to run through her fingers to relax herself. Emma taps her foot rhythmically over and over and over until Danny shouts. "Stop that!"

Nikki takes over. "It looks like we're all coming apart at the seams. Why don't you kids go outside and take a walk? Get some fresh air. I'll stay here to get updates. If anything happens, I'll call."

"I couldn't." Celeste argues.

"I insist. You've been here non-stop since the accident. You need to get outside and see the sun. Go now." Nikki ushers them out of the room.

At the exit of the ER Emma looks around and sees only the parking lot and some trees across the street. "Where can we walk around here?"

"Follow me." Celeste says. "We can cut through the University and join up with the bike path that runs along Chester Creek. From there, let's walk over to Goose Lake; it's less than a mile."

There is awkwardness between Danny and Celeste, but Emma says nothing. It is as though she is waiting for the right moment. When she works with recovering addicts she has a knack for being present in an approachable and non-judgmental way. The kids always open up when they are ready because she is a patient and sympathetic listener.

The water of Goose Lake sparkles in the sunlight filtering through the trees. Celeste walks ahead of them as though she is in a race. Danny and Emma have to jog to keep Celeste in sight. When she gets to the lake she walks straight to the beach through the running, yelling children and plops down onto the sand. Emma and Danny sit down on either side of her. None of them speak.

Fifteen minutes pass before anyone says a word. Celeste finally lifts her head and turns to Emma, "I really do love him. I know this sounds corny, but he's always been my knight in shining armor. Not once in all of our flights together did he ever criticize any of my decisions, even though he knew better and had so much more experience."

"Of course, that's how Rudy is." Danny says to her back.

"But I went and accused him of incompetence. Basically, that's what I did. He'll never get over it." She turns to Danny. "Did you see how he slumped in dejection when I questioned him? It was awful. It was like he was just giving up."

"He'll come around." Danny tries to sound confident.

Celeste shakes her head, defeated, while Emma jumps into the conversation. "No, you and Danny did the right thing. Rudy needs to face his demons. In a way he needs to hit bottom emotionally before he can accept that he may have used bad judgment and go on from there. We all do stupid stuff; he needs to admit that."

"But he's not strong enough right now."

"There is never a perfect time, but since you brought it up, this *is* the right time. From what I know of my cousin, he has a very healthy ego. His countless exceptional abilities make him so lovable, but also make the most problems for him. He's always been able to handle anything. I'm sure this will make him a better, safer pilot, because he should now recognize his vulnerability."

"If he ever returns to flying, that is." Celeste despairs.

"He will," Danny says. "He's never turned down a challenge."

"What should I do now? How can I support him and yet not seem like I'm overly protective? In a way, I want him to give up. I want to protect him from the dangers of flying and yet I know it is his life."

"There's always more to it than that. Like most people facing a painful experience, Rudy will probably reevaluate everything in his life. He most likely will appreciate the people he loves more and more. He will look to you and his mother and sisters—and cousins—for support and affirmation of his decisions." Emma voices her experienced estimation.

Celeste snorts. "That'll be the day!"

"No, really. Good always comes out of a traumatic experience like this—eventually. His relationships will mean more to him and you will be closer than ever—if you allow it—because he will realize how much he needs you."

"I hope that's true."

"It is. I can almost guarantee it. Not that it will be easy. I'm sure Rudy will have physical as well as emotional challenges. And we are all bound to do or say the wrong thing sometimes."

"I sure have done a lot of that lately." Celeste is morose.

"Well, that's life. But think of what his mother has gone through. I'm sure this has brought up memories of Uncle Pete's death. I bet it will be really hard for her to allow him to fly again. You're going to have to deal with her over-protectiveness."

"Hey, we'd better be getting back. I don't have much time left here before my flight and I want to see Rudy again. Maybe this time I can keep my foot out of my mouth."

Celeste gets up brushing the sand from her jeans. "Okay, let's see if they moved him to a better room."

"Only this time, could we walk a little slower? I'm not into racing right now."

"All right." Celeste laughs.

When they return to the waiting room Nikki is lying down on one of the love seats with her eyes closed.

Celeste turns around without entering the room. "Shh, look's like she's asleep. I'll go find out where Rudy is."

Danny and Emma sit down quietly. "Poor thing." Danny nods towards his mother.

"Well maybe if she wasn't running around in Chicago with other men, Daddy would still..."

"Don't start that, Emma. Let's wait to hear the whole story before we rush to make judgments."

"Well, she admitted to meeting another man."

"Please, let it go. Both of us are going to need to be mature about this."

"They haven't been very mature. Do you think they ever thought about us?"

"We're not kids anymore, Em. Besides, we'll still have both our parents, just not like it's always been."

Emma is struggling to hold back her tears. "I'm tired of trying to hold everything together. Why can't we go back to how it was before? Our house was always so homey. Mom was always there for us, except for lately."

"You've been doing your own thing for quite a while. At least she hasn't clung on to you. She's let you do things on your own."

"You're right. She has always allowed me the freedom to make my own choices and make my own mistakes. So even though I think this divorce is a mistake, I have to let her— them—do what they have to. I hate it, though."

Danny does not say anything.

"Well. Don't you care?"

"I do care. A lot. But what good does it do to bring up all that negative stuff? You'd just want to side with Dad and put all the blame on Mom."

"Come on. I..." Emma looks at her mother whose eyes are now open. "Did our talking wake you up, Mom?"

"No, I wasn't sleeping. I was just too tired to open my eyes. I guess jet lag has finally hit me."

"So you heard everything we said?" Emma asks, trying to remember exactly what she did say.

"Yes, sort of. I was doing a little daydreaming and only caught snatches of what you said. But I did catch the tone."

"I'm sorry."

"I'm sorry, too. I'm sorry to have to put you both through this. I just know that I cannot continue living a lie. I can't see how your dad and I will ever be able to reconcile. I am sorrier than I have ever been."

"We'll make it, Mom."

"Yeah," Danny says. "We'll all pull out of this mess along with Rudy. He's not the only one who crashed, is he?"

Nikki shakes her head. "No, it seems like my life is coming apart, too. Things are fraying faster than I can mend and to tell you the truth, some things are beyond the point of repair."

"But remember how you always told us some of the most beautiful patterns are born from chaos? Remember the quilt that got all those awards? When it was half done the fabric you had planned on using turned out to be the wrong color and texture and you had to patch it together with things you already had. It turned out to be much more beautiful than the design you had drawn."

"I guess life is like that—sometimes. We'll just have to take one day at a time and make the best of what comes. But, please, let's just try to be there for one another and not tear each other apart. Life is too short for hatred and bitterness. If Rudy's accident has taught me anything it is that family and loved ones can't be replaced. So I guess good has come out of it already."

Celeste, who has entered the room, nods in silent agreement.

"Rudy's awake and wants to see everybody. They've moved him to the fourth floor, room 434. Come on, he's waiting."

Chapter Forty-four

Details of the Crash

As they ride the elevator to the fourth floor Emma presses Celeste for all of the details about his condition.
She is acting like a nurse in charge so Nikki allows her to
run the show. On entering the room, Emma goes directly to
Rudy's bed. "Hi, Cuz. It's been a while since I've seen you,
but I must say you're looking well. You do remember me,
don't you?"

Rudy looks a bit confused and then notices Danny right
behind her. "Of course, you're the baby of the family. Here
to visit Natalia?"

"That's not the main reason, but I do hope to spend some
time with her. I'll be here for ten days."

Rudy notices Nikki and Celeste behind Danny and Emma.
"Wow, a regular family reunion—except, where's Mom and
Nat and Dom?"

"Your mom went home to rest. You know she's been here
almost non-stop since you got here," Nikki says.

"Where's your Uncle Dom?"

"Flying to Chicago for business. He'll be back in three
days."

"And Nat?" Rudy gives Celeste a worried look.

"She said she couldn't handle the stress. We haven't heard from her in a couple of days. But you know that's not unusual for her. Your cousin Emma here will deal with her problems once we find her."

Rudy sighs. "I know some of her hangouts. I'll give you addresses. We better get her butt back home before she falls off the wagon again. Her so called friends are bad news."

Danny looks from Rudy to Emma and then back. "I have to leave tonight. Gotta get back to school, but Emma should be able to handle her. You know she works with recovering addicts, don't you?"

"Yeah, I guess I heard something about that. I hope you can help Nat. She's a good kid. She just inherited some bad genes and found the wrong crowd in high school."

"But, let's get back to you. How are you doing now?" Danny focuses on Rudy.

"It's good to get at least a few of the wires disconnected, but this dang IV is irritating. Without it I would feel almost normal. Can't wait until I can get out of this bed."

"Normal? With all those bandages and bruises?" Danny laughs. "Anyway, I think you'll get your wish soon. PT starts tomorrow. I overheard the nurse talking about your treatment before they moved you up here."

"I bet their idea of PT is getting me out of bed to go to the bathroom."

"Well, you gotta start somewhere." Danny looks towards Celeste. "Hey, can I have a few minutes alone with Rudy? I'm leaving tonight and won't get a chance to visit with him again."

Celeste plants a kiss on Rudy's forehead and reluctantly turns to leave the room. The others follow with just a wave. "We'll be back in a jiffy."

As soon as the door closes, Rudy starts talking. His words tumble out in a rush. "It really was my fault, Danny. How could I have been so stupid? I've gone over it and over it in my mind. Like they say, it's always a chain of events that leads to an accident. I'm just trying to decide where that chain started. If I'm ever going to fly again, I've got to know when I can push it and when I can't."

"What do you mean, if?"

"Well, I think I will, but I still have a few obstacles. Or have you not noticed my smashed up body?"

"Oh, that! Nothing you can't deal with. Heck, I've had worse injuries than that and been back on the football field in a week."

"Come on, get real. You haven't had anything worse than a broken fingernail. What a baby!"

"You're just lucky I'm a gentleman and won't hit someone when they're down. Otherwise I'd pin you in a minute." Danny can't refrain from smiling. It feels good to be sparring with his cousin.

"Gentleman? I've never heard that word applied to you before."

"It so happens that I got the Osmann award for good sportsmanship last year. Not that I'm bragging, but very few freshmen ever earn that distinction."

"You're distinct all right, distinctly egotistical. But come on, I want to tell you about the crash before I lose my nerve— or forget the final details."

"Yeah, so what happened?"

"Like I said before, we landed at that strip to pick up some equipment and the weather was getting worse, so I told my passengers that we had to return to Deadhorse. They were grumbling and making remarks about other pilots they'd flown with. I guess I let that get to me."

"What jerks!"

"Yeah. I should have known better though. After I took off downwind, I think I delayed my turn back to the north hoping to get a peek through the pass. I thought if I could make it through the first mile or so, things would get better and we could press on, but they didn't. By the time I had to turn around, the valley was pretty narrow and my ground-speed from the tailwind must have been a lot higher than I thought."

"What does that have to do with anything?"

"We covered a lot of ground in the first part of the turn so I was much closer to the hillside than I realized. I still thought I was okay, though."

"What do you mean?"

"I lost visual references in the turn and rolled out on a heading that would take me out of the valley to the north. One of the new guys started yelling, 'Hey, I can't see the ground.' I turned and yelled at him to shut up. That's when we hit, I guess. I don't remember actually hitting the ground, or what happened afterwards, or anything about the trip to Anchorage, or much else for that matter. The next thing I remember is waking up with Celeste hovering over me."

"Well, you're one lucky guy." Danny's eyes fill with tears. He has a hard time getting the words out. "And, we're one lucky family to have you here with us in one piece."

"I'm glad to be here, too. I guess it wasn't my time to go. Or maybe my mom badgered God to let me stay a little longer. All I know is I'm grateful. I'm really grateful."

Danny nods in agreement.

Rudy continues. "I know I can beat these injuries. What I'm worried about now is, what am I going to tell the feds?"

"Just tell them the truth, man."

"But what if they take away my license?"

"How could they punish you after all you've already suffered? Just wait and see. You'll be fine."

"I hope so. The thought of being stuck on the ground for the rest of my life is too awful to even think about."

"Don't go there. No need to consider the worst case, not now. Think about getting better and let tomorrow's troubles take care of themselves. Now rest a little before the crowd descends on you again. Those women…"

Danny watches his cousin close his eyes. His breathing becomes slow and regular. Danny raises his eyes, whispers, "Thank you" and turns to leave the room.

Nikki, Emma and Celeste are standing right outside the door, looking down the hall. Danny almost knocks his mother down as he exits Rudy's room. She has her arms outstretched towards Leila who is walking towards them.

Leila says, "I panicked when he wasn't in the recovery room."

Nikki grabs her as she nears and hugs her close. "Sorry, I would have called but they just moved him. We talked to him for a couple of minutes, then Danny wanted some time with him alone, so we just came out to catch our breath. Anyway, I didn't call because I thought you'd be sleeping."

Leila pulls away and shakes her head. "Well…"

"I'm sorry LaLa. Please, let it go."

Danny interrupts saying, "Rudy just drifted off again, but he's been alert and in good spirits since he came up here. Why don't you go in and see for yourself, Aunt Leila?"

Leila takes Celeste's arm. "Come on. Let's check on our boy."

After they leave, Nikki ushers Danny and Emma down the hallway to a sitting area near the snack dispenser. "Don't you have to leave soon, Danny?"

"Yeah, I should probably be at the airport around midnight. So I have a little time yet."

"Maybe we should go over to Leila's house so you can take a shower and have something to eat."

"That would be good, but I just want to pop in and say goodbye. I didn't get a chance before, cuz Rudy drifted off while we were talking, but he did tell me the whole story. I'll fill you in later."

Danny heads toward room 434. He barges in, walks up to Rudy who is now awake and gives him a big bear hug.

"Hey, careful there." Celeste moves closer to the bed.

"Gotta hug my favorite cousin before I leave." Then addressing Rudy, "Take care, buddy. I'm leaving you in good hands with these two, but call once in a while, would you?"

"Okay."

"Maybe while you're recovering you can come down to Urbana and watch me win a few games."

"He's not going anywhere without me. But maybe we'll spend some of our honeymoon in your neighborhood."

"That would be great. We'll talk more about that, but I gotta run now. Love ya, Rudy. Get better fast."

Leila hugs Danny. "Thanks for coming. You've been good medicine for him."

Celeste, glancing at Rudy for approval, puts her arms out towards Danny for a hug. "You're two of a kind, Dan. It must run in the family. I look forward to getting to know you better—you and your whole family."

"Hey, that's enough, watch where you're putting your hands," Rudy protests.

Danny smiles. "See, he's almost back to normal. Your biggest job now is going to be holding him down."

Celeste blushes, "I think I'll manage just fine. I'm a lot stronger than I look."

Chapter Forty-five

Emma Encounters Natalia

D anny blurts out as soon as he sees his mother. "Okay, I'm ready to go. Maybe I can even catch a few winks before we have to leave for the airport."

"Why don't you stay here, Mom?" Emma offers. "Danny and I can go to Aunt Leila's house and order a pizza or something, no need for you to cook for us."

"It would be good to spend a little more time with Leila—and Rudy, of course. But let me see if that's all right with them." Nikki is gone for a few minutes and returns holding out car keys. "It's fine with them if I stay. Leila says you can use her car. If and when she's ready to go home, Celeste can drive her. Oh, and she says for you to make yourself at home in the guest room. You'll see my suitcase in there."

Danny embraces his mother and whispers, "Thanks for letting me come. Rudy's gonna be fine. You will be, too."

"I know."

"Don't let Emma get to you, though. She can be pretty stubborn about things."

"Don't worry. I know how to handle her. We'll work it out."

"I love you, Mom."

"I love you, too, Danny. God go with you."

"He always does."

Danny walks to the elevator with his head hanging, looking down at the floor. Emma joins him.

"Hey, it's not the end of the world. You'll see him again.

"I know. But I just hate goodbyes."

After dropping Danny at the airport, Emma returns to Leila's house on the hillside. The pizza container is still on the counter, but Emma turns toward the guest room. She showers in the tiled, walk-in shower, towels off and collapses on top of the covers. *I just have to lie down for a minute. I'll get the pajamas later.* She promptly falls asleep. Moments later, loud footsteps in the hallway wake her. She opens her eyes and looks around. "Where am I?"

She reaches for the edge of the bedspread, but before she has a chance to move Natalia walks into the room, turning the light on as she enters. A young man is right behind her.

"Emma, is that you? What are you doing here?"

Emma pulls the bedspread over her naked body. "Wow, Nat. I didn't expect to see you here."

"I could say the same thing."

Natalia sits on the edge of the bed and leans over to give Emma a hug. Emma notices her dilated pupils and her quick, nervous movements. She tries to hang on for a moment longer, but Natalia pulls away. She jumps up and grabs the hand of the young man with her. "Hey, this is Travis. Remember him?"

Emma, still groggy, studies him. The dark stubble of a beard on his thin face makes him appear like some of the homeless people seen on the streets of Chicago. He's dressed in blue jeans and a tank top revealing tattoos, one on his forearm and another on his shoulder muscle. Emma squints, trying to make out their details. She shakes her head.

"Trav, this is my cousin, Emma, from Chicago."

Travis says nothing, but grins at Emma. He glances at Natalia with a sort of leer. Emma frowns at his manner. "Hey, how about giving me a chance to get dressed? I'll meet you in the kitchen in a minute so we can talk and catch up."

"Nah, I can't stay, got to get over to Muldoon for an all-nighter. I just wanted to see if anyone was at home." Scratching her upper arm and then her neck, she looks around. "Hey, I'm dying of thirst. You got anything to drink around here? I could really use a beer."

"If you hang on a minute, I'll come and see."

"Right."

"Where is this place, Nat? Do I know anybody who might be there?"

"Maybe. It's the same old crowd we hung around with last time you were here—when we were just kids."

"Give me a minute to get some clothes on and I'll meet you in the kitchen. Maybe I can ride along."

"Right." Natalia and Travis turn and leave the room and as Emma dresses they rummage around in the kitchen.

She dresses as fast as she can. A door slams as she pulls on her jeans. She rushes down the hall to the entryway window and sees a car pull out of the driveway. Travis is driving and a passenger is slumped over in the right front seat.

Emma calls out, hopefully, "Nat, are you still here?" There is no answer. The only sound she hears is the ticking of the grandfather clock. "Oh, damn! I let her go again." Emma wanders through the house, aimlessly pacing. It's hard to tell what time it is with so little darkness at night. The clock on the mantel says it is twenty after midnight. "I should call my mom. Now, where did I leave my purse and my phone?"

Emma retraces her actions after returning to Aunt Leila's house. "Maybe I left my purse in the car." She goes out to the garage to look but it's not there. She checks the guest room and her luggage. "I know I had it at the airport." She shakes her head. *I must be more tired than I thought. It must be in the kitchen.* While walking there, a car pulls into the driveway. It's her mom and aunt. "Good, now I can tell them about Natalia."

They enter through the front door. Both seem surprised to see Emma awake.

"Honey, I thought you'd be asleep by now."

"I was. Well, almost that is. It's been quite a night. I can't find my..."

"What happened? Did Danny have trouble catching his flight?"

"No, at least I don't think so. I just dropped him off at the ticket counter. He said he'd call if there were any problems. His flight time was twelve-o-five and I haven't heard from him, so I assume he's okay."

"What's the matter, then?"

"She was here, Aunt Leila, with a guy. I don't know for sure, but she looked high to me. She said she was on her way to an all-nighter in Muldoon. I didn't stop her. How could I be so stupid?"

Nikki stares at Emma. "Nat was here?"

"Yeah. And I let her get away."

Leila touches Emma's shoulder. "It's not your fault. Nat's been on her own path for a long time."

"But she was right here. I could have talked some sense into her."

"I know. I've felt the same way. But, I'm afraid she'll have to hit bottom to realize she needs our help. I thought she had been there before—many times—but she never did ask for help. She just has to realize she can't do it on her own. We can't force it on her. I only hope she'll be safe until then."

"Me too."

"As hard as it is, all I can do is put her in God's hands and trust in His plan for her life."

"What's God got to do with it?" Emma throws her hands in the air. "I want to do something." She leans towards Leila and narrows her eyes. "What good is all of my experience with addicts if I can't help my own family? How can God allow such awful things to happen?"

Nikki shakes her head. "If I knew why God allows people to do stupid things I'd win the Nobel prize for sure. I guess the freedom to make choices is more important than doing the right thing."

"But why can't we have both?" Emma sounds desperate.

Nikki smiles at Emma. "That wouldn't be free will. Besides, that's not life, honey. That's just not how it is. We have to learn to accept what is if we can't change it."

Leila, remembering her experience in the chapel that morning, muses, "To love what is, to see blessings in every-thing—everywhere. I know this sounds like a platitude, but embracing the moment and sharing what you've been given does change things. All we can do is be fully present and give love. You said it yourself: love is always the answer."

"You're right. But sometimes love has to be tough."

Nikki has heard enough of this topic. "How about getting a snack before we go to bed?" She leads them toward the kitchen.

Emma, on seeing the pizza box, gasps. "Now I know where I put it. It was right here, hanging on a stool next to the counter. I was going to get rid of the pizza box, but didn't know where to put it, so I went to bed instead."

"Put what?" Leila asks.

"My purse. Nat, or her friend must have taken it."

"Oh, God! Now she's turning into a thief."

"We don't know that Aunt Leila. If anybody took it, I'm sure it was that Travis character. He looked kind of weird to me."

"Travis? That's who was with her? Oh no! He's the one who got Natalia started on the bad stuff. I think he even deals to support his own habit."

"Do you think we should call my phone and hope she answers?" Emma asks.

"I don't know. Maybe we should sleep on it. I don't want to push her over the edge."

Nikki puts on a pot of water to boil and hunts around the kitchen for some herbal tea while Emma gets oatmeal cookies out of the cookie jar. Leila sits like a guest in her own kitchen watching as her sister and niece prepare the snack. They share the pot of chamomile tea with warmed cookies before preparing for bed. Nikki moves her luggage to Rudy's room so she can have privacy.

Chapter Forty-six

Rescuing Nat

Emma begins to undress in the guest room. It is quiet in the house. Both her mother and aunt must have fallen asleep. She shakes her head. "No, I can't do it. I've got to find her." She slips her shirt back over her head and tiptoes into the kitchen. Picking up the landline, she calls her own phone number. It rings for a long time before someone answers. There is a lot of racket in the background. "Is this Nat?"

"What? I don't know any Matt. You must have the wrong number."

"No, not Matt, I'm looking for Natalia."

"What the...? You gotta know the right stuff to find what you need. Don't you get it, man? Don't give me any shit. You're just a..."

Another voice sounds on the phone. "Hey, who are you calling? How did you get this number?"

"Nat, is that you?"

"Who the f..."

"It's Emma, Nat! Come on. Just listen."

Only a few words are discernable over the background noise. Emma grips the phone, straining to understand what Nat is saying. She catches a few words.

"I think Travis OD'd. He's just lying there. What should I do? I'm scared, Em. I'm really scared. Now some guy is waving a gun around. I mean…"

"Hang on. Has anyone called 911?"

"I don't know."

"Well, do it. Right now."

"But what if the police come and find me here. They might think I killed him."

"Just do it, Nat. I'm begging you."

"Okay, hang on."

Emma can hear Natalia shout for someone to call 911.

She returns to the phone sounding hysterical. "What am I going to do? Oh, no, no, no…"

"Stay calm, Nat. Listen. I'll come and get you. Just tell me where you are."

"Remember the Cabin Tavern on Muldoon Road? The one with the grass on the roof?"

"Yeah, I think I could find it."

"Well, we're at the turquoise house right behind it. There's a wooden moose in the front yard. You'll see it."

"Nat, I need you to go outside and walk towards Muldoon Road. I'll be right there."

"Okay, I'm outta here. But hurry!"

Emma runs to the garage, grabbing the keys to Leila's car from the table by the entryway. When she opens the garage door, she glances back and sees Celeste's car blocking the driveway. "Damn. Now I'll have to find her keys. I didn't want to tell Aunt Leila until I had Nat safely at home."

Leila is in the hallway when Emma returns to look for Celeste's keys. "What are you doing?"

"I've got to hurry. Nat needs help. I'm going to pick her up."

"How could you think of going without me?"

"I didn't want to waste time."

"I'm going with you."

Emma grabs Leila's elbow. "We need to go now. Nat sounded desperate. Do you have the keys to Celeste's car?"

"Yeah, I'll get them."

Still in her pajamas, Leila snatches a jacket from the front closet. The keys are in the pocket. "I'm ready. Let's go."

Emma races down the hillside and drives across town, grateful for the light traffic at this time of the night. "I'm surprised at how much of this town I remember."

"They haven't added any new roads in the last few years. Even though there's construction everywhere in the summer, it's mostly fixing up potholes. Luckily, you chose the right way to get across town—no road closures. But, hey, how did you find out where Natalia is and what is going on?"

Emma pauses for a long time to compose her response. She doesn't want to upset Aunt Leila any more than she has to. She needs her to be calm. The family needs time to plan an intervention to coax Nat into accepting treatment. If Leila goes off the deep end now it may spoil any chances of Nat coming around.

"Look, we're almost there. I'll fill you in on the details later. Just—please, Aunt Leila—don't say or do anything that will upset her right now. Whatever she says or does, don't overreact. She's high. She's afraid. She might be hallucinating. We've got to get her home into safe, calm surroundings. She'll need to come down safely and that might mean medical intervention or hospitalization."

"Okay. I'll keep quiet. I want her back."

"Let me do the talking. I know what I'm doing. You have to believe that."

"I do. Just hurry."

Emma has slowed down to watch for Natalia along Muldoon Road. In the parking lot of the Cabin Tavern ahead, the flashing neon lights of its sign illuminate a small form slumped over on a bench.

"That must be her. I'll pull into the bus stop lane and park next to her. You can slide over to the driver's seat. I'll get her into the car."

Emma skids to a stop and races around the car, as Leila takes the driver's seat. She takes a hold of Natalia and steers her into the back seat. She is as limp as a rag doll.

"Okay, Aunt Leila, let's head home."

"Don't you think the hospital would be better?"

Emma notices the flashing lights of an ambulance turning onto the street beside the tavern, with a police car right behind it. *Thank goodness we got here before they did.* "I'll check her over and let you know. Go down Tudor Road, so if things look bad we can go to Providence."

Leila's hands are shaking as she drives south along Muldoon Road. *Keep her safe, Lord. I want my baby back. Don't let the drugs take her. Please.* Tears stream down her cheeks and she blinks to clear her vision. She can hear the girls moving around in the back seat.

Emma gets Natalia to sit upright and fastens her seat belt. She sits right next to her and allows Nat's head to rest on her shoulder.

"Can you hear me, Nat?"

"Ummm. I'm good."

Emma tries to rouse her from her stupor. She taps her chin and shakes her shoulder. "Nat, listen. Can you tell me what you took?"

Her head falls down onto her chest. "Don't know. I'm flying. It was…"

Emma lifts Natalia's head and tries to get her to open her eyes. "You have to tell me. Did you inject anything or was it pills?"

"Little, itty bitties."

"You took pills? What color?"

"Rainbow, oh, man, oh. I think I'm gonna…"

Natalia leans over and retches. Leila turns around to see what the noise is and shrieks, "Oh my God!"

"She's okay, Leila. Just keep driving."

Natalia throws up, covering one leg of Emma's slacks with vomit. Emma swallows to keep from retching herself and attends to Natalia, making sure she doesn't inhale any of the vomit. She pats her on the back.

"That's a good girl. Let's get it all out. You'll feel better."

Nat vomits again and again until nothing is coming out and then has dry heaves, moaning between each episode. When she is done, she leans her head back against the seat. Her face is pale and pasty. Her eye makeup is streaked down her cheeks making her look like a clown. She wipes her sleeve across her mouth and shudders.

"Did he die?"

"I don't know," Emma whispers.

"I wanna go back."

"We can't, Nat. The ambulance was coming. They will take care of him. You were too spaced out to be of any help. Come home with us and rest. You need to sleep it off."

Nat does not resist. "Okay."

She rests her head on Emma's shoulder again and falls asleep snoring.

"Drive home, Aunt Leila. She threw up some of whatever she took and she's going to be all right. I'm glad we got to her before she choked on her own vomit."

"Oh, God."

"She's fine now. Don't worry. I'll stay with her all night to make sure she doesn't bolt. Although, I don't think she'll be in any condition to run for a while."

All the lights are on in Leila's house as they turn into the driveway.

"Looks like Mom is awake."

Nikki rushes out to help Emma get Natalia into the house. Nat is limp and unresponsive. They carry her dead weight to her bedroom. Emma undresses her, lays her on the bed and washes her face.

"Watch her for a few minutes while I change and shower. I smell like a rotten brewery. If she starts to vomit again, be sure she's on her side."

Refreshed and clean, Emma returns to Nat's room. "I'll take over now, Aunt Leila. You and my mom better get some sleep. We have a rough couple of days ahead. We'll talk in the morning about what to do."

The sun is rising in the north, but Nikki and Leila return to their beds. Both fall asleep as soon as their heads hit their pillows.

Emma sits next to Nat's bed watching for any signs of distress. She checks her pulse from time to time and listens for regular breathing. Nat lies inert—unmoving. Even in sleep her flaccid face has the appearance of a drug addict.

Emma is accustomed to dealing with young drug users, but the fact that it is her own cousin in this state has her rattled. "How could I let this happen to her? Why her and not me?"

Nat starts to thrash. Emma shakes her head as though to clear it. "No. I can't let my feelings get in the way." Her professional demeanor returns and she keeps a close watch.

Nat settles down and returns to a peaceful sleep. Emma's eyes blink several times. They snap closed and her head drops onto her chest. Several times she lifts her head and forces her eyes to open. Fatigue finally takes over. She leans back in the chair and sleeps.

The room is bright and sunny when Emma wakes to find Natalia sitting up in bed, holding her head in her hands.

"How are you, Nat?"

"I feel really bad. My head feels like it's being crushed in a vise. My eyes hurt. My mouth is—ugh, like a manure pile. My body aches like the flu. But my stomach is the worst. I need something to take the edge off. You can get me something, can't you?"

"I can get you some ibuprofen, but that's it."

"Get me five or six. And how about a beer to wash it down?"

"Come on, Nat. Do you know how close you were to dying last night? You can't do this to yourself."

Natalia moans, gripping her stomach. "I'm gonna die if I don't get something. I know my mom has some pills around here. Get me something. Anything."

Emma rushes out to get the ibuprofen from her aunt. When she returns with a glass of water and three pills, Nat is sitting at the edge of the bed looking around for her clothes. "Here, take these. It will help."

"You're cruel. How can you make me suffer like this?"

Emma speaks with a stern, unsympathetic voice. She's businesslike now. "Your stomach can't handle anything right now. You might even throw these up, unless you take a bite to eat with them. Stay here. I'll go get you some crackers and milk. If you want me to help, you have to listen."

"Why should I listen to you, Miss Goody Two Shoes? What do you know about anything?"

"I'm all you've got right now."

Emma dashes to the kitchen, grabbing the crackers and milk as Nikki and Leila watch wide-eyed. She runs back to Nat's room.

"Take a sip. Not too much. See how your stomach does with this."

Nat holds the glass to her mouth with shaking hands. She sips obediently.

"Now eat a couple of bites of this cracker."

"I hate this kind."

"Just do it."

Nat takes the tiniest bite and washes it down with a little more milk. She gags.

"Hold it right there. Take a deep breath through your nose. That's it."

Emma nurses her through the next half hour until the effects of the ibuprofen begin to show.

"I've got to go and get something to eat, Nat. You stay here. I'll be back in a flash."

Nat lies down moaning. She clutches the edge of the bed and draws her knees up to her chin. She does not respond to Emma's statement.

In the kitchen Emma talks fast as her mother and aunt listen. "I don't want to leave her alone for long."

Nikki has fixed a plate of rolls, cheeses and lunchmeats for Emma to snack on. Emma begins to outline her plan between bites. "She's safe now. We know she can't escape because I locked the door. Her window opens onto the deck and it's a heck of a drop to the ground from there, so she won't get out that way."

"That's good. I wondered about that." Nikki looks relieved.

"She's in a lot of pain right now. I don't know what she took, but judging by her condition last night, it's highly addictive. It's going to be quite a while before her body stops craving another fix."

"So what is your plan?" Even though Leila has dealt with Nat's addiction for several years she still is quite ignorant about what to do.

"We need to have a family intervention to convince her to seek treatment. It will be a long road, but she has to take the first step, otherwise it will fail."

"What is involved with that?"

"Basically, the whole family needs to stick together and tell Nat that we will no longer support her addiction. If she wants to continue down that road, we will cut her off. We will not let her behavior hurt us any more. I think we should get Rudy and Celeste to help. I know Rudy is just getting back on his feet, but she is close to him and respects him. We have to ask. I'm hoping he will say yes."

"Oh, I'm sure he will." Leila knows her son and is confident of his love for his baby sister.

"You can share details with Rudy and Celeste when you visit today. Maybe by this evening or tomorrow morning I can bring Nat to the hospital and we can have it out. I'm pretty sure I can get her to come along under the guise of visiting her brother."

"You never did tell me how you happened to find out where she was."

"Well…you're not going to like this. When I called my cell last night, one of Nat's friends answered it. When she came to the phone she was hysterical and said that Travis had OD'd."

"He what?"

"She said he was lying there like he was dead. She told me where she was. I told her to call 911, get out of there and walk toward Muldoon Road."

"Do you know what happened to him?"

"I don't. I hate to admit it but it would be better for Nat if he did die. Still, I hope he makes it. It just seems like such a waste for someone so young to throw their life away like that."

"But he was—is—such a scumbag."

"Everyone deserves a chance. But our concern right now is Nat. I'm thinking that if we can get her to admit she needs help, I can take her back to Wisconsin with me right away—tomorrow if possible—and admit her into our program."

"That's a wonderful idea. I'll call right away to see if I can get reservations."

"We're not sure yet if it will work, Mom."

"Well, I'll just pray that it will. Look what Leila's prayers did for Rudy."

Chapter Forty-seven

Intervention

"How about some breakfast before we head to the hospital, La La? I think I know my way around your kitchen by now." Nikki is eager to help.

"No, I don't think I could eat any more. Those rolls you made were delicious, but that's enough for me. I ate more than I normally do. But you make everything look so appetizing. How do you do it?"

"I'm just glad to see you eating at least a little. You know you do need to keep your strength up."

"But I also need to keep my girlish figure for Dom."

"Dom. Yes. Can you tell me a little about him? Sounds like your romance got off to a flying start."

"It did. We just met in February of this year."

"And you're already engaged?"

"Yeah, well..."

"Isn't that a little fast?"

"I guess, but when I finally came out of my fog, I realized I couldn't stand to be alone any longer. It's hard to describe what happened, but you know how it is when two people connect."

Nikki nods and begins to say something, but stops.

"Listen, you're going to be here for a while. We'll talk more about it but now we should get down to the hospital to see how Rudy is doing."

"All right, but I'm not letting you off the hook. I want to know what he did to convince you to marry him."

"Don't worry," Leila says. "You'll get all the details. Now let's go."

"But I'm driving this time." Nikki smiles.

"If you insist."

Rudy is in good spirits when Nikki and Leila walk into his room. His first PT session just finished, he beams with optimism.

Leila gives him a hug. "You look pretty chipper this morning."

"Yeah, they got me out of bed for a few minutes and it felt really good to be upright and moving a little. Tomorrow I'll actually make it to the PT room."

When he hears about Emma's plan for a family intervention with Natalia, he whoops for joy. "Yes, it'll work. I know it will. She has to know how much we love her and what her addiction is doing to this family. She's got Daddy's strength and gutsiness somewhere beneath all that self-destructive behavior. Getting her out of Alaska is brilliant. She needs a different environment to thrive." Celeste looks doubtful.

"Remember how moving to Alaska, away from your California friends, changed your life, honey?"

"Yes, I guess it did." Celeste brightens. "How would I ever have met you if I hadn't moved here and started flying?" She gives him a hug. "Now tell them how your PT went today."

Rudy describes in detail his short walk down the hall, with a walker, making it sound like he has just completed a daunting endurance race. Leila listens with pride and gratitude. Nikki excuses herself to get an espresso. She puts her hand in her pocket, feeling for change. On touching the cell phone an idea pops into her head. Her hand tingles with excitement as she pulls the phone out and pushes the return call button on one of the recent calls. Her heart is pounding. She holds her breath, praying. *Let him answer, please answer.*

"Mitch Holden here."

For a moment, Nikki can't speak.

"Hello. Is anybody there? Hello."

"Mitch. It's me, Nikki." She doesn't know what else to say. She's called on the spur of the moment without planning what to say. She just wants to hear his voice.

"Nikki, oh my beautiful Nikki. Where are you? How are you? I've missed you. I need to see you again. My life has been hell since I talked to your daughter. I didn't know what was going on. I don't blame you for not wanting to talk..."

"I don't know what Emma said to you. I wasn't in the room when you called. When she saw me she turned on me like I was a criminal. But, listen. So much has been going on. I can't even begin to explain."

"You don't have to explain. It's enough that you called."

"We can talk when I get back to the Midwest."

"Where are you now?" Mitch asks.

"It's a long story, but I'm in Alaska with my sister and her family."

"When can we meet?"

"I'll be back next Wednesday. I just made my return reservations today. It could change, but I think my nephew will be okay by then. I'll call when I get home."

"Call before if you can. I'll be here waiting."

Relief spreads through Nikki's body like soft butter melting into warm toast. "I was afraid you wouldn't want to have anything to do with me. I was afraid…"

"Don't be afraid. I'm here for you. How can you doubt how much I care? Just hurry back. I'm so glad you're safe."

"Yes, I'm okay now. I'm more than okay. I'm great." Nikki feels lighter talking to Mitch.

"You sure are."

Nikki spots Emma and Natalia walking towards her where she sits near the elevators. "I've gotta go now, Mitch. Please pray for me, for us."

"I will."

"There's so much to say, but, later…"

"Okay, go now and think of me." Mitch says.

"I do. I will."

"Bye now."

"Till next week." Nikki holds the phone to her cheek and closes her eyes. She feels a surge of energy tingling down to her toes. Emma and Nat, only a few yards away, notice her sitting there holding her phone.

"Hey, Mom. What's up?" Giving Natalia a nudge, she says, "Look who I have here."

Nikki opens her eyes and sees Emma and Nat standing before her. Emma is holding Natalia's elbow, who looks like she would run if she were let loose.

Nikki stands to give Nat a hug. She knows the love she feels inside brims over and seeps into Natalia's spirit. Her niece does not pull away. Instead, she melts in Nikki's arms like a baby asleep. Nikki strokes her hair, clean now, and smelling like lavender.

"What a beautiful child you are!"

"Don't say that Aunt Elsa."

"But it's true. Now let's go visit your brother. He's eager to see you."

As they ride the elevator to the fourth floor, Emma taps her fingernails on the handrail. She rocks back and forth from foot to foot mechanically. It doesn't appear that Nat notices, but Nikki feels like telling her to stop. The tension of anticipating a difficult encounter builds as they near Rudy's room. Nikki tries to make light conversation, but neither Nat nor Emma seems to listen.

Leila rushes to the door as Nat enters first. Celeste stays close to Rudy's bed watching him hold his arms out to welcome his sister. "I'm glad you're here, kid. Where have you been?"

Natalia avoids answering his question. "I'm good, but how come you're still here?"

Rudy knows how Nat's drug use affects her and understands her inability to relate to the problems of others. He steers the conversation towards getting her to see how she is hurting others as well as herself. "Nat, you have no idea how close I was to dying. I was too out of it to know whether or not you were here, or even to care if you were. But since I regained consciousness, I've needed emotional support more than ever. Do you know how hard it is to admit that?"

He glances toward Emma to be sure he is not headed in the wrong direction. She nods encouragement.

Nat's face is unresponsive. She looks around the room as though to check for pills that might help her through her cravings.

"Celeste here has been a life saver to me. She talked me out of my coma. I could feel her love calling me back, when all I wanted to do was go deeper into oblivion. We're calling you back, Nat. Our love is surrounding you. All of us want you back."

"You can't give me what I need. You don't understand. I need a fix. I'm going to crawl out of my skin if I don't get something soon."

Having seen this response before, Emma has done her homework and knows how to reach the mental health physician on call here at Providence. She steps out of the room to call and explain the situation to Dr. Coleman. He listens without speaking. Emma is thorough. He doesn't need to ask any questions at all.

"Can you help, Doctor? I realize she's not a patient of yours and she's not in the system, but she needs something to help her make it to the treatment facility in Wisconsin. We're trying to talk her into it, but she's still coming down from a high."

"Where are you right now?"

Emma gives him the room number, saying, "I hope you're not too far away."

"No, I'm not. I'm just below you on the third floor. I can make my way up there in a couple minutes. I'll knock when I get there and you can let me know if it's okay to come in. If you want me to help facilitate, I can do that too."

"Thank you, Doctor."

Emma returns to the room in time to hear Leila say, "You have no idea of the torment you've put us through. You're killing us all."

"It's my life. I can't see what difference it makes to anyone else. Just leave me alone."

Emma steps in. "We can't. We love you too much to watch you slowly kill yourself with drugs. Give us a chance to prove that to you. Please."

Natalia folds her arms across her chest and walks to the window. The silence in the room makes everyone feel as though they are picking their way through a minefield.

"I know you need something right now, Nat. If I promise to do everything to help you come down easily, will you at least try to promise you'll go to rehab?"

"I've tried it. It doesn't work."

"It's your decision, then." Emma states. "We can't force you. But we are not going to enable you any longer. If you choose to run after drugs now, we won't stop you. Just don't count on any of us to bail you out if you find yourself in trouble. This is your last chance. From now on, you're on your own. But before you go you should know what happened to your dealer boyfriend."

"What? Where is Travis?"

"He didn't make it, Nat. He died on the way to the hospital."

"You're lying. Travis can't be dead. He's the best…"

Leila nods her head. "It's true."

Natalia puts her head down on the bed, sobbing.

Dr. Coleman knocks on the door. Emma hesitates before motioning to Nikki to let him in. He walks in silently, taking in the scene with a grim expression.

Nat cries. "I can't go on. I don't want to go on. Get me out of this hell."

Everyone in the room holds their breaths waiting for Nat's outburst to peter out.

She screams obscenities. Begs for help. Curses. "What's the point? I hate this life!" She pounds her fists on Rudy's bed, yelling, "I can't. I won't. Screw you all. I hate you as much as you hate me. You always hated Travis. You killed him."

In her thrashing and flailing she jars Rudy's broken hip over and over again. At first he grits his teeth and bears the pain, but finally can stand it no longer. He screams, "Stop that, you spoiled, selfish brat. You're hurting me. I know you're in pain. But don't you think the rest of us are too?"

His sudden outburst jolts Natalia. She looks at Rudy as though seeing him in the room for the first time. "Rudy how did this happen to you?"

"Come here, kid. Give me a hug." Rudy braces himself for another onslaught.

Nat leans over his bed. Still sobbing, she embraces him. "Will you help me out of this mess? I can't do it by myself anymore."

"I'd do anything for you. You know that. We're all here for you. You've got to trust Emma. She knows what she's doing. Go with her. Please, for all our sakes, go with Emma to Wisconsin and get yourself clean."

"Okay, I'll go. But first let me say goodbye to my friends."

Dr. Coleman steps in saying "No, Natalia. That won't work. It has to be a clean break." He continues talking quietly to Nat. His voice and manner are reassuring. After a few minutes Nat sits down. She slumps over in the chair, listening, nodding from time to time. They get up. The doctor takes Nat by the arm and ushers her out of the room. He glances at Emma, then at Leila, and gives them each a reassuring nod. "We'll be back in a few minutes."

Silence takes over the room. Nikki opens her mouth to speak but thinks better of it. Leila walks over to Rudy's bed and puts a hand on his shoulder. Emma stares out the window, biting her lip. Celeste and Rudy look at each other, with expressions of both hope and fear.

After what seems to all of them like hours, Dr. Coleman and Nat come back into the room. Dr. Coleman speaks quietly. Nat is now subdued. "She's going to be fine. She agrees to enter treatment with her cousin. I would recommend you get to Wisconsin as soon as you can, tonight if possible."

Leila embraces Nat while looking over her shoulder at Dr. Coleman. "Oh, Doctor, how can we thank you?"

"Just take care of this precious girl. She's a gift to all of us."

"We will, of course we will. Yes. She's my special gift from God."

Nikki grabs her phone. "I'll call right now to see how soon you guys can leave." She is able to get reservations on a red-eye flight to Chicago. She winces when she hears the price but shrugs and reads her credit card information to the agent. *I'm sure Gerik won't mind. If he does, screw him.*

The tension is the car is palpable as Leila drives Emma and Nat to the airport. Nikki comes along for the ride to say good-bye.

"Don't worry about my suitcase, Mom. I only had a few things and Nat will have a uniform issued to her when she checks in to the camp. We'll be fine."

Nikki is apprehensive, but hearing Emma's authoritative voice she relaxes somewhat. At the airport they embrace first in a group hug and then Emma and Nikki hold each other while Leila holds Nat as though she will never see her again.

"This is too hard." Leila moans and holds Nat tighter.

Nat is silent.

Nikki looks at Emma with a serious expression. "Take care of her now, Emma. I'll be home next Wednesday, but call if you need anything."

"Don't worry. Nat is in good hands. Love you, Mom."

"I love you too."

Chapter Forty-eight

Sisters Again

Returning from the airport after the tearful embraces, Leila and Nikki fall into bed, exhausted from the turmoil of the last few days. The next morning they are up early. Nikki puts a pan of blueberry muffins in the oven and makes them each a latte. They sit at the kitchen table holding their cups.

Leila studies Nikki across the table from her. Nikki is staring out the window at the Chugach Mountains, frowning occasionally. There's so much Leila wants to say but cannot put words together in a coherent way. *I love you Nikki. I'm glad you came. I hope we can continue to talk and get to really know each other and who we are now. I'm getting my life together, thanks to Dom. I want you to get to know him. How could Gerik betray you? My heart aches to think of your pain.* Words seem inadequate for what has happened between them since the accident. She doesn't know how to start. She notices Nikki fingering the cross at her throat, and sees a sudden warm expression light up her eyes.

Nikki has been thinking about the relationships in her life. *How could I have wasted all those years hating my sister, believing in Gerik and being duped by my best friend? Thank goodness for the kids, though. I'm awfully proud of them. The way Emma took over with Natalia, Rudy's strength—I know he's going to be okay, Danny's maturity—he's so gifted, and Ana—what a sweetie. I'm feeling much stronger now and even attractive. How different my life is since I decided to change my name! I'm a new person. I'm embarrassed to think of how I was turned on by Granite, but I'm grateful to him and the walking group for helping me to believe in myself. And Mitch, I'll never forget the night I met him. That was no coincidence. I'm sure it was meant to be. I don't know where it's going, but our connection is real. Who knows, maybe we're soul mates. He makes me feel alive. Please, God, let it be.*

Nikki turns, catching Leila's expression of—what? She doesn't know. Leila has never looked at her like that before. Their eyes meet and understanding between them needs no words. Their love and familial ties say all that needs to be said. Nikki sees her mother's expression in Leila's eyes. Leila, in turn, finds the look of their dad, whom she adored, on Nikki's face. They smile. Tears well up through their smiles.

"I never thought that through the worst of times I have ever had in my life the very best thing would happen, and that is getting my sister back. I'm glad I'm here, Leila."

In a choked voice Leila says, "Me too. It is good, isn't it?"

Silence caresses them and fills the room with light. Nikki nods. "Yes, it is. We are blessed, very, very blessed."

Made in the USA
San Bernardino, CA
07 March 2015